VICIOUS BONDS

SHANORA WILLIAMS

VICIOUS BONDS

NEW YORK TIMES & USA TODAY BESTSELLING AUTHOR

SHANORA WILLIAMS

Copyright © 2023 Shanora Williams

All rights reserved. This eBook is licensed for your personal enjoyment only. This eBook is copyright material and must not be copied, reproduced, transferred, distributed, leased, licensed or publicly performed or used in any form without prior written permission of the publisher, as allowed under the terms and conditions under which it was purchased or as strictly permitted by applicable copyright law. Any unauthorized distribution, circulation or use of this text may be a direct infringement of the author's rights, and those responsible may be liable in law accordingly.

Thank you for respecting the work of this author.

Cover Design by Emily Wittig Designs

Editing By Traci Finlay

Trademarks: This book identifies product names and services known to be trademarks, registered trademarks, or service marks of their respective holders. The author acknowledges the trademarked status in this work of fiction. The publication and use of these trademarks is not authorized, associated with, or sponsored by the trademark owners.

*To anyone feeling like they don't belong.
You matter. Always.*

MAP OF VAKEELI

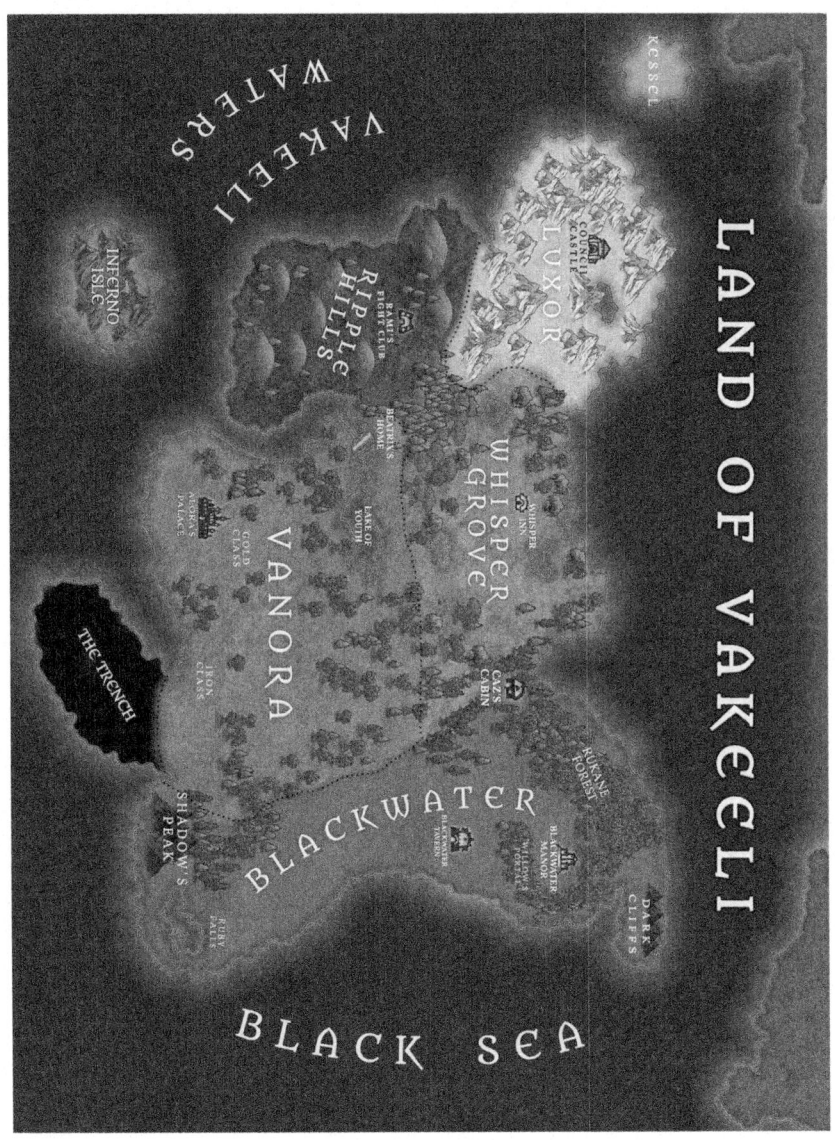

ONE

WILLOW

Never and I mean *never* go to a psychic when you're already down on luck. Especially a psychic who lives on the outskirts of the city, in a little home that reminds you of a tiny witch cottage. Even if you pass by the place several times a day to get to and from work, and constantly read the big white sign pitched in her yard with the words **I Can Tell Your Future** in bold font.

No matter how much the curiosity simmers in your throat, a quiet beckoning for you to see what that place is all about, it's best to swallow that shit down and keep it rolling. If you don't, you'll end up like me, Willow Austin, a woman who was told she'd *never* find love.

As I stand on a boat deck, my phone glued to my ear, all I can think about is what that tiny woman said. She sat at a two-top table, a sheer white cloth on top of it, and tarot cards stacked neatly. Crystals of all shapes and colors were lined up in a cardboard box, random bird feathers and patches of fur in a small, flat box beside it.

I expected her to use some of the items on her table, but instead she looked at me over the frame of her thin, rectangular glasses, reached across the table, and asked for one of my hands. She studied my hand as if she'd never seen another person's before and even sniffed it, which I found odd, but I didn't react.

"Oh, Willow," she finally said after some time, lifting her gaze from my hand to my eyes. "I'm afraid you'll never find love in this world."

It was strange of her to mention love because I wasn't searching for it, nor was I rejecting it. Love was a complicated factor in my life, one I preferred not to offer after so many disappointments.

I pulled my hand out of the little psychic's small, dry grasp, dug into my purse for cash, placed it on the table, and walked to my car while biting back tears. It didn't help that she'd told me this only two weeks after I found out my brother was missing. And maybe that's what I deserved to hear because seriously, who the hell goes to see a psychic only *two weeks* after their twin brother goes missing? Only a fool, that's who. And, several months later, I feel like even more of a fool while I have the phone pressed to my ear.

"You still there?" Garrett asks on the other line. Garrett, my friend. Well, more like my friend with benefits.

I blink at the sound of his voice, my eyelids heavy with mascara and eyeliner. It's been a long day, and the last thing I need is this call with him. "Yep. Still here."

"Well, like I said," he goes on. "You didn't tell me you were leaving last night."

I frown. "I didn't think I was obligated to right away, plus I texted you when I landed. You know I have to travel for work."

"A heads up that you were leaving town would've been nice."

I work hard to swallow while trying not to react to his passive aggressive tone. I can't argue with him. If I do, it'll just add fuel to his fire.

"Well, I'm sorry."

"It just seems like we're both on different paths, Willow. I don't ever get to see you. I also feel like you've been avoiding me lately. Not answering my calls as much. Not texting me back."

"I haven't been avoiding you." Sort of a lie. "It's just ever since my promotion, I have more work to do, which means more traveling." A door swings open behind me and music floods out, along with a train of women in cocktail dresses, all of them carrying a drink. One of the women in a ruby red sequin dress gives me a double take and grins.

"You're Willow, right?" the woman asks, stumbling toward me.

I smile and lower the phone a bit. "I am."

"Girl, you did so good with this event! Soooo good! Lou Ann has been going on and on about how all of this was mostly your idea! We're..." the woman hiccups. "We're having the time of our lives. I bet some *big* biddings are going up tonight!"

I force a smile at her. "Thank you. I'm glad you're having a great time."

The woman takes off, following the line of other women. They all giggle and shrill as they turn a corner of the boat and disappear, taking the joyous noise with them.

"You still there?" I ask, bringing the phone back to my ear.

"You sound busy," Garrett mutters. "Look, just call me when you're back home."

I close my eyes for several seconds, inhale, and then say, "Okay. Sure. Talk later."

I hang up quickly, wanting so badly to chuck my phone into

the lake and scream, but I don't because I need my phone tonight. Hell, I need it every day and night. Without it, I wouldn't be able to give my stealing boss event ideas for Townsend Corporate.

"Why the hell did I suggest a party on a fucking boat anyway?" I mutter. And not just *any* boat. Nope, I had to mention The Titan, a premium boat. Lou Ann was gung-ho for the idea—so much so that she wanted the best boat she could snag. It now rocks gently over the waves, and I place my elbows on the silver railing, staring out at the water.

My gaze tilts to the full moon and the splatter of stars in the midnight sky. It's a beautiful night—one I should be enjoying, but what's the point of enjoying any of this when there's no one to celebrate it with?

For a while, I thought the psychic was lying. I *would* find love. It *would* come to me. I deserved it. And when I met Garrett, we weren't serious at first, but we became sort of serious over the course of a year, and I thought the psychic lady was wrong.

But it turns out, with him he's been more of a placeholder—someone to occupy my time and my mind whenever I feel alone. It's nice having someone who can pop over with a meal and watch a movie with me. And at one point, I thought I could see myself marrying Garrett, until he revealed a different side of himself, one that woke me up and put me back in reality. Since then, I figured the witchy lady was right and because of it, I refuse to look for love.

Garrett isn't the man I thought he was and everyone I've ever loved has pulled away from me, either of their own accord, or because they had to, and I can't help wondering if it's because of me. Am I destined to be alone? Was I doomed from the moment I was born?

There was Warren. My mother. My father. All of them are gone. Am I truly that unlucky?

The door to the ballroom opens again. "Willow," a familiar voice calls. "There you are." I look over my shoulder to see Lou Ann, my boss. She didn't go with a cocktail dress like all the other women. Instead, she's in a coral pink women's suit. Dresses aren't for her. She's all business, even at parties. Come to think of it, I don't think I've ever seen her wear a dress in my whole three years of working for her.

"Is everything all right?" she asks.

"Yeah, everything's fine, I just..." I start to tell her who I was on the phone with, but by the way she darts her gaze over her shoulder toward the party, it's clear she doesn't really care what's wrong with me. It's a courtesy ask. I sigh and turn fully to face her. "Do you need me for something?"

"Yes. They're about to start the biddings," she says, waving the hand with her phone in it. "If you don't mind, can you tell the band to soften the music, and once that's done, request more champagne to top off the night. We want high bids, big smiles—you know the deal."

"You got it," I return with a smile.

"Thank you so much!" Just then, her phone rings and she says, "Ooh. Better take this. Hi, Charles? Yes, I can hear you now."

I watch her take off, disappearing around the same corner as the train of women. When she's gone, I draw in as deep a breath as I can, then look back at Lake Washington and the twinkling water. Warren would have loved this—sailing past Portage Bay to get to Lake Washington, the twinkling city lights and snow-capped mountains in the distance. The thought of my brother makes the center of my chest ache.

"Why do I have to deal with all this alone?" I whisper, then turn for the party, putting the biggest smile I can muster on my face as I enter.

TWO

CAZ

The gun is not my enemy, it's my friend.

The coolness of the barrel pressing against my temple provides a satisfaction I can't explain, especially when I remember all the horrors, the pain, and the violence.

With this gun, I could wash away everything I no longer wish to feel—agony, loneliness, the nightmares that continuously haunt me.

I've grown to love my gun,to care for it. To *feed* it. It craves the blood of my enemies and the pain of those who've caused me harm. It's not evil, nor is it good, but it *is* a part of me, like an extra limb.

I lie flat on my bed, bracing myself to give the trigger a pull with my finger. I stare up at the ceiling fan, the pointed silver blades spinning round and round, and for a fleeting moment it seems as if all the weight has been lifted. The world would be so much brighter without me in it. The sun will continue to shine, the grass will grow, flowers will bloom, and everyone will move on.

More pressure to the trigger, and I squeeze my eyes shut and think *this is it*. I'll leave this fucked up place and my body will turn to bone, then shrivel to dust. There's relief in knowing my grief will be washed away—that the burdens and worries will be no more.

More pressure to the trigger.

I squeeze my eyes shut tighter.

Why do I have to deal with all this alone? My eyes pop open and I stare at the ceiling fan again when I hear a voice so soft, so angelic, that my breath catches.

"What?" I whisper aloud. My breaths become ragged as I slowly pull the gun away from my head, and I wait...*wait...wait* for the voice to respond. To say something—*anything*. Just a whisper, at least, to let me know it's there. That I'm not alone.

But I don't hear it again. Just like a feather, it floats away, right out of my grasp, drifting into the dark depths of my mind. It's nothing but a hollow echo now, slowly fading away, despite how much I need it to stay.

I sit up on the edge of the bed, place my gun down beside me, and drag my fingers down the length of my face.

That voice in my head...it's not my mother. Not a friend. No one from my clan. It belongs to someone I'm sure I've never met before, yet I feel as if I know everything about her.

THREE

WILLOW

Relief washes over me when the boat docks and the partygoers leave. They stumble over each other, sweaty and drunk off their asses, but with smiles on their faces. For Lou Ann, that's a solid win.

I bid my farewells after checking in with Lou Ann and a few other Townsend colleagues, and don't waste a single second going to my hotel, packing up, and rushing to the airport for my midnight flight.

I board with first class to North Carolina (the highlight of this whole event—Lou Ann being able to afford first class tickets for us), decline the meal, but ask for a tequila and lime.

"Rough day?" the passenger beside me asks, a chubby man with a round face and even rounder cheeks when he smiles. He's balding and sweaty, despite his air vent being open and the A/C blowing on him.

"You could say that."

"Same here. Only the people who can handle the rough travel at midnight."

I laugh at that and raise a toast to him.

Once the plane lands, I book an Uber to take me home, tip the driver, and when they pull off, I stand in front of my condo building in Courtney Village with a relieved sigh. Looking left, I spot Bad Daddy's in all its rambunctious, late-night glory. It's one of the more popular hangout spots for a late drink and a burger. I don't have the urge to eat, and what I want to drink needs to be stronger than a couple of beers.

I drag my suitcase up the stairs, unlock my front door, and step inside. My place is just as I left it, clothes scattered all over the furniture, thanks to my last-ditch effort to pack for my trip. I overslept and was lucky I didn't miss my flight. The sink still has the two glasses from when I shared drinks with Faye, as well as a bowl I'd used for cereal, and plates from a few days prior. I sniff the air and wrinkle my nose. Something smells but I'm in no mood to figure out what it is right now.

With a sigh, I drop my suitcase by the door, kick off my shoes, and make my way across the studio to get to the kitchen. My liquor is lined up on a shelf on one of the walls, and I choose tequila again, pouring some into a glass tumbler, then retrieving a lime from the fridge to slice.

I carry it to my bed, which faces a window overlooking a parking lot. The lot is sparse, but seeing as it's four in the morning, I expect nothing less. Security drives by on a cart, the green lights flashing ever so slowly, alerting this side of the complex of its arrival.

I sip my drink. Suck the lime. I could grab salt, but not tonight. Tonight, I need the potency of the tequila swimming through my veins, the tanginess of the citrusy fruit to shock me.

I should be grateful to be alive, but lately I've felt nothing but sadness leaking in. After all, I have a roof over my head and I'm close to working my dream job of event managing. Sure, my boss takes my ideas and acts like they're her own—and yes, maybe I have an estranged father and my brother is missing, and my mother wanted nothing to do with me as a baby—but at least I'm alive. I should be happy, right?

Only...sometimes this life of mine doesn't feel worth it. Living, to me, is pointless if there's no one to share life *with*. There's always my best friend Faye who's there whenever I want to hang out, but there's still an emptiness inside me.

I miss my brother and my past life with him, laughing, joking, and grabbing chocolate brownie milkshakes on Sundays. I miss him telling me about the dumb girls he hung out with who he never understood or felt a proper connection with. Warren was always looking for love, always wanting someone to nurture and care for him. Someone who looked deeper than just looks and material things.

"Girls these days, Willow," Warren said one night over milkshakes. "They're weird, man. None of them talk like regular people. And what the hell is with them always saying something is *giving*?" He gestured to his milkshake, fluttering his fingers toward it. "This brownie and ice cream shake is *giving*! Let me put this on the gram for *errbody* to see, honey!" he said in a high-pitched voice, and I laughed so hard a chunk of brownie slipped out of my mouth. He couldn't help laughing either as I cupped my mouth, trying to contain the laughter. "Like, what does any of that shit even mean?"

I laugh at the memory, then take another swig of tequila while carrying my gaze over to the nightstand. I put my focus on the orange prescription bottle with the white label. I pop a pill out and shove it into my mouth, downing it with the tequila.

"You shouldn't take antidepressants with alcohol, Willow,"

Faye would say. She hates when I do it, but at least I'm taking them at all.

I lie back on the bed, staring up at the vaulted ceiling. The wood beams appear closer, the room spinning, and I close my eyes, breathing in and out.

What happens if I go missing too? Who would miss me? Like really, really miss me?

It's a thought so fast, so fleeting, that it terrifies me. My eyes pop open and I stare at the ceiling, but there's something different about it now. A purple streak of light is spread across it, waves bouncing on it like rippling water.

I narrow my eyes as I stare at it, and the purple streak forms into an oblong circle. It wobbles, the waves fading, as if someone is shaking a light onto the ceiling, and I sit up to look out my window. A projection or a person with a flashlight, I assume, but there's no one out there—no purple lights or flashing objects pointed my way. Not even security is nearby. I look up at the ceiling again, where the purple light still stretches.

I believe it's time for you to stop wallowing and pull your shit together.

I gasp when I hear a man's voice and shoot off my bed, peering around my apartment.

"Who the hell is that?" I shout. My pulse thumps in my ears like the foot of a rabbit. There are no corners to hide behind in my studio. It's an open floor plan and I can see everything, even the bathroom door, which is ajar, but there is the closet, and my eyes land right on the closed door of it.

I make my way to the kitchen, pulling out the biggest knife and holding it in front of me, then grab my phone from the counter.

"I'll call the police right now if you don't come out!" I move closer to the closet door, the knife shaking in my hand. I try steadying it, but with the tequila swimming through me and my nerves fried, it feels damn near impossible. It's not odd to think there's someone camping out in my apartment. After all, I'm hardly home and there are plenty of squatters looking for a warm place to crash.

I wipe my forehead with the back of the hand that's holding my phone and stand in front of the closet.

The police? Is that some kind of authoritative figure? If so, fuck them.

"Oh my God." I breathe out the words and build up the courage to grip the doorknob and open the closet door, ready to stab whoever is behind it, but I only end up stabbing air.

There's nothing inside but clothes and various shoe boxes stacked on the top rack. I turn on a light, shuffle through the line of clothing frantically, but it's empty. Completely empty.

A deep chuckle erupts, filling every hollow corner of my brain, and I whisper, "Who the hell are you?" before dropping the knife to the floor. I look for the purple light again, but it's gone now.

I don't hear the voice again for the rest of the night.

FOUR

WILLOW

It's the same dream again. I'm looking down at blood on my hands, blood smeared on clothes. My hands tremble as I try to decipher whose blood it is, but I can't. It's as if I have no memory—no recollection of who I am or where I've been—yet what I'm going through feels awfully familiar.

I peer up, surrounded by tall, lurking tress and a dense fog. I'm lost.

"Willow!" a man yells from a distance. "Willow, can ya hear me?"

This man sounds familiar—like he wants to help me. My heart beats faster, reacting to his voice. I try to scream—to call out to whomever he is, but I can't.

I grab my throat but it's wet and sticky. Pulling my hands back, I study them—more blood is on them now, wetter, thicker. It's spilling from my throat. I'm bleeding...but why haven't I died yet?

"Willow!" the familiar voice shouts again and I stagger to a stand, stepping on sticks and twigs that snap. A soggy leaf glues itself to my

bare foot, and the air becomes cooler. I try to find the voice, but I don't make it far.

Something grabs me from behind, its hands like ice, and I turn around to a figure in black. All I can see is their smile and the red eyes pointing upward at the edges like sharp crescents.

"*Go to him,*" *the dark figure growls.* "*So he can die.*"

FIVE

WILLOW

The sound of knocking pulls me out of my sleep, and I groan, rolling over in bed. Lifting a pillow, I bring it over my head, but the relentless knocking continues.

"What?" I yell. I lift one droopy eyelid to check the time on my alarm clock. "Are you fucking kidding me?" I hiss as another round of knocks sounds off. "It's seven in the morning!"

The knocking continues and I finally toss the pillow and comforter off, hurrying to the door. I check the peephole and my heart drops when I see who it is. *Really?* The one morning when I *don't* want to be bothered, he shows up? *Fucking Garrett.*

I debate ignoring it, but I know he'll keep knocking. Or he'll use the key I gave him...which I need back, by the way. Ugh. And he probably heard my voice just now. *Fuck.*

I drag a hand over my face, run a palm over my hair to smooth some of the frizz, rub the sleep out of my eyes, and then pull the door open. As soon as I do, Garrett says, "You didn't call."

I blink at him, letting the words register. Call? Oh. *Right.*

"Shit, yeah. I didn't. Sorry. I got home and completely crashed. I was exhausted." Garrett looks me over from the other side of the door, two coffees in hand and a box from his favorite New York City style bakery. His eyes swing across the apartment to the counter. I look with him at the bottle of tequila and the empty glass I used last night.

"Not exhausted enough to keep you from drinking, I see." He raises a judgmental brow.

"It was just one drink," I counter.

"If you say so." He shifts on his feet. "You gonna let me in or what?"

I step back, hugging the door as he walks past me. He places the coffees and bakery box on the counter, then takes a thorough look around. He does that a lot when he comes over, like he's looking for something—or *someone*, rather.

"Got your favorite." He offers one of the coffee cups to me.

"Thanks." I take it from him, moving across the hardwood floors and sitting on my sofa. I take careful sips and smile at him. "White chocolate."

"Yep." He carries his coffee with him. "So, uh, what time did you get in last night?"

"Four in the morning."

He huffs a laugh and I'm not sure what that laugh implies, so I don't react to it. We sit in silence a moment, sipping our hot beverages.

"You were right, you know," I finally say, and I hate the words as they spill off my tongue, but I can't stand the silence. Why is he even here? Why didn't he call first?

"About what?"

"About our...relationship." I glance at him, and he does his infamous brow quirk, waiting for me to say more.

"I know it's not fair of me to expect you to stick around when I'm hardly here," I go on. "I work a lot more so...I'm sure it's becoming frustrating for you."

"Yeah, it is." He sits back against the cushions. "But it's your job. That's why I came over to see you. Can't really be mad when you're making money to provide for yourself," he says with a smirk.

I force a smile and give him a onceover. He's dressed casually, jeans and a navy-blue T-shirt. He smells like sandalwood, and he's had his goatee trimmed into neat lines. His hair is the same floppy, curly top, trimmed around the ears. He looks nice, well-rested—the opposite of my current state. And because he looks so nice, it must mean he has to get to work himself. I find relief in knowing that.

I pick at the label on my cup with his name on it. "I was thinking, though..." I pause, letting the words marinate. "Maybe we shouldn't take what we have so seriously."

Garrett is quiet, so long I think he's upset. I lift my gaze, finding his. He's already glaring at me, his eyes hard and cold. "What are you saying? That you want to stop seeing each other?"

"What? No, I didn't say that at all!"

"Well, that's what I'm gathering."

"You're putting words in my mouth. I'm just saying, with my schedule I can't promise to always hang out. Plus, you have your job too. Life is getting busy for both of us." I lift the rim of my cup to my lips, but Garrett reaches over and clutches my wrist before I can take a sip. My heart drums faster as I glance down at his hand before finding his eyes.

"If you're tired of me, just say that." His voice is low, icy.

"I never said that," I reply evenly. My voice comes out steady and I'm glad. Any sign of hesitation and he'll question it.

Garrett glares, his hazel eyes intense, then he sighs and

releases my wrist, raising the hand he just held me with in the air and chuckling. "Look, I'm sorry. All right?"

I side-eye him.

"I just really wanted to surprise you with those movie tickets, so when you told me you weren't in town, I got a little upset. That's all."

"I understand," I whisper.

"Next time you'll let me know though, right? If you're going somewhere?"

"Of course."

"Good. I'm glad." He smiles, but it doesn't reach his eyes. "No hard feelings. Right, babe?"

I nod. "No hard feelings."

We both sip our coffees at the same time, and while I do, I try my best to control the beats of my heart. It's impossible. My pulse is in my ears, drowning out all noise.

This is what I mean. He's changed. There's an edge to him that I don't like—one I didn't realize was there until it was too late. At first, he was kind and caring. And when he'd show up at my door without a heads up, I thought it was cute. He'd always pop up with goodies, like flowers, baked treats, or coffee. But after a while, he became...territorial. And don't get me wrong, I love a guy who can prove he cares, but Garrett cares a little *too* much, to the point where it's unnerving.

There's one night in particular that made me realize Garrett wasn't the man I thought he was. I'd gone to help Faye unload a huge shipment of books at the bookstore she manages. We were there for several hours because she had to stock them and prepare for a launch day for a popular novel. When I was done helping her, I had four missed calls from Garrett and two text messages. I still remember the messages:

WHY AREN'T YOU ANSWERING ME?

WHERE THE HELL ARE YOU?!?

They were in all caps. I thought it was strange, and I called him back, but he didn't answer. However, when I got home, he was parked in the parking lot of my complex, waiting for me. He thought I was ignoring him. He got angry, then he grabbed me a little too roughly when I decided I wasn't going to argue with him about my whereabouts any longer. When he did that, I kicked him out and didn't speak to him for a week.

Then he appeared again, knocked on my door with cupcakes, put on that stupidly charming smile, and I took him in and forgave him.

I was stupid...but I also couldn't help myself because the truth was that without Garrett, my life was dull. I felt every dull, aching moment during the week I ignored him, and it sucked. All I did was drink or get high or sleep. It was depressing. Then I started thinking about how I possibly *was* guilty—that I should've spoken to him about everything like an adult, not gotten upset with him for wanting answers. Like I said, I was stupid.

There are times when I want nothing to do with him, like now...but then I remember, it's him or I drown myself in tequila and weed, and that makes me so damn lonely and desperate I can't stand it. But with the way he's grabbed me, he'll keep doing it. And I don't give a damn how depressed I am, or how much I wallow, I'd rather be alone forever than to tolerate a man who maliciously puts his hands on me.

"Oh—before I forget," he says pushing off the sofa and walking toward the counter. "Boris had the cinnamon rolls today. I snagged two before they sold out."

"You're kidding!"

"Not at all. Behold, the cinnamon rolls of glory, baby!"

I burst out laughing as I watch him sit next to me with the box open, revealing two large cinnamon rolls smothered in cream cheese icing.

"They look great. After I shower, we can dig in," I tell him, standing.

Garrett rises and walks to the kitchen. "Cool. Don't take too long. I'll have them nice and warm for you."

I smile at him as I make my way to my dresser, taking out a pair of sweatpants and a T-shirt. When I go to the bathroom, I close and lock the door behind me, start the shower, and then sit on top of the toilet seat, inhaling before exhaling.

I'm not sure how much longer I can keep this up. I have to officially break it off with Garrett. But when I do, I know he won't take it well. I don't know what he'll do, and that unknown terrifies the hell out of me.

SIX

WILLOW

I HAVE SEX WITH HIM. It only takes him six minutes to finish, and I only know because my eyes constantly slide to the alarm clock, waiting for it to be over.

After Garrett leaves within the next hour to go to work, I curl up in my bed again and sleep for two hours. When I wake up, there are three missed calls from Faye and two text messages. I release a breath, sitting up and pressing a hand to my head. Before checking the messages, I wonder why Faye would call so many times and realize there's only one explanation: She needs my help.

I trudge to the bathroom, brush my teeth, give my locs a rosewater and peppermint oil spritz refresh, and then call her back as I pick at some of my leftover cinnamon roll on the table.

"Um, hi. Why didn't you pick up the phone the first time I called?" she demands as soon as she answers.

"Don't I get a hello? Or how was your boat trip event thingy?" I ask, laughing.

"Oh, I'm sorry. How was your boat trip thingy, Willow?"

"It sucked donkey balls, thanks for asking."

"That's wonderful!" Faye shouts, her voice dripping with sarcasm. "No, I really do care about your event thingy, Willow, I really do, and you can tell me all about it very soon, but um...I have a huge issue."

"Okay. What is it?"

"Tonight is supposed to be the open mic at Lit and Latte's, but one of my employees called out, said she has a stomach bug. I could really use another hand, and you know I wouldn't ask you unless I *really* needed the help."

"Aw, Faye." I sigh then walk to my closet, shuffling through the clothes on the hangers. "Of course, I'll be there."

"Thank you soooo much, Willow! I owe you!"

"I planned on eating a burger and fries while binging episodes of *Bob's Burgers*, so yeah, you definitely owe me."

"Damn. That sounds amazing," she croons, as if longing for the same kind of mindless evening.

I laugh.

"Anyway, the open mic starts at seven. Please don't be late."

SEVEN

WILLOW

I DIDN'T EXPECT rain when I left my apartment, and I curse beneath my breath as I hop out of my car with a magazine over my head and rush to the entrance of Lit & Latte's.

I yank the front door open and lower the magazine as the bell above the door gives a light jingle.

"You made it!" Faye shouts from the middle of the bookstore. She bounces around a display table, dressed in a green midi-knit sweater and combat boots. Her thick, curly black hair is pulled up into a sleek bun, tendrils hanging around her heart shaped face and the nape of her neck. She pushes one of the tendrils off her tawny cheek, grinning from ear to ear, while I stand by the door, nearly damp and fighting a scowl.

"You're lucky I love you," I grumble as she approaches me, wrapping her arms tight around my shoulders.

"I know. I'm the luckiest bitch in the world." When she

releases me, I slide some of my locs behind my shoulders. She walks to the café counter and plucks a few napkins out of the holder. After I dry off as best as I can, she says, "Come on. Help me set up the chairs."

I follow Faye through the bookstore, walking past a round display table that contains the latest fictional book releases, then past the café counter with a "closed for now" sign pitched on top of it. There are cupcakes and other pastries behind the dome glass, and the espresso machine is still on, which means they'll most likely be using the café tonight during the open mic as well.

My eyes wander to the stairs leading up to the second floor. They've added string lights to the stair railing, as well as hanging plants above. I bet adding both was Faye's idea. It was her idea to add more lights and plants to the entire first floor to make it feel cozier and at home, give it a hygge vibe.

Faye moves past the seating area, where there are plush, neutral-colored floor pillows and green velvet couches. All the square, wooden tables that are normally organized in the center of the floor have been lined up and pushed against the backwall, replaced with three stacks of chairs.

Faye goes for the first stack while I continue looking around the store, pleased with the warmth of it. Weather sucks in North Carolina when it's mid-November and raining. Fortunately, the electric fireplace hums with life by one of reading nooks, the LED flames gleefully crackling, and the heater emitting enough heat to warm me up. I take off my jacket, feeling at ease as I begin to help Faye line the chairs into rows.

"You good today?" Faye asks as she sets up her last chair.

"Yeah. I'm okay."

"Just okay?" She eyes me as she picks up a clipboard.

"Could always be better," I return with a shrug. "You know that."

She lowers the clipboard with a sad smile. "Aw. What's the matter?"

"It's nothing," I tell her, waving a hand. I could tell her about my Garrett situation, but I don't feel like going there right now. "Listen, don't worry about me. Let's focus on your event tonight."

She gives me a onceover, her eyes traveling up and down the damp length of me, then she sighs and says, "When the night is over, you're telling me what's really on your mind," while pointing her pen at me.

I smile at her as she walks behind the counter of the café. She disappears behind the swinging door of the kitchen, and I turn to look at the front of the room where a red curtain hangs on the wall, a single microphone on a stand in the middle of the area. It'll be where the guests perform.

Faye returns with a tray full of fruits and cheeses and hands it to me. "You can set these up on the back tables," she says.

"Got it." I take the tray and head to the square tables to set the individual plates down neatly. By the time I'm done unloading the tray, there are people entering the bookstore already, shaking the rain off, and murmuring to each other.

Faye welcomes them all in, scans their virtual tickets from their phones, and as she does, one of the employees enters, apologizing for her tardiness. Faye tells her it's no big deal, but immediately gets her behind the bar of the café to get coffee going. Then she trots to me after getting some of the guests settled in, an anxious smile on her lips.

"I forgot the wine in the basement and more people are about to walk in," she whispers nervously, wringing her fingers together. She only does that with her hands when she's on edge.

"Hey, don't worry." I grab her hands. "That's why I'm here. I can go get it. Where in the basement is it exactly?"

"On the shelf straight ahead when you go down the stairs.

There's a whole case in a black crate. You can't miss it." She wipes the skin above her brow with relief, even though there's no sweat there.

"You've got it."

"Thank you so much, Willow."

A couple enters the store, and she smiles at me before rushing to greet them.

I make my way across the store, passing the employee lounge, which is set up with plenty of seating and tables, a refrigerator, microwave on the counter, and a box of what looks like donuts from Phil's. I approach the oak door that leads to the basement and grip the copper doorknob, swinging it open. It's dark as hell, so I immediately grab the switch above and yank it. The bulb in the ceiling illuminates the basement, buzzing as it clings to the light. Even with it, the idea of going down there creeps me out. Of course, I wasn't going to tell Faye this. She's my bestie and I can't fail her now.

I glance over my shoulder as a woman walks out of the restroom with a relieved sigh, then I draw in a breath, exhale, and make my way down the rickety wooden steps.

I spot the black crate she mentioned before I even make it to the bottom of the staircase, and relief floods me because at least I won't have to spend too much time searching for the wine.

I make my way across the basement, stepping between rumpled boxes and stacks of old books that smell like wet paper. There's a small window above the shelf, and I can see the rain really coming down, pelting on the blades of grass.

Reaching the crate, I pull out one of the bottles of wine. Riesling.

"Good choice," I murmur, studying the label. I check the alcohol percentage, but it's as I'm checking it that I feel a cool gust of wind drift past me, shifting a strand of my hair.

Frowning, I lower the bottle and turn around, but when I do, my heart plummets.

EIGHT

WILLOW

Fear seizes me when I realize I'm no longer in the basement. I'm standing in the middle of a dirt trail, surrounded by spiky, skyscraper trees. The air is cool all around me, nearly freezing, and I shiver.

Panic sets in because I don't know this place. I don't know where I am. Something heavy is in my hand—it's the same bottle of Riesling I took out of the crate. I still have the bottle, so that must mean I'm fine. I'm still at the bookstore...*right?*

I turn back around to face the crate again, but the crate is gone, replaced by a dirt path that leads to a foggy void. I can't see past the tattered gate at the end of the path.

I drop the bottle and wrap my arms around myself as the air grows colder. I'm in a forest I've never been in before. It's dark and the air feels and smells different. This place feels...*real*. But I'm at the bookstore. I was *just* at the bookstore.

All around me, there is nothing but silence and it's deafening.

The dirt crunches beneath my Chucks, proving that it's there—that this is really happening.

"How am I here?" I breathe shakily. "How am I here? How am I here?"

I swallow hard, tears welling in my eyes as I take a step toward the gate. If I move, maybe I'll snap out of whatever nightmare this is, but I can't move. I'm shivering again, paralyzed.

"Willow!" someone screams my name and I gasp. The voice is deep, familiar, and it's coming from the fog. "Willow, can ya hear me?"

I start to scream, to say something, but then I recall the dream last night—the blood spilling from my throat and onto my clothes. I reach for my throat, but there's no blood and I'm still in the jeans and graphic New York T-shirt I picked out before coming to Lit & Latte's.

"Willow!" the voice shouts, louder this time. It grows closer, closer.

Then a crackling sounds behind me, like a twig snapping, and it echoes. Something cold grips my arm—a hand digs into my flesh and forces me to turn around, but when I do, I face nothing but blackness. No trees. No light. No fog. Nothing but darkness and cold—a dark void where I can't see, hear, smell, or do anything.

The voice that was calling me is faint now. And before I can react, those red crescents from my nightmare—the evil red eyes—they watch me from above. The cold wraps around me like chains.

I can't move.

Can't scream.

Can hardly breathe.

I shudder and grit my teeth, no longer standing but floating closer to the eyes. Trying to withstand the pull, I kick my feet, pleading, but no noise escapes. Voice trapped, I float, thrashing and kicking, fighting for a way out.

Someone save me! Someone please help me!
Breathe, Willow. Breathe. Breathe. Breathe.
Willow!
Willow!
"Willow!"

I gasp as I open my eyes and come face to face with Faye.

"Willow? Jesus, are you okay? What happened?" she asks hysterically, looking me deep in the eyes. Her hand is on my arm, her head tilted in concern, but unlike the hand that grabbed me, hers is soft, her touch caring.

My eyes widen as I spin around, taking in my surroundings. I'm in the basement again. The cold is gone, replaced by humidity. I'm not floating, I'm standing in the same place I was when I was reading the bottle of wine.

"I…" I struggle to find words, my eyes bouncing around every corner, searching for those evil red eyes, but it's all the same. No forest. No fog. No cold. Just a basement with old shit in it…and now a shattered bottle of wine on the floor, liquid seeping into the cracks of the cement.

"I…I'm sorry, Faye. I—I don't know what's…"

"Are you sure you're okay?" she asks.

I look down at the wine. "Shit. I'm really sorry. I can go buy another one if you want me to." I can't help the shakiness of my voice. Something was just here. It tried to take me.

"Girl, no—what? Forget the wine! It's just a drink! You look like you saw a ghost! What the hell happened?"

I look into Faye's dark brown eyes, contemplating telling her what I saw and felt. It all felt so real, yet here I am. Standing still. Perfectly fine. Unharmed.

I touch Faye's face, making sure she's real, and her flesh is soft and smooth. She even has the sprinkle of light brown freckles on her tan skin, just as I remember.

"Okay...you're clearly not well. Come on. Let me get you upstairs." She wraps an arm around me and leads me past the shards of glass to get to the stairs.

I can hear jazz music playing before we leave the basement, and soon we're drowning in the noise as we move through the bookstore, past the mingling guests and the café, to get to the front counter.

"Sit," she insists, pointing to a stool behind the counter.

"I'm sorry, Faye. I—I really don't know what happened. I..." I swallow hard. How do I explain what happened without sounding like a complete lunatic?

I was in the basement and then it turned into a forest, and I was floating in darkness! Something grabbed me—no, you grabbed me! But it wasn't you, it was something else! Something evil!

"Willow," she murmurs, squatting in front of me. "Please tell me what's going on with you."

"Nothing's going on, Faye. I just...I thought I saw something in the basement but...it was nothing. It couldn't have been anything."

She considers that a moment. "Is this about Warren?"

When she says my brother's name, I freeze again and avoid her eyes. "No."

"Your birthday is this weekend," Faye continues. You're turning thirty. He'd be turning thirty too."

"Faye, please." I close my eyes and rub the center of my forehead. "Not here. Not right now."

"You have to talk about him, Willow. You can't keep holding it in."

"I'm not holding anything in. I'm fine, really!" I exclaim, a little louder than intended. "I'm—I'm medicated. I'm living and breathing. I'm fine."

"I called your name six times in the basement," she says, concern swimming in her eyes. "It's like you were looking past me and at something else when I tried to snap you out of—of *whatever* the hell that trance was."

I push off the stool and step sideways. "Don't worry, okay? I'm fine. I just think you're right about the meds and tequila. Maybe now is a good time to stop mixing the two." I laugh but there's no humor to my tone, and Faye can sense it because she doesn't laugh with me. She's still worried, and I don't blame her.

"Come on, let's go get that wine before people realize they're still sober," I say, steering the subject.

A smile pulls at the edges of her lips, but it doesn't reach her eyes and I know she's still thinking about the basement and about whatever the hell that trance of mine was. Hell, so am I. But Faye has guests and tonight must run smoothly, so she doesn't put up a fight, despite how badly I'm sure she wants to.

And besides, what happened to me has *nothing* to do with Warren, nothing at all. And even if it did, he's the last thing I want to talk about right now.

NINE

WILLOW

I ACT as normal as possible throughout the entire open mic, despite Faye coming to check on me every ten minutes. When the night is over and the guests are leaving, Faye thanks them all and waves them off, and while they exit, I help Mel (the employee who showed up to run the café) stack the chairs.

It's as we're dragging the tables back to their designated areas when Faye returns with a heavy sigh. "Just leave it. I'll be in early tomorrow to fix things before opening."

"Are you sure?" Mel asks, standing upright.

"Positive. It's been a long night and the storm is going to get worse. We should get out of here while we can." Faye walks down the hallway to get to the employee lounge and collect her things. Mel does the same, and when they return, I'm sliding into my jacket and pulling my car keys out of the pocket.

Faye wishes Mel a goodnight and watches her cross the

parking lot to her car, and when it's just us, Faye turns and asks, "So is it just tequila at your apartment?"

I ENTER MY APARTMENT, kicking out of my shoes right away as Faye follows me in. She slips out of her damp jacket and hangs it on the coatrack by the door along with her purse, and then looks around my place.

"Ugh! What the hell, Willow? This place is a mess." She walks to my dining table and picks up the empty box my cinnamon roll was in.

"What? I haven't been home long enough to clean it yet," I counter.

"I can see that." She scrunches her nose. "And *what* is that *smell*?"

I look around, as if I'll spot where the smell is coming from. "Hmm. So, it isn't just me smelling that then?"

Faye ignores my comment and marches to the kitchen, and when she notices the dirty dishes in the sink, she groans. Immediately, she rolls up the sleeves of her sweater, turns on the faucet, and begins rinsing the dishes.

"Faye, you don't have to do that!" I yell at her from the couch.

"If I don't, who will?"

"I will...when I'm in the mood."

She cuts her eyes at me briefly before putting her attention back on the dishes. "So are you going to tell me what that was about at the bookstore, or am I going to have to get you drunk and force the truth out of you?"

I knew this was coming, yet even with the question lingering in the air and having nearly two hours to think about it afterward, I still can't bring myself to present a solid answer.

"Okay..." I sit up on the couch. "It's going to sound crazy, but I've been having these really weird dreams. Or maybe they're hallucinations? I don't know."

"How long have you been having them?" she asks nonchalantly, as if I just told her I love chocolate. That's the thing about Faye. She's not easily shocked. She's normally calm and even-tempered.

"They started a couple weeks ago. Right after I returned from Atlanta." I chew on my bottom lip. "But the first dream was kind of tame compared to the one I had last night and today. The first dream I was in some house, lost. The house was huge and I heard people talking, but no one came to find me. I also hear, like, this voice—some man's voice. He has an accent. British, maybe?"

"Go on..."

"I don't know who he is or anything, but he feels familiar somehow. Anyway, when I was in the basement, I was in a forest. It was cold and the trees were really tall and scary looking. And I think something was hunting me or chasing me...I can't be sure. But that guys voice, I heard it again this time too. Like he's calling out for me or looking for me before whatever that thing is can catch me."

"Hmm." She scratches the side of her head. "Maybe it's stress."

"Why would it be that?"

Her eyes find mine. "Because you bottle a lot of shit up. Maybe it's finally starting to eat at your brain."

I roll my eyes then stand, going to the dining table to clear it. I might as well keep myself busy too.

"Maybe you should talk to a therapist," she offers.

"I don't think that's necessary."

"I'm telling you, Willow. When I saw Dr. Wan, she was incredible. She really put my mind at ease with the grief I had about my mom's death. She helped me heal...and I'm going to be honest, I think that's what you need to do. You need to heal." She turns the faucet off after filling the sink with water and suds and says, "I'm worried about you. I really am."

"Why?" I ask, laughing. "I'm fine. Please don't overreact. And why didn't you use the dishwasher?"

"You're drinking more, and the antidepressants don't seem to be helping," she goes on, ignoring my last remark. "You're seeing and hearing things, and I'm worried that you're secluding yourself. You're forcing yourself to be lonely."

"No, I'm not."

"Really? If I hadn't called you tonight, would you have called me to see what I was doing?"

I debate an answer. "I would have texted you...*eventually*."

She scoffs, rolling her eyes and going back to the dishes. "All I'm saying is I think it would be good for you. If you're seeing things and having bad dreams, maybe it means something, you know? Maybe it means it's finally time to talk about Warren's disappearance."

I avoid looking at Faye as I carry some of the trash to the trash bin. "If I take the therapists' number, will you stop bringing up Warren?"

She grins so big it nearly splits her face in half. "I promise."

Faye tidies up a bit more (what can I say, she's an incredible friend, with a nurturing side to her that I'm grateful for) and after she shares a chicken salad sandwich from Lit & Latte's with me, she gives me a tight squeeze and leaves before the storm gets any worse.

When she's gone, I walk to the liquor bottles lined up on the counter, grab the tequila, and pour some into a cup. I take a big chug, then drag myself through the living room, shut off all the lights, finish my drink, and flop on the bed to bury my face into my pillow and scream.

After my breakdown, the storm strengthens. Lightning strikes and thunder causes the thin walls of my apartment to rattle. I pop an antidepressant into my mouth, chug it down with water instead of tequila this time, and then shuffle through my nightstand until I find my joint papers and a little baggy of green.

I pause when I notice the polaroid picture of me and Warren. I pull it out slowly, staring at it. It's us, the year before he went missing. We were at a New Year's Eve party and I can't remember who took the picture, but they captured Warren with his arm draped around my shoulder and a "yeah, right," look on his face. I'm looking up at him, pointing and laughing. I was most likely teasing him about something, like I often did.

I stare at the picture so long my vision blurs and I bite into my bottom lip, not wanting the tears to fall. I breathe in, exhale, and then grab my weed before shoving the image back into the drawer and slamming it closed.

I roll a joint, spark it, take a deep pull, and then lie flat on my bed, peering up at the ceiling fan. It's not spinning tonight, but the more I smoke and the higher I become, the more it seems the fan is spinning, or perhaps it's the lightning outside. The blades start slowly, then begin to spin faster.

I huff a laugh, realizing I'm probably hallucinating again, but that's okay. At least I'm home. At least I'm safe.

Safe? I hear a deep voice ask. It's that same voice—the one I thought I heard in my apartment. The same one from my nightmares that calls out to me. ***No one is ever really safe, are they?***

I roll my eyes. "Nice try. You can't scare me tonight. I'm too stoned."

Stoned? What a strange word choice.

Okay. This is humorous, albeit freaky. I can hear this voice intwining with my thoughts. The voice isn't scary. If anything, it seems the voice is familiar with me, yet I have no clue who it belongs to. "Who the hell are you?" I ask. "Seriously—why can I hear you but not *see* you? Wait, are you my conscience?"

It's quiet for a long time, so long I think maybe I *am* making this voice all up in my head.

I've wondered the same thing. Who the hell are you? And why the hell has your voice been tormenting me?

"Holy shit," I breathe. *No. Not real. Not real.*

Trust me, this is very real, the voice says.

"What the hell?" I sit up to put out my joint. That's clearly enough of that. I go to my drawer, taking out pink pajama pants and an oversized Clemson T-shirt and changing. Then I lie back down and watch the ceiling fan, allowing it to distract my thoughts. But then it stops spinning, replaced by an oblong purple circle.

It's that purple light again. It shakes and moves, wiggles like neon purple waves. I blink slowly and, unlike last time, I don't get up to check if it's coming from outside. Truthfully, I don't care what this light is or where it's coming from, but I'm intrigued by it, and it's better than thinking I'm crazy by talking to some random voice in my head.

The light spreads across the ceiling and moves closer to me, and I raise a hand, reaching for it. I'm surprised when I touch some of it and the purple waves spill like liquid onto my fingers, slowly running down the inside of my arm and dribbling onto my cheek. I use my other hand to wipe my cheek while studying the purple glowing liquid on my fingers, then look back up—the light has spread more. It's rippling faster.

My body becomes weightless, and before the realization hits me, I'm floating toward the light. It ripples faster, faster, and I'm getting closer. I draw in a deep breath as if I'm about to go under water, and I think to myself that this is all comical. I'm so high that I'm imagining myself swimming in this purple pool of water, dancing in it. I feel the water on my flesh, illuminating my brown skin. My body floats higher, higher, and then I'm in the purple vortex pool, floating effortlessly. I turn over and look down, right at my bed. I can see my whole apartment from here, a bird's eye view.

And that's when I panic. I shouldn't be floating. I shouldn't be in the vortex. *How fucking high am I?*

I try to swim back toward my room, force my body down, but it's useless. This vortex is strong, and it sucks me in further and further. I kick my legs, spread my arms, and even try clawing onto something, but there's nothing to hold on to.

I continue floating, my room appearing smaller and smaller the more I'm sucked in. Eventually, my room is gone, and I'm swallowed whole. The purple light fades to a blinding black, and for the second time tonight, I belt out a helpless scream.

BLACKWATER

TEN

WILLOW

Breathe.

Breathe.

Breathe.

I repeat the words internally and finally open my eyes. To my surprise, the blackness has faded, but the entire front side of my body throbs in pain.

Groaning, I push up on my battered hands, then gasp when I realize I'm on top of damp dirt. I scramble upward, hands shaking as I stare down at the clumps of soil on them, then look up. I can't believe it. I'm *here* again—in the forest from my nightmares.

My breathing becomes shallow as I spin to look all around me. I'm surrounded by the same skyscraper trees that give no light or leeway, and there's nothing in view for miles. I have the urge to walk, but where the hell am I supposed to go? Which way? *What do I do?*

My eyes drop to the dirt path below me that runs from left to right. If I follow it, maybe I'll find out where I am.

I start walking to the right, telling myself this isn't real. I'm dreaming again, that's all. I got really fucking high and now I'm dreaming.

"Wake the fuck up, Willow," I whisper. "Wake up. Wake up." But the words are useless. And perhaps this isn't a dream because my shin is burning. It's a pain I've never felt before, and it causes me to stop walking. I lower into a squat, yanking up my pajama pants to check my shin, and there's a large gash. It's not deep, but there's blood dripping down to my bare foot.

I work hard to swallow, then look around for something to stop the bleeding, but nothing here will stop it. I need to find help. Fast.

"Damn it," I mutter. I must be dreaming, and if this is a dream, I can control it, right? I can find a way out—a wacky way that will take me back to reality.

I almost laugh at the thought until I hear a low growl ahead. My stomach drops as I freeze, eyes widening as the growling becomes louder.

Slowly, I look up to where the noise is coming from, and fear paralyzes every fiber inside me. Ahead is a wolf with all black fur. All its sharp teeth and even its magenta gums are revealed because it's snarling so hard. The wolf's hazel eyes bore into mine and it takes a step closer, lowering to its haunches, ready to pounce.

Every part of me wants to scream, but if I scream, it will attack me. *But this is a dream. It's not real. I can get out of this.* I stagger to a stand, and the wolf growls louder, then barks.

"Easy," I whisper, my voice shaking as I hold my hands in front of me. "Please just...go away."

The wolf moves closer, barking again, gnashing its teeth, and the warmth drains from my body. "Please," I whisper. *It's not real. This isn't real...is it? Please, God, tell me this isn't real.*

My heart is beating twice its rhythm, I'm so scared.

I take a step back as the wolf moves closer. If I run, he'll run after me. If I keep standing here, he'll attack me. I look down at my leg again. The blood is dripping between my toes, mixing with the black dirt.

My best bet is to run. Fuck my leg. Fuck this dream. I can't just stand here and get mauled. I have to do something, so I pivot and run, allowing the adrenaline to course through me. My run is weak, and I feel myself limping, but I don't care.

The wolf barks again. It's coming after me.

I dash through the trees, glancing over my shoulder at the wolf. Branches scratch my cheeks and leaves slap me in the eyes, but I *run, run, run,* my heart beating madly, my mouth going dry.

My shin sears with pain as I glance back, and the wolf continues snarling at me. Looking back was my mistake because as soon as I face forward again, my ankle catches onto something, and I fall.

I land flat on my stomach, roll over, and scoot backwards. The wolf's paws pound into the earth and then it leaps forward, landing right above me.

"No!" I whimper as it cages me between its legs.

It growls in my face, its damp snout touching my nose, and I close my eyes, pleading silently.

Please don't kill me. Please don't kill me. Please don't...

"Cerberus!"

My breath hitches when I hear the voice, and immediately the wolf's snout is off mine. I open my eyes, keeping my body perfectly still as the wolf runs away.

My heart gallops in my chest as I listen to sticks breaking, footsteps approaching. I hear the panting of the wolf again, and before I know it, it's standing right beside me, wagging its tail. And then a man appears only a couple steps away, dressed in all black.

ELEVEN

WILLOW

A FLAT BLACK cap is on the man's head, creating a shadow over his eyes. Worn black leather gloves are on his hands, which are at his sides, and he stands only a few feet away, wearing a creaseless black trench coat. I have a feeling he's staring at me, but I can't tell due to the brim of his hat being so low.

"Who are you?" the man asks, voice gruff.

His voice. I know that voice. I just heard it moments ago, in my apartment. It's deep, an English accent—a dialect I'm not familiar with. I've heard many people with all kinds of accents, thanks to my line of work, but not his. His is different and hard to forget—a voice that has haunted my dreams and played tricks with my mind.

I try to find the words to speak, but my tongue feels like a dead fish in my mouth.

The man moves forward, only now his hands aren't empty. There's a silver handgun in one of them, and he's pointing it right down at me. The gun is twice the size of a regular handgun, the barrel so wide I can see into it without squinting an eye.

I throw my hands in the air. "No—wait!"

"I asked who you were."

"I—I'm Willow. Willow Austin."

"And where did you come from, Willow Austin?" he asks, the gun hovering inches from my face.

"I—I don't know. I landed here, and that—that wolf started chasing me! If I'm not supposed to be here, I'm sorry! I'll leave, I swear, j-just please don't kill me!"

The man remains steady with the gun, and he tilts his head upward. When he does, I see his eyes. Icy blue, surrounded by thick, dark lashes. His eyes are both intimidating and alluring as he glares down at me.

"Are you from Ripple Hills?" he demands.

"I—no, I don't know what that is."

He squints his eyes, only slightly. "Vanora? Did Alora send you?"

"Please," I plead. "I don't know what you're talking about. I don't even know where I am!"

The wolf growls at my outburst.

"Oi!" he shouts at the wolf. His eyes don't leave mine. "Home. Now, Cerberus."

The wolf doesn't hesitate to dash away. As it does, the man lowers the gun and steps back. "Get up."

I do as I'm told, wincing as I bring myself to stand. I face him and angle my chin upward a bit because he's tall. *Really* tall. His jaw ticks as he looks me all over.

"You're not dressed like you're from Ripple or Vanora. Where are you from and why the hell are you on my property?"

"I told you," I breathe raggedly. "I—I ended up here somehow. I really don't know."

He narrows his eyes at me, angling his head. "Have we met before?"

"I...I don't think so...unless you work with Townsend a lot too, then maybe. Probably through Lou Ann."

"Lou Ann?" He raises a brow.

"My boss."

He stares at me blankly.

"Um...I'm sorry...do you happen to have, like um...a cellphone or something I can use?"

"A cellphone?" he asks, frowning now.

"Yes—like an iPhone or something? Even an Android? iPad?"

He grimaces, and by the way his jaw ticks repeatedly, I can tell he's becoming aggravated. Okay, I get that we're kind of in the middle of nowhere, but how the hell does he not know what a cellphone is?

"What territory are you from?" he demands.

"Territory? I, uh... *What?* I don't understand the question. I'm so confused right now." I swallow hard. "Look, I just want to go home," I tell him, holding my hands up. "That's it. I don't want any trouble."

"So you *do* have a home. Where?"

"Um...an apartment...in North Carolina."

"What the hell is a North Carolina?"

"Oh, God." I scoff, then I laugh because this man can't be serious. I'm standing in front of a person who doesn't even know what state we're in, who owns a wolf, and has a gun. All red flags.

"I'm sorry, were you born under a rock? How do you not know what North Carolina is?"

He frowns but doesn't respond. Instead, he lifts his gun again and aims it directly at my face, and I throw my trembling hands in the air.

"Turn around and walk."

"I—where am I supposed to go?"

"Follow the path north."

"North...north. Um...okay." I turn around with a limp and hobble through the forest until I spot the path. I can either go left or right. Right feels like going north, so I turn that direction, but he clears his throat. I glance back, and he points the other way with the gun.

"Yep. Got it," I whisper.

I limp my way along the path, and within two or three minutes, an iron gate appears. It reminds me of the gate that was in my dreams. Only there's no heavy fog, and I can see what lies ahead very clearly: land—lots of land. The grass is cut neatly, and a rocky path leads to a gothic black castle. It stands tall, the tips of the dark roof flirting with the gray clouds in the sky. I stop walking to take in the view, my jaw nearly dropping. Where the hell am I?

"There's an exit that way. Go to your *North Carolina* and don't come back," the man says behind me. I turn a fraction to look at him. He still has the gun pointed at me.

"You're going to let me go?"

"I don't care where you go, just don't ever come back here."

I swallow hard, but the saliva is rough going down. I wobble to the right where he's pointing, and though I don't see an exit, I don't care. It's better getting lost than being faced with a gun that size again.

I need to find help from someone nicer than this asshole.

"What was that?"

I spin around and face the man again. He's lowered his gun a bit, just enough to see me clearly past his hand.

"What was what?" I ask.

"You just said something."

I frown. "I didn't say anything."

"I heard you speak," he retorts.

"I—I didn't say a word."

Frustrated, he lowers the gun. "Do that again."

"Do what?"

"Think about something."

"Um...okay." I swallow hard and try to think of something random. Or clever. Faye would know what to think of. Knowing her, she'd think of a penguin or a baby chick...or books. She loves books.

Who the hell is Faye?

I shift my gaze up. "She's my best friend."

"What?" he asks, shock written all over his face.

"You asked who Faye is..."

"I didn't ask that out loud." He looks at me sideways. Then as if a realization dawns on him, his blue eyes expand. "*Shit*." His throat bobs. "You're that voice," he says. "You're *her*."

"Who?"

The man looks me up and down, as if seeing me for the first time.

You can hear me.

My eyes stretch when I hear his voice, loud and clear, despite his lips not moving.

"H-how are you doing that?"

"Shit," he curses again. The man clears his throat and tucks his gun away, then digs into his trench coat. He opens a silver case and plucks out what looks like a cigarette, except it's all black. Pressing it between his lips, he lights it with a silver lighter, inhales, and then puffs out a large cloud of smoke. It doesn't smell like an ordinary cigarette. It's scent is sweeter, like maple syrup and spices.

"You're her," he says, nodding. "You're that other voice in my head." He gives his head a shake. "All this time I thought I was insane."

This conversation is starting to feel real, and it's weird, so I say, "Maybe we're just dreaming?"

"Trust me," he rasps, pulling from his cigarette thing again. "This is no dream."

"What do you mean?"

He drops his eyes to my foot, and I look with him at the caked dirt and blood. "You're bleeding. Follow me." He walks past me toward the castle-like home.

I hesitate a moment as he marches away without looking back. I peer over my shoulder at the forest that was behind us, then toward whichever exit he pointed at that I still can't make out, and figure it's probably best to follow him than to wander around, lost. I don't know this man, and I don't know where I am, but he has shelter...and possibly a phone.

He also has a gun, I think to myself.

"Don't worry about the gun," he calls out, still walking toward the castle. "I won't use it on you unless you make me."

TWELVE

CAZ

I don't trust this woman, and yet I'm leading her into my house. I'm clearly losing it. But I heard her voice...heard it without her lips even moving. That's the voice from my head, now in the flesh. The voice has a face and a body and a bloody heartbeat. The voice breathes and hums. It's her, I know it is, but what the hell is she doing here? Or better yet, how did she find me?

I open the front door, leaving it wide so she can follow me inside. I carry myself down the marble foyer, past the dark columns wrapped in vines, until I'm in my kitchen. There's a bell by my backdoor and I pull the rope down, ringing it twice.

When I glance over my shoulder, the woman isn't there. I march around the corner, and she's standing in the middle of the foyer, gawking at one of the portraits on the wall.

"What the hell are you doing?" I demand, and she turns her head to look at me.

"Is that you?" She points up at the painting from Aunt Maeve

—the one she had done for me when I first built this place. Black horses with manes of fire, and a shadowy man riding one of them toward total darkness. The horse the man is riding reminds me of Onyx.

The woman turns to look at me, awaiting an answer.

"Come to the kitchen," I order, giving her my back. She appears this time, and I tell her to sit at the table.

"Any chair at the table?" she asks, pointing at the twelve-top.

"Would you please just sit?" I grumble, and she does, taking the chair closest to her.

I'm glad when I hear footsteps and Della appears. She smiles at me, light wrinkles forming around her eyes and mouth, and says, "You rang for me, sir?"

"Yes, Della." I gesture to the woman in the chair. "I need you to stitch her up. She's bleeding on the leg. Where, I don't know, but the sooner it gets done, the sooner I can send her off."

Della focuses on the Willow woman, and her smile stretches even more. "Of course, sir." Della walks to the Willow woman, grabbing her hand and helping her stand. "Right this way, dear. I'll have you all stitched up and ready to go."

"Do you have a phone?" the Willow woman asks.

"I beg your pardon?" Della looks between her and me, confused.

"She keeps asking for this *phone*. I don't know what she's talking about."

"Right." Della wraps her hands around the Willow woman's and leads her toward the stairs. "Come with me, and we'll learn more about this phone thing you speak of."

I watch them go. The Willow woman looks back at me with a frown before snatching her brown eyes away.

How the hell do they not know what a phone is? Her voice echoes in my head, and as Della takes her upstairs, I don't hear anything else. I'm glad.

When they're completely out of sight, I grip the edge of the wooden counter and shake my head. This cannot be happening—not right now. This Willow woman—she's a distraction. She must be.

I leave the kitchen and make my way back down the foyer toward my office. My transmitter is on the desk where I left it, and I pick it up.

"Tell Maeve there is an emergency. Meet me when she can. Allow her to track my location."

The transmitter blinks red, then neon blue, and I watch the screen load the words before sending my message off. I replace the transmitter, set my gun on the desk, and sit in the chair behind it.

Is he always so on edge? I hear the Willow woman's voice, which is strange considering she's probably near Della's chambers a floor up. I shouldn't be able to hear her, yet I do. How the hell does this mind-voice thing work exactly? Now that she's closer, does that mean I'll hear her conversations too? Can she hear mine? I pray for the person who has to suffer through my thoughts.

"Don't you answer that, Della," I grumble.

Ever since I've known him, yes.

I refrain from rolling my eyes and work my jaw instead.

It must suck working for him, the Willow woman says, huffing a laugh.

Not at all, actually. Mr. Harlow takes very good care of me.

I smirk. *Take that, Willow Woman.*

Is he angry sometimes? Yes. Della goes on, and I work my jaw again. *But he's not as horrible as you may think.*

So, I was right. You are *a jackass. Good to know.*

"Right. That's it." I push out of my chair and march back to the kitchen, heading up the spiral iron staircase until I'm on the second floor. I make a left turn and stride toward the wide-open French doors. I'm in Della's wing. It's been a while since I've set foot here. She's spruced the place up with Vanorian flowers, a few Blackwater plants, and mauve wallpaper.

"Are you about finished?" I ask as she wraps a bandage around Willow Woman's leg.

"I am, sir. I would like to give her some new clothes—these are...unique. And filthy, might I add. Perhaps I can find some in Juniper's closet?"

"I don't think Juniper would approve," I counter.

"Juniper will live. It's either that, or you take this young woman to the village and let her pick out her own attire. You don't want her walking around in dirty garments, do you?"

Oh, for fuck's sake.

My eyes move to Willow Woman's and she's smirking. Shit. I can't let her stay in my head. I frown and envision a wall of rocks surrounding my brain. Then I cock a brow at her, and she narrows her eyes, confused.

"Fine. Borrow something from Juniper's. When you're done, send her to my office."

"Understood, sir."

I turn and leave the room, but not before hearing, **Eww. Why is he walking around like something's stuck up his pale ass?**

I don't bother looking back, despite my fists clenching at the remark.

THIRTEEN

WILLOW

Della leads me down the iron stairs, and I can't help noticing how sharp the rods connected to the railings are. I have the urge to touch one of them but fear I might injure myself if I do, and I don't think Della is in the mood to stitch me up again.

I'd already given her a hassle when we went to this Juniper person's room. Della sifted through the closet, trying to find something that might fit me while telling me that Juniper and I are about the same size. She finally settled on a black and white two-piece tweed outfit with a white blouse to wear beneath.

The outfit, though a bit stretchy around the waist, is tight and ridiculously itchy and I told her that, to which she said it was either this outfit or a dress. We debated about the dress and two piece and, finally fed up, Della said, "Trust me, it's this or he'll have you walking around half naked until the clothes you have on right now are clean." I finally decided to let it go, and she smiled triumphantly as she led me behind a steel room divider for privacy.

Afterward, she brought me a gray liquid in a vase and told me to drink it. "It will heal your leg," she said, and sure enough it did. I no longer feel pain or limp when I walk. The scar is still there, raw beneath the bandage, but I feel almost back to normal. Almost because I still have no idea where the hell I am.

When Della rounds a corner and enters the kitchen, she stops at the middle of the wooden counter and plucks something out of a bowl. "Here. Eat this," she commands lightly.

I take the charcoal gray object from her, frowning. It's odd shaped, with deep grooves, like a dog toy. "What is this?"

"Fruit, dear," she says. "You eat it."

"Yes, I know you eat fruit, but what *kind* of fruit is this, exactly?"

"It's a blackfruit. Fresh from the lake trees."

"Blackfruit?" I blink twice at it before meeting her eyes and forcing a smile. "Thanks?" I raise it in the air. That's the most she'll get because I won't be eating this random black fruit.

"Mr. Harlow is in his office." Della points toward the foyer we came from when I first walked into the castle. "Go straight down and you'll see it on the left. If you'll excuse me, I must go to the village to pick up tonight's dinner."

Della pats my shoulder with a smile before walking out of the kitchen. She turns a corner and disappears, and I have a feeling I won't be seeing Della again—well, I hope I don't. Hopefully by the time she returns, I'll be home again, in my bed.

Sighing, I clutch the mysterious blackfruit in hand and make my way through the foyer. As I do, I drop my gaze to my feet, at the pointed shoes with silver tips that remind me of the tip of a sword. The shoes are odd and a little too snug on my feet. There's no way I'll be able to walk in them for long. I'm better off going barefoot. "These are most certainly popular right now," Della had said as she handed them to me. They most certainly *shouldn't* be.

Papers rustle as I move closer to the office. As I step around the corner, I spot a bush of black and gasp. I leap backwards as the black bush wags and realize it's that wolf again. It stands on all fours when I walk closer, eyes locked on me like I'm prey.

"He won't bite unless I command him to," a deep voice says. I shuffle to the right, and the man—this Harlow person—is sitting behind a desk, going through sheets of tan paper.

"He almost attacked me in the forest," I counter.

"I intervened before he could."

"Yeah, at the last second," I mutter.

He drops the papers to snap his fingers. "Here. *Now*, Cerberus." The wolf immediately walks around the desk, sitting on its hind legs beside his owner. He doesn't take his eyes off me.

"Take a seat." He gestures to the metal chairs on the opposite side of the desk. I swallow hard as I move forward carefully, pulling one of the chairs back and sitting.

"You should eat that," he says. "Blackfruit is extremely rare and good for you."

"I've never had one."

He stares at me, carefully assessing me, then goes back to fingering through some of the papers.

"What do I call you?" I inquire.

His eyes flicker up to mine briefly before dropping again. "Caz." He finally stops fiddling with the papers, giving me his full attention. "You said in the forest that you *fell* here." His hands fold on top of the desk. "What did you mean by that exactly?"

"I mean that I literally *fell* into that forest. I don't know where I am, or how I got there, but it's not my fault I ended up there."

"What is the last thing you remember before falling?"

"Um...well, I was smoking on my bed."

"Smoking?"

"Yes, weed." I eye him, and he appears confused. "It gets you high."

"High? Like quish does?"

"Quish?"

He shakes his head. "Never mind. Continue with the last thing you remember."

"I was on my bed, then I saw a purple light on my ceiling. I touched it, and it's like I was brought closer to the light. I remember looking down at my bed, trying to get back to it, but then everything went black. The next thing I know, I'm on the ground, surrounded by trees, and my leg is bleeding."

He doesn't react. Just stares at me, and it makes me uncomfortable, so I sit up straighter in my chair. Cerberus growls, and a yelp forms in the heart of my throat.

"He doesn't like sudden movements," Caz informs me.

"Oh...um...my apologies, wolf."

"Is there anything else you remember?"

"Uh...well, before I saw the light, I heard a voice." My eyes lock on his as I debate whether I should tell him *whose* voice it was. I decide to bite the bullet. "I'm pretty sure it was yours."

He's quiet a moment, his gaze lowering. "I heard you in the forest when Cerberus was chasing you. Not your actual voice. The one in my head. I knew exactly where you were without any kind of lead."

"How?" I ask.

"I don't know."

Why didn't you stop your damn wolf sooner then?

Caz tips his chin. "You should watch your thoughts. I can hear them."

I frown. "Then stop listening."

"Kind of hard to do when it seems I'm meant to hear them."

I press my lips. "Why can't I hear all of yours?"

"Because I'm not allowing you to."

"What? How can you do that? Do you know about this—*whatever* this thing is we can do?"

"To me, it seems like a form of telepathy. I don't know how it works, or why we share it, but I know someone who may have an idea. She should be on her way to me soon. She'll be able to figure out where you came from and, hopefully, how to get you back."

"Okay. Finally, some good news. In the meantime, what about a phone?"

He sighs, clearly exasperated. "I'm assuming a phone is a form of communication for you."

"Yes, that's exactly it." I sit forward. "Do you have one?"

"We don't have phones. We have transmitters. Unfortunately to have one, it must be assigned to you and if it isn't, you must ask permission to use it, so I can't let you use mine."

"Not even if I ask for your permission?"

He picks up that same silver case from before, plucking out another black cigarette thing with a simple shake of his head.

"Wow. Okay, so how do I get in touch with someone? How can I get my own transmitter thing?"

"You really aren't from around here." He exhales, sitting back in his chair. "Transmitters in Blackwater are only given to those higher up in ranking and the people who work to have them. I have absolutely no clue who you are other than your name and I don't know where you're from, therefore it will be nearly impossible to provide you a transmitter."

"That's...really stupid. Where I come from, anyone can have a phone as long as they can pay their bill."

"Their bill?" he frowns. "Does that involve trading goods and rubies?"

"No." I pinch the bridge of my nose. This is incredibly frustrating. "Look, I seriously need to get back home. I appreciate you taking me in and helping me out, but the sooner I can get back, the better."

Just as I air my statement, the front door bursts open and a man barges in, nearly out of breath. He's tall, wearing a dark-gray tweed suit. A black cap similar to Caz's is on his head, and the jacket of his suit is open, revealing a gun in a holster, but it's no ordinary gun. The gun he has is black and massive—bigger than the one Caz had in the forest.

"Caz!" the man hollers, huffing as he enters the office. "We're gonna need you at The Tavern! Yusef's at it again, but this time he has the fucking Rippies with him! Killian is still there and he's pissed 'bout it. If you don't get there soon, I have no doubt Killian'll kill 'em all."

Um...what? The man talks so fast it's hard to understand a word he's said, and his accent doesn't help me discern much of it, other than there's trouble.

"How many Rippies other than Yousef?" Caz asks, much calmer than what seems ordinary for an outburst like this.

"Three, but they're big bloody fuckers. Ugly sons-a-bitches too." As if he's just noticing me, the man steps deeper into the room and grins. "Ello, who's this?"

Caz stands, walking around the desk. "That's what I'm trying to figure out."

"She coming with us?" the man asks.

"She damn sure isn't staying in my house alone." Caz stops at the door of the office to look at me. "Get up. Follow along." His eyes then dart to Cerberus. "Cerberus, on guard."

The wolf dashes past the random man and Caz, heading out through the crack of the front door.

"Where are we going?" I ask, following them out of the office.

I tail them out the front door and a car is parked up front—

made of dark gray metal. There are no headlights. Instead, the lights are on the side of the car, the rims sleek, black. It's so...*futuristic*—nothing like I've ever seen before. And when the other man opens the back door and gestures inside, I realize this Caz person must be more important than I thought.

"Don't ask questions. Just ride," Caz says in response to my question.

"Ride what, exactly?" the man asks behind the wheel, grinning, and I roll my eyes.

Caz gives him a glare. "Shut up and drive, Rowan."

FOURTEEN

WILLOW

So far, I've learned that Rowan has a hookup tonight with a *delicate thing* from a place called Vanora, he has an obnoxious laugh, he doesn't take many things seriously (unlike Caz, here), and he's Caz's cousin and one of his right-hand men.

How do I know he's a right-hand man? Because when we pulled up to this tavern he spoke of at the mansion, he parked, pulled out his massive gun, looked at Caz, and said, "If you want, I can go in there and pop all their fucking heads off. It'd take me a minute, probably less."

Now, Caz is shaking his head. "I'll handle this, Rowan."

"Suit yourself." Rowan shoves his car door open, and Caz does the same.

"You," Caz says, dipping his head back into the car and pointing at me. "Wait here and don't fucking move." He's gone before I can say a word, slamming the car door and marching toward the black building. A black and silver sign is attached to the building with the words *Blackwater Tavern* in bold lettering. The windows are square and prison-like with bars over them. I'm not sure if that's to keep danger out, or to prevent escape for those who go inside.

Anxious, I sit forward and watch the men go inside, then take a sweep of my surroundings. This place is dark and cloudy, despite the sun lingering behind thick clouds. Everything is black and gray, including the dirt on the ground, and every building appears to be coated in a thin layer of ash.

Deep voices rise behind me, and I watch as three men in all black walk toward the tavern.

"Shit—Caz is here!" one of them shouts.

"Oi! Blackwater Monarch is in the tavern!" another whoops. "It's fucking on, now!"

The men dash toward the tavern, bursting through the double doors. Bright gold light pours out as the doors swing apart, then darkness again when they're closed.

I have to get out of here. I'm not about to sit like some damsel in distress, waiting on this Caz character to come back. I smell trouble all over this tavern, and I don't want to be here when the crazy shit goes down.

I open the car door and step onto the dirt. There's a magnetic pull to it; it clings to the silver tips of my shoes. Stepping forward, I close the door behind me and take another thorough look around.

I'm surrounded by buildings that look like they were built decades ago—some homes, some stores. A restaurant is nearby, black umbrellas pitched above the outdoor tables. People walk by themselves or with horses along the street. What time period is this? They have no cellphones but do have these fancy cars and guns. None of it makes any sense. I'd think I time traveled, but it's like I jumped forward and backward and ended up here, somewhere in the middle.

Someone around here must have something I can call home with. If I can get in touch with Faye, or even Lou Ann, I can get out of here. I can't be too far away from home. For all I know, I blacked out or sleep-walked to this place—this foreign place where the air is thicker, the atmosphere darker, and I can taste salt in the air.

I spot a woman walking in a dress. Her hair is pulled into a fishtail braid and she has a child with her. A mother will help. I start to make my way toward her, but a loud *bang* causes me to gasp, and I stop dead in my tracks.

I spin toward the tavern and the doors burst open as a large dark-skinned man comes barreling out, gripping the collar of a white man's shirt. The dark-skinned man shoves the other one onto the ground, mounts him, jerks an elbow back, and slams a large fist into his face.

"Oh, shit!" I back away as he continues punching the man over and over again.

A crowd files out of the tavern to watch the fight, throwing their hands in the air, hollering and cheering for this man, and drowning out my screams. Even as the big Black guy conjures blood from the one on the ground, they cheer. He punches the man until his face is bloody and raw, then he hops to a stand with his crimson fists in the air and roars, "Who's next?"

"Enough, Killian." Caz makes his way through the crowd, unbothered, like this is the norm—as if he's constantly watching bloody fights between men around here. Meanwhile, I'm still cupping my mouth, stunned by what just happened and too afraid to move. "Bring them here," Caz demands.

Two men stumble through the crowd, and Rowan is right behind them, his big gun pointed at their backs. "You try anything, and I'll blow your fucking heads off," Rowan says with a sneer. "I wouldn't test me either. This here's a new gun and my finger's been itching to pull the fucking trigger."

"I'm going to ask you this one last time," Caz says, standing in front of the men. "Who sent you?"

The men stare at Caz. One of them, a skinny man with a bald head, quivers, while the other, plump and hairy, wears a tight grimace on his face, chin tipped defiantly.

"Fuck you, Caz!" the defiant one spits. "You'll be fucking dead soon!"

Caz doesn't react. He only stares at the man. Then he says, "On your knees."

The man grimaces harder but doesn't move. Caz gives a simple nod of the head, and the Killian man charges forward with his bloody hands and grips one of the defiant man's shoulders, forcing him to his knees, and then gripping the back of his neck. The man winces but remains insolent.

"Who's telling you I'll be dead soon?" Caz asks. "Go on. Say his name."

"I'm not telling you shit," the man hisses.

"You came to *my* tavern, knowing damn well you were in *my* territory, and you gleefully stirred shit up. You caused a scene like this to drag me here. So tell me, who wishes me dead?"

The man raises his chin, nostrils flared, and Caz sighs before taking a step back, opening his coat, and drawing out his gun. Killian moves away as Caz points the gun at the center of the man's forehead.

"Very well."

Those are the last words Caz says before pulling the trigger and sending a bullet flying through the man's skull.

My heart drops and I back away again, but I can't bring myself to make a single noise, afraid he'll use it on me next. He just... killed that guy—murdered him in cold blood, and everyone is still standing around, watching this man bleed out like he was slapped or something. Oh, God. Am I in hell?

Caz swings the smoking barrel of the gun toward the quivering man, who immediately throws his hands in the air.

"It—it was Rami! Rami sent us!"

"Why?" Caz barks.

"I—I don't know, I swear, I don't! T-they paid me! I just took the rubies and did what they said!"

"Yousef, you dumb fuck," Rowan grumbles.

Caz keeps his gun pointed at Yousef, then he takes a step closer, pressing the hot barrel to his forehead. It sizzles on his skin, and Yousef whimpers. "Anything for rubies, eh, Yousef?"

The man squeezes his eyes shut, his hands in the air, silently pleading.

"Do me a favor. Run to Ripple Hills—and when I say *run*, I do mean *run*. Run the whole fucking way and don't stop until you're at Rami's door. And when he opens that door, you tell that filthy fucker that he'll be dead before he gets the chance to say my name again."

"Y-yes. Yes. I will. I—I promise. I'll tell him," Yousef pleads.

Caz stares at him a moment longer, then lowers the gun and steps away. "Okay then." He tucks the gun into the holster inside his coat. "Run. *Now*."

Yousef nods and scrambles away, not daring to look back. Rowan lifts his gun and points it at Yousef's back, and Caz raises a hand to the top of Rowan's gun, lowering it to the ground.

"Let me use it once today. At least a shot in the leg," Rowan says in a near pout. "He'd still make it to Ripple Hills."

"If Yousef ever returns to my tavern, you can aim for more than his leg next time."

Rowan rolls his eyes, but he doesn't protest as he puts the gun away.

"Right! Show's over!" Killian barks, waving his bloody hands. "Get the fuck back in the tavern or go home!"

The bystanders grumble as they make their way inside again, and as they do, Caz turns and looks at me, as if he's just now noticing me.

"I told you to stay in the car," he snaps.

"Who's this?" Killian demands.

"He won't tell us," Rowan says. "He's being all secretive about her. You think that means he has a thing for her, brother?"

"Depends on where she's from," Killian says, still glaring.

"Fuck off, both of you," Caz grumbles. "Have either of you seen your mother?"

"Last I heard, she was visiting Helen."

"I need her," Caz says, then he looks at me again. "And you." He points a stern finger at me. "Since you clearly have a hard time following orders, come inside where I can watch you."

I can't believe there's a place I'm more terrified of than his home or the forest that surrounds it. This tavern doesn't seem like a place for a woman to be, but he doesn't wait for me to protest. He doesn't seem like the type to wait for anything.

Caz marches into the tavern, the two men trail him, and I draw in a lungful of salty air before entering the tavern too.

FIFTEEN

WILLOW

The tavern has a historic vibe, which I find interesting because here are these men with their big guns and fancy, futuristic cars, and yet everything inside this place looks to be made of items from the 1920s. Even down to the way they dress, in their dark clothing, thick trousers, and black caps. All of it feels aged, yet there's something about it that screams it's ahead of my world.

They have unique clothes and guns. Even the liquor on their bar doesn't look like ours. Theirs is in bigger bottles made of steel instead of glass, with black and brown labels. The glass tumblers they use are a crystal-like vintage. Folk music blares from the speakers, and men are shouting as they slam cards and poker chips down on a table during a heated card game.

Women dressed in short dresses sit on some of the men's laps, and behind the bar is a man and woman in all black serving drinks. It's like *The Great Gatsby* and *Blade Runner* had a baby.

Caz and his henchmen march past the bar, and most of the

people steer clear. A woman literally leans back so she doesn't touch them as they pass. They continue down a dimly lit hallway and make a left.

I hurry along, keeping my head down as a few men in a corner become rowdy. Another set of men stare at me, probably wondering who I am.

When I take the left, two French doors are ahead, propped open and revealing a dark, spacious office. The office walls are covered in shelves, filled to the brim with books. A rolling ladder is perched in front of one of the shelves, and I have the urge to walk over and climb on it, just to swing around all the shelves and discover what kind of literature is in this office, but I don't. They're already looking at me like I have two heads. It's best that I blend in.

Caz walks around the large wooden desk in the center and pulls back a leather chair, taking a seat. Rowan and the big Killian guy sit in wooden chairs on opposite sides of the room. Killian begins wiping his bloody knuckles with a damp towel, and Rowan places his new gun on his lap like it's a pet, lightly stroking the metal with a cloth to remove smudges.

"Have a seat. Maeve won't be long," Caz says to me, gesturing to the chair on the opposite side of his desk.

I look from him to Rowan and Killian, who both cock a brow before returning to what they were doing. Their mannerisms are identical, yet they look completely different. Killian is dark skinned—darker than me—with a bald head. He's buff and appears to be made of muscle. One of his ears is pierced with a steel hoop, a red jewel engraved into it. Rowan is strong looking in his own way. He's not buff like Killian, but there's something hardy about him that warns you not to cross him. His skin is paler than Caz's, freckles peppered across his cheeks and the bridge of his nose. His hair is a dark reddish-brown.

I move across the room, pulling a wooden chair back and sitting. My eyes drop to a stack of leatherbound books and notebooks near the corner of the desk. Three fountain pens lie in angles atop a scattered set of papers, and a brown stain in the shape of a ring is on the upper left corner of one of the papers, most likely from a cup of coffee or tea.

Behind Caz is a rusted black gas lamp, lit and flickering, and on each wall at least two to three pillar candles, offering warm glows. "Who is Maeve?" I ask after clearing my throat.

I look into Caz's eyes as he removes the worn black gloves from his hands. He doesn't answer. Instead, he pulls out yet another black cigarette thing from his silver case. When he sparks it, I sigh. What I wouldn't give to get high right now. Or maybe I'm still high and that's why I'm imagining all of this.

"She's our mother," Rowan answers, and Caz cuts his eyes at him before returning them to me.

"Wait...she's your mother and who else's?" I ask, because I could've sworn Rowan said they were cousins in the car.

"She's *our* mother." Rowan gestures between himself and Killian.

"You two are *brothers?*" My brows lift with surprise.

"Where the hell did you find this woman, Caz?" Killian grumbles, clearly agitated by my question.

"In my forest," Caz replies as he exhales, letting a chain of smoke spill through his full lips.

"Your forest?" Killian continues a frown. "What was she doing there? Spying?"

"No," Caz says, and nothing more.

"Is she wearing Juniper's clothes?" Rowan sits forward in his chair. "She looks like Juniper right now. That's literally the weird shit Juniper would wear."

"Rowan, please." Caz rubs the center of his forehead.

Someone knocks on the door, and I look back to see a short, pale boy with a gray cap on his head, his hands folded in front of him.

"Mr. Harlow, sir," the boy says, his head slightly bowed. "Maeve and Juniper have arrived."

"Good. Send them back."

Caz puts out his cigarette, placing it on an ashtray, and then clears his throat as he leans back in his chair. Moments later, a woman appears between the double doors of the office. For the first time, I see someone dressed in color. She's wearing a red skirt with a color-block white and black blouse tucked into it. A red hat with black and white beads is on her head, and her hair is in tight pin curls beneath the hat, not a single hair out of place. Red rubies wrapped in gold dangle from her ears. Her heels click as she enters the office saying, "This'd better be important, Caz, or so help me..." The woman stops in the middle of the office, staring at me.

"Who's this?" she asks, but by the way she looks at me and the way her jaw drops, it feels as if she knows *exactly* who I am. I feel like I should know her too, but I don't. I've never seen her before.

"Maeve, this is Willow Austin," Caz announces, "and she's the reason I've called you here."

The woman continues staring at me, her mouth slightly ajar.

"By the stunned expression on your face, I'd say you know exactly who she is," Caz goes on.

"No—I...I mean, yes, but...*how?* How is this happening *again?*" Maeve finally closes her mouth, pressing her red lips together and looking from me to Caz.

"Um...I'm sorry. Is anyone going to tell me what's going on?" I ask.

I glance at Rowan, and his eyes are wide as he shrugs hard, his shoulders practically touching his ears.

"Mum, why don't you have a seat?" Killian suggests, rising from his chair.

"Yes. I'll do that." Maeve walks across the room, sitting in Killian's chair. He rubs her arm, and she gives his hand a quick, affectionate pat. She pauses on the pat, stiffening as she studies his knuckles. "What happened to your hand?"

"Had to kick a Rippie fucker out," Killian says, pulling his hand away.

"Language, Killian!" Maeve snaps, releasing his hand and then shaking her head. "Back to the issue at hand. Caz, where did she come from?"

"She landed in my forest, Maeve." Caz folds his fingers on the desk. "She doesn't know how she got there, or how she ended up in my territory, but she was there. Cerberus found her. Fortunately, I got there before he could rip her to shreds."

Oh, fuck him! I frown at Caz.

He stares back at me, one eyebrow cocked. **Fucking me should be the last thing on your to-do list right now.**

My jaw drops, and I start to say something, but Maeve shifts in her chair and clears her throat. She's staring at me again. I shift uncomfortably.

"You'll have to pardon my gawking, darling. It's just—well, the last time I saw you, you looked different. Your hair was...not like this. It was shorter. Curlier."

"What do you mean? My hair has always been like this," I tell her.

"Right...to *you* it has. But the last time I saw you... my word, that was nearly ninety years ago."

"Ninety?" I ask, confused. "Do you mean nineteen?"

"No, *ninety*."

I frown. "Uh...okay." I'm nowhere near ninety so it couldn't have been me. "I'm sorry to ask, but how old are you exactly?"

"One-hundred and fifty-eight," she replies casually.

I blink several times, trying to process the number that just came out of her mouth. She doesn't look any older than fifty—if that.

"Okay. This...um. This is all *really* weird and confusing. Do you think you can tell me how to get back home, please?"

A woman rushes into the office with a crystal glass in her hand. The liquid in her glass sloshes over the rim, spilling over her tan knuckles. "Late, sorry!" she chirps. "I needed this very badly before coming back here to deal with you lot!"

"Juniper, if you're going to drink, just stay at the damn bar," Caz grumbles.

"Oh, shut up, Caz. I had a long day, all right? Do you know I was in the village today and some woman tried to *fight* me? She was out of her bloody mind! I calmed her down, but she kept calling me a bitch, because apparently, *I've* been sleeping with her husband." She takes a swallow of her drink. "You should've seen that greasy fucker! Like I'd ever waste my time having an affair with a man like him!" Juniper sips her drink again, and her eyes bounce from Caz to me. "Ohhh...who's this?" She grins.

"Just sit and be quiet," Caz orders.

Juniper frowns and makes a face at him before slinking her way across the office and sitting on a black bench against the wall.

"Anyway, Willow, I suppose getting back would be the same way you got here," Maeve informs me.

"I don't even know how I got here. It's not like I was planning to come to this place."

"What's the last thing you remember before arriving?" she asks.

"She was smoking and was high on something called *weed*," Caz drawls, rolling his eyes.

"Weed?" Rowan and Killian ask at the same time. "What the fuck is that?" Killian asks.

"Is it like quish? The shit that made Newton lie in the middle of the street and get trampled by a fucking horse like an idiot?" Rowan laughs.

"Language!" Maeve snaps again, rolling her eyes.

"It's a narcotic," I explain. "It...makes me feel good. Probably like whatever you just smoked, Caz," I say, gesturing to the half-cig on his ashtray.

"That's not called weed. It's bloom," Caz says. "And it doesn't make me high, or whatever you call it. It just calms me down."

"Well, that's exactly what weed does for me. It calms me down and clears my head."

"Bloom is the finest you can find," Caz goes on. "I'm sure your *weed* holds no comparison."

"How the hell would you know? You don't even know what it is," I argue.

"She was doing drugs," Killian interrupts, cutting his eyes at Caz. "Can we really trust a junkie?"

"*Excuse me?*" I turn to glare at Killian. "I am *not* a junkie," I growl. How fucking dare he?

He ignores me, still looking at Caz. "I don't trust her, or this whole story about landing in the fucking forest."

"You don't even know me," I counter. I don't give a damn if he just beat some guy to death or whatever the hell he did, he's not about to treat me like I'm scum on the bottom of his shoe.

"What if she's here to hurt you? You led her right into your home, your place of work—she could be working with the Rippies for all we know!"

"I *would* know," Caz responds calmly.

"How?" Killian demands.

Caz pauses before looking at each person in the room, and

then me. "Because I can hear her thoughts—well, the important ones, it seems."

"What?" Killian asks, irritated.

"If she were here to harm me, I would know it, Killian. She and I have already gone over this. I don't know what kind of fuckery it is, but we can hear each other without saying a damn thing."

"You mean like telepathy?" Juniper asks, perking up on the bench.

"Exactly," Caz answers.

"Just like the woman from ninety years ago, only it wasn't with Caz. It was with Tepper," Maeve says, looking me over.

"Who's Tepper?" asks Caz.

"He was a friend from Whisper Grove. I met the old Willow through him. He was close friends with your mum."

"And where is this Tepper now?" he asks.

Maeve lowers her gaze. "Dead."

I don't know why, but my eyes lock on Caz's when Maeve says that, goosebumps sweeping across my skin.

"So let me get this straight. There's someone in this room who can get into Caz's mind? Shit!" Rowan laughs, nudging his brother in the ribs with his elbow. "We can use that, brother! Talk about a loaded gun!"

Killian folds his arms, still frowning, finding none of this amusing.

"Unlike her, I can control my thoughts," Caz informs them.

"How?" I ask again because he's never explained it.

"I practiced when I first started hearing you. Months ago. I didn't know who you were, didn't trust you, and I knew deep down I wasn't going out of my damn mind, so I learned. I had my own mind and I wanted to keep it to myself, just like everyone else gets to."

"Yeah, but *how*? How do you block me out?"

He shrugs.

"How can I block *you* out?"

A smirk tugs at the edges of his lips. "Practice, I suppose."

I groan in frustration. That answer doesn't help me.

"If all of this is true," Maeve interjects, stepping forward, "then I think the bigger question is why is she *here*? Why now, during the middle of this feud with Ripple?"

Caz studies Maeve before shifting his eyes to the left. "I'm trying to figure that out myself."

The room falls silent. We bounce our eyes over each other, listening to the music amplify from the bar, the rambunctious chatter gravitating down the hallway and sneaking into the office.

"I know who we can go to," Maeve finally says. "But you won't like it."

Caz narrows his gaze, looking into Maeve's gray eyes, and Maeve cocks a brow, giving him a silent answer that I can't grasp.

"No," Caz growls, pushing out of his chair.

"She can help us, Caspian. You know it."

Caspian? Is that his full name?

"I will *not* go to her. Not after her truce with Ripple Hills. And you stop worrying about my name." He points a stern finger my way.

"She made the wiser choice, and you know it. She didn't want to pick sides anymore," Maeve goes on.

"Which is exactly why we *can't* trust her! She can easily use that to her advantage to keep us against one another."

"Well, if you don't lower your pride and go to her, you'll never get this girl back to whatever world she came from. Alora has connections to powerful Mythics. She'd know who to talk to about this."

"Oh—no. No, I *have* to get home," I say quickly. "I can't stay here. This place is dangerous and, no offense, but I feel really sick here—like this whole place gives me nausea."

Juniper snorts into her glass while Killian grumbles something incoherent.

"If we don't go to Alora, Willow might be stuck here," Maeve urges. "And I'm sure the last thing you want is this woman in your hair during this mess with Ripple. She'll become a liability—one we don't need, especially if people find out she can hear what you're thinking, Caspian."

Caz's head shakes, but he doesn't disagree. With a sigh, he cuts his eyes at Killian, who says, "I'll send the message," and immediately stomps out of the office.

"Juniper, Rowan, tell Veno to get a car ready," Caz orders, planting his fists on top of the desk. "Looks like we're taking a bloody trip to Vanora."

SIXTEEN

CAZ

***I just want** to go home. I can't stay here. I need to get back. Oh my God, is that kid skinny dipping?*

I stare out the window, trying my hardest to block out Willow's thoughts. The car is completely silent, yet it feels as if she's screaming. I can't take it. This incessant whining has to stop. The interesting thing is I can block her out, but there are times when I can't stop her thoughts from tangling with mine. It seems the closer she is to me, the easier her voice can slip through the cracks of my mind's wall. I'm not sure I can hear her deeper thoughts, just the thoughts that bubble to the surface. They seem louder when she's afraid or worried. Either way, it's incredibly annoying.

Besides, she's the one who dropped here. All of us have far more important things to do than getting her back to where she belongs.

Oh my God. What if Faye came by again? She'll be worried

sick, especially after that stupid basement nightmare. Oh—and Garrett! Damn it, Garrett. He has a key. He's gonna see I'm not there. Didn't tell him I was going out of town again either. What am I going tell him when I get back? He's going to be pissed. Am I ever gonna get back? Yes, I have to. There has to be a way.

Garrett. I've heard her say that name—I'm not sure when, but it's someone she knows. Someone she cares about. Either way, the name annoys me.

Veno drives slowly through Blackwater Village. We're in the SUV, Maeve seated upfront. Willow is in the second row, wedged between me and Killian, and Rowan and Juniper are in the back row. I'd have taken the front seat, but Maeve is older and I'm courteous.

"I was going to wear that outfit to a party, you know." Juniper places her chin on my shoulder, looking sideways at Willow.

"You were?" Willow looks over her shoulder. "I'm sorry—I told that Della woman that I didn't want to wear these clothes, but she insisted."

"Della is lucky she works for us," Juniper gripes.

"Juniper, sit back."

"Caz, will you shut up? I'm getting to know our new friend here!" I know Juniper has just rolled her eyes. She's lucky she's my damn cousin—the only person who gets away with telling me to shut up. "Anyway, Willow, I think it looks great on you. Suits you better than me."

I press the pads of my fingers to Juniper's forehead, pushing her back lightly to remove her head from my shoulder. I feel her scowling at the back of my head.

"You know I don't like people touching me." Which is why it's taking everything in me not to lose my shit being in such a tight space, seated next to a woman I don't even know. Her thigh is too close to mine, the heat of her skin radiating through the material of her clothes, and I feel her breathing. Not to mention she smells different...not like the women in Blackwater, who usually smell like sand and water. She carries a sweet smell, something subtle and foreign. I've never smelled anything like it before.

We should've driven separate cars.

"Why?" Willow asks, turning her head to look at me.

"What?" I meet her eyes.

"Why do we need separate cars?"

I rip my gaze away from hers. For the love of Vakeeli. How the fuck did she hear me?

"You're not as quiet as you think you are," she murmurs. I glance at her, and she rolls her eyes, then turns to look out the window next to Killian. "How long will it take to get to wherever we're going?"

"Ten hours to Vanora from Blackwater," Maeve says from the front.

"Great," Willow replies sarcastically.

I don't want to sit next to you either, trust me.

Willow whips her head and glares a hole into the side of mine.

Why are you such an asshole?

I don't acknowledge her. Instead, I look out the window again toward one of the villages as we pass it. Shadow Village. Darker buildings, sharper roofs, grumpier citizens.

Now you're going to ignore me?

I roll my eyes. I need my wall again. I think of it—big rocks wrapping around my brain. My eyes close briefly as I draw in a breath, and then exhale.

"So, if you can read Caz's mind, can you ask him if he's the one who stole my TC-15?" Rowan asks from the back.

"You're still going on about that damn gun!" Juniper laughs.

"Yes! That was a brand-new, high-quality TC-15! Highly rare, might I add! I killed Wesley with it, remember? That pig."

"Why would Caz steal it?" Juniper asks.

"To sell it. I don't know," Rowan grumbles. "He has a habit of taking shit that doesn't belong to him and tossing them on the barges."

"Not from family," Maeve says over her shoulder.

I don't bother acknowledging either of them, but I can feel Willow looking at me.

"Veno, stop at the Barix," I order.

"The Barix, sir?" Veno glances at me through the rearview mirror, confused.

"Yes. Now."

"Yes, sir."

"What are we stopping at the Barix for?" Maeve peers over her shoulder at me.

I don't answer, but I feel all their eyes on me. It takes less than ten minutes to arrive at the Barix, and when Veno pulls into the vacant parking lot and unlocks the doors, I climb out and rush toward the building. The Barix is my third home in Blackwater, the tavern being my second and the mansion being my first. It's where I keep my cars, my money, and many of my guns.

Slipping my hand into my pocket, I pull out a set of keys, finger to the designated one, unlock the metal door and swing it open, then I head for the keys hanging on the wall, belonging to my cars. I grab the key fob to my favorite black X-Stinger, then slam my fist on the garage door button to open it.

My X-Stinger sits beautifully in the garage, amongst other cars of various styles—SUVS, pick-ups, two-doors. All of them are mine, and I breathe a sigh of relief as I march to the first black one and climb behind the wheel. I reverse out of the garage, close it, and then tap a button to lock the building back up.

"Seriously?" Maeve shouts out the window. "A ten-hour trip won't kill you, Caspian!"

"It will when I'm with this family. I'm driving alone. Don't wait up."

Maeve scoffs and rolls her eyes, but she doesn't argue. She knows she won't win. She tells Veno to go and he pulls off, hitting the main road that leads to Vanora.

I watch the car grow distant and allow my mind's wall to lower. Just as I do, I hear Willow's voice again, asking so many questions. None of them bother me but one: **What the hell is wrong with him?**

I drive, leaving the vacant lot of the Barix and trailing behind Veno. It's a great question—one I'm sure she doesn't want the answer to. Because if she knew, she'd never look me in the eyes again.

VANORA

SEVENTEEN

WILLOW

The ride to the Vanora place feels like forever. I'm not sure if it's because of the anxiety I have, riding to this unknown place, or because it seems everyone in the vehicle is watching me, including the driver. I feel them all stealing glances, wondering what my true intent is when I have none.

Regardless, I've dozed off several times, not to my liking, but the cars are different here. The SUV has heated seats, and even the backseats recline for added comfort. The car rides smoothly along the blacktop roads, hardly hitting any bumps. It's impossible not to fall asleep. Other than a bathroom break about four hours in, we haven't stopped.

I wake up when the vehicle loses speed, and when I open my eyes, I can tell we're not in Blackwater. The sky doesn't look the same as before, that gloomy gray that lingered. Now, the sky opens up, the clouds parting, a picturesque sunset revealing itself. Then the trees appear, bright green and lush, leaves swaying in the wind. Some of the leaves are gold, with more gold dripping along the bark of the trunks. Fascinating. We pass an abundance of land and go through several tree groves until Veno slows the SUV more.

I look through the windshield at a gold gate ahead. In front of the gate are armed soldiers wearing ivory suits, their matching hats pulled down to their brows. Veno stops the car as one of the soldiers approaches.

"Identification," the soldier requests after Veno lowers his window.

Veno looks to Maeve, who is already shuffling through her black leather handbag and pulling out a shiny black card. Veno takes the card from her and hands it to the soldier, who reads it and then tips his head, eyeing Maeve.

"Nice to see you again, my lady." The soldier smiles and hands the card back to Veno, and she returns the smile, taking the card and sliding it into her bag again.

"Alora is expecting us," she informs him.

"Yes, we've been told. You're free to go."

Veno bobs his head and rolls his window back up. The gold gates ahead split apart, and when he drives through, I notice pearls twinkling in the golden rods. As he drives farther in, a sign appears, made of gold and edged with rubies and pearls.

You have entered the land of gold.
Welcome to Vanora.

I thought the land we'd passed outside the gates was beautiful, but as we enter Vanora, my jaw drops—I'm stunned by the city's splendor.

Veno takes us along a paved white road, passing gilded horse carriages and markets. The people are dressed beautifully, coming in all shapes, skin tones, and sizes. There are smiles—lots of them—as they make trades, and children run in silky clothing, bouncing through tall grass. I glance up at children on a bridge in bathing suits. They scream as they jump off the bridge and land in a body of water that shimmers like gold glitter.

Hills of green make the distant land, and only a short run away are the bluest waters I've ever seen, stretching out farther than the eye can see. It's nearing sunset so the sky is a mass of purples and pinks, with splashes of orange from the sun that causes the water to sparkle. I'm nearly pressing my face to the glass as I drink it all in. I've never seen anything like this. It's all so miraculous. A place a human could only ever dream of.

We pass another market, where soldiers walk on foot, patrolling the area. Not too far away from the market are houses, some big, some small—and even those that look like duplexes. The homes are simple colors—white with brown roofs, or brown with white roofs. Gold gutters and décor. From what I see, none of the homes are more than two stories high... that is until I spot a palace in the distance.

Marble upon marble, with columns throughout and pillars that sparkle. Statues stand outside the palace, lined with gold, the doors gilded too. We drive along a bridge, cerulean waters beneath us, and I capture a view of waterfalls below. It's like a dream, this place.

"Beautiful, isn't it?" Juniper's voice is in my ear. I look over my shoulder and she's leaning over the leather seat, resting her chin on top of it.

"Very."

"I'd live here if I could."

"Why don't you?"

She shrugs. "I belong to Blackwater. It's where I was born. I'm also in the Blackwater Clan. Makes sense to stay."

I'm not sure how to perceive that. Perhaps the rules are different in their world as far as where a person can live.

Juniper sits back, and Veno swings around a roundabout driveway, parking next to a large fountain with a statue of a woman in the center. The woman is in a long, flowy dress, reaching to the sky.

When Veno kills the engine, everyone climbs out and I follow suit, popping my door open and stepping onto smooth, white cobblestone. The cobblestone shimmers beneath the sunset, like tiny diamonds have been crushed into it.

I hear the tires of a car approaching and look back. Caz pulls up behind Veno, and it's astounding how much the Blackwater cars stand out in this place. Black with silver rims, next to all this white and gold. It represents them and their wicked demeanors for, sure.

Caz steps out of his car, looking right at me with a grimace. *Shit.* Did he hear me? He cocks a brow, and it's enough for me to know he probably heard every thought.

His eyes finally peel away from me, and he tips his chin, looking upward. I follow his gaze, and up the stretch of stairs, standing at the very top of the palace, is a woman.

She stands there, donned in white, with gold threads weaved into her dress. She's adorned in gold jewelry that shines beneath the sunset, the bottom of her dress blowing with each breeze. A large hoop is pinned in her left nostril, connected to her left earring, and she looks down at us with kind eyes, a smile gracing her ruby lips.

"Welcome, my Blackwater friends!" she greets us, smiling harder.

Caz walks around me, immediately marching up the stairs. As he does, a large man with deeply tan skin steps beside the woman. He's even buffer than Killian, with long black hair braided down to the center of his back. Brown ink embellishes the majority of his visible skin, and he wears leather pants and a very thin, sleeveless white shirt.

"Is that Alora?" I ask when Juniper steps to my side.

"That's her," Juniper responds. "Queen of Vanora herself."

I swallow hard, following everyone up the staircase. Caz reaches the top first and gives Alora a quick bow, to which she smiles, delighted.

When I reach the top of the stairs, nearly out of breath, my legs aching and on fire, I notice Alora is barefoot, but there is brown ink lining the edges of her feet, her ankles wrapped in diamonds.

"Willow Austin." Her voice is light, sweet. She smiles at me, and I'm taken aback by her beauty. She's gorgeous up close, her tan skin flawless—not a blemish in sight. Her glossy black hair is parted at the crown, in a half-up, half-down style. "My word, are you a lovely sight."

"You know my name?" I ask as her hazel eyes lock on mine.

"I do."

I want to ask how, but I don't, and she smiles, turning her eyes to Caz.

"It's a pleasure to have you here, Caspian." He sighs, and I hear him internally grumble something about not liking to be called by that name. "How may I be of service?"

EIGHTEEN

WILLOW

Alora is a welcoming queen. I can see why she's...well, a *queen*. She's patient and calm, even with Caz and his temperament. Any question she asks him, he answers as if annoyed, but she doesn't react. She simply takes the answers in stride while walking through her castle—ruler of all, beneath no one.

I'm too awe-struck to think much about how rude he's being. The palace is something out of a movie. I've traveled to a lot of cities and have seen *many* places, but this tops every single one. She guides us through several corridors, passing a dining hall, the kitchen, and even the regal room, where a throne is on an altar.

"I don't like the throne much," she confesses. "In fact, I only use it when I want everyone to take me seriously, or if I have an important announcement." She smiles at me, and Juniper laughs at her remark.

"When will we discuss why we're here?" Caz asks from the other side of the room.

"In a moment. I'd like to show my guest around. She's never been to Vanora before, and it'd be rude not to give her a tour. We won't be long." Caz grumbles something beneath his breath as Alora takes my hand, leading the way out of the regal room.

"I'm coming with you," Juniper says, tailing us.

Alora shows us her tailoring room, her meditation center, the spa, an aquatic room (which I find the most interesting—glass walls with colorful fish and tiny black sharks swimming behind it), another kitchen that's for larger events, a music room, and then a ballroom.

"Down there, you'll find the garden room," she says, pointing down a stairwell. "It's quite relaxing in there at night. There's also storage down there, where we stockpile barrels of our youth water."

"Youth water? What's that?" I ask.

"It's basically essence from the Regals—water they created that keeps you youthful and healthy," says Juniper.

Alora makes her way up a staircase and walks along a wide corridor with skylights in the ceiling. Her guard (Proll, as she introduced him to us) is trailing behind us while keeping a safe distance.

"I figured you'd like to see this part of the place." Alora pushes a tall, white door open, leading us into a library that's two stories high and bigger than a gymnasium. Every shelf is lined with books, a pearly staircase leading to the second floor. She takes us up the stairs to two wide glass doors leading to a balcony that overlooks the ocean. We step outside, all of us, as the sea breeze floats by and the cerulean waters whisper to us.

"Wow," I murmur. It's the only word I can muster. There aren't many words that can perfectly describe this view. "Why doesn't Blackwater look like this?" I cut my eyes to Juniper who releases a harmonious laugh, then shrugs.

"Every territory has its differences, I suppose," says Juniper. "Vanora is known to be the most beautiful, but also *very* expensive to live in."

"While Blackwater can be affordable, but *very* lethal. However, that doesn't mean there isn't beauty to it. You simply have to look for it," Alora says.

"But even your clothes are...better," I confess.

"Meh." Juniper interjects. "Depends on the person. I prefer Blackwater clothes over Vanora's. With all the corsets and the stifling bras and panties—ugh, I would *die*."

"Didn't you say you'd live here if you weren't from Blackwater?" Alora asks, smirking.

"I did...but only if I could wear my own clothes most of the time."

Alora chuckles, then meets my eyes and says, "Speaking of clothes, come with me."

She guides us through the castle, beneath large chandeliers and intricately designed ceilings, pillars, and statues, until we're approaching a large door bathed in gold. She pushes the door open, and reveals a room full of dresses. Most of them are white, some gold, but the colorful set near one of the ocean-front windows catches my eye most.

I step up to one of them, running my fingers along the silk fabric of a pink dress. I finger an emerald dress with red rubies lining the bosom, and then an orange gown with silver threads.

"You look like you're wearing Juniper's clothes," Alora says to me.

"She is," Juniper confirms.

"Well, we'll have to fix that, won't we?"

"What are you saying? That I don't have good taste?" Juniper counters, a hand pressing to her hip.

"No, no, it's not that," Alora says, fighting a smile. "I just think

I can find something to better suit Willow, is all. Don't be so feisty."

Juniper fights her own smile, and says, "As long as I get to pick out some clothes too."

"Of course." Alora turns to me. "You look like more of a pants woman." She walks past and opens a closet, revealing pants, blouses, and shoes in many styles and colors. "Pick a few outfits and I will have them tailored to fit you. I know the reason you're here is because of the Tether you share with Caspian, and the only person I can think of who knows anything about that is Beatrix, and for her, you must be presentable. She's quite picky about how people look when they come to her, actually. Hopefully she'll answer my requests, and if she reaches back out, I'd like us to be prepared to see her."

"Oh...um...okay." I step next to her, surveying each piece of clothing, then decide to go with twill khaki trousers and an ivory cotton blouse. Normally, I wouldn't wear twill, but it seems to be what all the pants are made of here. I pick another outfit that's simpler, black pants and a sheer pink blouse, and Alora gives me a satisfied smile as I collect it all.

"Wait a minute." Juniper walks past me, opening one of the glass drawers and pulling out brown suspenders. "This will complete the look of the first outfit you picked."

"Good eye," Alora praises.

Juniper places the suspenders on top of the clothes, giving me a triumphant smile. "I'd fit right into this place if I had the chance."

Alora walks out of the room, calling for someone to tailor the clothes I selected, and I don't know why I'm surprised that they get my measurements and clothes fitted all within thirty minutes. She even sent someone to fetch a new pair of shoes from the city. They were brought back within twenty minutes.

Now, I stand in one of Alora's bedchambers looking into a wide mirror, surprised by the new look. I've never dressed like this, but dare I say, it suits me. And Juniper was right about the suspenders. They add a nice touch.

"We should eat!" Alora declares when everyone has gathered in the regal room again. A woman walks up to Alora, whispering something in her ear. Alora doesn't move her head as she listens, and when the woman scurries away, Alora releases a sigh.

I step around Alora and can't help it when my eyes snap to Caz. It seems no matter what room we're in together, I *have* to look for him. It's like a stupid, compelling force—one I can't stop from happening no matter how hard I try, and as if it's the same for him, he looks at me too. Some of the irritation washes off his face as he looks me up and down in my new clothes. His eyes soften, and for a split second I think he'll compliment me, but instead he swings his gaze to Alora and says, "Let's get on with this already."

"Oh, unleash your patience, Caspian." Alora gestures to two women in a corner, giving a dainty wave of her hand. They nod and hurry around a wall, disappearing. "I already know why you're here, and we would be going to see Beatrix, but she hasn't gotten back to my transmitter requests, unfortunately. But, rest assured, we will figure out your Tether." When she says that, Caz cuts his eyes to me. "The Tether you're denying, might I add."

"I'm not denying anything," he counters.

"Oh, Caspian. Always so serious." She walks around him, wrapping an arm around my shoulder. "She's a beautiful woman. You'd be a fool to reject her."

Red splotches appear on Caz's neck, a tight grimace on his face now. "Please realize that just because I'm in your graces, doesn't mean you get to embarrass me in front of my clan."

"Am I embarrassing you?" She presses her lips, then glances at me. "Willow, here, doesn't seem to be the least bit bothered."

"I'm not as uptight as he is," I tell her, and that sets Caz ablaze. His whole face is red now, his fist clenching, and I'm fighting a laugh.

"Fine. Dinner," he says through gritted teeth. "Then you'll give Beatrix another try, correct?"

Alora smiles. "Absolutely."

NINETEEN

CAZ

I can't bring myself to eat. There's no point, especially with Alora. She likes to play games, and right now, I don't have time for them. Hell, I never do, but I try to be lenient with her because she's queen, and I'm in her territory with my own requests.

Dinner is more like a feast, with all sorts of vegetables, fruits, and greens. No meat, because Vanorians don't eat it. There's a plate in front of me, topped with a fresh green salad and a bowl of Vanorian fruit next to it. A sparkling pitcher of youth water is on the center of the table, our glasses filled to the brim.

This water tastes weird. I hear Willow's voice echo in my head. I look up at her, seated across the table from me, and she's studying her glass of water with a slight frown.

I avoid rolling my eyes and instead, let her hear me. *It's youth water, not regular water from the springs. It's used to keep people young and healthy in Vakeeli.*

She picks her head up, locking eyes with me. ***What's Vakeeli?***

This world you're in. That's the name of it.

Should I be drinking this?

I don't see the point. It's not like you'll be staying here much longer.

She scowls, narrows her eyes, then lifts the cup to her lips, guzzling it all down.

Alora laughs from her end of the table, and I cut my eyes to her. She's seated in her gold, throne-like dinner chair, looking between me and Willow, clearly amused by the interaction.

"So, Alora. How is your treaty with the dirty Rippies going?" I ask.

Alora picks up a goblet, sipping from it. "It's going well. In fact, they've given me their highest quality Vakeeli steel."

"Have they?" I sip my water. "A bunch of ass kissers if you ask me."

"Oh, don't you worry, Caspian. Your rubies are still in high demand around here. Couldn't live without them."

"They're not *my* rubies," I mutter.

"No, they're not. But they're found in *your* land and *your* people dig for them." Alora turns her eyes to Willow, who is nibbling on a slice of fruit. "Willow, when did you drop into Vakeeli?"

"It was yesterday...I think."

"Were you scared?" Alora places a hand beneath her chin, resting her elbow on the table.

"I was."

"Caz and his guns. It's terrifying, really, the way he swings them around at people."

I work my jaw.

"How do you know so much about what's happened?" Willow asks.

"I can read people."

"*Read* people?"

"Yes. Well, not exactly read your thoughts, but I get a sense of the energy, and the most highlighted parts of what you've experienced are revealed to me, sort of like a vision. For example, your name is attached to you, so that's easy, and when I asked about you dropping into Vakeeli, your mind immediately went to the word *gun* and wrapped itself around a paralyzing fear. I just sort of put two and two together." She sips from her goblet again. "It gets quite annoying, actually. But it's also how I can tell you two are Tethered. You see, the energy sort of floats off the both of you. It's a purplish hue that shoots back and forth, like a game of Chetnee."

"Chetnee? Do people still play that?" Rowan asks from the other end of the table, picking up his steel beer mug.

"They do, yes," Alora replies eagerly. "We have matches every four days."

"Chetnee," Rowan mumbles, then chugs a mouthful of beer. "I was always really good at it."

"Chetnee is just a game with a paddle and a ball," Alora explains to Willow. "The ball bounces back and forth on a golden table. Whoever misses the ball with their paddle three times, loses."

"Oh. So similar to ping pong?" Willow asks, her eyes lighting up.

"Is that what it's called where you're from? Interesting." Another sip from Alora's goblet. "Anyway, I'm glad I had you select more clothes because Beatrix is really doing her best to ignore me, which tells me she's either not home, or doesn't want to be bothered. She's a stubborn old woman, hates when I ask things of her. We'll have to go to her by morning if she doesn't answer my next transmitter request. In the meantime, you all can stay here for the night, but you'll have to leave your guns with Proll. Just to be on the safe side."

"Yes!" Juniper hisses, elated.

"Wonderful. A night of Vanorian women," Rowan cheers, raising his drink in the air. "What a night it shall be!"

Killian just folds his arms, and Maeve yawns before taking a small sip of wine. Juniper refills her wine, and asks, "Alora, may I borrow clothes from your wardrobe?"

"Of course, you can."

"I sleep with my guns," I tell Alora, going back to the topic.

"Well, tonight will be the exception if you plan on staying here," Alora says, rising from the table. "You know the rules."

I pull my eyes away. I can't argue with her. Not here. This is her territory, so her ruling goes. Still, I have a hard time trusting her. Well, I take that back. Out of all territory monarchs, she's the one I put my faith in most. But this treaty she has with the Rippies grates on my nerves. She settled with them two months ago, making trades with them, swapping gold and steel. She knows I hate them, yet she tolerates them. It drives me mad.

"Luzian and Clara will show you all to your chambers for the night," Alora announces as two women dressed in sleek gold gowns approach. "If there is anything you need, just call for them and they'll assist you."

Alora looks between me and Willow. "Will you two be sharing a room?"

"Hell no!" "Not on my life."

I glare at her. She glares back at me. I feel a dull aching in the middle of my chest, not painful, but irritating.

Alora's laughter swims through the dining hall as she turns to leave. "You two have the most stubborn Tether I've ever encountered."

TWENTY

WILLOW

I STAND in the garden room, where one of the walls is made of crystal-clear glass, the other white walls covered in vines and various colored flowers. I wandered through the castle and found this room down the stairs, where Alora said it would be. Outside one of the windows is a waterfall pouring into the ocean. The water is still surprisingly blue at night, the moon bold and bright, nearly burning like the sun. She was right. It is relaxing here.

"Your energy is serene." Alora's voice slices through my thoughts and I gasp, turning to find her. She's changed into a sleek, copper night gown. All her jewelry is off, she's not even wearing lipstick, and she's still so freaking pretty. It seems so natural for her to be that way, whereas for me, I have to put in the work to make sure I'm somewhat appealing.

"You scared the hell out of me," I breathe, pressing a hand to my chest. A glass goblet is in my other hand, half-full of wine. The wine here is much stronger and more delicious. Sweet, not too bitter. The perfect combination. And I admit, it's making me tipsy. "I'm sorry for wandering," I tell her as she stands next to me. "I couldn't sleep."

"Is your bedding not comfortable? If not, I can have that fixed straight away."

"No, no. It's not that. The room you gave me is perfect." And it truly is—overlooking the city, the glittering lights and infinite number of stars in the indigo sky. The bed is comfortable, the feathery duvet plush and cool. I showered in the bathroom before coming down here, which was an experience. Everything I could think of was there, from robes to towels, wash cloths, loofahs. There was even a selection of soaps, perfumes, and lotions to choose from. All of them smelled divine.

"After the shower, I tried lying down, but couldn't close my eyes," I go on. "It was weird being in that room, surrounded by so much luxury. Then I remembered I'm not home—that I'm in some other world where everything is new and unlike anything I've ever experienced. None of this feels real, and I can't help thinking I've lost my damn mind. That wouldn't be too far of a stretch to consider, honestly. My mother lost her mind and became suicidal when I was three." At my last sentence, I cup my mouth and stare at Alora. "Oh my God. Why did I just tell you that?"

"Could be the wine. It has that effect on people. You're new to it, so perhaps you shouldn't drink too much more of it tonight."

"Yeah." I set the glass down on the nearest surface.

"Do you know why?" she asks.

"Know why what?"

"Your mother lost her mind."

"Oh." I rub the tip of my nose, getting rid of an itch. "She kept saying someone was following her—that she had a stalker who wanted to take her children. Her psychiatrists would say it was because she had a hard time conceiving me and my brother. So, when she *did* get pregnant with us and gave birth, they think she may have suffered a psychotic break." I shake my head. I hate getting into that topic. It's one I still can't fully wrap my head around. I can't believe I'm even telling Alora about it. It's not something I discuss much with others.

"And what about your father? Was he around when this happened to her?"

"Yeah. He's actually still alive, but he's hard to catch on the phone and he hardly ever visits me, so…"

"So, other than having incapable parents, what's the matter?" Alora asks, looking into my eyes.

"I just…" I pause. "I guess I realize that I don't belong in this place."

"Oh." Alora presses her lips, mulling it over. "Well, I'd say that's far from the truth. If anyone doesn't belong here, it's Caz and Killian. They're a couple of brutes, aren't they? Rowan is decent. I like him very much."

I laugh at her comments, then sip my wine. "I never thought there would be so much out there. I mean, sure, the world isn't small, but me being *here*, in this other universe…it just makes me feel miniscule."

"Darling, you are far from miniscule. You have the Cold Tether. That's grand."

"I don't even know what a Cold Tether is. What's so grand about it?" The question comes out laced in sarcasm. "'Cause I can tell you, being forced to hear that psycho man's thoughts is not a pleasure."

Alora laughs, then draws in a breath. When she exhales, she tilts her head and wraps a hand around my wrist. She leads me to a rusting gold bench that faces the waterfall and brings me down to sit with her.

"When I was a little girl, I came across a couple who were Cold Tethered. There are many couples who can be Tethered in Vakeeli. Tethers are a common thing, but most are simple, really. It's no greater than someone claiming that the person is their soulmate. But a *Cold* Tether...well, it's similar, but a bit more complicated. It derives from the original Tethered people—the first kind Regals ever made. From what I was told, Cold Tethers are rare and, unlike a regular Tether, your mind and body is instantly drawn to your mate. Doesn't matter if you've never met them or seen them, you're bound to them, and regardless of where you are, you will find a way to one another." She pushes a loose tendril of hair behind her ear. "You also feel things simple Tethers don't feel with each other. I always hear the senses are heightened in every way, and when you're away from your mate for too long, it comes with great pain and misery. Apparently, it was designed this way to prevent loneliness and for the Cold Tethers to be with each other forever, but I'd say that didn't age well. Anyway, a simple tethered person can be with whomever they want and live a full life. But not a Cold Tether. They *have* to be with their mate or else they die."

"Oh my gosh."

"Very unfortunate, yes. Anyway, when I was young, I was such a diehard romantic," she says, smiling. "However, I was a queen in training, so my father didn't approve of my romantic antics. He wanted me to be strong and resilient, to not waste time on boys unless I was ready to find a king...which I still haven't done, by the way." She waves a hand. "Despite his disapproval, I would write letters to random boys in the city. None of them were personalized, they were just letters, and I'd walk to the city on weekends and hand them to the boys I found most handsome."

"Really?" I laugh.

"Yes. Oh, the boys got a kick out of that one. Here they all were, thinking the princess of Vanora wanted to marry them one day." She titters, rocking a bit, her pearly teeth sparkling. "But one day when I was in the city, I gave my letter to a boy who was unlike the others. He had the most beautiful brown eyes, and his skin was so pretty—like it was made of ground coffee. He was a stunning human, and he took my letter and ran to his mum. His mum smiled at me, and then a man stepped up beside her. And...I didn't know it back then, but this couple had a Cold Tether. I could feel their energy from so far away. And the way they looked at each other, the way they held hands, the way they did *everything* together—it fascinated me. Their love was *colossal*, and I remember thinking I wanted a love like that. I wanted a man to love me with all his heart. I wanted someone I could have beautiful brown babies with, with bright brown eyes. When I put a read on that couple, I was *overwhelmed* with joy. It's hard to explain the joy I felt that day, but if I had to describe it, I would say it was the sun, moon, and stars all wrapped up in a cool bed of flowers, somehow blossoming inside me."

"Wow," I murmur. "That's beautiful, Alora."

"It is. And everyone in the city loved that couple. They were gifted. The man built swords and shields for the people, and the woman was very good at designing custom dresses for women. I recall her dress making skills being very popular for Armistice Night."

"What's Armistice Night?"

"It's the one night in Vakeeli when all territories agree to get along. There's a big ball in Luxor, everyone from all walks of life attend, and for one night there are no feuds or fighting or wars. There is only dancing, laughter, peace, drinking...and sex. Love of Vakeeli, is there a lot of sex." Alora laughs a bit, shaking her head, then her face changes beneath the moonlight, saddening, her lips twisting. "But one day...that couple was found just outside of

Vanora's gates. Their faces were hollow, eyes black, mouths ajar. The beauty and joy were gone. Someone had killed them." She works hard to swallow. "Or *something*, rather." Her eyes flicker up to mine. "The downfall of a Cold Tether is that you're hunted for that beautiful joy you share. I'm not sure what it is that hunts you, but what I do know is that you and Caspian have a Tether that is just as strong as that couple who once lived in my city, whether you like each other or not. And I have a feeling once you give in to this Tether, it will be stronger than theirs, which will make it all the more beautiful to witness for me, but much easier for the malevolent to find you."

I clutch my glass tight in hand, lowering my gaze. "Well, we shouldn't have to worry about that. There's no giving in to a man like him."

Alora smirks. "Do you think so? Because I see him burning bridges for you."

I scoff. "Trust me, he *hates* me. He wants me gone and, frankly, I'm ready to go back home."

"Are you, though?" She tilts her head, locking eyes with me. She searches my face, and it makes me uncomfortable, especially remembering she can read my energy. She knows I'm lying.

"I mean...it would be nice to get to know the person I'm somehow connected to, but he makes it hard to do that."

"Sure, he's a hard man to figure out, but don't let that fool you. He's your Tether, and whether he cares to admit it or not, he feels something for you. He can't quite explain it yet, as these feelings are new to him, but he does. A Tether of any kind is inevitable. I've been conducting business with Caspian for years and never have I seen him look at a woman the way he looks at you."

"He hardly looks at me, your majesty."

She smiles. "It's when you *aren't* looking that he does. And when you think he isn't listening, he most certainly is. I bet you he's listening right now."

I let her words marinate in the crevices of my mind. I even try listening for Caz's voice, but I hear nothing. I'm knocking and he won't let me in.

She gracefully stands. "I'm going to finish off the rest of my duties for the night. We have an early start in the morning, so I'd like to get to bed as soon as possible. I hope you enjoy the rest of your night. And if you can't sleep, ask Luzian for a cup of mulled wine with gold clover. It'll put you right to sleep."

When she leaves the garden room, I stand back up and walk to the window. I drop my gaze to the waterfall tunneling into the ocean, studying it a moment, before making my way back to my room for the night.

Before I can get to the room, I spot Juniper, whose room is two doors from mine, only she's not in the clothes she had on earlier (a tweed suit and brown cap). She's in high-waisted black trousers, a blood red blouse tucked into them, and a thick black belt wrapped around her waist, accentuating her hips. The belt doesn't look like Vanora material, and when I see the red rubies in the buckle of it, I figure it's a Blackwater belt she had with her.

"There you are!" she chimes when she hears my steps.

"You're looking for me?"

"Indeed I am. I want you to come to the city with me."

"To the city?"

"Vanora is a beautiful city at night. You'll love it! Let's get you changed. Alora gave me access to her closet, and she hardly wears pants as it is. She may as well give all her clothes to me." She links elbows with me and wanders down the hallway, taking the stairs up to the wardrobe Alora presented to us earlier.

"Is it safe going out there at night?" I ask.

Juniper chokes on a laugh as she opens the closet. "Much safer than Blackwater, I assure you." She reaches for clothes, taking down black pants that match hers, and a silky blue shirt with gold moon and star designs. "This should work." She brings it to me. "Get dressed. And hurry. I don't want Caz to see us leaving."

"Why not?" I ask, changing out of my clothes. I'm not opposed to this. From what I've seen, Vanora *is* beautiful, and I'm curious about the city, what it's like, and if it's anything like Blackwater. Hopefully it's better.

"Because he'll send Killian with us, and Killian ruins all the fun."

I slide into the trousers as Juniper taps her chin while looking at the accessories. She plucks a gold belt from a rack, and then a set of gold, dangly earrings. After she places them on a velvet stool, she moves to the necklaces, taking down way too many.

"There are two sides to Vanora," she goes on, studying the jewelry she's selected. "There's Gold Class, which is where all the richer Vanorians live. They're the classy type, very boring, really, with their fancy parties and silk gloves." She picks up two necklaces and carries them to me as I slide into the shirt. "Then there's Iron Class. They still have riches, but they don't really live by the rules. They know how to have fun, make a good drink, and party."

"And let me guess…Iron Class is where we're going?" I watch as she walks around me to clasp the necklace on.

"Damn right."

"Is it not dangerous?"

"Sure, it is…well, it can be. But I have a gun."

"I thought you had to give your guns to Alora's guards?"

"Yeah, but I have one in the SUV they don't know about." She walks around me, takes a thorough look at my clothes, and, satisfied with what she's put together, she smiles and looks me in the eyes. "You're so beautiful. No wonder Caz can't stop looking at you." Her words fly right through me. I'm not sure how to digest them, and I'm glad when she leads the way out of the room, shuts the lights off, and says, "Let's go get your boots," over my shoulder.

When I slip into my boots, we walk down the stairs and through the spacious corridors of the palace to get to the front door. I almost think we're in the clear as the door opens and we step into the coolness of the night, but as Juniper opens the back door of the SUV and reaches under the seat, someone clears their throat.

I turn and look back, and Caz moves out of the shadows by the pillars, a bloom pinched between his lips, the tip lit in fiery embers. He pulls it away with a gloved hand, releases a cloud of smoke, and says, "Where the hell are you two going?"

Juniper slams the car door and groans, tucking something into the back of her belt. Her gun, I think. "We're going out."

"Where?"

"To the city."

"Take Killian with you," he says, pulling from the bloom again. Smoke trickles out of his nostrils, and his icy eyes cut to me.

Juniper frowns. "No. We'll be fine."

"You're trying to go to Iron Class, and you're not going without protection," he counters.

"I can protect myself. Besides, I have a friend in town. Remember Hannie? She'll show us the good places."

"Willow is not from here. They'll sense it a mile away, Juniper. You must be forgetting the Rippies spend a lot of their time in Iron Class too."

She sighs. "Oh, buzz off and let her have a little fun, Caz! Love of Vakeeli! It's bad enough she has to suffer listening to your thoughts all day."

That annoys him, clearly, because he drops his bloom on the ground and steps on the lit end, squashing it. "Killian goes with you, or you don't go at all." They're the last words he says before switching his eyes to me again, looking me up and down, and then turning away.

He makes his way around the palace, and I have no idea where he's going, but even with his disappearance, he can't escape what I saw his eyes do, or the thoughts of his that whispered through my mind. His eyes lingered, not on my face, but the split of my shirt at my breasts, and as they did, he said, **No way in hell she's going out dressed like that without one of us.**

TWENTY-ONE

CAZ

"Did I say you could put your bloomy hands on my books?" Alora's voice rings through the library, and I glance over my shoulder as she enters.

I ignore her, putting my focus on the book again. "Do you have any books on Tethers?"

"I'm afraid not," she says. "The Cold Tether is a sacred study, and with all the Gilded running around Vanora, The Council believe it's better that they don't digest too much of it here. After all the rumors about Decius overpowering Selah, well...I try not to have them at my people's disposal."

"So you'd rather they be ignorant to their history?"

"Not at all. If they wish to learn about the Cold Tether, they're more than welcome to do so. It's just not something we teach to our own very much—and don't act like it's *my* fault the rule is in place. I didn't create it. I suppose The Council doesn't want anyone getting any big ideas about using their energy to overthrow their superiors."

"Hmm."

"Why aren't you sleeping?" she asks, sitting on a chaise in the corner.

"I don't sleep much. You know that."

"Ah, yes. How miserable that must be. Are you still on those black tablets then?"

I cut my eyes at her. "How is that your business?"

"Of course, you are." She sighs, placing an elbow on top of the chaise, resting on her side. "For the love of Vakeeli, Caspian, when will you learn to unwind? You allow your traumas to fester and hold you down. It's no way to live."

"You don't know anything about traumas, Alora, so stop talking to me about them."

"I know a thing or two."

I close the book in hand and slide it back in its place on the shelf. "A few slaps on the wrist from *King Papa* doesn't count as trauma."

I take the seat across the room.

"Why do you pretend you don't feel anything for Willow?"

I frown. "Where the hell did that come from?"

"You know what I can do, Caspian. You know what I can see. It is abundantly clear how intrigued you are of her."

"She literally dropped into my forest, an unknown woman from another world. Who wouldn't be the least bit curious?"

Alora narrows her eyes. "You know what I mean."

I lean back in the chair, spreading my legs apart. "Mind if I light me bloom?"

"The smell of bloom gives me headaches. You know that."

"Then I suppose you should leave then, eh?" I pull out my

silver case, plucking out a bloom. When I find my lighter, I spark the end, and Alora rolls her eyes.

"Stubborn mule."

"Leave me be."

She stands, sauntering across the large room. "You should stop rejecting what you feel for her," she says at the door.

"I feel nothing," I respond through a haze of smoke.

Alora chuckles. "I don't believe you." Then she leaves the library, and I'm grateful for the silence. It would be quieter in my chambers, but I can't sleep in that bed. I can't sleep, period. We're too close to Ripple Hills, and this truce she has with them means they can come and go as they please.

Another reason why I didn't want Juniper going out with a woman who isn't from this world. She stands out far too much for someone *not* to notice. Plus, who knows what her energy brings, or what she's brought from her world that could cause trouble here.

Fuck, I never should have let them go out. But there's Killian. He'll watch them. He'll keep me posted.

I close my eyes, and the sound of music fills the hollows of my brain. People are yelling. Strobe lights bouncing. The smell of bloom and sour scent of tonics.

This place is different. Oh shit. Is that guy staring at me? No, he's not. He's looking past us. Right. What kind of top is that? Eww, where are their pants? Jesus. I should've stayed at the palace.

Juniper and Willow must be in Iron Class already. I feel Willow's heart racing, her mind running through a million thoughts. It's all so new to her. The problem is I can sense her excitement. She's thrilled to see these new things, but I also get a glimpse of her worry, as if she knows something bad will happen while she's out.

And because of it, I keep listening to her thoughts, praying to Vakeeli that the night goes smoothly enough for me to ignore her again.

TWENTY-TWO

WILLOW

KILLIAN DRIVES THE SUV, grumbling the whole way through Gold Class, something about his time being wasted and never being able to relax for one night.

Despite it, I'm able to see Gold Class for what it is—bright, shiny, and classy. The people dress very nice, not a wrinkle in sight or a hair out of place. They ride in chariots, their white horses leading the way. There's an air of optimism and elegance, and it doesn't fit the Blackwater people. If we hung out there, we'd stand out like sore thumbs. Juniper mentioned Gold Class doesn't like to be around people from other territories, just their own, and that they're very strict about guns and dress code. It's no place for people like Juniper and Killian, or even me.

"You know you could've stayed at the palace," Juniper says to Killian, finally breaking the ice. "No one *made* you come."

"Caz wanted me to come," Killian returns.

"You and I both know I can handle myself. He just wants

someone keeping an eye on Willow because he's scared of what this Tether does to him."

Why is she bringing me into this?

"Whatever it is, I don't care. I could be back at the palace, eating, sleeping, or fucking."

Juniper snorts, gazing out the window. "Fucking what? Your hand?"

Killian grumbles something else and speeds up, purposely making Juniper slump back against her seat.

Shortly after, we're in Iron Class. Nothing says it, but it's assumed by the way it looks. It's a bleak contrast to Gold Class. Iron Class has slightly smaller buildings, gold lights, and the people appear younger. Their clothes are casual—not upscale and classy like Gold Class. There are people standing outside of buildings and bars, smoking long black sticks. Fancy cars zip by with neon lights beneath them, not a horse in sight. This is where the people of Blackwater would fit in.

Killian parks the SUV in front of a tall white building with tinted windows, and Juniper hurries to climb out.

"If you try to run, I'll shoot you in your leg, Jun," Killian warns, stepping out the car.

Oh my goodness. Would he really shoot his own sister?

"I'd like to see you try," Juniper claps back.

"Don't test me. I'm not in the mood."

She rolls her eyes and looks at me. "Come on." Leading the way toward the building, Juniper opens the door and walks inside. It's dark in the building, strobe lights flashing, gold lights bouncing off the walls. I realize it's a club, humming with bodies, a wall-to-wall bar ahead. Juniper goes straight for the bar, pushing through the crowd with her arm linked through mine. When she finds a clearing, she waves for the bartender's attention, and he approaches—a skinny, brown-skinned man dressed in a gold vest and white pants.

"How can I help you ladies?" he asks, a casual smile on his lips.

"Two gold tonics, please," Juniper requests, taking a satchel from her pocket. She plucks out six rubies, and the bartender glances down at them before looking at her again.

"You two aren't Vanorian, are you?"

"No, we're Blackwaters. Will that be a problem?"

The bartender smirks, accepting the rubies. "Not at all. Drinks are coming right up."

When he turns away, Juniper says, "One thing you must learn about *all* men of Vakeeli: don't let them walk over you. Once they realize they can, they'll use it against you. Oh—and rubies get you very far. Always have rubies on hand." She turns her head and gasps. "Hannie! *Hey!*" Juniper rushes away to wrap her arms around a woman approaching us in a black dress. The woman lets out a shrill yelp as she hugs Juniper back, kisses her cheek, and then leans back, keeping her hands on Junipers shoulders. She's beautiful, with coily black hair and umber skin.

"I've missed you!" Hannie squeals. "Blackwater has been keeping you busy, eh?"

"Oi, has it," Juniper sighs. "There's always something happening. You know how it is."

"You ought to move here, stay with me," Hannie suggests, shining her pearly whites as she drops her arms.

"As I always tell you, one day." Juniper turns to me. "Hannie, this is Willow. She's from Blackwater as well. It's her first time in Vanora." She winks at me.

"Oh, we'll break you in good!" Unexpectedly, Hannie reels me in and hugs me.

"Oh...uh." I force a smile as I hug her back. She smells like flowers and sea salt. It's a pleasant scent.

"We don't know each other, but we'll become family by the end of the night," Hannie assures me.

"That's if we can escape that brother of mine," Juniper says, rolling her eyes.

Hannie swings her eyes to Juniper again. "Is it Rowan? He's lots of fun, eh?"

"No," Juniper grumbles. "It's Killian tonight."

"Two gold tonics!" The bartender slides two gold cups across the counter to Juniper and she takes them, handing one to me. I take it, thanking her with a smile.

"I don't think I've met Killian yet. Well, not properly." Just as she says that, Killian pushes his way through the crowd like a mountain, meeting up to us.

"Don't drink a lot. We have to be alert tomorrow," Killian grumbles, looking between me and Juniper.

"What are you, my father?" Juniper rolls her eyes again.

"Jun, stop it with the smart-ass comments. I don't want to be here anymore than you don't want me to be."

"So leave." Juniper supplies him a shit-eating grin before taking a sip of her drink.

"You're a big guy, aren't ya?" Hannie looks Killian up and down. "A bit wound up too, eh?"

Killian steps back, glaring down at Hannie. "Who the hell are you, and why are you talking to me?"

"I'm Hannie Keery. Eldest daughter of the Keery family, and I'd shake your hand, but it seems you've been struggling to dig the arrogance out of your ass for a while, so verbal greetings will do."

Killian squares his shoulders and grimaces. "You should watch your mouth."

"And you should watch your temper." Hannie's eyes that were once brown, light up and flash gold. I gasp at the sight of them.

Killian bellows a laugh, which is hardly a reaction to me. "You think your fiery little eyes are gonna intimidate me? I'll pop them out your head before you even have a chance to use 'em on me."

"Is that a challenge?" Hannie stands taller, raising her chin.

"Only if you want it to be, love."

Hannie's gold eyes turn brown again, and she narrows them, then huffs a laugh. "It'd be a waste of my time and energy."

Killian shakes his head. "Whatever. Off to take a piss." He points a finger at Juniper. "Stay put."

We watch him go, and when he's out of earshot, Hannie turns to us and says, "There's a guy named Tomán having a party at his house. Booze, wine, gold dust, tonic—it's all there. What do you say?"

"Oh, hell yeah! What are we waiting for?" Juniper gulps down the remainder of her drink, and Hannie lets out a belly-deep laugh. I finish mine off, and Hannie grabs us both by the wrists, leading the way out of the club. When we're outside, I draw in a cool breath and follow Hannie and Juniper's lead down the block.

"What do you think Killian'll say when he finds you gone?" Hannie asks, laughing.

"Oh, he's going to lose his shit. I just know it," says Juniper.

"Do you have your transmitter with you?"

"No. Left it at Alora's palace."

Hannie stops in her tracks. "Okay, before we get any further, promise me you will *not* repeat those words."

Juniper blinks at her. "What words?"

I look between them, confused.

"That you're staying in the queen's palace. If these loads of shit find out you're staying there, they'll manipulate the hell out of you and Willow. Not to mention, Tomán is gifted, so..."

"Will he blow off my head with his eyes like some of the other Gilded can?"

"Nah," Hannie responds, turning to walk again. "What Tomán can do is *much* worse, so don't test him."

Hannie's words don't sit well with my gut, and I'm tempted to tell Juniper that I'm ready to go back to the palace. I love having fun, but knowing these people have powers and can blow people's heads off...well, I believe that changes my description of fun.

"Oi!" A deep voice booms behind us, and Juniper gasps and then shouts, "Ah, shit! Run, Willow!" before taking off in a full sprint herself. I look back, and Killian is pushing past people, charging toward us.

Hannie has already started running, and seeing them kicks me into high gear.

"Get your asses back here!" Killian shouts, but Juniper runs faster, laughing. She's light on her feet, unlike me. I hate running. Hate it with every fiber of my body. I consider stopping and getting caught. Killian can't hurt me, he'll just take me back to the palace, and honestly, the palace seems like the safer place to be right now.

Just as the thought rides through me, my lungs working overtime and my breaths short, a hand catches my arm and yanks me to the side. I scream as I'm swallowed in darkness, and a hand claps around my mouth.

TWENTY-THREE

WILLOW

I smell her before I can see her.

"Quiet," Hannie whispers, her hand still covering my mouth. My heart thunders in my chest, but not louder than Killian's feet as he stomps past the opening.

Finally releasing me, Hannie steps past me, peeks around the corner of the opening, then moves away. As she turns to look at me, her irises shimmer gold and she releases a sigh of relief.

"He's gone."

"Are you sure?" I hear Juniper ask, but I can't see her. Hannie walks past me to flip a light switch on, and we're in some sort of warehouse with mannequins inside. The mannequins are headless, their bodies made of steel.

Yeah," Hannie breathes. "I saw him turn a corner. We can get to Tomán's this way. Come on."

She walks through the warehouse made of brick and metal and out a backdoor, but not without keeping watch. Down an alley we go, and I hear people hollering, men bellowing. My heart beats a little faster, and I don't miss the way Juniper rests her hand on her gun as we approach. As her shirt lifts and she moves a step ahead, I notice another weapon tucked between her back and waistband. This weapon looks like a thick, metal stick.

Finally, we round a corner, and relief sinks in when I see the houses ahead. They're beautiful homes, simple, white, clean. All glowing gold with decorative lights. One house in particular stands out most. The roof is sleek and gold, so shiny the moonlight reflects off it.

The bass of music increases as we approach the house, and Hannie fluffs her hair as she walks up the white stairs, stopping when she approaches a man dressed in all white.

"Hannie, my love. Took you long enough," the man says, a pompous smile riding his lips.

Hannie grins, running a hand over the man's shoulder. "These are my friends." She gestures back to us.

"Not Vanorians?"

"No, Blackwaters. They're cool."

The man looks us all over, hesitant. "Not sure if that's wise tonight, Han. We've got Rippies coming in and out of this place."

Hannie sighs, then stands on her toes and whispers something into the man's ear. Whatever she says makes him reveal a smile worth a billion watts, and he steps aside to let us pass.

"You know the rules," he says to Hannie. "No powers from the Gilded. Tomán has his at rest tonight."

"Of course."

Sauntering into the house, Hannie tosses her spring-like black hair over her shoulder, and when I look back, the man is watching her, licking his lips. I have no idea what she said to him, but it must've been good.

The music grows louder, livelier, a mix of folk and pop as we enter. People stand everywhere—on the stairs, in the living room, the kitchen. It's like an American house party, but with people who are dressed ten times better, and look like gods and goddesses. I've never seen people dressed so nicely, with their gold jewelry and shimmery clothes. It seems custom here. If not dressed well, you'd stand out like a sore thumb.

Juniper hooks an arm through mine, and I look at her. "You all right?" she asks as Hannie is whisked away by a petite woman who is thrilled to see her.

"Yeah," I breathe. "All good."

"Don't go dobbing on me to Caz in that head of yours."

I laugh. "Trust me, he's the last person I want to talk to right now." My chest tightens after those words, making me short of breath. I don't know what the feeling means. Maybe it's from all the running we just did?

I let the feeling roll over me, shaking it off. It seems to only happen when I talk shit about Caz...or maybe my body is realizing the lies and reacting to them. Truth is, it wouldn't be so bad to talk to him. Too bad he's an asshole.

We enter the kitchen, where there's a beautiful display of drinks on a waist-high table. The tablecloth drips with silver and gold, the glasses lined up neatly, some of them stacked. An ice sculpture is in the center, a swan with the beak of a crane. It's all so beautiful that I don't even want to touch it, but Juniper swipes a glass for herself, and I follow suit, picking one up and sipping it. The alcohol is sour, and my face puckers.

"What the hell is this?" I ask.

"Vinnel," Juniper says. "Disgusting, but it really puts you in your element."

"It's really gross." I place the glass back down. "Is there anything else to drink? Some wine?"

Juniper turns for another table, picks up a gold goblet and a steel bottle, and pours red liquid into the goblet. She carries it to me. "There you are, miss prissy."

I take the goblet from her, sticking my tongue out before giving it a sip. "This is much better."

"So, are there parties like this in your world?" Juniper leans against the wall, casually sipping.

"No." I take a thorough look around. A guy in the corner is blowing fire into the air from his mouth with a bronzed liquid. Three women are belly dancing—one in the main living area, one in the kitchen, and another outside. A gay couple makes out by the back door, their tongues lodged down each other's throats. A group hovers over a bar counter, sniffing gold dust up one nostril. When they inhale, their eyes sparkle like stars have exploded in them, and they grin. "Nothing like this."

"Vanorians know how to party. I will give them that."

"What made you want to come out tonight?"

Juniper shrugs. Sips. "I don't know. Just needed a little fun, I suppose. It's always so serious in Blackwater. Always about business and bloody rubies. Sometimes it's nice to *not* think about any of it."

"I get that. It's the same with my job. I take days off, just to lie in my bed and read…or drink…or get high."

A laugh bubbles out of Juniper. "You're basically the female version of Caz, only he gets lifted off red tablets."

"What are red tablets?"

"They're a medicine created by Mythics that cures someone's aches and pains. Caz has a sensory issue—doesn't like to be touched much—so he has to take them, but they come with lots of side effects. The main one being that if you take too many, you're lifted higher than the clouds."

"Oh." I shift on my feet. "Well, regardless, I'm sure he's ready for me to get out of here."

"Nah." Juniper pushes off the wall, chugs the rest of her drink down, and then grabs another glass. "If he is, it's only so he can be serious Caz again. It's all he cares about. Seriously, it's better that he's out of Blackwater right now. That place will end up driving him mad if he lets it."

The kissing couple is now making their way outside, stripping out of their clothes and slinking into a glittery pool. I can't help watching them as they sink under the water, lip locked and tongue tied, then re-emerge, their hair shimmering in the night, like its coated in glitter.

"Do you date anyone?" I ask, turning to Juniper.

"I don't date," she says, waving a dismissive hand. "Waste of time, especially with Blackwater men. But I do get laid here and there by a guy who works at Blackwater Tavern." She grins, taking pride in that. "Only thing is he's the equivalent of a wolf in heat, so yeah, he's suitable in bed, but downright awful with women."

I swallow a mouthful of my drink and turn my head as Juniper does to focus on the people in the wide-open living room. The song changes to some kind of folksy song with a lot of bass, and I spot Hannie still chatting with the petite woman, both of them laughing, joyous.

A guy walks into the kitchen just as I'm about to take another mouthful of wine and bumps into me. I gasp as my drink tips over, spilling onto my shirt, sinking into the material. He brushes past Juniper to grab a drink, chugs it down, and then grabs another. Juniper looks at my shirt, her eyes stretching, before turning to him.

"Excuse me, love. Did you not feel yourself bumping into my friend here?" she asks, her head going into a slight tilt.

"No, Juniper—it's okay." We *are* standing in the way of the drinks. "Let's just move."

"We will. After he apologizes to you."

"Oh, fuck off," the man snaps. "I've had a long night."

Juniper sets her empty glass on the table, then squares her shoulders, facing him full on. "Let me guess. You're not a Vanorian. You're a Rippie, and you think women are beneath you, so you talk to them any way you want."

The man turns, nostrils flaring, reddening at the edges.

"Juniper." I tug on her arm, my heartbeat ratcheting.

"I said. *Fuck. Off*," he growls, stepping closer to her.

Juniper gently pulls her arm away from my hand, and before I can even blink, she's drawing her gun and pointing it at the center of the man's forehead.

The man tosses his hands in the air, his grimace transforming into sheer panic, while bystanders watch the encounter, their eyes wide with worry. Some of them back away, trying to get out of the room, as if they sense something very bad is about to happen.

"Would you like to repeat those words?" she asks, pressing the barrel to his forehead.

"H-how the hell do you have a Blackwater gun?" the man demands.

"Oh this?" She smiles as she studies the side of it. "I own it, and I do love to use it. Now, do me a favor." She pulls the gun away and walks around the man, pointing it at the back of his head. "Apologize to my friend, and we'll squash this."

The man's hands are shaking, his face turning redder, but not from anger. From fear. She nudges the back of his head with the gun. "I—I'm sorry," he mumbles.

"Louder. I couldn't hear you." She presses the barrel harder into his head.

"I'm sorry!" the man bellows. "Damn!" He moves away and Juniper steps back, a satisfied smirk on her lips.

"There," she says, tucking the gun back into her waistband, "See how easy that was? It's not hard being kind to women." She grabs another drink and then presses a hand to my shoulder, ready to guide me to another part of the room.

"You fucking *bitch*!" The words come out in a roar, and the next thing I know, glass is shattering over Juniper's head. She buckles forward, stumbling, and I gasp as the shards trickle off her dark hair. She freezes, stunned, and the house falls quiet, minus the music.

Then, her whole upper body vibrates with rage, from her head to the tips of her fingers. Her face crumples into a deep frown.

In one swift motion, Juniper snatches her gun and swings her arm behind her, shooting the man in the head.

TWENTY-FOUR

WILLOW

The gunshot makes my ears ring. I drop my drink to cover my ears, and the glass shatters on the floor.

"That *fucking asshole*!" Juniper's accent is thick and heavy with rage. "I wasn't really going to shoot him, but he asked for it, the fucking prick!"

A man stomps in from the back of the house, a wide-barreled gun in his hand. He sees the body of the man on the ground, blood pouring from his head, then hollers, running straight for the only other person with a gun in the room. Juniper.

"Juniper! Behind you!" I scream, but it's too late. He grabs her by the throat, slamming her against the nearest wall.

"Let me go. Right now," she growls through clenched teeth.

"Fuck you," the man growls back.

"Fine." I don't know how she manages it, but Juniper raises something between them. It's not a gun, but some kind of thick, long metal weapon—the same one I saw when her shirt lifted on the way here. She presses it to the man's chest, generating a large volt of electricity, and it zaps him so hard, he flies backward and crashes through a glass window. I look over my shoulder at where the man went, and he lies there, unconscious. Then I look back at Juniper, and she's holding the weapon in hand, smirking.

Another man stomps into the kitchen, and then another. They're coming from all angles, armed with guns, and I freeze, unsure where to go or what to do. What the hell is happening?!

"You lot better back the fuck off right now or you'll regret it," Juniper pants raggedly, rubbing her throat. "You saw what happened to your friends. Let's be wise here."

One of the men growls and lunges for her, but she grips him by the wrist, twists it, then cracks it, all in one swift motion, causing him to cry out in pain. As she forces him to his knees and uses the electrical stick thingy to put him out, one of the other men points his gun at her and shoots, but she ducks just in time for the bullet to miss. Retrieving her gun, she points it at the shooter and the bullet pierces him in the chest, just as another man charges toward her from behind and tackles her to the floor.

A gasp escapes me, and I rush forward, attempting to yank him off. "Leave her alone!" I shout, but he shoves me off and my back hits the edge of a counter. Pain seizes me and I cry out, crumpling over. I knew I should've stayed in the palace. What is Juniper thinking? She's killing *everyone* and I'm in the midst of it. What if she goes prison? What if I have to testify? There's a room full of witnesses! Is she out of her fucking mind? Damn it! Now I see what Caz was worried about.

"Get the fuck off me!" Juniper screams, but her scream doesn't last long. The man's body lifts in the air and goes flying across the room, smashing into glass that leads to the glittery pool. People shriek and scream (as they have been doing since Juniper's first bullet), jumping out of the way.

Hannie rushes into the kitchen, her eyes glowing, her hand up in the direction the man went flying. The man tries to get back up, but Hannie curls the tips of her raised fingers, and his nose bleeds. He hollers in agony as he bleeds out on the ground, clutching his head, and in a matter of seconds, the hollering ceases.

Everything is quiet now. Even the music has stopped. Juniper grunts as she stands, dusting herself off, and wiping blood off her cheek.

"WHAT THE HELL IS GOING ON HERE?" A deep voice fills the room. Hannie drops her hand, looking back as a tall man shoves his way through the crowd.

He's much, much taller than anyone here, his eyes blazing gold, his jaw clenching on and off. He studies the mess in the kitchen, the dead bodies on the ground. But his eyes settle on one person. The man outside, who has just bled out because of Hannie.

"Brother!" he cries, rushing for him. "No! Brother!" he wails, dropping to his knees next to the body.

"Oh, shit." Hannie looks at Juniper. "We need to go. *Now*."

"Who did this?" the man demands, but it's all I hear before Juniper has my arm and is rushing with me out of the kitchen toward the front door.

We reach it—the door wide open for our escape—but it slams closed on its own, and Hannie sucks in a sharp breath as she spins around, watching as the tall man floats into the main area. Yes, floats. His feet are off the ground, but he's moving toward us.

"Did you do this?" he demands.

"Tomán, I—I didn't know he was your brother," she says, her hands up, as if trying to calm a wild beast.

"*You* did this!" he roars this time, and he glides forward, slamming into Hannie and knocking her through the closed door. The front half of the house is gone from the smash, now an open crater that faces the street, and outside is Hannie and Tomán, battling in the air. Both of them are floating. Both of them letting off streaks of gold as they punch and kick.

"Shit! We'd better go!" Juniper says behind me.

"Oh, no you don't!" A man grips Juniper by the hair, and she cries out as he twists it around his large hand. "You started this, you Blackwater bitch!"

The party becomes rowdy as the man tosses Juniper across the room. She lands on a display table full of glass and tumbles over, hitting a wall.

"Juniper!" I scream.

The crowd swarms me, rushing out the hole in the wall, running from the chaos. Hannie and Tomán are still fighting, and the man attacking Juniper is roaring as he picks her up and throws her again. Across the room, a burly man looks at me, points a finger, and asks, "Are you Blackwater too, ya darkie?"

"What?" I shriek.

"You are, ya darkie bitch!"

Get down.

Caz's voice rings loudly in my head, and I don't think as I react to it. I lower to a squat, and the sound of another gun goes off. When I look up, the man who was pointing at me no longer has a head. It's been blown off, nothing but blood and membrane. The body falls to its knees and hits the ground with a heavy thud. More screams. More cries for help. More people running.

Panicking, I scramble away, bumping into someone's legs. When I look up, I'm staring into Caz's blue eyes.

"See what happens when you listen to Juniper and not me?" He reaches down, grips my arm, and helps me up. "Let's go!" He charges through the back of the house, where more men are coming in, dressed in brown and grimacing at him. With one hand holding my wrist, he uses the other to aim and shoot. He doesn't miss. Each man goes down, and he runs past their bodies like they're meaningless creatures.

Behind me, I see Killian tearing through the rowdy crowd, and I have no idea where he came from, but I assume he showed up with Caz. How did they know where we were?

Killian rescues Juniper from the other man who is giving her hell, and when she's up, their guns go off. Rounds of bullets fly in the air, Juniper screaming and Killian roaring, their backs pressed together, taking each man on. When they have a clearing, they run after us, and when we're far enough, Caz releases my arm, demanding me to run to the black vehicle parked down the cobblestone street. It's his car, and he presses a button on a fob, unlocking it and shoving me inside.

Juniper and Killian are at the car in a matter of seconds, hopping into the backseat. As soon as they do, Caz starts the engine and speeds off, driving away as fast as he possibly can to get out of Iron Class.

"Your head is as hard as steel, Juniper!" Caz barks.

"It's not my fault that fucker was rude to us!" she shouts back.

"You're always starting something! *Always*!" he snaps. "You know we aren't to fight or use our guns like that in Vanorian territory! If Alora gets word of this and hears about your gun, she'll ban us! You *know* this!"

"Oh, don't play the innocent, like you didn't keep a gun or two yourself!"

"That's beside the point, Juniper! Mine is for emergencies! Look at you! You almost got yourself *killed*! You almost got *Willow* killed!" I don't know why hearing him say my name makes my heart beat harder. I mean, it's already beating pretty hard, but his voice causes a different effect on me.

I glance back, and Juniper does look bad. Gashes are all over her face and her nose is bloody.

"Caz, you have to understand. It was never my intention to—"

"Oh, fuck off!" he barks. "Just sit back there and shut the hell up! For once in your life, just listen to me and *shut up!*"

The car becomes quiet, and I face forward again in the passenger seat. The tension has mounted, and it sticks like glue in the confines of his car. It's a short ride back to Alora's castle, but the silence is deafening.

When we pull up to the palace, Caz has them store their guns in a lockable compartment beneath his driver's seat, where there are more guns hidden, and then he says, "I'll do all the talking to Alora. You all go to your chambers and don't come out until morning. Fucking hell. I swear." He pushes out the car, slamming the door behind him and storming up the stairs.

"You never listen," Killian grumbles, getting out the car. "I told you not to run. You're lucky I don't shoot you now, where you sit."

When he's gone, it's just me and Juniper in the car. She sighs and tosses her head back, resting it on the seat. Silence ticks by, and then Juniper blows a breath.

"As terrifying as that was," she says. "It was also pretty fantastic."

I'm not even sure what to say or how to react. And I don't know if it's my shock from everything that's happened—the glowing eyes of Hannie and Tomán, the floating, the guns and violence, people literally getting their heads blown off by guns—or if I'm losing it, but I laugh. I laugh so hard it hurts my stomach.

Here I am, facing death at every corner, in a world I never knew existed, and I'm *laughing*. It's all I can do.

"Hannie will be okay," Juniper says after a while. "She always takes care of herself."

"Yeah." I wipe a tear from the corner of my eye. "I hope so. But is what just happened a normal thing around here? Won't you all get in serious trouble for it? There were so many witnesses. So many men are dead, and you fled a crime scene. You killed like, ten people, Juniper, but Caz is treating it like a slap on the wrist."

Juniper holds up a finger. "Actually, I only killed three of them. The rest were stunned beautifully. Besides, why wouldn't I have killed that guy? He was a Rippie who threatened you *and* hit me—with very thick glass, might I add. I'm sure he'd have done much worse if he had a weapon on him, and in Blackwater, we leave no loose ends. It's our motto. Do you *not* kill people who threaten you where you're from?"

"Not exactly," I murmur. "We just get the authorities to handle it."

"Wow. People must get away with awful shit there then." Juniper rubs my shoulder and I meet her eyes. "For what it's worth, I wouldn't have let *anyone* hurt you, Willow."

I pat her hand with a smile. "I know."

TWENTY-FIVE

CAZ

I'VE SPOKEN TO ALORA, and I've taken blame for our guns. It's my fault for not checking my clan and securing the weapons beforehand, though I never would've let them go out without at least one. It's my fault nine men are dead in Vanora, but to be fair, all but one of them are Rippies, so I'm not feeling too sympathetic about that.

Still, this has caused a bit of an uproar, and instead of resting, Alora has had to meet with her team to come up with a speech for the Vanorians about the violent acts from last night, which stemmed from *my* people. Everyone who attended the party was seen by a Vanorian Mythic and has had Juniper's face erased from their memories, as well as mine, Killian, and even Willow's. Many people saw us and if word gets out that *we* killed those Rippies, our feud will only get worse.

Alora will cover me, she always does, but I'll owe her—especially now that she has her treaty with the Rippies—and she'll make sure I don't ever forget it. I know if it weren't for me offering double the rubies in the next shipment, she'd have thrown me to the wolves.

When I leave Alora's office, I walk down the staircase to one of the palace's balconies, needing another smoke. I light my bloom as soon as I step foot outside, then walk along the marble balcony until I reach a dark corner. I pull from my bloom, my focus ahead, on the sea.

As I take another pull, I notice a shadow in my periphery and glance over my shoulder. Willow is seated on a bench behind the shadow of a pillar. She's changed into a white night gown, much more suitable than what she was wearing to go out with Juniper.

Honestly, I'm not surprised there *was* trouble tonight with how she and Juniper went out. They weren't dressed the classy way. It was clear they were looking for a good time, which was an invitation to let anyone in. What she's wearing now isn't so subtle either, the gown sheer and her nipples slightly pebbled beneath, but at least she's here, where I can keep an eye on her.

"I can hear you," I mutter, facing forward again. I can't look at her breasts again. I'm almost positive she saw me eyeing them earlier.

"I know you can."

"No one's being mean to Juniper."

"You kind of are." She stands and walks next to me. She's showered. I smell the soap on her skin, oat and honey with a splash of vanilla. Without asking, she plucks my bloom from my fingers and brings it to her mouth, taking a pull from it. Then she says, "Hmm. My stuff is stronger. Yours tastes like reggie." She keeps smoking it and I stare at her, confused by what she just said. "Never mind." She waves it off.

I watch her a moment before pulling out another bloom for myself and sparking it.

"How did you know where we were?" she asks after a stretch of silence.

"I didn't at first, until I heard you panicking. Felt your fear." I take another pull. "It's almost like my mind knew exactly where to find you."

"Hmm. Interesting." She leans forward, resting her elbows on the marble railing.

"Juniper knew better than to take you to that party."

"I wanted to go with her."

"Yes, courtesy of that rebellious streak inside you. What is it about women that makes them not listen?"

"What is it about men always wanting things to go their way and *mansplaining*?"

"Mansplaining?" I frown. "What the hell does that mean?"

"It's when a man feels the need to explain something to a woman in a condescending way. Maybe if you didn't do that, Juniper would listen to you more."

"Oh, please. Juniper listens to no one. She does what she wants."

"Seems all of you do."

I say nothing to that, only because it's true. I take a harder pull from my bloom. "Do you not think about what could happen if you die in Vakeeli?"

Her head turns, her eyes latching on mine. Her brown irises are bright beneath the moonlight, her skin satiny smooth, warm. I haven't seen skin like hers in ages. Natural light seems to favor her complexion, especially the glow of the sun and moon. I haven't seen anyone with skin like hers since my mother. "It's not like there's much to live for in my world."

Confused, I say, "I thought you wanted to go back."

"I do...but there's not much to go back to, other than work."

"Do you not have any friends?"

"I do...like, two." She shrugs.

"Family?"

"My father, but he doesn't keep in touch much. My mother and brother are dead." There's a sharpness in my chest when she says that. It's mildly painful. Is it her heartache?

I drop my gaze. *I'm sorry to hear that.* I can't say it out loud. I don't know why. Saying it out loud will make this thing—whatever the hell this Tether is—feel concrete.

I don't have to look at her to know her eyes are on me. I fight the urge to look at her too, because I know, one look into them, and I'm done. I'll cave to something I'm not even sure about.

I don't know what it is about her, but I can't get her out of my head. Sure, all these feelings could be because of the Tether, but I won't give in to it. Even if I wanted to—which I *don't*—there's no way she can stay here. If I give her even an inkling of hope that she can, she probably will. Then it becomes a liability for me and everyone I love. I can't have that.

I stab out the lit end of my bloom, stand tall, and move back. "Anyway, there will be no more one-on-one time with Juniper while you're here. We go to Beatrix tomorrow and get you back to your world, so there'll be no point in getting chummy with her or anyone else. Do you understand?"

She eyes me, her brown irises sparkling in the moonlight. Her jaw drops just a bit, her eyes hardening, and there's an ache in my chest again—sawing at my heart like the dull blade of a knife.

I ignore it, walking around her and making my way inside the palace without looking back.

TWENTY-SIX

WILLOW

For breakfast, we're given fruit and water. Everyone eats in groups—Caz, Killian, and Rowan on the balcony, Juniper and Maeve seated at a table with me. While we eat, Alora announces that she still hasn't heard from Beatrix, and seeing as she doesn't want to waste any more time, she figures we better head her way so she can deal with her in person.

I can't help noticing Alora is much more stressed today than she was yesterday, and I'm pretty sure it's because of the Blackwater group. They're heavy people who drag the residue of their problems with them, and here she is cleaning it up.

Before we leave, we watch Alora stand in her palace, giving a speech about the violence from last night as the people of Vanora stand in the courtyard below. She has a powerful voice, one that touches the soul. She's a good queen who gives hope and carries herself with grace—not that I would know what it's like being a queen. But if I were to imagine myself as one, I'd want to be like her.

The Vanorians leave with smiles on their faces and go back to their lives, so I suppose all is well for now. She promised them that the guards would be patrolling both Gold and Iron Class to better protect and serve them, and apparently that gives the people some peace of mind. Violence in Vanora isn't as common as it is in Blackwater, but according to Maeve, it does still happen, especially when one of their gilded becomes out of control. After witnessing the fight last night with Hannie and Tomán, I can sense just how out of control they become.

Veno drives along a tall bridge that stretches for miles, and I cling to my seatbelt when I realize how high in the air we are. The bridge is built over the blue waters. One wrong turn or jerk of the wheel, and we're all going down, but no one seems to be worried about it but me.

I clear my throat, and Maeve looks back at me. "Afraid of heights, love?" she asks.

"Not usually," I say, then peer out the window again. "But this is *really* high up." It's taller than the bridge that led us to Alora's castle, not to mention the waves are rowdier, crashing against whatever surface they can reach below.

"Beatrix had it built by the people of Vanora. She made it so that if you want to reach her, you have to be willing to cross this bridge to get to her," says Maeve. "She's a very powerful Mythic. Been around for centuries, even before Alora was born. Some say she was one of the first Mythics around."

"When exactly was Alora born?" I ask.

"If you're asking her age, I believe she's two hundred and seven this year."

What? "And how old is Caz?"

"One hundred and twelve."

"I'm one hundred and ten," Juniper says proudly. "Rowan is one hundred fourteen and Kill, here, is one hundred sixteen." I glance at Killian and he's frowning at me, like he didn't want me to know that bit of personal information.

"I don't understand how you all look so young even though you're so...*old*. No offense."

Maeve laughs. "The youth water was created by the Regals but could only be found in Vanorian territory, hence the reason Alora has full rights to it. It does wonders. Has healing properties, rejuvenates you from inside and out. It even gets rid of plagues—the kind that can kill you within a day or two. But not everyone can afford it, you see. So, while some of us have the luxury of obtaining youth water and living a very long time, many don't. The Rippies are just now getting access to it, courtesy of the treaty Alora recently made with them, but us Blackwaters have had it for a very long time. It'd be worth more than rubies if there were people out there who actually enjoyed life."

"I see. And what happens if you stop drinking it?"

Maeve considers my question, pressing her lips. "I suppose your body just adapts to its age, which probably would cause someone like me to become frail and more prone to sicknesses. Weaker bones and teeth, all that. Hmm...not many people think about not taking it. It's become a staple for us, really."

I nod, then look out the window, at the vast waters beyond the bridge. "This Beatrix...she really doesn't like to be bothered, does she?"

"She doesn't," Maeve says, "which is why only you, Caz, and Alora will be allowed inside. She most likely won't let us in." Maeve switches her gaze to Juniper. "So don't even think about getting out of the vehicle."

Juniper sucks her teeth and rolls her eyes. I start to smile, but I feel eyes on me and look over. Killian is glaring a hole into my face. He's been like this since this morning—staring at me, watching me carefully, as if I'll attack someone at any given moment.

"Do you have a problem?" I ask, frowning.

"Yeah. *You*," he growls.

"Look, the sooner I get out of here, the better for us all, right? But having you stare at me isn't gonna get things moving any faster."

"You have a smart mouth on you," he spits back.

"I've been told."

Killian's frown deepens and his nostrils flare.

"Killian, you will be nice to Willow from here on out, do you understand?" Maeve twists in her seat to get a look at him. "If not, I'll toss you overboard. Do you hear me?"

Killian's eyes don't move from mine as he says, "Yeah, mum. I hear ya."

I pull my eyes away, glad when Veno drives onto flat land again. A winding trail leads up a green hill, and at the top of the hill is a house. It's not very large, like the homes in Vanora, but it stands out with its copper roof and tan walls. The door is wide, rectangular, with copper trimmings.

Looking through the back window, I spot Caz's car trailing behind us, and a bright white car behind his that has Alora. Veno pulls over next to a large tree and parks, and I draw in a breath as Caz parks beside us and immediately climbs out of the car. He marches to my door and snatches it open.

"Out," he demands.

I'm tempted to tell him to ask nicely, but I feel we're closer to getting me home and I don't want to delay it any more than necessary, so I climb out. Plus, after his rude words last night, I see now that I really shouldn't be here.

He slams the door behind me and gestures toward the house, and as he does, Alora walks past us in a bronze dress and sandals, focused on the front door.

There are two windows on either side of the door, both covered from the inside by dark curtains. One of the curtains shifts to the side, and I see a dark figure, but just as quickly as I see it, the curtain moves back and settles in place.

"Beatrix!" Alora calls from the bottom of the stoop. "I know you're here!" She pauses, waiting for a reaction, but nothing happens. "There's something that must be discussed and it's quite urgent, so if you could open the door, that would do us all a world of good!"

Caz stands beside me, shoulders squared and chin up as he faces forward. Proll walks ahead, standing next to Alora. He grunts, and Alora shakes her head and lifts a hand to him, as if telling him, "No."

What would he do? Break the door down?

There's a moment of silence, as if we're all holding our breath, and then I hear a deadbolt clink, another lock, a chain rattling, and the door slowly opens.

A woman appears on the other side—petite and old. Her skin is a very dark brown with a gray undertone. She appears to be in her sixties or even seventies, but in this world, there's no telling how old she really is.

The woman walks onto her porch, and a smile spreads across her lips as she says, "My queen! What an unexpected surprise."

"Oh, cut the crap, Beatrix. I gave your transmitter several contacts. You may not have answered, but I'm sure you saw them."

"Did you try to contact me?" Beatrix gives a sheepish smile. "I don't think I've checked my transmitter in days. The damn thing is hard to keep up with, and you know I'm not good with devices."

Alora rolls her eyes. "As my message stated, there is a couple in crises."

I frown at Alora. "We're not a couple."

"Right. Well, there is a...*friend* of the Blackwater Monarch who needs your assistance. Apparently, she is from another world, and I believe you will know how to get her back."

"Another world?" Beatrix takes another step forward, narrowing her eyes as she scans me. "She smells like the other world."

What? How can she smell me?

"Will you perform a reading on her?" Alora asks.

Beatrix pulls her eyes from me to take a sweep of Caz. "She may come in, but *he* may not."

"What?" Caz snaps.

"There is a darkness in you. I don't want it in my home. You'll taint the whole place with it."

"Alora, what is the point of me coming all this way just to be dismissed?"

Alora raises a graceful hand at Caz, giving him a stern look, before passing her gaze to Beatrix and softening a bit. "Beatrix, you *will* allow him into your home just this once, tainted darkness or not. It will only take a few minutes."

"You know, my queen, when you gave me this land a great distance away, you promised I would be left alone, so long as I did what you asked."

"And you have been left alone for the most part, but unfortunately, I need your help again. There is no one else we can turn to for this that I trust, Beatrix, otherwise I wouldn't be here." Alora steps forward, her face turning serious. "I believe they're Tethered. And not just a simple Tether. A *Cold Tether*."

Beatrix's smirk falls right off her face and her eyes shoot over to me and Caz again. This time she looks at us—*really* looks at us—before blinking rapidly, stepping back, and saying, "Come in. *Now*."

TWENTY-SEVEN

WILLOW

B<small>EATRIX</small>'<small>S HOME</small> isn't very big and wouldn't suit a claustrophobic person, but it's cozy in its own way.

The walls are painted a deep brown, and wooden shelves line them with books and trinkets—things most people would ignore rather than buy if they stumbled across it. Old books take up most of the shelves, loose sheets of paper hanging out of some of them. It smells like herbs and spices in here, as well as old, wet paper. Taper candles are neatly placed throughout the cottage, the flames lit, their wax melting and dripping onto whatever surface it can reach.

Beatrix hums as she moves through her home. She reminds me of the psychic woman from my world who swore I'd never find love. What a time that was.

"Right this way," Beatrix chimes. She leads us through her living room—past two brown chairs, a wooden coffee table, and lamps on the side tables that look like they'll break with a simple breath—until we're greeted with an oval table near the kitchen that seats four.

"Have a seat," Beatrix says, taking the chair closest to two double doors. She sits and folds her hands on the table. I take the chair to her left, and Caz claims the chair on the opposite side. Alora remains standing, choosing to watch while Proll stands guard behind her.

When I look down, there are foreign symbols etched into the table. Triangles with lines, oblong circles, and other shapes I've never seen before.

"How did you get here?" Beatrix asks, fixing her eyes on me. "I assume it happened quickly—a suction in and then a sudden drop?"

"Yes," I say. "It was exactly like that."

"And, let me guess. *This* dark soul found you." She jerks a thumb at Caz, who flares his nostrils. I get the sense he hates being talked about like he's not in the room.

"His wolf found me first, actually."

Beatrix smirks, and Caz's jaw ticks. Then his eyes swing to the right, dropping to the floor, and he tenses in his chair. I frown and lean over a bit to see what he's looking at. At first, I don't see anything, not until it moves. A spider—but it's unlike the spiders where I'm from. This one is big, black, and hairy—like a miniature tarantula.

Beatrix looks at the ground with him and continues a smirk as Caz slides his chair to the left.

What? Is he afraid of the spider?

"Worry not," Beatrix says, grabbing an empty jar from the shelf near her. She removes the lid, scoops up the spider, gives the jar a light shake, then replaces the lid. Once the lid is secured, she places the spider on the table right next to Caz, and I watch as Caz draws in a deep breath before putting his focus ahead again.

"Those spiders can be pesky. They love my home. Sometimes I feed them. That one's named Ori. Or maybe Ori is in the kitchen and this one is Hurn. Hmm. I'm not sure."

Caz's jaw pulses. "Can we get on with this, please?" he demands.

"Of course. Lend me your hand. You as well." Beatrix extends both arms in opposite directions so Caz and I can take them.

Caz frowns at her hand before carrying his gaze up to hers. "Is there another way this can be done?"

"Touch," Beatrix says, smiling at him. "You hate it, you poor thing. You have no idea what you're missing out on by covering yourself up so heavily." She sighs, as if bored with him. "Don't worry. You're from my world. I don't exactly need to *touch* you to see what will come." She looks at me. "But I do need *your* hand." I place mine in hers, and she wraps her dark, nimble fingers around it before closing her eyes.

As she does, the room darkens, a heavy shadow hovering above us, and I refrain from gasping as the lights flicker. Some of the symbols on the table illuminate in a striking neon purple, each one coming alive as Beatrix inhales then exhales with her eyes still shut.

I glance at Caz, who keeps his eyes fixed on Beatrix, then switch my sight to Alora who is watching it all, fascinated. Beatrix grips my hand tighter, hers becoming cold like ice until finally, the glowing symbols turn back to normal, the lights stop flickering, and she opens her eyes, exhaling again.

She turns her gaze to mine, not blinking, then she turns to Caz. "She must be gone within the next week."

"How do I get her back?" he asks without hesitation.

Beatrix pushes out of her chair and marches through her tiny home. My eyes follow where she goes, and she stops in front of a tall bookcase, snatching a book from the third row, and returning to the table. She drops the thick book and flips it open, fingering through the pages.

"You were right, Alora. They share a Cold Tether."

Alora nods, as if she knew it all along.

"It's been so long since I've encountered *this* kind of Tether though," Beatrix goes on, a dip forming between her brows. "What you two have is powerful. I—I haven't seen this kind of Tether in so long. The kind pulled from two universes. "You can hear his thoughts." Beatrix is still flipping through the pages. "And the longer you're around him, you'll eventually begin to feel his pain. And he will feel yours. *Here*." Beatrix lands on the page she's been looking for and places a finger on it. "The Cold Tether," she says. "The Cold Tether is so powerful, so extreme, that within only a few days, things can become fatal for both of you. The more you two are together, the more dangerous it will become for you to be around one another."

"How?" asks Caz.

"Yeah, how?" Because last night, Alora made it seem like a Cold Tether was a beautiful thing. Now this Beatrix woman is telling me it's a fatality?

"There is a Vakeeli being who hunts for Cold Tether mates and harnesses their energy because it's pure and still has the power of the Regals. It wants to keep it for itself, use it for to grow stronger. And it has, with time." Beatrix flips the page, and a chill runs down my spine when she reveals an image of something I've seen before—something from my nightmares.

It's a figure in all black, wearing a hood. It's sketched on the page in what looks like charcoal, so the image is smeared, but the crescent eyes are as red as blood. It's similar to the grim reaper, but deadlier, scarier.

"They call it Mournwrath. It isn't defined by gender, and according to legends, it does not have a face, yet it can turn into anyone it wants to get what it needs. It has hunted the Cold Tethered since they were created by the Regal, Selah. It was over a century ago that I last encountered a couple with a bond like yours. Two days later, they were found dead. Their bodies were pale, their faces sunken in, as if all the life had been drained out of them, and their skin was cold. Colder than the ice of Luxor."

I work hard to swallow. I don't know what Luxor is, but the way she describes it sounds serious.

"That sounds like the couple from Vanora," Alora murmurs, her face ashen. "No one could explain their deaths."

"Yes," Beatrix goes on. "I warned that couple; I knew that if they stayed together, they'd probably not see the next week—that Mournwrath would look for them, absorb their Tether, feed off of them like a leach, until they were no more. They didn't listen." Beatrix looks between us. "I get the sense you two don't very much care for each other, so the sooner you separate, the better."

"Okay, but how do I get back home, to my world?"

"Right. Here." Beatrix flips the page again, revealing a paragraph written in very small script. "You'll say this chant in the place you dropped. Wherever you landed is where your portal home is. You'll see it open when you say the words, and it'll take you back. But when you return, he *cannot* be there." She turns her eyes to Caz. "If you're near the portal, there's a possibility that a trace of you may trickle into her world, making it much easier for Mournwrath to find her. And believe me, it *will* haunt her, if it hasn't been already. It'll get inside her head, make her think crazy things just to get her to open the portal back up. It can only feed when you're together and *in love*—which will happen, whether you want it to or not."

"Trust me. We won't have to worry about that," Caz declares, and I roll my eyes because I knew a smart-ass remark from him was coming.

"Is there no way to stop this thing regardless?" I ask.

"There's always a way to stop something," she says, smiling a bit. "But whatever method is used is not heard of. You see, the Cold Tether is so rare that when one encounters it, it's too late to learn what to do or where to go next. Many believe Selah had a way to work around it before her disappearance—a possibility for the Cold Tether to last without being attacked by Mournwrath—but after so many centuries, Mournwrath has only become stronger and is practically unstoppable. We can only learn when the Tethered are together, and when they agree to become one, or as I said, fall in love. That's when the bond is most powerful. I believe you two have been safe thus far due to your clear disdain for each other."

"So, I say a chant in the forest where I landed, and it'll take me back home?" I ask. "That sounds easy enough."

"It's that simple." Beatrix scribbles something on a sheet of paper and slides it across the table to Caz before slapping the book closed. "Go today, back to where you came from. Get it done and get it over with. And whatever you do, don't go falling in love along the way. It'll only make your lives harder."

I push to a stand just as Caz does. "As I said before, you'll have no concern there. No one's falling in love. She'll be home before we all know it. Thank you for your time, Beatrix."

Alora smiles graciously at Beatrix, but just as she starts to speak, the house shakes, like an earthquake is passing. Trinkets on the shelf clatter, the windows rattle, and the floor vibrates beneath my feet. I look across the room at Caz, who is drawing his gun, but it's too late.

An explosion so powerful rips a hole in the side of Beatrix's house and causes everyone to fall.

TWENTY-EIGHT

WILLOW

"Get up." Caz's voice is gruff. I try looking up at him, but he's not clear. A cloud of dust surrounds us, and I've landed outside the back of Beatrix's house. I push up on my hands, cough, then wince from a sharp pain in my upper thigh.

"Ow! *Shit*," I hiss. I look down and a piece of metal is stuck there. It's ripped through my pants. Blood drips from the wound it's created, and the sight of it instantly makes me nauseous.

"Oh my God," I breathe out shakily. "It—it's stuck in my leg."

"Can you move at all?" Caz demands. "We *have* to move."

"No, I can't fucking move! I have a piece of metal stuck in my fucking leg, Caz!"

"Give us a look." He lowers to a squat to examine it. "If I remove it, you'll bleed more." He sighs and stands, but then there's a loud bang. I gasp, and Caz whips his head up to find the source of the noise. Another bang goes off, and he ducks, cursing beneath his breath.

"It's the fucking Rippies!" a deep voice shouts from a distance. It sounds like Killian. "They've brought a fucking tank!"

"Shit," Caz curses again, side-eyeing me. I can tell he's tempted to leave me here. I wouldn't be surprised if he did. He looks from me to study his surroundings.

"What the hell is happening?"

"What's it look like? We're under attack by the fucking Rippies."

"What is with your family and these fucking Rippies?" I try to bend my knee but wince again and hiss through my teeth. It's useless. I can't move my leg or bend it without pain searing through it.

Love of Vakeeli! Of course, this would happen right now! We get this close and those bloody Rippies come to fuck it all up. And I can't just leave her here. They'll enslave her for sure.

"Enslave me?" My eyes stretch wide as I stare into his eyes.

"Stay out of my fucking head," he growls, pointing a stern finger at me, then he grips my arm and helps me stand. I cry from the pain, not surprised that my reaction is a swift punch to his chest. "I know you're in pain right now, but I told you, we have to move. We're sitting ducks here."

"I—I can hardly walk," I say as he turns and starts walking anyway.

"Hardly is better than not at all."

I grimace as more gunshots sound off. To my left, I spot Alora and Proll running toward a line of trees. She's holding handfuls of her dress as she runs, and when she glances back at me, her eyes widen and her lips part. Ahead of them is Beatrix, who is covered in debris, her hair even grayer from it, and isn't slowing down for anyone.

"Up ahead," Caz says. He eyes me, and with a huff he rushes back to drape my arm around his shoulder and assist me. We're getting closer to the trees. We can hide, and maybe we'll be safe.

Well, that's what I think until Caz's grip loosens around me. He grunts, and I fall to the ground as he stumbles forward. A cry breaks from my lungs as I land on the damn piece of metal again.

"Fuck!" I scream, flopping onto my back and gripping my thigh.

I turn my head to see what the hell just happened, and Caz is standing just a few steps away. There's a trickle of blood dripping down the back of his head that wasn't there before. He's facing a man in a distressed brown fedora who's holding a thick, black club. Caz glares at the club before staring into the man's eyes.

"If you're going to have the audacity to hit me," Caz growls, "At least be smart about it and finish the job."

"Oh, shut up, you pussy," the man snarls at him, and he's missing teeth. A lot of them, clearly, because his words sound like they're coming out the mouth of a snake. The man withdraws a gun from his holster, but before he can lift it in the air, Caz reaches for the club to distract him. The man punches him, but Caz eats the blow, tackling him to the ground and pouncing on top of him.

Picking up the club, Caz raises it in the air and brings it down, hitting the man in the face with it repeatedly. Blood spatters onto his clothes and his face, the *whack, whack, whack* getting louder and louder. Even so, Caz doesn't stop. He hits him so many times the man's face is nothing but a bloody pulp by the time he's done.

Tossing the club aside, Caz pulls himself to a stand before picking up the gun the man had and pointing it at his chest. Two loud bangs sound off, two bullets through the man's chest, and Caz steps away, tucking the gun in his back pocket before using the forearm of his jacket to wipe away some of the blood from his face.

He then turns to me, offering a bloody hand. This is the third time I've seen his ruthless side, and each time has gotten worse. What the hell will it be next time? Slicing someone's skin off bit by bit?

"Let's go," he orders. I clutch his hand, allowing him to help me up. We stagger toward the trees as more guns pop off.

"What about the others?" I ask.

"They know how to protect themselves. This is a regular day for us."

"A regular day? Are you serious?"

He says nothing as he helps me through the forest. The banging noises echo before fading, but Caz doesn't stop, and I'm curious if he knows where the hell we're going or if he's just moving as far away from the chaos as possible.

The pain in my leg is becoming numb, and I don't think that's a good sign. What if I lose my leg? No, I can't lose my leg here! I never asked to come to this place.

"Can we stop to check my leg? Maybe we can take it out now," I insist.

"I'd advise against that. I take it out now, and you'll probably bleed to death before we make it somewhere safe."

"How do you know?"

"I can tell," he says. "It's too close to your artery."

"Well, I'm not sure I can walk much longer."

"Do your best."

"Do you even know where we're going?"

He ignores me, and I stop walking.

"What the hell are you doing?"

"*Where* are we going?" I demand.

"Would you just come on?"

"Listen, I'm in a lot of fucking pain right now, I'm in a world I don't belong in, and I've watched you and your family kill several people like their lives mean nothing to you! Tell me where we're going or I'm not taking another step!"

He frowns at me as if I've lost my mind, and perhaps I have lost it because seriously. How can any of this be real? I'm convinced I'm still dreaming, and that I'm in a lucid state that's hard to pull out of.

I don't have time for this shit.

I fold my arms across my chest and raise a brow. *And you think I do?*

His gaze narrows, as if I'm challenging him. Maybe I am. I'm sick of this. The demands, the violence, all the damn pain! I've been in pain since I landed in this place, and it's only been close to seventy-two hours.

"Fine. Have it your way." Caz marches toward me and picks me up, cradling me in his arms. I fight against him: one because I don't want him manhandling me, and two because I'm not your average-sized woman. I'm what they call *thick* on Earth. Despite it, he holds on tight, and I gasp when I feel like I'm about to fall, but his hands are secure around me.

"Put me down," I snap. He's going to drop me, I know it. I'm too heavy.

Shut up. His voice rings in my head. ***You're not too heavy for me. Now be quiet before I toss you over my shoulder to press the metal deeper.***

I huff a dry laugh. "You really are an asshole."

Caz continues walking—I'm not sure for how long or how he manages to do the trek with me in his arms. As he does, the sky becomes darker, birds stop chirping, and I hear the sound of crickets.

He pushes through a thicket, takes a trail, and when he stops walking, we're on a hilltop. Just down the hill is a small village. The buildings are white and brown with round windows, all about two to three stories maximum. I have no clue how the day just transitioned to night, but it's dark in this area, the stars bright in the sky, twinkling with glee.

Gold bulbs of light are attached to the buildings, and they stand out in the darkness, giving a warmth that cools some of my anxiety. Several bonfires burn in the distance, spaced throughout the fields of grass, and people surround them, laughing, chatting. It's all so...*peaceful*. Nothing like Blackwater or Vanora.

"Where are we?" I ask as Caz marches downhill. I can't look away from this place. It's magical, really. While Vanora has its own uniqueness and regality to it, this place gives more of a cottage core appeal. Everything is touched with green—green grass, green vines on the buildings, green trees planted on every corner. The buildings are neutral, the houses sturdy, surrounded by lush greenery. The streets are made of cobblestone, horse carriages are parked near the curbs.

"We're in Whisper Grove," Caz finally says. "Where they'll have a bloody doctor who can take a look at your leg."

WHISPER GROVE

TWENTY-NINE

CAZ

I'M ready to toss her onto the nearest surface I can find. My eyes flicker down to hers as we approach Whisper Inn, and I can see the aggravation in her eyes, feel the irritation spilling off her skin. It's electric, feeling her this way. I never thought I'd be able to feel a person's temper, yet I can feel hers like heavy weights, and it doesn't help that I can also hear every thought and name she's calling me. *Asshole* this, and *jackass* that. She's ridiculous.

The rustic building of the inn stands bold in the night, it's arched windows revealing silhouettes behind sheer curtains as people move about in their rooms. As I approach, I hear laughter from inside, a foreign sound to me. Where I'm from, people hardly laugh unless they're drunk or high. They're all so hardened and cold. Like myself, I suppose.

I make my way up the stoop and drop Willow into one of the two chairs beneath the awning. "Wait here," I order. She grunts, then scowls at me as she adjusts herself as best as she can with her injured leg. I dust off my hands and jacket before entering the inn.

The laughter is louder, as well as the music from the three-man band in the corner. Men and women sit at two- to three-top tables, sharing drinks of what I'm sure are gin, because that's all they drink in Whisper Grove. Gin and water. Such purists.

A man behind the bar—wearing a white shirt made of linen, with dark, long hair—eyes me as he dries out a glass and places it on the counter. The lobby falls silent as I walk deeper into it, and as I approach the counter, eyeing the barman, he stands tall and looks me hard in the eyes.

"Doctor Manx. Where can I find him?" I ask.

The man glares at me with stormy teal eyes. "I don't think that's how you ask for someone to come to you, mate."

"I need him."

The man glances over his shoulder at a round-topped black door, then back at me. "Haven't seen him."

"Is he behind that door?" I ask, pointing at it. "And don't lie to me because if you lie, I'll know, and it won't be pretty for you."

"Listen, mate, don't come into my place of work starting trouble with me, all right?"

"There won't be any trouble if you lend me Doctor Manx."

"What do you need him for anyway?"

Just as he asks that, the front door of the inn opens and Willow limps inside. Everyone in the room stares at her, and when they notice the blood on her clothes and the metal in her leg, some of the women gasp while the men mumble. Even the band's music comes to a pause.

She swallows hard as she peers around the lobby, then she limps her way toward me, her eyes hot on mine. "I'll bleed to death by the time you come back," she snaps, and I turn to face the barman again.

"This is why I need him," I mutter.

The man looks between me and Willow, who clings to the counter with bloody fingers. "Tell me what happened first. I'm sure if you know Manx, then you know the rules. Bringing violence is a violation in Whisper Grove."

"This happened *outside* of Whisper Grove, back in Vanora. Right in your backwoods, actually."

The man makes a face like he wants to frown but is more intrigued by what I have to say next.

"I don't come with violence, otherwise I would've been blown to bits. I've only come so Manx can take a look at her leg, and then we'll be on our merry way. Now do me a solid and go behind that door of yours and tell him Caz is here, and that I need to see him right *now*."

THIRTY

CAZ

I'm not allowed to see Manx until I hand over my weapons, which is downright fucked, but I knew that coming into Whisper Grove, and for now, it's the sacrifice I'm willing to make. The sooner Willow sees Manx, the quicker she can be patched up and I can find a way back to Blackwater to get rid of her.

After handing over the weapons to the barman, who tells us his name is Alexi, he turns for the door behind him and walks through, quickly shutting it. I glance over at Willow, who eyes me and shifts onto her good leg to stay steady.

"You should sit," I tell her.

"Sitting makes it hurt more."

Stubborn mule.

I look away, but I know she's glaring a hole into the side of my head. Fortunately, she doesn't react, and whatever thoughts she has, I block them out as the door swings open and Alexi returns. Trailing behind him is Manx.

He looks the same as I last saw him, only his beard is gone now. His face is naked, but his hair is still shoulder-length and snow-white. He wears a white robe that's as bright as his smile as he steps around the bar.

"Caspian Edgar Harlow," Manx greets, and if I didn't have so much respect for Manx, I'd slap him for saying my full name out loud. He opens his arms to me, ready for an embrace, and I stiffen. Noticing, he tosses his hands in the air in surrender, smiles, and says, "Ah. I thought maybe you'd have gotten over that old touch thing by now."

I step toward him. "Manx, I need a favor."

"Don't I get a hello? How are you doing? What's life like?" he asks, frowning at me.

"I wish I had time to ask how your life has been, but as you can see..." I step aside, gesturing to Willow's bleeding thigh. "I need assistance."

Manx steps around me to get closer to Willow with a tilt of his head, then he drops to one knee before her, lightly grazing a finger over the metal. "Just a small shard. Isn't touching a nerve or an artery, fortunately."

"You were wrong," Willow says to me.

I work my jaw, holding back on whatever rude remark tries to surface. Not that it would matter. She'd likely hear it anyway.

Manx smiles up at Willow, and she returns one to him.

"Alexi, help this young woman to my office, please."

Alexi finishes topping off someone's drink, then marches around the counter to Willow. "You're in pain so I'll carry you there," Alexi offers. "Is that okay?"

Willow looks into his eyes, bounces her gaze to me, tips her chin, and says, "Yes. That's fine."

He scoops her into his arms carefully, and she wraps her arms around his shoulders, avoiding his eyes, but clearly enjoying the attention judging by the small smile on her lips.

Glad there are people here who know how to treat a woman.

I watch Alexi carry her down a hallway and turn a corner, and there's a flare in my chest as they go. It feels as if I've suddenly developed heartburn, or that I've swallowed a ball of spice that hasn't digested properly. The feeling blazes inside me, unwanted, unwavering, and I form a fist at my side, clenching my teeth together. I don't know what it is. I've never felt it before, and I don't fucking like it, but what I do know is that I *don't* like Alexi having his hands on her. It doesn't sit well with me and downright pisses me the fuck off.

Why wasn't she grateful when I carried her? All she did was gripe about it mentally and squirm, but one touch of this stranger and she thinks he's some kind of god?

My eyes shift to Manx, who is already looking at me with a smile.

"What are you looking at?" I grumble.

"Is she yours?"

"I don't have anyone."

Manx smiles wider, his eyes turning bright. "I see."

"Just heal her so we can leave, Manx. I don't need any of your wise-old-man bullshit right now." I walk past him, going to the office.

THIRTY-ONE

WILLOW

ALEXI SMELLS NICE, and while being pressed against his body, I can tell he's fit. He's also kind, which I can appreciate—a true gentleman, which is refreshing.

He enters a room painted white, with wooden accents and wooden beams in the ceiling. A floor-to-ceiling bay window is ahead, and outside of it are other buildings of the town, houses peppered in the distance. Bushy green trees tower outside the window, the leaves gently brushing the grainy glass panes. Alexi carefully places me on the soft bed against the wall with pillows propped against the headboard.

"Can I get some water for you?" he asks, stepping back. I notice an entire wall of shelves filled to the brim with books behind him.

"I'd love that. Thank you."

Alexi smiles and turns to leave, but he doesn't make it out

before accidentally bumping into Caz. Alexi stumbles back, alarmed at first.

"Oh. Pardon me, mate. Didn't see you there." He claps a hand on Caz's shoulder.

Caz's jaw ticks as he looks through the corner of his eye at Alexi's hand. "Take your fucking hand off me."

Alexi snatches his hand away as if it's on fire, shakes his head at Caz, then looks at me. "I'll be getting that water for you."

I smile. "Thanks, Alexi."

When he leaves the room, Caz fixes his hard blue gaze on mine. He narrows his eyes at me a moment before moving them across the room and standing in front of the arched window with his gloved fingers crossed in front of him.

I wait to see if any of his thoughts will trickle in with mine, but they don't. His mind is like a vault right now. I feel myself knocking, demanding to be let in, and as if he senses my knocking, he cuts his eyes at me before putting his focus out the window again.

Dick.

Manx enters the room, and I rest my back on the pillows, looking the man over in his white robe. He has a pair of wiry, round glasses on the bridge of his nose that he didn't have on before, and he approaches the bed, still wearing that kind smile.

"The man you're traveling with is a rude one, isn't he?" Manx asks. "He didn't tell me your name, so forgive me for inquiring."

I huff a laugh. "It's Willow. And yes, he's a very rude man." I glance at Caz. He's working that jaw again, like he always does when someone's talking about him.

"Willow. That's beautiful. Okay, well I'm just going to take a look here, see what I can do. Mind if I...?"

He points to the rip in my pants, and I nod. "Go ahead."

Manx turns for a pair of scissors on the desk and cuts the

fabric of my pants so he can see the injury better. As he examines it, Alexi walks into the room again with a glass of water. A piece of fruit is floating in it that reminds me of the shape of a blackberry, but it's not black. It's green.

"A verdeberry," he says when he notices me staring at it. "It'll do you wonders right now. Eases pain and has a very sweet taste. Try it."

I sip the water, and the juices of the berry leak into that tiny sip. I take a big gulp the second time, then lower the cup, nodding. "Wow, yeah. That's *really* good."

You'll drink his bloody berry water but won't eat our blackfruit. Tasteless.

I glance at Caz. He isn't looking at me. He's still staring out the window, as if on guard.

If you have so much to say, why don't you say it out loud?

Caz doesn't move, but he does let out an agitated breath.

"Can I get you anything, mate?" Alexi asks Caz, and it's clearly a reluctant ask. Alexi is only being polite.

Caz turns his head, his ice blue eyes locking on Alexi. If his eyes could shoot daggers, they'd be stabbing Alexi a dozen times right now.

Alexi sighs, then looks at me. "Some friend you have there."

"Not my friend," I say after another gulp of water.

I feel a cramp in my chest, tight and uncomfortable. And cold? How is it cold? It's painfully cold—like something is trying to freeze my heart. It lasts only a few seconds before disappearing. Caz's eyes are on mine when I look up, as if he felt it too.

"Ah, there we go."

My eyes avert to Manx, who is now holding up a bloody piece of metal in his hand that's about three inches long.

"Wait. Did you just—"

"Pull this out of your thigh while you weren't looking? I did, yes."

"But I—I didn't even feel it."

"I used an herb to numb it. Now I'll clean it up, use my healing elixir, and within six to eight hours, your leg will be as good as new. Won't even have a scar by the time you're healed."

Manx lifts a tiny amber vial up as well as two clusters of cotton. He pulls the dropper syringe out of the vial and drips a few honey-colored drops on the wound, then rubs it around with the cotton ball. I don't feel a thing as he does it, and it's incredible. What kind of sorcery is this? Sure, there are numbing and healing agents where I'm from, but none this powerful or fast-acting.

"Did you say six to eight hours?" Caz takes a step toward Manx.

"Yes," Manx looks over his glasses as he tends to my wound. "She won't be able to walk until then, I'm afraid. The numbing agent I used is very strong. It makes the whole limb numb. She'll be dragging it like deadweight if she tries moving it too much before then."

"Manx, are you serious? We don't have that much time."

Manx finishes up then tosses the damp cotton balls in the trash. I gulp down the rest of my sweet water as he stands and faces Caz. "Are you willing to carry her to your next destination?"

"Find me a car or something."

"You know we don't allow cars here."

"Then send for someone to pick us up outside of Whisper Grove. It can't be that difficult."

"Caz, I'm not sure what your hurry is. No one can come into Whisper Grove with violent intentions, so you'll be safe for now."

"Yah, *for now*. They'll be camped outside of this place waiting for me at every corner by the time we leave."

"Who are you referring to?" Manx asks, his nose scrunching.

VICIOUS BONDS

"The bloody Rippies. They just attacked us less than an hour ago. That's why she had the metal in her leg."

"Did you start it?"

"*What?*"

"Never mind. Look, whatever the issue may be with you and the Rippies, this young woman cannot leave until tomorrow."

"You've got to be fucking kidding me." Caz pinches the bridge of his nose.

"Alexi can send one of our troops out, make sure no one is lurking around the Grove, and if they are, we'll send them away. In the meantime, I suggest you use a room in the inn and take the night to let her heal."

Caz's head shakes, clearly not in love with this idea, but he finally releases a deep breath and says, "Fine. Give us our rooms."

"Alexi, which rooms do we have left for the night?"

"Well, there was the Yeung wedding last night and some of the guests are still here, so we only have one room vacant." Alexi slides his gaze from me to Caz. "Comes with only one bed, but we do have extra cots available that we can send to the rooms."

"Fuck that," Caz rasps.

"I'll take it," I say, raising a hand. "And some more water with the verdeberries, please."

Alexi smiles and walks up to me, taking my glass. "You've got it, love."

Caz looks between us, his eyes wide and wild, before shaking his head and storming out of Manx's office. We watch him go, and when he's disappeared, Manx looks at me and says, "That boy is a hard one."

"Don't know why you tolerate him," Alexi mutters, walking away with my glass. "I'll bring a wheelchair and the keys to the room. I can help her to the room when I return."

"Thank you, Alexi," says Manx.

When he leaves, Manx makes his way to his desk, organizing some of the tools on top of it and then straightening the vials.

"How long have you been around Caz?" he asks.

"Um...just two days now. Maybe three."

"You saw Beatrix," he says, smiling over his shoulder.

"We did. We ran from her house after the attack from the Rippies. How did you know?"

"That woman's energy lingers. It's powerful. I could feel it before even touching you."

"You can *feel* people's touch?"

"Oh, I can feel lots of things. See lots of things." He pauses. "Just like I can see that you and Caz share a bond, one he's not ready to surrender to yet."

"He doesn't have to surrender to it. Trust me, I want nothing to do with him." Just as I say that, I feel that cold cramp in my chest again, but it's much tighter this time and nearly stops my breath.

Manx's eyes broaden. "You felt that, yes?"

"Yeah," I breathe.

"Denying your Tether." He makes a sucking noise with his teeth. "It'll pain you to deny it. Better to give in to it."

"There's no way anyone will *ever* give in to him. Have you met him?"

"I have. I've known him since he was a boy. He and his mother were patients of mine for a few years."

"Oh." No wonder he tolerates him.

"I always knew he was special, but this? A Tether? It's astounding. Where did you come from?"

"Earth...I think." I bite my bottom lip.

"Earth." He laughs. "I've heard of that place in my studies, yes. Well, Willow, I encourage you to be patient with Caz. He's in need of people like you. The kindhearted and selfless. He just has to accept that people like *you* are here to help him, not hurt him."

Alexi returns to the room with a wheelchair and another glass of water in the cupholder of the chair. "Ready?" he asks.

I nod, and Alexi helps me off the bed and onto the seat. He swivels the chair around and guides me out of the room, but Manx calls my name.

"Yes?" I answer.

"When Caz finds his way to the room, tell him to come to me if he develops any black veins on his body."

I frown, confused, but Manx turns away, going back to tidying up his tools and medicines, and Alexi rolls me out of the office, down the hallway, and through the lobby.

As he pushes me, I can't help looking for Caz. The lobby is full of people in ivory and tan clothing. He'd stand out amongst them in all his black clothing, yet as I surf the crowd, I can't find him anywhere.

THIRTY-TWO

WILLOW

Alexi leaves me on the bed inside a large room that overlooks the Whisper Grove village. Just outside the window are groves of trees, the green leaves vibrant even in the night.

Behind it, the sky is a velvety purple, dotted with bold white stars and a full moon. According to Alexi, it's one of their better rooms, and they normally save this room for royalty or monarchs whenever they visit.

The bed is plush and comfortable and is doing my thigh a world of good. Alexi even had fresh clothes sent up for me from one of their clothing boutiques next door, but I can't shower and change into them until the numbing elixir wears off.

"Give it two hours, then it won't feel so numb," Alexi had said before leaving the room. Thirty minutes later, there was a knock at the door, and a woman with a gold tray walked inside. She placed the tray on my lap with a smile, and I looked down at the meal.

It was potato soup, slices of sour bread, tea in a cup, with cubes of sugar in a square dish, and more verdeberries in a bowl. I smiled at the verdeberries. This had to be the work of Alexi.

"Enjoy your dinner," the woman said, then she left.

Now, I'm sitting here with a full belly, examining the room. The walls are ivory with green trimmings. Wooden beams are built into the ceiling, the floor made of smoothed out rocks. It's similar to the cobblestone on the streets, but darker.

I shift my gaze to the window, watching the stars twinkle as I pop a verdeberry into my mouth.

Where are you? I wonder, hoping Caz can hear me.

I wait to see if I'll get a response. Nothing comes.

After another hour, my leg doesn't feel so numb anymore, so I scoot to the edge of the bed, tapping my foot on the floor to see if I can add pressure to it. My leg feels like it's fallen asleep, but I *can* move it, and Manx was right. The wound is starting to fade. It's shocking how quickly it's going away.

Feeling good enough to stand, I get up. When I don't feel any pain, I wobble to the bathroom.

In the bathroom, green vines crawl up the walls, and a porcelain clawfoot tub sits in the center.

A shower is in the corner, the gold showerhead gleaming beneath the leaves strung around it, and fortunately there is a built-in bench inside for me to sit on. Fluffy tan towels are neatly folded on a shelf, and I grab one, carefully making my way toward the shower. I unwrap the prepackaged bar of soap, and it smells earthy, like cinnamon and moss. It's not a horrible scent, but also not one I'd choose if I went shopping.

When I'm done showering, I dry off with the towel and spot a robe hanging on a hook. I slide my arms into it, stand in front of the mirror, and sigh.

I'm still here, in a world I don't belong in, but at least I'm clean and healing. Even the scratches that were on my palm from the fall in the forest have begun to fade.

There are boxes of new toothbrushes on the counter, and I break one open. The toothpaste comes out black with gold chips in it, and I scrunch my nose, but it smells minty, so I use it anyway. After rinsing, I leave the bathroom, and my leg feels about eighty-five percent better.

I wobble to the bed, lie on it while in my robe, and stare up at the ceiling. As I do, the door of my room opens, creaking on the hinges, and in walks Caz.

THIRTY-THREE

WILLOW

I sit up as quickly as my body will allow, watching as he moves across the room, stripping out of his jacket, an unlit bloom pinched between his lips. He sits in a chair in the corner, pulling off one of his gloves, then another. He's quiet for a while. I'm quiet too—literally twiddling my thumbs as I wait for him to say something.

When he doesn't, I tell him, "Alexi says if you're hungry, there's food they can bring."

He glances at me before taking out a lighter to light the end of his bloom. A quiet sigh leaves me.

I don't want to argue or fight with this man anymore. We're adults and should be able to speak to each other like so. Plus, what Manx said earlier has gotten to my head. He needs someone like me, and I have good qualities. I'm patient and understanding. I don't know why Caz is so bitter and angry, but I don't want to feed into that negative side of him any more than necessary.

"Not hungry," he finally says.

"Are you going to try to sleep?"

He cuts his eyes at me before putting his focus on the door. "I don't sleep."

"Everyone sleeps."

"Well not me."

No point in arguing with a crazy person. "Are you always like this?" I ask, exasperated.

"Like what?"

"So...*blegh*."

"I don't know what that means."

"So uptight and mean."

He cocks a brow. "You haven't seen my mean."

"So, you're just a dick because you like being one?"

"What did you want earlier, when you were looking for me?" he asks, rapidly changing the subject.

"Nothing. I just thought you'd left me stranded here."

He snaps his gaze on me and frowns. "Why would I do that?"

"I don't know." I shrug hard, even though I know the reason. If he'd left me here, I wouldn't have known how to get back to Blackwater. I wouldn't have been able to get to my world.

"I wasn't abandoning you, if that's what you're thinking. I went back to Beatrix's to see if I could find the book," he says. "The one with the chant in it. I lost the paper she gave me during the explosion."

"Oh." I pause. "Did you find it?"

"No." He frowns. "Beatrix hasn't returned, and I couldn't use her transmitter because she wasn't there to allow me access to it. Mine was in my car, but the car wasn't there when I went by."

"So...no one knows where we are? Do they not have transmitters here?"

"No. That's the thing about Whisper Grove. All their communication is done either verbally or by written letter."

"This world is so backwards compared to mine. I mean, the medicine is clearly ahead of ours, but not having phones or ways to communicate right away? That's different."

"I don't think our technology is like yours, and that's probably for good reason. If technology was too advanced here, it'd be genocide. We'd all be dead by now. The Council agreed a long time ago that to maintain power and limit chaos, there must be restrictions. Direct communication and too much technology is one of them, I suppose."

"Why is everyone trying to kill each other here anyway? It's so violent. Doesn't make any sense."

"It's not violent *here*," he says, his head shaking as he takes a hard pull from his bloom. "Not in Whisper Grove."

"What's so special about Whisper Grove?"

Caz looks from the window to me, then back out the window again. "Whisper Grove is a piece of land wedged between all four major territories: Vanora, Ripple Hill, Luxor, and Blackwater. It's the only land that happens to be free of command, and by not having someone in command, the people thrive here. They take care of one another, treat each other as equals."

"That's how it should be everywhere, right?"

"You'd think." Caz's shoulders tense. "Whisper Grove was created by a tribe of men and women who left all other territories in search of a place more peaceful. Somewhere quieter. Safer. A place where children could run free without the risk of a bullet piercing through their skulls." He closes his eyes a moment before peeling them open again. "The people here are good people until you cross them. Their weapons are most threatening, and they don't trade with other territories. It's how they maintain their power. There's also something here in Whisper Grove that instantly scans your intentions as you cross their borders. It's assumed that a former Mythic who promised to always protect the original tribe put it in place. The Council don't share how it's done, nor have they revealed which Mythic designed it, but you can't see this weapon, or feel it scanning you. If your goal is to come into Whisper Grove and start a row with someone, well...it detects that. And when it does, it blasts you to bits."

"Wait." I hold up a hand. "So, if you were coming to this place trying to hurt someone with *me* in your arms, it would've blown us up?"

"Correct."

"Oh my God. I knew it was a bad idea having you carry me."

He fixes his eyes on me. "You had no problem with the barman carrying you."

"His name's Alexi," I retort. "And no, I didn't have a problem with him carrying me because, unlike you, he was nice."

Another eyeroll as he digs into his pocket, pulling out a pill bottle. He opens the lid and dumps a red pill into his palm.

I study him, watching as he tosses the pill in his mouth and gulps it down. "There's nothing wrong with taking care of someone or being taken care of, you know."

"From what I recall, I'm the one who brought you into my home, had you patched up, and gave you clothes to wear," he counters. "I'm the only reason you even had the chance to meet that barman tonight, so keep it in your pants."

"Well, first of all, there's nothing coming out of my pants for Alexi, so how about you stop being a dick about it. Alexi happened to show me great hospitality and I'm grateful for that. And let's not forget, you pointed a gun at me only *seconds* before helping me. Maybe you should've been a little nicer."

"Nicer?" He scoffs, then folds his fingers on his lap. "Being nice is a weakness, and it gets you killed."

"Well, like I said, Alexi is nice."

"Please. He's an arrogant brute."

I laugh so hard I flop onto my back. "You can't be serious," I tell him, wiping a tear from the corner of my eye and sitting up again. "*He's* the arrogant brute? Have you looked in a mirror?"

He glares at me, waiting for me to stop laughing.

"You done now?" He pushes out of his chair, making his way to the closet and taking down several blankets and a pillow. He spreads one of the blankets out on the floor, places the pillow on top of it, and then lies on both.

"You should get some rest. We have a long way back to Blackwater in a couple hours."

"You know you can take half the bed if you want. It's a pretty big bed." And it is. I've never seen a bed so large. It's not a king, or even a California king. It's wide—big enough to fit three burly men.

"I'm fine here."

"Suit yourself." I turn over in the bed, resting on my comfortable side and facing the window. The wind pushes the leaves of the tree against the glass, and I inhale before exhaling, wishing I could just go home already, though I am tired.

I feel the fatigue in my body, and I'm convinced that those verdeberries make you giggly, or give you some kind of high, because I'm feeling a bit loopy. Or maybe it was Manx's elixir?

Shit.

I frown when I hear Caz's voice echoing in my head.

Is that a fucking... Oh, fuck!

I glance over my shoulder as Caz springs off the floor to sit on the edge of the bed.

"What is going on with you?" I ask, confused.

He swallows hard, staring down at the floor. With a frown, I lean over to see what he's looking at and notice something crawling near his pillow. It looks similar to the spider that was at Beatrix's—like a baby tarantula.

"Wait a minute..." I stifle a laugh as Caz moves his feet farther away from the spider. "Are you *afraid* of spiders?"

"Fuck off," he grumbles.

"Oh, wow. You are! *Wow*!" I stare at him, surprised by this new discovery. "And here I was thinking you're this fearless man who can't be bothered."

I climb off the bed, picking up the empty teacup from my tray and wobbling toward the spider. It's crawling onto his pillow now, and I see him shudder in the corner of my eye.

I can't. This is hilarious and ridiculous. What kind of grown man is scared of spiders?

"I'm not scared of them," Caz counters, and I forget he can hear me. "I just don't like them."

"I admit, these are some hairy little beasts..." I scoop the spider into the teacup. "But they're not much to be afraid of. They're not poisonous, are they?"

"Not that one. Plus, they're disgusting to look at."

I'm instantly reminded of all the spiders that'd come into me and Warren's bedroom when we were young. We stayed in an apartment in Sugar Creek, a two-bedroom unit with walls as thin as paper, and our room hardly had space for a twin sized bed. Despite it being one of the worst places we ever lived, a lot of memories were created there.

There was this one corner in the room the spiders would always build a small web. I'd never been afraid of them, but Warren did warn me about poisonous ones, like the brown recluse.

"I think it's kind of cute, actually." I walk toward Caz with the teacup. "Would you like a closer look?"

"Willow, if you bring that teacup any closer, I swear I'll—"

"You'll what?" I ask, smirking. "Kill me? You can't incite violence in Whisper Grove, remember?"

"Then it'll be payback as soon as we're past the border. Seriously—back the hell off with that thing."

"Tell me why you don't like them," I say, taking another step closer. He stands, huffing as he moves around the bed to get farther away from me.

"I just don't."

"But this one is harmless, so what's the big deal?"

"I just don't fucking like them, all right? Never have and never will."

"There has to be a reason."

Caz's head shakes as he takes another step back with a frown. "Fine, if I tell you, will you fuck off?"

"Sure." I smile, bringing the teacup to my chest.

He draws in a breath, clearly relieved that I've stopped coming closer, then shakes his head as he exhales. "First of all, let's set the record straight. I'm not fucking *afraid* of them. I'm *traumatized* by them."

I blink. "How?"

"I was running in a forest one day with some friends and fell down a well. I was maybe nine or ten. Anyway, I was stuck there for maybe an hour or so while my friends went to get help. Shortly after they'd left, I moved around in the well and stepped on a spider's nest. They crawled all over me—under my clothes, into my shoes, my hair." He shudders. "I tried getting them off, but it seemed the more I smashed or swiped at them, the more they kept coming. Someone finally got me out of the damn well, but not without me being bitten over thirty times. I had to stay in the hospital for a week so they could clear my body of their poison. My doctor told me had I been in that well any longer, I probably would've died. Since then, I don't fucking like them."

"Oh my God." I step away, my stomach sinking. "That's... that's so traumatizing. I'm sorry that happened to you." Now I feel like a complete bitch.

He doesn't say a word, just looks away, as if ashamed, and now I *really* feel bad. He hates spiders because of a childhood trauma. That's awful.

I wobble around the bed to get to the window, twisting the lock open and lifting it. I dump the spider onto the windowsill, and it scatters away quickly. Then I close and lock the window before setting the teacup on the shelf next to me.

Caz climbs off the bed, walking to the chair and picking up his jacket. **Not staying here.**

He carries the jacket with him, marching to the door, and my heart pounds as I watch him go toward it. "Wait—Caz," I call as he wraps a large hand around the doorknob.

He stops, and I feel a slight ache in my chest again, only this time it doesn't hurt. It's pulsing, like it has its own heartbeat above my own heart. A chill sweeps through my body, but unlike the coldness before, this one doesn't paralyze me. Instead, it soothes the marrow in my bones and causes my scalp to tingle.

"You don't have to leave," I tell him. "I'm not judging you about the spiders. After hearing that story, I understand why you're afraid of them, and I'm sorry for taunting you about it."

He turns fully around, glaring at me. "I'm *not* afraid of them."

"Right—well, it makes sense why you hate them."

He tips his chin, clearly finding that statement more suitable. "You tell anyone, and I'll bury you."

I fight a smirk. "No, you won't."

"What makes you think I won't?"

"Because apparently we're Tethered." I step closer, but not without wobbling. "And I have a feeling burying me would be just like burying yourself."

He's quiet as I take another step. Then he says, "Look at you. You can hardly walk and you're talking about some Tether."

"Don't change the subject."

If I'm not mistaken, his eyes soften as he looks into mine. It's very brief, but they do, and he clears his throat, looking away to break his trance.

"Look, I know you feel this...*whatever* this is that happens when we're arguing or disagreeing with each other," I go on.

His throat bobs and he works his jaw, like he often does when there's a topic happening he doesn't want to discuss. I've noticed that about him. In only a matter of days, I've noticed many of his quirks.

"I have a feeling if you leave this room tonight, that cold cramping we're feeling will only get stronger. For all we know, that pain might really start to cause damage." I pause, debating whether I should tell him what I felt, but either way he'll probably hear my thinking about it. As I look into his eyes and notice them swimming with curiosity, I shoot for it. "Earlier, when you walked out of Manx's office, I felt cold, and like I couldn't breathe for a second, and I don't know what that means for us, but I don't want to feel that again, so if you'd just *stay*, I think it'll be best. For both of us."

Caz looks deeper into my eyes, holding my gaze a few beats before snatching his away and sighing. Without a word, he walks across the room, moving past me to get to the cushioned chair in the corner.

"Fine. I won't leave, but I won't be sharing a bed with you either. Nothing to take personally, I just don't like people near me for too long."

I start to ask him why, but for now I'm just glad he didn't go. Oddly enough, I feel safer with him around than when he's not. And sure, Whisper Grove may have a rule that doesn't allow violence, but who's to say someone can't find a loophole and attack us anyway?

Despite it all, it's a victory to me. He's staying, and I'm tired, so I think I'll sleep. I climb into the bed, lying on my good side again, and pull the plush white duvet over me.

This bed is so comfy. You have no idea what you're missing out on.

I peek at Caz, and his eyes are already on me. With an eyeroll, I hear his voice in my head saying, **Go to sleep already, Willow Woman**.

I close my eyes with another smile.

THIRTY-FOUR

CAZ

She's right. If I'd left the room, I'm sure the cramping in my chest would've gotten more intense. Normally, I'm okay with pain. Pain has only made me stronger, but this is a different type.

It's not a normal hurt, just a relentless ache that intensifies when I'm away from her, and the more I try to pull away and ignore her, the worse it becomes. It's like a toothache that's taken over my whole body—a pain I wish would disappear but instead lingers.

When we're in the same room, sharing the same space, that ache dulls and cools. It's as if by being near her, my aching is soothed, her presence my painkiller.

I'm not sure what this Cold Tether is all about, but I don't like it. Becoming attached emotionally *and* physically to someone I don't even know? It's bogus, and I never asked for any of this shit.

She's asleep now, breathing softly, making small noises. I watch her a while, wondering if this was meant to happen. Was she meant to land here and pop into my life? Was she meant to hear my thoughts, feel my emotions, read me like a book? It's hard for many to get a read on me, but Willow does it with ease. It's as if this Tether was created for us to be soulmates, but I can't help feeling like that's impossible for me. She's nothing like me, and there's no love left within me to give.

I'm a fucked-up man with fucked-up urges, and she's this delicate thing who would have no idea what to do with me. It's not fair to her, to me, but by morning, we'll be able to move again. We'll find Beatrix, we'll get that chant memorized, and it's back to her world she goes.

With the thoughts running rampant in my brain, I stand and make my way to the door. Before I go, I glance back and watch Willow's chest rise and sink as she sleeps soundly. Truthfully, I feel bad for her. Being stuck here, in a place as awful as Vakeeli. The woman is terrified to be here. I have to find out more about this Tether.

Fortunately, Whisper Grove has one of the largest libraries, and it's a short walk from the inn. I leave the room, close the door behind me, and walk down the hallway. As I pass the bar, I spot Alexi behind it, wiping down the counters. No one else is around.

"Going out?" he calls.

"Fuck off," I mutter, already walking out the front door. I don't know what it is about him that I hate...well, I take that back. I *do* know. It's that he had his hands on Willow. I can't figure out why it angers me that he held her, but it does, so *fuck him*.

I walk along the cobblestone street, passing lit lanterns and horses tied to poles, until I spot the library ahead. It stands tall between the village hall and a bakery. A brown three-story building, half of it swathed in thick, green vines. There are two balconies, both laced with vines as well. A gold glow emits from the upper window. I used to call it the candle that burns forever because, no matter the time we visited, it was always burning. No one is probably in there; it's nearing midnight. Fortunately this library never closes.

I remember it as a child—the late hours wandering through Whisper Grove with my mother. She was a night owl. She didn't like going out much during the day. She'd bring me here to study, because to her, reading was essential. And not only that, but Whisper Grove also had the finest literature. A lot of the books go back centuries upon centuries. She'd find a book for me (normally about something she wanted me to learn, like the names of flowers, or the types of clouds), plop me down in a corner, and tell me to read. Then she'd find her own books and read for hours, scribbling notes like mad in one of the leatherbound notebooks she carried. I never knew what she was writing in those books, but it always seemed urgent. That is until the day she burned every single one of them. That was a week before I never saw her again. Clearly those journals had information inside them that she didn't want anyone figuring out.

I brush the memory away as I grip the handle of the library door and pull it open. As soon as I'm inside, I'm greeted with the scent of aged books and cinnamon. Candles in sconces line the walls, and what looks like infinite rows of shelves are ahead, overflowing with books. I pass the front counter, which is vacant, a white sign perched on top of it with the word **CLOSED,** and move through one of the shelves. I pass fiction, non-fiction, Greek mythology, and textbooks for math until I spot the section I need.

Vakeeli History.

It's the largest section of the library, a circle of bookcases surrounding sunken-in leather sofas, wooden chairs, and desks. I'm not sure what I'm looking for, but I'll know it when I see it, so I spark a bloom, pick up a pillar candle, and make my way to the first shelf.

There are books on certain wars and battles, the battle of Luxor and Kessel, for instance, and the four-year war between Blackwater and Ripple Hills. Ripple lost, of course.

Monarchs of Vakeeli, going back 10,000 years.

Maps.

Resource guides and explanations.

I stop when I see the section I need.

Selah the Regal.

I place the candle on a shelf, put out my bloom, and scan the row of books. I'd heard about Selah through my mum, very rarely. It's been deemed that Selah still exists but is impossible to reach. Many say she lives on an island she created herself, deep in the Vakeeli waters. I suppose no one would know because there is only so far a person can venture into the waters before the waves become large enough to drown your boat and kill everyone on it.

I spot a book with the title *Selah's Creation of the Tethered* and take it out, carrying it to a table and flipping it open. There's passage after passage of what the Tether is, exactly as Beatrix described it. There's the simple Tether, which is common in Vakeeli. Soulmates who link eyes, connect, and marry off like normal people do. And then there's the *Cold* Tether and the story of how it was created.

THERE ARE **arguments that out of the three Regals of Vakeeli, Selah was most powerful. Hassha, Regal of the sun, moon, and stars, and Korah, Regal of water, air, land, and vegetation, were the creators of all Vakeeli territory. Selah was the Regal of animals and men. The Regals possessed the power to create all living things, building each territory in a unique way.**

After all the land was formed, Selah created the first of

Vakeeli mankind, the Tethered. There were seven Tethered total. Three females: Jesha, Rotan, and Oriah, and four males: Valkee, Busk, Decius, and Lehvine. It is said that this number is all Selah could produce. Her powers would not let her create more than seven at once.

After Hassha and Korah had created and split the lands, each Tethered was given a territory where they created their own laws. Selah created each Tether to be completely unique. They were not family. They did not know each other. She'd separated them as children, raised them individually, and allowed them to develop their own characteristics. The Tethered kept to themselves, growing roots in their lands, and making each territory the best that they could, but she soon realized her Tethered were lonely, just as she was when Hassha and Korah stepped down to become Mythics among the land of Vakeeli.

Selah allowed the Tethered to seek each other when they became old enough to mate. When it was time to mate, they'd know because their hearts would beat harder, their bodies would develop, and their feet would move without guidance until they were where they needed to be. According to the text, when they found their mate, the bond was undeniable. They would become protective and could smell their mate from miles away. With their mates, they would create children, who would also carry the power of the Tether.

Jesha mated with Valkee.

Rotan mated with Busk.

Oriah mated with Lehvine.

However, by creating seven Tethered, Selah had conjured a downfall. One of the women would accidentally mate twice, and that was Oriah, who not only mated with Lehvine, but Decius as well.

This did not sit well with either male, because as mates, a solid bond is created so that procreation can begin. The Tethered males become very territorial, digging into their primitive ways for their mates, and this was hard for Oriah because her heart had mated to two.

Lehvine was strong, with arms as thick as tree trunks and hair as dark as a raven. He was ruler of Blackwater. Decius was the mighty ruler of The Trench, which was once known as Titan before he abandoned it.

It's rumored that Oriah begged Selah to let her have both men, to let her bond and procreate with both of them, but Selah told her she could not because it would disrupt the sacredness of the Tether. But of course, Selah loved Oriah, and she did not want her to suffer, so to spare Oriah's heart, Selah agreed to take whichever man she didn't choose and put him to rest, so that Oriah would live with one mate peacefully and without guilt.

With a heavy heart, Oriah chose Lehvine. And when Decius found out that he was going to be put to rest because of Oriah's choice, he was not pleased. Selah gave Decius three full moons to live, and he lived angrily, bitterly. Then, he found out Oriah was pregnant, and that her procreation with Lehvine was beginning.

With this news, Decius' anger only intensified, but he hid it from Selah. On the day Oriah gave birth, Decius paid her and Lehvine a visit and confronted Oriah, begging for her to take him back. Oriah told him she couldn't—that she'd already bonded with Lehvine. They were going to live the rest of their lives procreating for Selah in peace.

Still angry, Decius argued with Oriah until Lehvine interfered and tried breaking it up, but it is said that when Lehvine touched Decius, his anger was so powerful that Lehvine's hand turned as black as coal and his arm lost its strength. Lehvine retreated and managed to get Decius away, but it would not be the last time Lehvine saw him.

Decius had gotten a taste of Lehvine's power through his wrath, and he craved it more than he did the bond with Oriah. He wanted all of Lehvine's strength, so Decius returned to Blackwater, the land Lehvine ruled, appearing twice his size, with arms as large as Lehvine's. It was there when he attacked Lehvine, wrapped his hands around his head, and sucked the life from him to become even stronger.

Once Lehvine was dead, his body hollow and cold, he gave Oriah an easy solution. She could be with him now that Lehvine was gone and they could continue to procreate, but Oriah was mortified. She'd watched as Decius took the life from her mate and felt a pain she'd never felt before. Her heart was breaking, and she became freezing cold.

She shivered as she ran away with her son and hid him in the fields, and when Decius found Oriah and she still refused him, he clasped her head in his hands and drained the life from her too, and he felt full.

Realizing what he'd done, and that Selah would soon come, Decius fled and went into hiding. And when Selah visited and found two of her Tethered dead, she was broken-hearted.

Selah figured out who'd done it, and she sought to destroy Decius immediately, get rid of the abomination she'd created, but it was too late. Decius's hunger for Tethered souls became too much for him to bear, so he found Rotan and Busk and drained the life from them too. And then, when he became hungry again, he went after Jesha and Valkee, all of whom had procreated. Jesha and Valkee had created twins, and Royan and Busk, a daughter. With no more Tethered to take,

Decius hid, and Selah collected all the Tethered babies, casting a protection spell over them.

Selah knew once the babies grew, the spell would weaken because of the strength of the Tether, and that Decius would come out of hiding to hunt them too once they were of age, so she created three uppers, known as The Council, who could also procreate but could not be harmed by Decius.

The Council had children, and their children had children. Some of the children were born with gifts to further protect themselves and their families from Decius and beings like him, and they are known as the Gilded. The Gilded were once pulled together to create an army, but as time progressed and Decius revealed less of himself, the army dispersed and lived normal lives.

All of The Council's children and the Gilded procreated, filling up the world of Vakeeli, just as Selah had planned. Then, when the Tethered babies were old enough, she blessed their souls with the power to be reborn and used all that was left of her energy to send each baby into hiding. Two of the babies remained in Vakeeli and were looked after by the Regals and The Council, while the twins were sent to a different universe, one Selah had never ventured to, but figured was best in order to keep them safe.

However, these precautions did not stop Decius from finding them. The four Tethered babies remain, and each time they are killed by Decius, they are born again months later. According to the text, Selah did not want to destroy the babies because she wanted to find Decius and destroy him only, so they could live peacefully and carry her gift on. She could not create anymore Cold Tethers. She didn't have the energy or power to do so. Because of this, each baby was reborn again and again until she could find a solution.

For centuries, Selah protected the cold Tethered from Decius each time they were reborn by allowing them to mate, and once mated, she'd harness the power of their Cold Tether herself, which in turn would weaken Decius and allow the Tethered to prosper as normal beings for as long as their lives went on.

However, Selah's disappearance has counteracted that. Cold Tethers are still being hunted and drained before they can procreate, and it is said that Decius may have gotten strong enough to place his own attack on Selah, which has resulted in her disappearance.

The Cold Tether continues to be studied. It is a sacred bond, passed down from the highest Regal. Some believe it to be a curse, while others consider it a gift...

I STARE at the last page of the book. I'm can't even form a coherent thought. Decius was originally a Tether created by Selah...and now he's Mournwrath?

"Shit," I mutter. This is worse than I thought. I flip the page, and as I do, I hear footsteps drift through the library. Who the hell is here so late?

I glance down at a fountain pen on the table and pick it up, gripping it and moving behind a shelf to hide. The footsteps move closer, and I lift my hand, angling the pointed tip of the pen ahead of me. I may not have my gun, but I have this. I just hope it doesn't trigger any alarms. *But if it's a Rippie, or someone else out to get me...*

A person steps into view, and when I see who it is, I lower my hand and release a breath.

THIRTY-FIVE

CAZ

"Manx?"

Manx spins around, his eyes nearly bulging out of his head. "Oh! Caspian! What are you doing here?"

"What am I doing? What the hell are *you* doing in here? You almost got yourself stabbed!"

"You were going to stab me?" He presses a hand to his chest.

"If I had to. You could've been a Rippie."

"Hmm. Glad I'm not one then." He shrugs, peering around.

I stand taller. "You didn't answer my question."

"Why am I here? Right. I presented a study to a group of teenage boys in this section earlier and I left my notes." He wanders around the desks until he's in front of a wide table, then picks up a thick notebook chockfull of papers. "Ah. Here we are. Essays. I have to grade them tonight."

"Right." My eyes slide to the book on the table, and Manx looks with me.

"Still up to your old habits?" he asks, smiling.

"Something like that."

"What are you studying this time?"

"Vakeeli History," I tell him, purposely keeping it vague. The last thing I want is to get into a conversation about the Tether with Manx.

"Interesting. Well, don't let me keep you." He walks past me, raising the notebook in the air. "I just came for this. But do let me know if you need anything."

"I will."

He pauses. "How's Willow's leg?"

"Not sure. Didn't ask."

"Of course you didn't," he chuckles. "You should be nice to her. Can you imagine how she feels, stuck in a world she knows nothing about? I'm sure all she wants is to get back home, where she feels safe."

"Yeah, well, I'm working on that."

Manx tilts his head, looking me over briefly, before waving a finger in the air. "One day you'll learn to soften up, Caz. One of these days, you'll just have to."

With that, he ambles through the library and is gone. A door creaks on the hinges and slams closed, and when it does, I swipe up the book and take it with me, leaving the library too.

THIRTY-SIX

CAZ

When I return to the inn, Willow is still asleep. I strip out of my jacket and slump down in a chair in the corner by the window, flipping the book open again and reading more about the origins of the Tether by moonlight.

As I get to the next passage, Willow startles in her sleep, moaning. I glance up and she's still again, so I return to the page of my book.

But then I feel a cool draft whisper by, like a breeze has snuck through the window. I look over my shoulder, but the window is closed. Willow whimpers and gasps, and I snap my gaze on her again, leaning forward with my brows dipped.

She moans again and rustles about, as if fighting something. I close the book and stand, moving closer to the bed. She must be having a nightmare and I figure I should wake her, but as I lift my hand to touch her, something tight wraps around my throat. I stumble backwards as what feels like a pair of hands chokes me, squeezing as tightly as possible. I struggle for breath, my gaze shifting to the bed as Willow makes strangled noises while thrashing and moaning louder.

"Willow!" I choke out. "Willow—wake up...wake...up!" I flop onto my back as the grip grows tighter, suffocating me.

Willow sits upright in the bed, staring at me while holding her throat. Her eyes are nearly bulging out of her head, her lips turning purple, before she finally bursts a gasp and sucks in a large amount of air. After her gasp, the grip around my throat weakens, but I still feel the essence of it lingering.

"What the bloody fuck was that?" I pant, rubbing my throat.

"I—I saw it," Willow says, breathless.

"Saw what?" I snap, sitting up.

She doesn't answer. Instead, she climbs out of the bed, and clearly her leg has healed because she rushes to the bathroom without so much as a stumble.

I push to a stand, still rubbing my throat as I follow her. She turns on the lamp built into the bathroom wall and looks at her reflection in the mirror. Tears form at the rims of her brown eyes as she rubs her throat, and as I stand behind her, I see exactly what she sees. Red marks are on her throat, the shape of fingers, as if someone grabbed her tight and refused to let go.

Then I look at my reflection, and there are markings around my throat the shape of fingers too, but they're not like hers. They're as black as ink. I glance at hers again, then mine. The fingers are the same size and in the same angle, like the person wrapped their hands around my neck from behind me.

Her eyes flicker up to mine in the mirror, and it only takes one name from her mouth for me to realize just how much danger we're in.

"Mournwrath."

THIRTY-SEVEN

WILLOW

"Manx said something to me before I was brought to this room." I face Caz, and he's rubbing his throat, trying to get the black marks off, but they're not going anywhere. It's sinister, seeing the fingerprints around his neck, but what was even more sinister was seeing Mournwrath in my dreams.

I was in the forest again, but this forest looked different—not like the one I landed in when I first came to this world. This forest had trees as tall as skyscrapers, the branches and pine needles frozen, and despite the wind blowing, the trees didn't move. It was so quiet I could only hear myself breathing.

I tried finding a way out of the forest, but something came after me, swift and strong. Its fingers wrapped around my neck from behind, and I couldn't see it at first, not until it lifted me into the sky. I floated there as the grip was released from my throat, but my body turned, spinning in a 180, and there it was. Mournwrath, floating in the air with me, those red crescents boring into my eyes. It started to lower the hood of its black cape, and black talons slipped from beneath it, wrapping around my throat again. The talons were cold and tight, and for a moment I couldn't breathe. Then I woke up, and Caz was on the floor, holding his throat.

"What did Manx say?" Caz asks, bringing me back to the present.

"He said to come to him if you develop black veins on your body or something like that."

Caz frowns a moment, then lifts his arm. He's wearing a long-sleeved black shirt, so I can't see any of the skin on his arms. The only thing revealed are his pale hands.

His blue eyes flicker up to mine before he takes a step back and grips the hem of his shirt. Without a word, he pulls the shirt over his head, and I blink rapidly, taking a step back, my eyes growing wider. Black veins run up both his forearms and even the center of his chest, but that's not what catches my attention most. It's the scars on his body and old wounds that catch me off guard. Some of them look like bullet wounds, while others like marks from a whip, as if he was beaten repeatedly. A tattoo is on the heart of his chest, the name *Azira* in a bold, script-like font. I'm curious who that is.

Beneath the scratches and whip marks, his pecs are lean and smooth like marble, as well as his biceps. His belly has more markings the shape of healed bullet wounds. One is wedged between his ribcage and one of his six abdominal muscles.

Caz steps around me to investigate his reflection. The veins on his arms aren't extreme, but the ones on the center of his chest are prominent, and they're spreading outward, as if they'll eventually leak to the rest of his body.

"What the hell is this?" he rasps.

"I think it's part of the Tether," I whisper.

Caz looks through the mirror at me, then he turns and slips back into his shirt. He marches to the bedroom, and I follow him as he picks up his jacket and gloves.

"We need to get Manx." He slides his fingers into the leather gloves. Once his boots are on, he's heading toward the door.

I slip into the white shoes Alexi brought up for me with the change of clothes and follow Caz out the door.

THIRTY-EIGHT

WILLOW

Caz marches down the hallway, making a rapid turn toward the lobby. It's empty and quiet, chairs stacked neatly on top of the tables and the floors shining, like they were waxed not too long ago. The lights are dim, and the bar counter is clear, minus a few napkin holders.

Caz walks behind the bar toward the round top door and bangs on it.

"Maybe don't be so loud," I whisper, peering around.

Caz glares over his shoulder at me before banging again, even louder this time. The door swings open, and Alexi appears on the other side, bleary-eyed and grimacing.

"What the hell?" he croaks. "Why are you banging on my door in the middle of the night?"

"Where's Manx?" Caz asks.

"He's probably home, asleep, like other normal people do at this hour," Alexi declares. "And whatever it is you need him for, I won't be taking you because it's very early and you've interrupted my sleep."

Alexi starts to close the door, but Caz plants a firm hand on it, pushing it back open.

"Lead me to Manx," he demands.

"You know, you'll get nothing in life by making every demand of yours sound like a threat." Alexi looks Caz up and down, and I step around Caz to stand next to him.

"Alexi, I'm really sorry to interrupt your sleep like this." I grip Caz's arm and lower it, taking his hand off the door. Alexi stands taller, giving a smug smile. I hear a growl in Caz's throat but ignore it. "Manx told us to come and see him. It's important, otherwise we wouldn't be here. Do you think you can get him for us?"

Alexi is still staring at Caz, both of them having a stare down. When he finally snatches his gaze away, he drops his eyes to mine. "Anything for *you*, Willow."

I smile. "Thank you."

"Of course. Give me a moment."

Alexi closes the door and I glance at Caz, who shakes his head and moves away from the door. "Wish you'd stop kissing his ass," he mutters.

"I'm not kissing his ass," I counter. "But he's right. Demanding people to do things won't help you."

"Don't believe that. It's helped me thus far. People listen when demands are made."

"Probably because they're afraid you'll blow their heads off."

"Alexi would be afraid too if he weren't in this bloody territory."

Just as he speaks his name, Alexi walks out of the room, tugging a shirt over his head and pulling it over his sculpted belly.

I pretend I don't notice as he moves from behind the bar counter and says, "Follow me."

I follow him first, and Caz reluctantly does as well. He leads us out of the inn, where the stars twinkle in the sky and a cool breeze floats by. The air smells like sweet honeysuckle and fresh cut grass, and I understand why people enjoy staying here. If we weren't in such a hurry, I'd stop a moment and drink it all in.

Alexi strides along a cobblestone street that has grass prodding between the cracks, passing several cottages until he approaches one made of brown bricks and surrounded by low hanging trees.

The trees are green and plush, and a thin, stoned trail leads to the front door of the house. The windows of the cottage are tall and rectangular with green vines winding up to the roof.

We walk past waist-high bushes that are trimmed neatly, as well as flower beds. I've never seen these kinds of flowers before, bursting in yellows and blues. Alexi approaches the door and gives it a knock before planting his hands at his waist.

Caz and I wait a few steps back as footsteps drum through the house and the door is pulled open. Manx appears on the other side, dressed in tan linen, his white hair glossy. There's a brush in his hands and a soft smile on his lips.

Alexi opens his mouth, but Manx holds a hand up. "I know what this is about." His eyes land on Caz and me. "Come inside, you two. I'll see what I can do."

THIRTY-NINE

CAZ

"Why didn't you tell me this would happen sooner?" I turn away from the window, focusing on Manx. "You could've told me in the library when you saw me."

"I wasn't sure if it would happen."

"How did you know it would at all?"

"As I told you, I've studied the Cold Tether. Black veins are always a symptom."

"You seem to know a lot," I grumble.

"Years and years of studying, my boy."

I look out the window again. I don't know what I'm looking for, but I don't feel safe in Whisper Grove anymore, despite the security rules.

"If it helps, the perimeters of Whisper Grove were canvassed. There was one Ripple Hills member hanging around the border," Manx says, carrying a tray of tea to the table. He places the tray on the center of the table and disperses the teacups. I move away from the window and stand by the table while Manx pours tea into Willow's cup first. She smiles and thanks him, and then he pours some for me.

"What was he doing there?" I ask.

"He wasn't really doing anything. He had a fire going, and we told him to leave."

"Well? Did he?"

"Yes. Without hesitation."

Willow helps herself to a few cubes of sugar, plopping them into the hot liquid.

"However," Manx says, sitting at the head of the table. "He did leave a message before he went."

I slide my eyes to Manx's, and he pushes a folded sheet of paper across the table to me. There's blood on the paper, and I avoid a grimace as I pick it up and open it. When I read the message, I clench my jaw and crumple the paper in my hand.

"How long ago did he leave?" I ask.

"Two hours ago."

"What does it say?" Willow inquires, eyeing me.

I control my breathing. No use in getting angry here, plus I don't want to trigger any alarms with hostility. I walk toward the window, peering out, and the sun is spilling over the rooftops.

"Can you help us with the problem at hand?" I glance over my shoulder.

"You mean the black veins?" Manx stands, making his way toward a shelf and pulling down an amber vial. "I can." Approaching, he offers me the vial, and I take it.

"What does it do?"

"It'll slow the spread," he says. "People have come to me with many infections and diseases, and I remember reading once that calla flora and green herbs help Tethers." He turns his attention to Willow. "As for you, I can offer a protection morsel, so those nightmares you've had don't happen again. Unfortunately, I only have one more, and it lasts for two days. That should be enough time for you to get back home, yes?"

"More than enough," I tell him, popping the lid off the vial. I chug down the liquid, and the bitter taste swims around my mouth before I gulp it down. I gasp a breath as Manx returns to his shelf of elixirs and pulls down a small purple bottle. He pops something into his hand and carries it to Willow.

"Take it with your tea," he says. "It's quite disgusting."

She accepts what he offers, and I step closer to see what it is. It's a silvery chunk, looks like metal. She presses her lips, studying the chunk before asking, "Do you have a remedy for everything?"

"Almost," he says, sliding the teacup on the saucer closer to her. "There's one thing I'll never have a remedy for though."

"What's that?" She pops the chunk into her mouth. Her nose scrunches as she chews, and she picks up the tea quickly, chugging down several hot gulps. I'm surprised she doesn't burn her tongue.

"A broken heart." Manx takes his seat again. "That's the one thing all people must live with, no matter what world they're from." He raises a brow at her. "I'm sure you know a thing or two about that."

She brings the teacup to her mouth and sips before asking, "Are you reading me?"

"I can read your energy and I can tell something has broken you before. A few things, actually."

She says nothing to that. Just shifts her eyes down to the table.

"What do the black markings mean exactly?" I moce closer to the table. "And how do you know so much about it?"

I avoid looking at Willow because I can hear her thoughts, but right now those aren't the priority. She's thinking a name repeatedly but trying to bat it away. **Warren. Gone. He's gone. Probably won't ever come back. The tea. Focus on the tea. It's good. Could use some honey.**

"They simply mean your Tether is becoming stronger," Manx says, bringing my focus back. "I've studied the Cold Tether for centuries. The black veins always pop up when the Tethered form a bond."

I cut my eyes to Willow as she locks on my face. Was a bond formed between us? If so, it can't be that deep. Not enough to cause all of this—the nightmares, Mournwrath's attack, the veins.

"I've always been fascinated by it," Manx continues. "And your mother...ahh, she did say you'd be special." He pauses, stroking his chin. I try not to let the mention of my mother get to me. "I would say it's as simple as your Tether becoming stronger, but I'm afraid if you don't get her home soon, something worse will happen to you, Caspian."

I tip my chin. "Like what?"

"A fatality. *Death*, even." He looks at Willow. "Are the nightmares scarier, Willow?"

"Yes. And in this one, it was Mournwrath. I'm sure of it. It was...*choking* me."

Manx winces, as if he can imagine the pain. "The protection morsel should help. You'll be able to sleep peacefully in the meantime. And once you return to your world, the nightmares should cease completely. As long as you don't come back to Vakeeli, you're safe. According to what I've studied, it's when you're in the same universe as Caspian that it's easier for Mournwrath to latch on and attack."

"Well, I appreciate your help, Manx. But we must go now."

Manx tilts his head up at me. "You're going to Ripple Hills?"

"I have to."

"For what?" Willow asks.

I ignore her. "If I don't go now, they'll kill them."

"That's what they want you to think," says Manx.

"No. It's what I *know*. They're getting bolder, Manx. Bold enough to kill monarch clan members if they have to. If I don't go now, it'll make me look like a joke."

"I think you should get Willow home first. I can send a troop to retrieve your cousins."

"No." The word comes out louder than intended. "I *have* to go for them. I can't waste any more time here."

Manx releases a long breath, glancing at Willow. "Taking her with you is dangerous. You know how the people of Ripple Hills are."

"She'll be fine as long as she sticks with me. Once I get my cousins back, I'll take her to Blackwater and send her home. I'll be there long before the protection morsel wears off."

FORTY

WILLOW

It doesn't seem like a good idea going to Ripple Hills with Caz, but he insists, even when I tell him it may be better for me to stay in Whisper Grove.

"I won't be able to make it back in time to Whisper Grove to get you and then return to Blackwater before the morsel wears off. Once I have my cousins, we'll head there." He says this as we leave Whisper Grove, both of us carrying black sacks containing water, fruit, and dry foods like nuts and berries, courtesy of Manx.

"What did the note say?" I ask as we climb a hill. I feel a cramp building in my side from all the walking. I haven't walked this much in ages.

Caz stops at the top of the hill and looks toward the valley ahead. A forest is nearby, the leaves of the trees rustling with the wind. There's no telling what's in that forest.

Caz digs into his pocket, waiting for me to meet up to him before handing the paper to me.

· · ·

We have the girl and the darkie. If you want to see them again, bring 600 rubies.

"The darkie?" I don't know why I'm surprised by that word again. Darkie. It's so...*ignorant.*

"They're referring to Killian," Caz mutters, already marching down the hill.

"Yeah, I gathered that, but why are they calling him that?"

"Why do you think?"

"So let me get this straight," I huff, clutching the paper and following him downhill. "Even in another universe, there's hatred for someone's skin color?"

Caz side-eyes me before putting his focus ahead. "Unfortunately."

"So, it's a universal thing." I suck my teeth. "Got it." I glance at him before saying, "I'm glad you're not hateful on that front."

"Why would I be?"

"I don't know." And I really don't. I just see this clear-cut white guy, and one like me would assume he has an inkling of racism buried inside him.

"Human is human. And a piece of shit is a piece of shit. If they want to hate someone for the color of their skin, that's their problem, but I choose not to be a part of it. Makes no sense."

"No, it doesn't. In our world, it's called racism, and it's a hatred that has killed many people."

Caz is quiet a moment, taking long strides, making it harder for me to keep up with him. "My mother was a brown woman."

My brows tilt upward. "Was she?"

"Yes. She had nearly the same skin tone as yours."

I don't know why that makes me smile. "So, I remind you of your mom?"

He cuts his eyes at me. "Don't get carried away."

I fight a laugh, and I see his mouth twitching, like he wants to laugh too but refuses to do so.

"So, what else should I know about you, *Caspian Edgar Harlow*?"

"You should know that I don't like being called by my full name."

"Clearly. What else?"

"And that it annoys me when people ask me too many questions."

"That's not news to me."

"Didn't think it would be."

"Are you always so stubborn, Caspian?"

He stops walking to look me in the eyes, pointing a stern finger at me. "Stop calling me that."

"What's wrong with your name? I think it's a nice name. It's unique."

"It's Caz."

"Why do Manx, Maeve, and Alora get to call you by your real name?"

"Because I've known Manx my whole life and I have a deep respect for him. As for Maeve, she's my aunt and she partially raised me, so she can call me a stupid asshole and get away with it for all I care. And Alora is...well, *Alora*. She says and does what she wants regardless of how anyone feels. I've only met you, so you don't get that privilege. You shouldn't take it personally. My cousins don't call me by that name either, not unless they want to fuck with me. It's just Caz, to everyone."

"It's weird for someone to hate their own name so much. I mean, if you do, why not just change it?"

"Names cannot be changed in Vakeeli. The name you're born with is the name you keep. Modifications are acceptable, but changing your name amounts to an insurmountable disrespect. It means there's shame within you, and people find that a weakness here."

"But...you're ashamed of your name."

"But others outside my circle don't know that, and they *won't ever* know it." There's an underlying threat in his tone.

"I'm not going to run around telling people you hate your name."

"I know you won't."

I roll my eyes, pushing one of my locs off my forehead. "This world is insanely complicated."

"You get used to it."

"I see." I look him over again. "It seems this world makes people...*hard*. Are the children even happy here?"

He doesn't respond, and if I'm not mistaken, he picks up his pace, taking a trail between a line of trees. I stay behind him this time, dropping the questions for now, not only because I know he's done answering them, but because I'm getting tired. I've truly gotten lazy. My word.

I'd do anything to be home in my bed, rolling a joint, getting high, and then curling up in a blanket to take a nap. I suppose if I shut up, we'll get there sooner, so I pick up my pace, but end up bumping right into Caz's back.

Gasping, I stumble backwards, but he turns and catches my wrist, preventing the fall. With his other hand, he has a finger pressed to his lips, his eyes wide with warning.

What? I ask, and the thought is loud and clear in my mind, so I know he can hear it. *What is it?*

Something's hunting us.

I freeze, staring into his eyes, too afraid to look around. Caz releases my wrist, and I steady myself as he pushes his jacket back and slowly retrieves his gun from the holster. I still remember how pleased he was to see his guns when Alexi dumped them outside the border. He'd even checked the bullet chambers, to make sure all the bullets were there.

Caz takes a thorough look around. Raising his gun, he points it past me, and murmurs, "Whatever you do, do *not* run."

I don't. I stay where I am, trembling as he narrows his eyes.

"Cover your ears." He says, and I lift my hands, bringing my palms to my ears and squeezing my eyes shut just as Caz pulls the trigger.

Despite my ears being covered, the gunshot makes them ring, and my initial reaction is to duck down.

"*Shit.*" Caz curses beneath his breath, and he aims the gun forward again, letting off a round of shots. I hear rapid steps, the crunching of gravel, the snapping of sticks and twigs.

A beastly growl erupts in the air and a blur of white dashes past me, tackling Caz to the ground.

FORTY-ONE

WILLOW

My body trembles as I remain squatting, too afraid to look around me, or even ahead of me, where Caz once stood.

He's dead. It's my first thought because I don't hear his thoughts, and I can't hear him breathing. Whatever that thing was that was hunting us just killed him, and now I'm on my own and won't be able to get back to my world. Shit, maybe it'll kill me next.

No, no, no. He can't be. He can't...

I dare myself to look up, and there's a bushy white tail in my face, streaked with silver. Beneath it are a pair of human legs, clad in black jeans. They're Caz's legs, perfectly still, and above him is a wolf. The wolf's body is white; I can't see its face, but its shoulders are hunched as it growls down at him.

Willow, be still. I hear Caz's voice and relief floods me.

Oh, thank God, you're not dead!

My gun.

He moves his hand to the right, his fingers twitching, and I look in that direction. His gun is near a tree, the silver glistening beneath a streak of sunlight.

I start to move, but Caz's voice in my head demands me to do so slowly.

I crawl toward the gun, breaths coming out rapid and panicked. Just as I'm about to grab it, there's a rustling and a white paw touches my hand. My heart drops to my stomach.

Slowly lifting my head, I peer up at the wolf, and it stares down at me. Its eyes are silver, and there's a patch of silver on top of its head. The wolf doesn't snarl nor growl at me like I expect though. It cocks its head instead, as if it's wondering why I'm reaching for the gun.

I stare into the wolf's eyes, and a vision fills my head—one I've never had before. *A pack of wolves. A baby wolf, running in a field. The wolf being fed by a faceless woman in all black. She pets the wolf. The wolf is happy—I can feel its happiness coursing through me. A memory it's fond of.*

"Willow, the gun," Caz demands, snapping me out of whatever trance I'm in.

The wolf breaks our stare, turning its head to growl at him again.

My brows dip as the wolf stands in front of me, as if on guard, and Caz glares at it, confused.

"Is it..."

"She's protecting me." I say the words without fully understanding them.

Caz's eyes narrow a split second as he keeps his focus on the wolf. "How is that possible?"

"How is what possible?"

"You're not even from Vakeeli." He steps back, blinking.

The wolf walks around me, sniffing at my legs and feet, before deciding to sit next to me. I lift a shaky hand and stroke its fur, and it rests it's chin on its front paws.

Caz walks forward and starts to pick up his gun, but the wolf bares its teeth and growls at him. He raises his hands, a guiltless gesture to show he's not trying to harm her, and she stops growling, allowing him to pick up the gun and put it away.

"This is strange. Not everyone can have a wolf." He studies her a bit more. "But she's protecting you, which means she's yours. Have you been to this world before and don't remember?"

"I...don't think so."

"Maeve." Caz combs his fingers through his thick bed of hair. "She mentioned something about this—the Tether. Seeing you before, years ago, but it wasn't really *you*. Perhaps..." Caz's voice trails off as he loses himself in thought.

"How did you get your wolf?" I ask, standing cautiously.

"My mother bonded him to me when he was a pup, only I didn't know it then. Not until he came to me when I was nineteen. When I became monarch." He pauses. "She used to be like Manx in a way—could make her own elixirs, created remedies to help protect and heal people. She also had this way with animals. She could bond them to humans forever, so that they're willing to protect that human at all costs. My mother, and others who could manage it, would create these bonds for their children mostly, as a way to protect them when they couldn't be around."

I can feel my brows pulling tighter together as he speaks. "When I looked into her eyes, I saw a woman in all black feeding and talking to her. Do you think..." I pause. "Do you think that could've been your mom?"

"Perhaps..." He stops talking to shake his head. "No. It's not possible, unless...unless she *knew* this day would come. Unless she knew the woman you were before."

"What do you mean?"

Caz locks on my eyes. "It wouldn't be possible unless she knew you'd end up here, in Vakeeli."

"How would she have known that?"

Caz doesn't answer, and I don't think it's because he doesn't want to, but because he genuinely doesn't have the answer. Instead, he turns around with his back to me. "We should keep moving."

"What do I do about the wolf?" I ask.

"There's nothing you can do. It's here to protect you, so it'll follow you from here on out. Well, while you're in Vakeeli, I assume."

I glance down at the wolf, and her silvery eyes meet mine. I'm not sure what it is I feel, but when my eyes connect to hers again, a warmth courses through me, and there's a squeeze in my chest, one that demands I protect her at all costs too. She whimpers, then licks the back of my hand.

I follow Caz as she walks by my side. "What should I name her?"

"How do you know it's female?"

"She looks like it. Plus, when I was on the ground, I didn't see a penis, so..."

Caz sighs, and I glance down at the wolf again. She's panting, her pink tongue hanging out as she peers around, like she's on the lookout for trouble.

I have a wolf now. That's insane! I mean, it was already crazy enough that Caz had one. My wolf is the opposite of his—white, husky, and furry, but there's a viciousness to her that would make anyone hesitate to approach her. The silver streak on top of her head brings out a fierceness in her, and as I study the streaks throughout her fur, it's settled.

"That's a terrible name," Caz grumbles.

"Get out of my head!"

"Can't help what I hear."

"And I can't help what I think. Silvera is a pretty name. It's unique."

"If you say so."

I frown at his back. Then I ask, "How do you do it?"

"Do what?"

"Shield some of your thoughts."

He releases an exasperated sigh. "For the last time, it takes practice." He stops walking and picks up a clunky rock. "Just picture millions of these tiny rocks surrounding your brain. You use the rocks to guard your mind and protect it. Some of the rocks crumble in my mind—usually when I'm focused on something else and not fully concentrating on blocking you out—and that's when you can hear me. I assume you have no rocks surrounding your brain and no kind of guard because I can hear *everything* running through your head. It's quite annoying actually. You should get it under control."

He tosses the rock at me, and I clumsily catch it. "Well, I guess I'll start building my wall of rocks now."

"Good. It'll spare us both."

I glance down at Silvera who has her head cocked as she looks from me to my hands. "If you feel the urge to maul him, I won't stop you this time." I rub the top of her head, and I don't know why I keep the rock in my hand, rolling it around in my palms, but I do as I follow Caz along the trail.

FORTY-TWO

CAZ

"What is that pill you keep taking?" Willow asks.

We've stopped to rest, and it's a good stopping point because Ripple Hills is only a few miles away. I chug down some water after taking two red tablets.

Why do you care?" I ask after a gasp.

"You've been taking them every day since I met you."

"They help me."

"With what?"

"For the love of Vakeeli, could you stop asking so many bloody questions?" Fuck, she talks too much. It's astounding she's not tired of her own voice. I swear she's no better than Juniper. It's no wonder they've gotten along so well.

"If I don't ask questions, how the hell am I supposed to know anything? You forget I'm in a new world, with new rules and terrifying shit around every corner." She rolls her eyes.

She has a point. But still.

With a sigh, she presses her back to the trunk of a tree and slides her eyes down to the white wolf beside her. I still can't wrap my mind around that damn thing. I mean, if my mother had planned this so far in advance, why didn't she warn me? Why didn't she tell me some woman would fall out of the sky and I'd be chained to her forever? I wish she were here...

I look up, and Willow is staring at me. *Shit.* I hope she didn't hear me. I draw in a breath and exhale, making sure the wall around my mind is sealed tight.

When she says, "I don't understand why you're so bitter," I assume she didn't hear me because she's still stuck on my last question, which I admit was rather rude.

"I'm not bitter."

"You really are," she laughs, but with hardly any humor. She pauses then, her head moving into a slight tilt. "Is there a reason for all the scars on your body?"

I dig into my bag, pulling out a pouch of green nuts. Snatching out a handful, I stuff them into my mouth.

"I'll answer your question about the red tablets instead," I say around a mouthful.

"Okay." She sits up taller, giving me her undivided attention. I let the quiet steep a bit before speaking again.

"I have a thing about people touching me." I clear my throat before popping more nuts into my mouth. "I don't like people's hands on my skin. Never have. The red tablets were made by Mythics, for people like me. People who are extremely sensitive to touch."

She nods, as if she understands, but I have a feeling she doesn't. Her brows are puckered, her eyes pleading for a clearer answer. I look past her at a thin tree with thorns on its branches.

"I'm not sure why I was born that way, but I was. When someone touches me, it's not a normal sensation for me like it is for everyone else. It doesn't bring me comfort, and it doesn't soothe me. Instead, I'm hyperaware of the touch, and at first it just made my skin crawl. But as I got older...well, anyone's touch would hurt, and it made me angry."

"Wow." She blinks. "I wonder why that is."

"Just does." I'm not about to tell her anything more than that. There's a deeper reason for my anger, and it has nothing to do with being touched. Besides, there's no need for her to know so much. I put up my wall, making sure none of the thoughts slip out for her to hear.

She nods again, lowering her gaze. I chomp a few more nuts, side-eyeing her.

"That's why you cover yourself up."

"I suppose. It's still annoying having people touch my clothes, but at least it's not my skin."

"That must suck."

I say nothing to that.

"But you've touched me several times," she says. "Once at that insane party in Vanora, and when we were escaping Beatrix's. You carried me the whole way."

"I had no choice."

"Did it not hurt for you to hold me?"

I remain quiet, mulling it over. Truthfully, it didn't hurt. It was almost instinct to carry her and get her to safety. I didn't think twice about whether it would hurt me or not.

"I suppose it didn't."

"So...maybe there are exceptions."

Yeah, with her, it seems.

"Maybe that's why you're so bitter," she goes on. "You don't let anyone embrace or hold you. *Comfort* you."

"I prefer it when people stay away from me."

"Why do you want everyone away?" Her question catches me

off guard, and the curiosity of it burns in her eyes. She truly wants an answer, but I have none to give. Well, none I want to voice out loud.

I stand up, collecting my bag. "Gotta take a piss. Once I'm back, we'll move out."

RIPPLE HILLS

FORTY-THREE

WILLOW

I FIND it hard accepting what Caz has told me. Humans were made to touch and be touched. It's what makes us, well, human.

And, sure, this is a different world, but that doesn't make him any less mortal. He has flesh, bone, and a beating heart, and everything else that makes him man. He bleeds, just like I do, and he breathes, same as I. There really is no difference between us, and I'm curious how someone else's touch can anger him.

I think back to when he mentioned his mother. He speaks about her in the past tense, as if she's no longer here. What happened to her? Or better yet, what happened to *him*? There's a reason he's so closed off and guarded, and a part of me is lured to that, desperately wanting answers.

Unfortunately, he hasn't given me much leeway to ask. And I take it I won't be asking anytime soon because we've now made it to Ripple Hills. There was a wooden sign we passed along the way with the territory's name, and now we're lurking in the woods,

Caz warning me to stay low. Silvera lingers beside me, her ears perked up, fully alert.

We're in a thicket of trees, the ground ripe and wet. The land is squishy beneath my feet, like walking on a wet sponge, yet the air is desert dry.

Caz stops in front of a tree and looks ahead. I look with him, and there are hills of many sizes, covered in brown grass. Judging by those hills, it's understood why it's called Ripple Hills now. The hills are like waves of the sea, as if that's what they once were before being permanently solidified into land. Clusters of houses and buildings are perched on top of each hill, and black roads weave around each one, connecting one hill to the other.

The sky is a hazy gray, no flowers or anything of color in sight. Even the trees' leaves are brown. It's just like Blackwater, only the dirt isn't black, it's brown. There is no plush green grass, no signs of life outside the people there. I see thin cows munching on dead grass near a few farmhouses, and my curiosity simmers, wondering what other creatures are around that I can name.

"Stay here." Caz's voice slices through my thoughts as he hurries down a hill with his gun in hand. I bend down, watching as he approaches a house smaller than a shack. The home looks abandoned, but it can't be because black smoke is pumping out the chimney.

Walking onto the porch, Caz gives the front door a knock. When a man answers the door, Caz wastes no time pointing the gun directly at his face. The man throws his hands in the air and backs away, and Caz invites himself inside, nearly shoving the man out of his way.

"What the hell?" I gasp. Silvera stands next to me, her soft fur rubbing against my leg. I feel the heat of her body, hear the growl forming in the pit of her throat. "No, it's okay," I whisper to her. "Well, I think it is."

I put my attention back on the house, and Caz is coming outside again, holding something black. He's speaking—to whom, I'm not sure—and then he turns around, pointing his gun at the man. The man trembles in a corner, and Caz points the gun at a chair on the porch. The man immediately sits, and Caz looks ahead, where he knows I'll be.

Come. His voice is loud in my head, a direct command.

I hesitate, watching as he drops his arms, waiting for me. What the hell is he doing? I'm sure this isn't the way to go about entering Ripple Hills, especially if they're as bad as he and everyone else makes them seem.

"Why are we doing this?" I whisper when I approach him.

"No need to whisper. No one can hear you."

"How do you know?" I carry my gaze to the man on the porch. Up close, he seems to be nearing his seventies, but he's probably older, and that makes me feel awful for him. The poor man is shaking like a leaf.

"He'll be fine. I won't hurt him unless he makes me." Caz walks up the porch. "Mind if we make use of your place until our ride arrives, Tom?"

"N-no, I don't mind," the man stammers.

"Great." Caz gestures to the inside of the house. "Lead the way."

The man rises out of his chair and ambles inside.

"Caz, this is wrong," I tell him. "Maybe we should just go wait in the forest."

"That's more dangerous."

"Than being in this random man's house? Isn't he a Rippie or whatever?"

"He is now, and there's a reason he lives on the outskirts. Right, Tom?" Caz enters the house and I follow him in just as Tom bobs his head reluctantly. I look back before closing the door, and

Silvera sits outside the house, her back to the door, keeping watch.

"I don't want any trouble, please," Tom pleads. "I've kept to me self. I swear."

Caz ignores his pleas, cocking a brow instead. He's being so rude.

"Why do you stay here?" I ask, and the question sort of blurts out of me.

"I have no choice." Tom's eyes glisten as he looks from Caz to me. "I *have* to stay here."

"You can't move to another territory? A safer one?"

"Not allowed," Caz mumbles, standing near the window. He moves the curtain aside with the tip of his gun, keeping watch.

"Do you need a passport or something to leave?"

"A passport?" Tom's face crumples with confusion, and he swings his eyes to Caz.

"Enough with the questions, Willow." Caz turns to face Tom. "We won't be in your hair for long. Just stay quiet, and we'll be gone before you know it."

Tom sits back in his chair, his eyes bouncing around the room, trying not to look Caz into his eyes. Leaning against a wall, Caz folds his arms and stays that way, icy eyes on Tom, until we hear gravel crunching outside.

Caz tilts the curtain and, pleased with what he sees, moves away from the window. He steps in front of Tom, holding up the black object he had earlier while on the porch. It's a transmitter. After tinkering with it, he says, "I'm going to give this back to you, Tom, and when I go, you won't contact anyone, right? You'll behave?"

"I—I won't. I promise."

"Especially not with those Rippie pigs." Caz tosses the transmitter to the man, and he catches it, but barely.

"I won't contact anyone, Mr. Harlow. I promise."

"Good on you." Caz gives Tom his back and looks at me as he bobs his head at the door. "Let's go."

I follow him out of the door, but not without looking back at Tom. Tom lifts a hand and gives me a small wave and a smile. I wave back before walking past Caz to get outside.

FORTY-FOUR

WILLOW

When I make it down the rickety steps of Tom's porch, I spot the same car that was in front of Caz's house my first day in Vakeeli. The metal gleams in the daylight, the rims covered in a coat of dirt, and standing outside of it like a soldier with a large gun in hand is Rowan.

"Caz! Nice to see you, brother!" Rowan shouts.

Caz marches around the car. "Get us to that bloody club now. Willow, get in the back."

I resist the urge to argue as I open the back door of the car. I hear the pitter-pattering of paws, and Silvera makes her way out of the trees, trotting to me.

"Oi! Where the hell did that thing come from?" Rowan's eyes nearly bulge out of his head as he gawks at her.

"She's Willow's now," Caz responds.

Silvera jumps into the back row of the car and sits on the seat obediently. Rowan looks at me, his chin down and mouth ajar,

SHANORA WILLIAMS

before he shakes his head and climbs into the car. I get in and shut the door, and Rowan says, "That thing better not shed on my fucking seats. Even Cerberus isn't allowed in my car."

Silvera growls, her eyes on Rowan, and I rub her back, hoping it'll calm her down. "Careful, Rowan. Silvera doesn't seem to like men very much. She almost chewed Caz's face off earlier."

"Oh, if only Cerberus were here," Rowan chuckles.

Caz points ahead. "Drive."

Rowan puts the car in gear, driving away from Tom's house. I look through the back window at the lone shack, and when I do, the house explodes.

A scream escapes me as chunks of debris fly toward the car, and I duck as pieces slam against the back window. Silvera barks and I glance at Caz and Rowan, but they haven't so much as flinched.

"C-Caz," I stammer. "W—what just..."

Caz doesn't look back as he says, "I told him not to make contact with anyone."

"What did you do?" My words come out strained, breathless.

"I gave his transmitter a timer. He only had to give us five minutes to get away. If after five minutes he hadn't made any contact, Tom would've been fine. I expected him to make contact about us being here eventually, but the fact that he did it within a minute...well, that says a lot about him. He contacted the pigs, the transmitter picked it up and...well, I assume you know the rest."

Rowan makes a whistling sound, then utters the word, "*Boom.*"

"No, I *don't* know the rest. How can you *do* that to someone?"

"I don't carry just guns with me."

I blink at the back of Caz's head.

"He was a nice old man. He was harmless!"

"He wasn't harmless. You're just impressionable and you trust way too easily." Caz turns his head a fraction.

"You're ridiculous. You're killing people for no reason!"

"No reason?" he shouts.

"Yes! He did nothing wrong! So what if he called someone, we would've gotten away regardless!"

"The fucking audacity," Caz growls.

"Calm down, brother," Rowan warns, glancing at him.

"No—she needs to fucking hear it!"

"Sure! Tell me! What is it that I need to hear? What could possibly justify you killing an old man?"

"Do you know that old man is on the outskirts of this shitty territory because he used to *molest* young girls—girls *twice younger* than you?"

My heart sinks. *"What?"*

"He was a teacher in Blackwater for a long time—a hundred and twenty years, in fact—and he took advantage of that role. He'd invite girls to his home when he lived in the city, pretend to tutor them, when really, he was forcing himself onto them. He'd tell them that if they didn't cooperate, he'd make them fail his class, or worse, report them as unteachable, which could cause them to end up in The Trench. And that's a very bad place, Willow. You basically go there to rot to death."

I stare at Caz, stunned, and notice Rowan's grip on the steering wheel has tightened.

"He wasn't lying to you when he said he couldn't leave," Caz goes on. "He was sent from Blackwater to Ripple Hills to live on the outskirts as a form of punishment. He has no job, no money, and he's fed twice a week. The only reason he has a transmitter is because he's under parole and has to be checked on every two to three hours. He's not to be around anyone, especially women, because he's been restricted. If he makes one wrong move, he's to be sent to The Trench to rot. The *only* reason he wasn't there after what he did was because he had a little pull with The Council—favors he'd done for them prior to his deception. I did the world a favor by getting rid of that piece of shit, and believe me when I tell you I'd do it all over again in a heartbeat."

"H-how do you know he did all this?"

Rowan's head drops a bit, but he keeps his focus on the road. Caz's jaw ticks as he fights with the words, until finally it relaxes and I hear his voice in my head. **Because he did it to Juniper.**

My heart is in my throat now. "Juniper? Are you serious?"

Caz says nothing. Neither does Rowan.

I work to swallow, fighting the bitterness building in my throat. "I'm sorry. I didn't know."

"No, you didn't. You just made your own assumptions. And for the record, I don't just go around killing for no reason. I only do it to people who threaten me, my clan, or to people who fucking deserve it."

I sit back against the leather seat, dropping my eyes to the dirt stains on my knees from kneeling so much in the forest. The tension radiates through the car, nuclear, and as uncomfortable as it makes me, I allow the tension to marinate.

It's warranted in this moment. I shouldn't have assumed...and Juniper. *God.* It's no wonder she drinks so much—no wonder she got so angry at that guy at the party and shot him. She's taking control of her own life and fighting the corruption of pig-like men. And I can understand it because I deal with similar issues in my world.

Women aren't seen as equals to men like Tom. We're objects—toys for men like him to play with, whether it be our bodies or our emotions. The thought of that lights a fire inside me, and it burns so deeply I clench my fists. There is no escaping the misogyny of men, no matter where we women turn. It's bullshit.

"I want to help," I say after several minutes of silence. The wheels of the car bump along the road as Rowan continues driving. I lean forward, gripping the tops of the leather seats. "If we're going to save Juniper and Killian, I want to help."

"The Rippies will eat you alive," Caz grumbles.

"Then make it so they don't."

"How the hell are we supposed to do that?" he demands.

"I don't know. There has to be some way!"

"The only way I can see that happening is if we dress her like a..." Rowan clamps his mouth shut instantly, swinging his gaze to Caz.

Caz's nostrils are flaring, his fists clenched on his lap. "You just had to open your big fucking mouth, didn't you?"

"Dress me like what?" I ask.

"It could work," Rowan says, shrugging. "If there's one thing the Rippies think women of her nature are good for, it's that."

"It's too risky. She might not even be able to pull it off. She doesn't know shit about them."

"What do I have to dress as?" I demand.

Caz doesn't say the words, but he damn sure thinks them loud enough for me grasp. ***A whore.***

FORTY-FIVE

CAZ

THIS IS A TERRIBLE IDEA. I know it, Rowan knows it, and even Willow understands the detriment. She senses how all of this can go wrong if she fucks up even once, and after asking us nearly a million questions about why she had to dress like a whore to fit in Ripple Hills, I could feel her anxiety ratcheting up with each answer. Despite it all, she wants to do it, not for herself, but for Juniper.

The plan is to for Willow to go into the club and find exactly where Juniper and Killian are. Sure, my cousins could be in the caves, but if I know that sly bastard Rami, he could have them somewhere else, being tortured. Rowan and I could go in ourselves, but our faces are too recognizable, and to avoid a blood bath, it's best to send a woman none of them have ever seen. That's where Willow comes in. If she can't fine Jun and Kill on her own, she can find Rami...and hopefully he'll be swimming in enough arrogance to lead her straight to them.

We didn't have much to work with for her. She'd left Whisper Grove in comfort clothes—a white shirt with soft gray pants. Rowan stopped along the way at a Ripple Hill shop so Willow could grab makeup, hair accessories, and a crop top. As she did, we kept watch by the car, the brim of our hats low and our fingers on the triggers of our guns, prepared for any surprises.

I glance back as she pulls the crop top over her head. Her eyes slide to mine after she digs in the bag for the makeup, and she pauses. I contemplate telling her never mind—that I'll find another way to do this that doesn't involve her, but instead, I look away, putting my focus out the window again. It'll be fine. She's a smart girl.

"I really am, though," she says, and I roll my eyes. *Mind's wall. Mind's wall.*

Once Rowan finds a decent spot to hide the car, I use the blade of my knife to cut her pants and make them into shorts. *Very* short shorts.

"This is too much," she says, covering her chest. "My ass is hanging out!"

"Honestly, it's not enough," Rowan counters, then presses his lips. I hate to agree with him. It's not enough, really, but it will do, and as the thought crosses my mind, my eyes shift to Willow's. She's already looking at me, eyes wide, curious.

We call the Rippies pigs for a reason—they're disgusting, and they have terrible hygiene, even the women. But the women get by with their assets—tits, ass, pussy. Whatever. They flaunt it, and it's how they get what they want. And it's how you'll get what you want.

She shakes her head. **Great.**

After collecting as many guns as possible from the trunk, Rowan and I strapping up to the teeth, we move down an alley behind Rami's Fight Club, one of the hottest spots in Ripple Hills. Rami's Fight Club is where the Rippies meet up religiously for a drink, a dance, and bet money on fights in underground caves. They shout and holler as they watch two opponents tear at each other, breaking noses, biting flesh, ripping hair, and whatever else to incite violence.

The thought of it sinks into my core and a wave of nausea runs over me. The memories are impossible to forget—*fists smashing into my face, arms locked around my throat, someone kicking my shin in, breaking it.*

I close my eyes a moment and breathe, just like Manx taught me when I was younger, and it helps. But I remember the feeling —*all of it*. I swallow the bitter memories down and focus on the present. I have family to save. Memories be damned. And of course, when I turn to look at Willow, she's already looking at me. She heard it all. Damn it. Mind's wall, for fuck's sake.

As we approach the end of the alley, we spot several guards surrounding the building. Some of them stand with their arms folded, deep frowns on their faces. Others are smoking, or whistling at women as they walk by.

"The basement entrance never has many guards," Rowan says. "We can get in that way."

I nod and he leads the way around a corner, going down a set of damp cement steps that need repairing and venturing through another dark alley. This alley is leaky and smells like cat piss. Willow follows me and I feel her breath on my skin as she stands closely. I try to ignore the warmth of it, the smell of her. I swear she's becoming harder to disregard.

A light appears at the end of the alley, and deep voices echo, bouncing off the walls. Rowan stops, pressing his back to the wall with a grin. "It's fucking showtime."

"How many?" I whisper.

"Three. I've got it."

Rowan leaves no room for hesitation. He pushes off the wall, his gun aimed in front of him, and rushes down the rest of the alley. I hear scuffling, thudding, men crying out in pain, and in a matter of minutes, Rowan is running back to us.

"Let's go."

I follow him to the end of the alley, my gun aimed in front of me. I lower it when I see three bloody bodies on the ground.

"Did you have to stab that one's eye out?" I focus on Rowan.

Rowan shrugs, unbothered. "He tried going for mine first."

Willow makes a gagging noise, and when I look back, she's covering her mouth.

"Get over it," I tell her, and I hate to sound so harsh but this is serious. If she fucks up even once, we'll never get my cousins back. I have everything riding on her tonight, and something tells me she can do it. "I need you to focus."

"Juniper and Killian are inside, probably in the caves," Rowan says. "Juniper's transmitter has been at this location for hours. They must have it."

"Right. We send Willow in, and she can find out where exactly they're keeping them." I turn to look at Willow, and her eyes widen as she stares down at the bodies again. "Don't look at them. Look at me."

She swings her gaze up, but that doesn't stop her from shaking like a leaf.

"When you go in, see if you can find any doors that lead you to a holding cell or cages. If you can't find any, look for a man with a shiny red tooth. He goes by Rami. When you find him, let me know."

"What if I can't find him?" she asks.

"Oh, you will. You can't miss that fat, arrogant cunt," Rowan grumbles.

"How am I supposed to let you know?" she asks me, panicking.

I tap my temple, and when it registers, she nods. "What if you don't hear me? You always have your mind wall up and—"

"I'll hear you."

She looks me deep in the eyes, then nods. "Okay."

"Just be confident," Rowan tells her, reloading his gun. "They love confidence. But not *too* confident or you'll have them fighting over who gets to fuck you first."

"You make them sound like dogs."

"They are dogs," Rowan goes on. "Disgusting ones at that—like stray dogs, you know? The kind who eat their own shit."

"Good to know." Willow sucks in a deep breath.

"Take this." I hold out one of my handguns.

"Where do I put it?"

I look at her from head to toe, then settle on the waistband of her shorts. I pull the waist of them out, careful not to touch her belly, and she shudders a breath when she feels the coolness of the metal pressing against her pelvis. "Keep it hidden unless you need it."

"I've never shot a gun before."

"It's not hard. Just aim and pull the trigger."

"Okay." She steps back and makes her way to the door. "When I call for you, you'll come right in?"

"Yes. Just make sure you find out which cave Juniper and Killian are in first."

FORTY-SIX

WILLOW

Rowan opens the door ahead, revealing a dark tunnel. "That door down there will lead you into the club," he says. I tug on my shorts, then press a hand to flatten what's left of my shirt. I don't feel appealing at all in these clothes, but I have to remember what I find appealing may not be to the people of Vakeeli.

I walk in, swinging my eyes to Caz and Rowan. Suddenly, I'm scared shitless. What if I'm caught? Or one of these Rippies tries to take advantage of me because they do think I'm a whore.

"I won't let anything happen to you," Caz says. "Just call for me. I'll be there."

I nod, sighing.

Rowan bobs his head at me, providing a boost of reassurance, and then closes the door. When it clinks shut, I draw in a breath and face the other end of the tunnel.

Lights attached to the wall, ensconced in metal, give me just a bit of leeway to see the battered door at the other end. The hallway reminds me of an underground tunnel, one that would've been used to help people escape, and I wonder if that's what it was to Ripple Hills before. Did they keep people like *me* enslaved, and this tunnel was made to help them flee? The idea makes me shudder, but I keep walking.

I'm fortunate not to see bones scattered on the floor, or anything out of the ordinary, just a simple dirt path leading to another door. Through the gaps of the door, flashes of neon lights fill the spaces. I make my way toward it, the music growing louder, the bass drumming, until I'm standing in front of it. I twist the rusted handle, and the door lets off a light moan when I pull it open, and as soon as it is, the music grows twice as loud. The bass thrums through the soles of my shoes, and the lights are damn near blinding, flashing all over the place.

The stench of sweat and body odor smothers me when I close the door behind me. The crowd is thick, and for a split second, I don't think there's any way I can get through. People are shoulder to shoulder, facing a stage of performers, cheering wildly. Couples dance and gyrate, bumping into other people without a care in the world, and half-naked women stand on tabletops and counters in thick, platform heels.

Two large men stand over a naked woman in the far-right corner. She's lying on her back on a large table, gripping her breasts, and smiling up at them. The men pour liquid all over her, and she spreads it through every line, hole, and crease of her body.

I look past the filthy display, pushing my way through the first gap I spot. The performers play metal rock that drowns out almost every noise, even though people are yelling. I can already sense a headache coming on.

Stand by the bar. Tell me what you see. I hear Caz's voice in my head and look around, as if he'll appear.

Can you see what I see?

No, but I can hear it. And I feel your heart beating. Relax. Blend in. No one will notice you unless you make a scene.

I swallow hard, bumping into some of the rocking bodies. A woman ends up grabbing my hand, wanting to dance with me, but I shake my head and brush her off. Men stare at me, some glaring with disgust, others licking their lips with interest. I keep going until I've reached the bar. I can't see a thing on the dancefloor.

The counter is surrounded by a metal cage. There are no stools or chairs to sit on. The bar is its own entity, and the people outside it are beggars, thirsting and desperate.

Two people stand behind the bar—a female with oily hair and red highlights, and a bald, thick-necked man who is shouting angrily at one of the drunk clubbers through one of the windows of the cage, asking what he wants. I decide to go to the woman. If I'm going to blend in, I'll need to at least hold a drink.

I approach the bar woman, and she peers through the window at me. "What will it be?"

Ask for a gold tonic. Caz's voice is firm. "A gold tonic, please."

The woman scoffs, I'm assuming at my manners.

Don't be so nice. Rippies are rude by nature.

I sigh, letting his voice pass, waiting patiently for the drink.

What do you see?

I take a look around the club. *People dancing. Another bar. Sofas near the back wall.*

Any other doors besides the one you walked through?

I scan the room, my eyes stopping on a door by a hallway. *I see one. Next to the bathrooms, I think.*

Give it a try.

The bartender brings back my drink, sliding it across the counter to me, not caring that some of the liquid spills. "Thirteen rubies," she says.

I dig into my black pouch and pluck out some of the rubies Caz gave me for this very moment. She extends her hand out, and I drop them into her palm.

"Keep the rest," I tell her.

With a quick bob of the head, she turns away, and I leave the bar, moving across the room to get near the restrooms. The band seems to be playing harder on their instruments, their heads bobbing wildly, hair swinging all over the place. I reach the hallway, and there's a black door. I pull it open, but nothing is inside but dirty mops and brooms. Damn it.

It's just a utility closet.

Shit. I don't hear Caz's voice for a few beats. **Right. Well, let's go for Plan B. Find Rami.**

My eyes shift to a staircase leading up to the second floor, and as the music transitions and the crowd hollers, I hear a man's bellowing laughter.

Stepping to the left to get a better look, I see him standing behind a barbed-wired gate. His clothes are different from everyone else's. He's not like the others in their simple solid-colored shirts and dark pants. Everyone is uniform but him. His clothes appear cleaner, his brown and white suit crisp, and his jewelry glinting beneath the lights. He's a tubby man, short, greasy looking, but obviously with money judging by all the gold jewelry he wears. As he laughs again, I take note of the red tooth and how the lights flicker off it. It's him.

Do you see him?

"Yes," I say out loud this time.

Good. You know what to do. Be careful about it.

I suck in a breath and weave through the crowd, taking the

stairs up. I put a few of my locs in place with one hand while gripping my drink tighter with the other.

A pale man stands at the top of the stairs, donned head to toe in dark brown. He's bald, his inked arms folded across his chest. A tight grimace sweeps over his face when he sees me.

"Who the fuck are you?"

I clear my throat. "Here to see Rami."

"Rami hasn't said anything about visitors. Now fuck off."

"I know, but I was thinking I could surprise him." I wrap my lips around my straw and make my eyes bigger, hoping this type of flirting works. I'm terrible at flirting.

The man takes a look over his shoulder before focusing on me. "He won't like you. Too dark. Stop wasting your time."

I swallow hard, working down the bile building up in my throat.

Get Rami's attention, Caz says.

How the hell am I supposed to do that? I look to my right, at Rami —who is glancing my way. He's talking to someone, but his eyes cut to me.

You're gonna hate this. Push the guard.

"What?" I shriek, and I don't mean to say it out loud.

"All right, off with you. Get out of here," the guard snaps, shoving me hard on the shoulder and forcing me a step downward.

Did he just hit you?

"Yes!" I yell.

Good. Rami likes violence. Hit that fucker back.

Furious, I drop my drink and push the guard back on the chest, and when he stumbles, he glares at me. His large hand wraps around my upper arm, and I wince as he reels me inward.

"Who the fuck do you think you are, huh? You fucking darkie."

"What's going on here?" Another voice rises behind the guard, and the guard glares me down a second longer before giving the man his attention.

"She fucking pushed me," he grumbles.

"He pushed me first," I snap back.

The man steps around the guard to get a closer look at me. Rami. His eyes roam my face, my body, then he looks at the guard. "Well, why'd you push her first?" he asks, then breaks out in a laugh. "Right. Get over it. Let her go."

The guard releases me, but not without continuing his stare down.

"Never seen you before. What's a girl like you doing 'round here?" Rami asks, grinning.

I tip my chin. "I came to see you."

"To see *me*?" He licks his lips as he looks me from head to toe. "And what have I done to deserve the pleasure?"

I shrug. "You're Rami. You deserve everything." **Lay it on thick, why don't ya.** I ignore the sarcasm in Caz's voice, keeping my eyes on Rami, who only smiles harder at the compliment.

"I like her. Let her through." He swats the guard away with an impatient hand, then reaches for me, clutching my wrist. "What's your name?"

"Layla," I lie, forcing a smile.

"Well, *Layla*, it's your lucky night. You get to hang with the big boss. I was just on my way to watch one of the fights." He drags me along with him, walking across the room until he's reached another staircase. "Watch your step here." He says it, but he's the one dragging me and making it impossible to do so.

I take the steps down with him quickly, glad I don't trip and fall flat on my face.

The floors are black, the walls painted a muddy brown. The music from the club fades into the background, and I look back. Two guards are following us. The one I pushed is still there, grimacing at me. I snatch my eyes away from him as Rami stops in front of a red door with a black handle.

When he opens the door, I'm relieved to see we're in a quieter space. A wall of windows is ahead, and I can't believe my eyes when I see the large fighting ring below. It's bigger than the MGM Grand Arena down there. Spotlights beam down on the cage, a wild crowd surrounding it. Some of them are gripping the metal gates and rattling them, shouting as two large men inside the ring fight. One of them is *very* familiar.

I feel my mouth go bone dry as I whisper, "Killian."

You see him? Which cave? There should be a number on one of the walls.

I look for a number. There's a large 5 on the wall next to the exit.

Cave five, I think. Take the stairs down. Red door with a black handle. He has two guards standing outside it.

"What will you have?" I turn at the sound of Rami's voice. He's closed the door so it's just us.

"Gold tonic, please."

"Ah, don't be a bore. *Here*." He pours something from a slim silver bottle into a glass and brings it to me. "Drink this. It'll loosen ya right up."

I take it, but I don't drink it right away, and as if that bothers him, Rami stares at me.

"Drink," he commands.

I lift the glass to my lips and sip. The liquid is sour and acidic, but I swallow it and do my best not to make a face.

"That's a good girl." He smiles, pleased with himself. I avoid rolling my eyes. Men like him make me sick. "You know, I fancy the ones like you."

"The ones like *me*?" I ask, as if confused.

"Believe it or not, I have a weakness for darkies. But shhh...

don't let anyone else find out." He winks, like it's our little secret. "Darkies know how to have a good time. Suck a good dick. They take it up the ass very well too, or at least pretend to."

I take another sip of the drink instead of responding.

Stop drinking. We're moving in.

I lower the glass and turn to face the window instead. Killian is on top of a man, beating his damn face in, blood splattering onto the mat. The man will probably die if no one stops him.

"Do you run this fight club?" I ask.

"Now what kind of bloody question is that?" Rami laughs. "Of course, I do! I'm Rami, the fucking Ripple Hills Monarch! All this is mine."

"Ah."

"Yeah. Make lots of rubies and gold from this little gig, too. Come," Rami says, taking one of the recliners. He spreads his legs apart then pats his lap. "Why don't you sit with me?"

I clear my throat. "I'm okay here."

"Sit down. *Now.*" He continues a smile, despite the words coming out through gritted teeth. I start to set my drink on a nearby table, but he says, "No, no. Bring that with you. Wouldn't want it going to waste, would we?"

Carrying it with me, I walk toward him and ease myself onto his lap. As I do, I feel Caz's gun digging into my waist. "You like that, yeah?"

I fight the urge to vomit. There's a pinch in my belly, but I focus on the fight. "My money's on the one doing all the punching."

"What? That darkie brute?" Rami laughs. "Eh, believe it or not, that fucker is from Blackwater. People are betting a lot of money on him." Rami grabs one of my locs, twirling it around his fingers. I fight the urge to swat his hand away for touching my hair without permission. "Not only that, but he's part of the monarch's inner circle. And we've got him. The rubies and gold will be rolling in."

"Is he the only one you have from Blackwater?"

Rami shakes his head. "No. There's another, and she's a delight." Rami claps when a bell rings and Killian's fight is over, though I'm sure no one can hear it but me. A man with a thick device in his hand escorts Killian off the stage. The end of the device lets off an electric current, and he places it on Killian's back, tasing him while shouting at him. It's just like the weapon Juniper had at Toman's party

Rami looks at me, and I fidget on his lap. Pressing his fingers to the bottom of my glass, he forces the rim of the cup to my lips. "Drink up."

I take another sip, and my stomach churns. The drink burns going down and my head spins, but I try to stay present.

Willow, stop drinking whatever he's given you!

"He's...he's making me."

"What was that?"

My eyes swing to Rami's, but now I'm seeing double. I blink hard, hoping it'll clear my vision. It doesn't.

"Nothing. So...um...where is she? Juniper?"

Rami is quiet a second, glaring at me. "How do you know her name?"

I blink slowly, keeping my double-focus on Rami. He watches me carefully, then a slow smile spreads across his lips. "You think I don't know who ya are?" His voice has changed. It's deeper. Huskier. I drop the glass and it cracks, splintering on the floor. Rami's hand comes to my throat, tightening, and I clutch at it as he forces me to look at him.

"You're Caz's dark little whore. There are pictures of ya leaving his pub. I saw ya with him and his clan, you dumb bitch. You think I'm stupid? That I'd just let someone like *you* back here? What the fuck are ya doing here? Where is he?"

"I—I don't know what you're talking about—"

Rami clutches my throat tighter and lifts me in the air before tossing me on the floor. I land on my back with a grunt, trying to get up, but it's impossible. I'm dizzy now, my legs going numb. I can't move them. He stalks toward me, sneering, revealing that red tooth dead in the center.

"You spyin' for him?"

"N-no."

"One thing I hate is a *lying* darkie."

I weakly slide back on my elbows as he closes the gap between us. When he bends down to clutch my ankles, he drags me toward him and pins me down between his legs. I dig into the waistband for the gun, but he yanks it out of my hand and tosses it across the room.

"Stop!" I scream.

"Oh, now you want me to stop?" He's grinning down at me. I take a swing at him, but he catches it and shoves my hand back down on the floor. His other hand strikes my face, a heavy slap, and my cheek stings so badly my eyes well with tears. "Be still!" he barks. "You dirty darkie bitch. I'll teach you what happens when you work for Caz Harlow!"

"Caz!" I scream. "Caz! Now!" *Take the stairs down. Red door! I'm here!*

"Are you calling out for that filthy fucker?" Rami grins as he flips me onto my belly, and I try to fight him off, but I feel like I'm losing complete control of my body. I feel his hands tearing at my shorts and then my panties. He groans, as if pleased with what he sees, and I hear a buckle jingling. A zipper noise is next. *No, no, no.*

"Get off me!" I scream, and I use whatever's left of my energy to throw my head back and smash it into his face. Rami howls in pain and goes flying backward, and I dig my fingernails into the carpet, forcing myself to move, even if I have to get away like a dying slug.

"You fucking *bitch*!" A hand drops to my head and grips a handful of my hair tight. I scream.

Caz! Caz, please!

The tears burn as they run down my face, and in a matter of seconds I can't breathe because Rami has turned me onto my back and has his hands closed around my throat. His nose drips blood, but that doesn't stop him from choking me. There's anger in his eyes I've never seen—it's satanic, really. I've never seen someone so wicked—so excited to end another person's life.

I weakly tap at his hand, fighting for my next breath. A pressure builds in my head and just when I think this is it—this is my end—there's a loud thud, a gunshot, and the pressure around my neck subsides.

When I look up, coughing and panting, Rami's left eye is gone. There's a hole the size of a golf ball in its place, blood gushing out of it. His body crumples forward and lands beside mine, and I suck in a sharp breath, wiggling away from him.

Footsteps thunder on the floor, moving toward me, and when I look up, I'm met with ocean blue eyes. I breathe in again as Caz drops to one knee beside me.

FORTY-SEVEN

WILLOW

"Easy," Caz murmurs when I try to move. His eyes fall to my pants, which are halfway down, and a shadow spreads over his face. He looks at Rami's body again, grimacing. One of his fist clenches, like he wants to further mutilate his dead body, but instead, he looks at me, breathes evenly, and the shadow is gone. I try to read his thoughts, but I can hardly keep mine straight.

He reaches down, helping me pull my pants up. "I should've known that dirty fucker would pull something like this. I never should've sent you in here to do this. I should've found another way."

I stare at him a long time—so long I wonder if any of this is real. There's no way this has become my life. Being constantly attacked and surrounded by blood and gore. I don't know what comes over me, but as Caz helps me sit up, I throw my arms around his neck and hold him as tight as I possibly can.

He grunts and tenses, but I don't let go. I *can't* let go. Holding him like this feels like it's where I belong. As I hold him, I feel his heart beating against mine, and the stubble on his jawline and chin grazes the side of my face as I bury it into the crook of his neck. It takes me a while to realize his body is still tense and he's not holding me back.

And then I remember.

I snatch my arms away from him. "I'm sorry," I whisper. "I touched you. I'm so sorry."

Caz looks me in the eyes, and when they drop to my lips, I almost *want* him to kiss me. I want what just happened by Rami to be erased and replaced by something else—anything that'll take my mind away from that paralyzing fear.

A tightness grips me, and a coolness runs from my throat to my stomach, and as if Caz can feel the same, he drops his eyes and places a gloved hand on top of mine.

"I took too long. I apologize."

"It's okay," I whisper. I don't think I've ever heard him apologize.

"Did he hurt you?" he asks in a low voice.

I drop my head, looking away. "A little."

"Hey. Look at me."

But I don't. I can't.

Caz's presses his fingers to my chin, lifting it and locking eyes with me. "He won't *ever* hurt you again. Do you understand?"

My eyes slide down to Rami's body on the floor, the blood pooled around his head.

"Can you walk?" he asks as he helps me up.

"Not really. What did he make me drink?"

"It's a suppressant. It's a famous kind here in Ripple Hills. Makes a person's lower body go numb, causes dizziness, and many other side effects." He leads me to a recliner and places me down gently.

"It should wear off within the next thirty minutes. Until then, I need you to stay in this room."

"What?" I panic, reaching for him before he can go. "B-but I can't stay here. What if more of those Rippies come?"

"They won't. We took out all the guards. Now we have to stop *that*." Caz points toward the windows, and I follow his finger to the ring.

I can't believe my eyes when I see Juniper in the center of the ring. She has a cut beneath her eye, her dark hair hanging in her face. She looks battered and awful. A man is standing in the middle of the ring, announcing the two fighters. When he points at Juniper, the crowd boos her and some even throw food and drinks at her over the fence.

"Stay put. I'll be right back for you." Caz leaves the room, aiming his gun ahead. When it's clear, he shuts the red door behind him, and my heart thumps violently in my chest as I shift my gaze to Rami's body, then out the window at the fighting ring.

A bell rings and makes my head throb, and I'm not sure what kind of suppressant I was given but I feel the urge to vomit. I lean forward, pouring out whatever contents are in my belly onto the floor, then wipe my mouth with the back of my arm.

When I look back up, I hear gunshots, and people are running, screaming, and scattering like roaches. More gunshots, and a bullet hits the screen hanging near the ceiling. One side of the screen falls off the brackets and dangles, and when I drop my gaze to the floor again, Rowan is running into the cage, aiming his gun at the referee and Juniper's opponent, a beefy pale woman with cornrows.

He collects Juniper from the ground with one arm while barking orders and his gun still aimed, and the referee and opponent flee the ring.

Not too far away, Caz and Killian are standing outside the

ring, holding their guns firmly and shooting at the armed guards bursting through one of the entrances.

They'll be outnumbered if they don't leave soon.

Another dizzy spell hits me, and I groan, slumping back in the chair. I breathe in and out. In and out. It doesn't help. I wheeze as weakness plagues me.

I need you.

My eyes begin to close, despite trying my hardest to keep them open. The last words I hear before I slip into darkness are his.

I'm coming.

RETURN TO BLACKWATER

FORTY-EIGHT

CAZ

Dealing with Willow was meant to be a simple exchange. I figure out how to get her back to her world, and things go back to the way they were. That's no longer the case, and I realize that as she lies on my lap and the worry has seized me. I had one job—to get her back—and if she dies, I've failed. I hardly ever fail. That alone is eating me alive.

Rowan drives, and Killian rides passenger. Juniper is in the back seat with me, Willow's legs on her lap, and Silvera is on the floor of the car, nuzzling Willow's hand. We'd left her in the car before going into Rami's club. Juniper gives me a look, but I pull my eyes away before I can digest what that look means.

I'm sure she's wondering why I have Willow so close to me. No one would believe it. Hell, I can't even believe it. Here this woman is, lying on my lap, and it *doesn't* bother me. I've never let anyone lie on me, but with her...it's different. And I felt that when I shot Rami through his fucking skull. When she threw her arms around me, it was as if I could see the world a bit more clearly. I expected to feel anger or pain, but when she buried her nose into the crook of my neck, I only felt...*peace*. A tidal wave of emotion rushed over me, and I couldn't quite grasp most of what I was feeling, but it felt good. That fleeting moment of her skin on mine was otherworldly. I didn't want her to let go. I was lost in her touch, wanting more to ease her pain and allow her to ease mine.

"What'll we do about Rami?" Juniper asks in a low voice. I glance at her. Her left eye is swollen shut, and there's a cut above her lip. Her hair sticks to her forehead, still sticky with sweat.

"Nothing we can do," I mumble, and I can tell that answer doesn't satisfy her, but she won't argue. Not right now.

Rowan pulls up to the front of my house, and I ease Willow off my lap to get out of the car. I reach inside to pick her up and carry her into the house, and as I do, I feel my cousins' eyes on me from behind. I bet they're looking at each other now, wondering how the hell I'm allowing any of this—*holding* her, *carrying* her—but I don't care.

"Della!" I shout, marching through the door.

Footsteps clamber around the corner, and Della rushes from the kitchen. "Yes, Mr. Harlow?"

"I need you to take care of her," I order, marching past her to get up the stairs. "She's been given a Rippie suppressant. I think there was too much in the drink. It's been hours and she still hasn't woken up."

"Do you think it's an overdose?"

Fuck. I hope not. An overdose is lethal. It'd paralyze her for years. "I'm not sure." I place Willow on the bed of one of my guest rooms. She doesn't make a sound. If her chest weren't moving, I'd think she'd have stopped breathing. "Just do what you can."

"Yes, sir." Della goes straight to work, leaving the room to go to her chambers. I hear bottles clinking, the sound of Della getting all the items she needs, and as I study Willow's motionless body on the bed, the guilt eats me alive. I shouldn't have let her walk into that situation with Rami. I should've known he'd pull something as low as drugging a woman just to try to get his way. He was luring *me* there, not her, and he was ready to pull all the stops if it meant taking me down...even if that meant killing her.

The moment I saw her pants down and him on top of her, strangling her, something inside me snapped. My vision turned red, and the agreement I'd made with The Council years ago about not killing another monarch slipped my mind. I couldn't let him kill her.

I'd fucked up by murdering Rami, and I'm going to hear about it soon, I'm sure of it, but if I hadn't killed him, he would've killed her. I'd do it again if it meant saving her, which is highly unlike me, but I've come to realize there are a lot of things about Willow that I'd never do for anyone else. She's just...different. That's all I can say. She's different and she's grown on me.

Willow whimpers, and I take a step closer.

"Della!" I call.

She scurries into the room, cradling several vials in her arms.

"Her lips are turning blue." My heart beats harder, faster. "Is that normal? What should we do? We can't let her die—we have to get her back to her world—"

"Mr. Harlow, stop worrying!" Della drops all the vials on a desktop, and they clatter, some dropping onto the floor, but she doesn't care as she turns to me, placing her hands on my shoulders. I feel her touch searing through my jacket and pull away. "I'll take care of this. Now go."

Della returns to her medicines, dumping some into a silver bowl and mixing them together. I step back, giving Willow one more look before leaving the room.

I shut the door and walk down the hallway, a tightness developing in my chest—one that I'm sure is connected to Willow. I work twice as hard to breathe and almost double over in the hallway, but I grip the corner of a nearby wall, collecting a few breaths.

Her pain is mine, and I won't rest until I know she's all right.

FORTY-NINE

WILLOW

When I open my eyes, there's an ache in my belly. I wince and groan as I clutch my stomach. The warmth of my skin clings to my fingers, and I realize I don't have a shirt on. Just a bra.

Frowning, I sit up and lift the blanket to see I'm in my panties too. I'm half naked, and at the realization, a jarring memory hits me.

Rami taking my pants off, trying to force himself on me. The slap. The anger in his eyes as he choked me. The hopelessness.

Tears fill my eyes just as someone clears their throat, making me gasp.

Looking up, I find Caz sitting in a chair in the corner of the room. He's dressed in all black—pants, shoes, and a T-shirt that hugs his upper body. His arms are out, muscled, with those dreadful black veins all over them. Everything about him looks refreshed but his eyes. His eyes are tired, dark bruises around them, as if he hasn't slept in weeks. He's leaning forward, elbows on his lap, his fingers laced together beneath his chin. His blue eyes are locked on me.

"Nothing happened to you," he says, then sits up, dropping his hands. "Nothing of *that* nature, anyway."

"Oh." Relief swims through me. Something shifts to my right and Silvera pops up, her front paws on the bed.

"Oh. Hi, girl." I rub the top of her head as she nuzzles her damp nose into me. I wonder how long she's been here.

"She hasn't left your side since we got here. We've had to bring her food because she wouldn't leave."

"Really?"

"Really."

I start to stroke her back but notice my hands are shaking. The shakes are bad. I can hardly control it.

"It's the aftereffects." I meet Caz's eyes again as Silvera hops down. "Della had to create some concoction to throw off the suppressant. It zaps the nerves, but it clears the suppressant out of your system. Which reminds me, you should probably go take a piss before you end up going in the bed."

I blink at him, realizing my bladder does feel full, before attempting to climb out of the bed. As I place one foot on the ground, one of my knees buckle, but Caz is up in an instant to catch me. I cling to him as best as my shaky hands will allow and carry my gaze up to his. Our eyes connect—his cloudy, tired, and swimming with mild concern.

He breaks the connection. "This way," he says, guiding me to the bathroom. He places me on the edge of a clawfoot bathtub then steps back, taking a look around, as if he isn't sure what to do next.

I huff a laugh. "I think I've got it from here."

"Are you sure? I don't want you to fall."

I smile. "I've got it. Thanks."

With a quick nod, he leaves the bathroom, shutting the door behind him, and I sit for a moment, taking in the details. The walls are a shimmery black, the floors made of gray stone. The silver tub is in pristine condition, not a scratch or dent on it, and I'm almost certain it's never been used. I run my hands over the silver knobs and faucet, then make use of the toilet, because I really do have to pee.

When I've relieved myself, I catch a figure next to me. There's a mirror on the wall, and the figure is...*me*. I wobble toward the mirror, taking careful steps. My shaky fingers reach to one of my locs and I wrap it around my finger, but I can't help noticing the reflection shows a girl I don't know. She appears thinner, and there are bruises on her body, around her ribs and her neck. She's been beaten and attacked, and the reminder of that brings tears to my eyes. She isn't the Willow who landed here only days ago. She's *even more* broken now.

I close my eyes as reminders of Rami fill my brain again, and I flinch when I remember the way he slapped me. Hot tears run down the length of my cheeks, and my throat closes at the sheer reminder that I was alone in that moment.

And then it hits me about Garrett and what it will be like when I go back. The way he tries to control me, the way he grabs me, shakes me. Rami was an example of what Garrett would eventually become and feeling the wrath of it was horrifying.

I'm abused.

I'm damaged.

I'm useless.

It's no wonder I'm so depressed.

A pair of hands take hold of my face, and I open my eyes as two thumbs stroke my tears away. I suck in a sharp breath when I see Caz standing in front of me, holding my face, stroking my wet cheeks as he studies my eyes. I try to find the words to tell him

I'm fine—that this is just a misunderstanding and that I'll be okay.

But he says, "You're not okay."

I look into his eyes for a long, long time, until my vision blurs and I can no longer see him, and the tears break out like a flood. My stomach is sore, and it hurts even more as I try to hold in the sobs, but the sobs are uncontrollable and they burst out, and that feels much better than fighting it.

Caz releases my face, and I think to myself, *Don't go.*

He doesn't. He picks me up in his arms, and I rest my head on his chest. **I'm not leaving you.**

"I'm sorry," I whisper. I hate when people see me cry, and he of all people is witnessing it. I'd think he was laughing on the inside if I couldn't hear his concern.

He doesn't say anything as he carries me out of the bathroom and places me down on the bed again. I'm surprised when he lies next to me. He doesn't touch me, just lies there, waiting for my wave of sadness to pass. As he does, Silvera comes over, looking between us. It's almost like she's asking, "Did he do this to you?"

I force a smile at her, pat her head, and she gives us another thorough look before sauntering through of the crack of the bedroom door.

"You have to stop thinking about it," he finally says.

I turn onto my side, peering out the window. There's an ocean out there, the water nearly black. The water ripples beneath gray clouds, crashing at the shoreline. A barge moves along the water at a snail's pace. "I'm trying."

He's quiet a moment. "Is it only Rami that has you this way?"

Truthfully, no...but I'm not telling him that. Doesn't matter anyway. He'll read my mind and figure it out. I really need to learn how to do that mind wall thing.

Caz sighs. "Willow, will you look at me?"

I don't move. I keep my focus ahead.

"Who is Warren?"

I whip my head, glaring at him. "Don't worry about it."

"Why shouldn't I? You keep thinking his name. Him and some person named Garrett. And Garrett is clearly no good for you, so I don't understand why you allow him to take up so much space in your mind."

"I should get back to my world," I say, steering the subject.

"Look, you can't let the things Rami did beat you down."

His statement, though true, infuriates me. I sit up and face him, frowning. "How can you say something like that?" I shout, and he stares at me, unflinching. "I came to this world with no clue what was going on or what I was doing! I've been getting attacked *constantly*, Caz! I've been called names that I *never* thought I'd hear, and a man almost *raped* me!"

"I stopped him," Caz counters.

"Yeah, when it was almost too late!" I'm battling tears again. "I called for you—I *kept* calling for you, but you didn't say anything back, and I thought..." I bite hard into my bottom lip, so hard I think it'll bleed. "I thought you wouldn't come. I thought you'd left."

Caz's brows dip and his head goes into a slight tilt, but I don't look any longer to find out what else he does. Instead, I draw my legs to my chest and place my forehead on my knees. "I just want to go home."

"That's the second time you've said something like that."

"Like what?" I mutter.

"That you thought I'd left you. You said this before when we were in Whisper Grove for the night. Why do you think I will abandon you in your times of need?"

"Because you hate me!" I shout, glaring at him, and his eyes widen. He's slack-jawed. "Ever since I've gotten here, you've made it *very* clear that you don't want me around. And I don't want to be! I didn't ask for any of this!" I drop my legs and realize I sound like a whiny little girl with my next statement, but I say it again—"I just want to go home."

Caz climbs off the bed, walking around to the bottom of it. "You think I hate you?"

"Don't you?" The question comes out snarky. I don't mean for it to, but at this point, I'm tired and in pain and I don't want to talk anymore. He won't answer anyway. He's too fucking stubborn. He may as well just leave the damn room.

He marches around the bed and stops when he's next to me, his knees hitting the edge of the mattress.

"Just go, Caz. No one's forcing you to stay and look after me. I can take care of myself."

I rest my back against the headboard, lowering my gaze, and when I do, he bends down and brings a hand to the back of my neck.

I look up into his crystal eyes, and a surge of energy hums through me as his lips fall down on mine. It takes me a moment to digest what's happening, but not long because the energy is so potent, so powerful that I moan into his mouth. *He's kissing me.*

A coolness courses through my veins, like tiny ice chips have been pumped into my bloodstream, and Caz buries his fingers into the hair at the nape of my neck, deepening the kiss and groaning. I'm not sure what to do with my hands, but I kiss him back just as deeply, just as passionately. He tastes like he's just eaten fruit, crisp and tangy.

With a groan, he climbs on the bed to mount me, cupping my face in his hands, and I lace my legs around his waist. I feel him growing hard as he grinds his dick between my thighs, and this kiss...it's *incredible*. If there were meant to be fireworks going off for the best kisses, they'd be loud and booming for ours right now.

Heart beating harder, I curl my fingers into his silky hair, and he releases a guttural noise, like what I've done hurts him but feels good all the same. Our lips part, then connect. When they part again, I run my tongue over his bottom lip, and he hisses.

"Fuck, Willow," he rumbles.

His voice sets me on fire. He dives in again, losing himself in my touch, my lips. His body becomes rigid, his dick harder, rubbing against me. It skims over my pussy, and I whimper, aching. I can't help myself when I reach down to grip him.

He breaks the kiss, hissing again, and we take a moment to study each other's faces. There's a confused expression on his.

"Am I hurting you?" I whisper.

He studies my eyes, then shakes his head. "No." Then he coaxes my lips apart again and lightly wraps a hand around my throat. I thread my fingers through his thick hair, giving it a tug, and a strained noise fills the base of his throat. His dick strains in his jeans, skimming the fabric on my clit. I clench for him. Damn my panties. I want our clothes off. I want him inside me. God, why do I want him so much? I know he wants me too. I can hear him.

She tastes so good. Fuck, I don't know if I can do this. Her hands... I'm so fucking hard. How is she doing this to me?

More. I beg for it, and I know he can hear me. I *need* more. I need him to wash away everything and make all of what happened to be worth something, so I grip the ridge of his dick again, rubbing it. I drop my other hand, working to unbutton and unzip his pants, but it's when I'm about to push them down his waist and free him, that he grunts and tears his mouth away.

The weight of him is gone, as well as the heat of his body. When I look up, he's standing, and he takes a few steps back, breathing raggedly. Using the back of his hand, he wipes the corner of his mouth and stands tall, clearing his throat.

Once he's gained his composure and has fixed his pants, he asks, "Did that feel like hate to you?"

I don't answer. I'm trying to catch my breath and digest what's happened. I've kissed men before, but *none* of them have felt like *that*. None have made me want to be swallowed whole by a kiss, to be buried with it. No man has *ever* made me ache the way he has right now.

He clears his throat again, swiping his palms down the length of his shirt. "Regardless, we've found Beatrix," he says, and I try focusing on his words, but my eyes drop to the erection in his pants. He's still hard. Why doesn't he just take me? I'm right here. Just *take* me. "She gave me the chant," he continues. "Della will bring some clothes for you, and then you can go home, back to your world, like you want." He says the final statement with a whisper of disappointment. After he does, I feel a sharp pain in my chest, tight and constricting. I lift a hand, rubbing my chest. He doesn't react, but I'm sure he feels it too, and it bugs me that I can't hear him. His wall is high and thick, not a single thought escaping.

Caz looks me over, eyes glossy, then makes his way toward the door, leaving the room and shutting it behind him.

I run a finger over my lips, staring at the door, wishing he'd come back to do that all over again, but he won't. He's proved his point. He doesn't hate me, but he also doesn't want me staying, and I need to get back home, so I'll go because this world is nothing but a vicious fantasy, and my real life is much safer.

Regardless, knowing he's walking away physically hurts, and the wider the space grows between us, the more I feel the pain inside cutting deeper, like a sharp knife through the heart.

FIFTY

CAZ

I sit in my office chair, clutching my chest with one hand and stroking the top of Cerberus' furry head with the other.

It's been an hour since that bloody kiss—well, it was more than a kiss, and I can't stop thinking about it. In fact, the more I think about it, the more pain it causes me. I want to be back in that room. I want to kiss her again. I want to bury myself so deep inside her that it eases the pain, but I can't do that.

She doesn't belong here, and she doesn't belong to me. She almost *died* because of me, so she can't stay. If she leaves, then maybe the urges won't be so intense. Manx said the Tether is getting stronger the more we're around one another, and I realize whatever he gave me is wearing off because more black veins have appeared across my ribcage and are running farther up my neck.

My eyes move to the gun on the desk. The silver glimmers from the light pouring through the window, despite it being a cloudy day. I release my chest to pick up the gun and weigh it in my hand.

The reminder of being around that fighting ring eats at me. The metal cage. The whistles. The people shouting. The sweat and blood and anger. I sit back with the gun, close my eyes, and bring it to my temple.

Not my enemy, my friend.

"What are you doing?" The voice fills the room, and I open my eyes to find Willow standing on the other side of the office. She's dressed casually, black jeans and an oversized T-shirt. Her hair has been pulled up into a ponytail, the ends sprouting out like individual flower stems. Her brown eyes swim with concern, and she looks from me to the gun. I lower it, placing it back on the desk. Cerberus stands and walks to Willow to sniff her, before turning away and leaving the room.

"Nothing."

"Why were you pointing that at your head?"

"Are you ready to go home?" I counter.

She shifts on her feet. "I'm hungry."

"Della is in the kitchen."

She frowns, lowering her line of vision to the gun again, before locking on my eyes. "Where's Silvera?"

"She's outside, roaming the forest. Probably hunting."

Willow nods, and after giving me one more concerned onceover, she turns from the door and walks away. I sit back, blowing out a breath and closing my eyes. When I start to get up from my chair, my transmitter illuminates on the desk.

"Council. Council." The transmitter repeats the name of the people trying to contact me.

Shit. I knew this would come. I just didn't think it'd be so soon.

FIFTY-ONE

WILLOW

DELLA SERVES me eggs over easy and two strips of a yellow fruit that tastes like apples, and I gobble it down before sheepishly asking for seconds.

As she prepares another plate for me, Juniper enters the kitchen, wearing a black jumpsuit and chunky boots. Her hair has been washed and appears fresh and curly. She looks much better than she did when they had her in the ring, though her left eye is swollen and bruised, and her upper lip is stitched. She has a steel cup in her hand, her other wrapped in bandages, but blood is seeping through them. They'll need to be changed soon.

"It's quite early to be drinking, Juniper," Della says, cutting her eyes at her as she cracks an egg.

"It helps me think." Juniper sits on the stool next to mine. "Can I have breakfast too?"

Della nods, fetching more eggs from the fridge. With a sigh, Juniper lifts the rim of the cup to her lips and takes a long sip.

"What is it that you're always drinking?" I ask.

"Blue tonic," she answers. "They call it that because it eases a bad case of the blues." She winks, and I can't help smiling. I study Della's back as she works on the eggs, then side-eye Juniper again.

"Listen…I know about…the teacher thing." I glance at Juniper, who freezes.

"Who told you?"

"It sorta came up in conversation when we were on the way to get you and Killian from those fighting caves."

"Hmm." She sips, avoiding my eyes.

"I'm sorry that happened to you, Juniper."

"Don't be," she says, waving a dismissive hand. "It's over. Happened so many years ago."

I clamp my mouth shut and plant my elbows on the counter. Through my periphery, I see her take a bigger gulp of the drink, and I sigh for her.

I can't imagine what it must be like being a woman living in this world—given no respect whatsoever. It's a mid-century approach, this place. The women are only looked at for sex and meals. Fortunately, Caz and his crew don't seem to be that way entirely, but encountering men who are is infuriating.

Della brings our food, setting it on the counter in front of us, then tells us she has to go to the garden for more fruit. She wipes her hands on her apron before leaving, and when it's just Juniper and me, I smile at her. She returns a half-smile, then sets her cup down.

"Thought she'd never leave," she says, rolling her eyes.

I huff a laugh, cutting into one of my eggs. "Do you not like Della?"

"Oh, I *love* Della. I fancy her very much, actually. She can just be a bit…overbearing."

"She seems very motherly."

"Hmm. Yeah. She was a mother once. A good one, I hear."

I stop chewing. "What do you mean *was*?"

Juniper bites into her fruit. "Her son was killed by Rippies."

"Oh my God."

"Yeah, it was horrific. He was only fifteen at the time, walking home from a friend's house. We assume he took a trail home because they found his body near there. The Rippies had carved an upside-down U on his forehead and two bullets were found in his chest. That's how we knew it was them. The U represents the hills where they're from."

"That's awful." And suddenly I don't have the stomach to eat.

"It was very tragic, but surprisingly Della didn't cry. Not right away, anyway. She came to Caz's door and asked him to find the people responsible. Caz found them and he put them on a stake for her in the village, lit the stakes on fire, and let her and all of Blackwater watch them burn. It was all anyone could talk about for weeks."

"Are you serious?"

"Absolutely. Why would I not be serious?" Juniper looks at me as if she's insulted by my question.

"I'm sorry—I just mean...well, I didn't know Caz had that much power to do something like that for the whole town to see. Aren't there police or authorities in Blackwater?"

"Caz *is* the authority here," she says, laughing. "As well as Killian and Rowan. Sure, there are coppers around, but they work for Caz. He pays them and tells them what to do, so they can't stop him. He rules all of Blackwater. It was handed over to him after his father died."

"Wow. That's a big role to take on."

"It's actually quite calm here until someone steps out of line."

"So, is there anyone above Caz who can tell him what and what not to do?"

"There's The Council, but they hardly tell him what to do. They're just a group of high-grade Mythics who oversee Vakeeli and make sure there is more peace than chaos, I suppose." She rolls her eyes. "In my opinion, they're doing a shitty job. Just a group of bored, superior people."

"Wow. Everything is so different here compared to where I'm from. There are no people with gifts on Earth."

"How can you be so sure?" she asks. "Maybe they just hide it."

I press my lips. That's a possibility.

"What's it like where you're from anyway?" she asks, turning toward me.

"Well, there are different countries, which I suppose is similar to how every territory in Vakeeli is different. But there is more... freedom, I suppose. And way less violence. I mean, don't get me wrong, there is still violence where I'm from, it's just not so open like it is here. People do unspeakable things to one another there, and most times they're not punished for it. Justice is hardly ever served. And just like there is hate for darkies here, it's the same in my world, only we call it racism."

"Wow. That sounds pretty shitty."

"It is. There are police. They're like public servants, there to protect the people...but there are some who are corrupt and do the opposite. And the food is not like the food here. Most of it is...well, most of it is unhealthier, actually." I laugh. "But, man, would I love a cheeseburger right now."

"A cheese-what-er?" Juniper asks, gawking.

I laugh again. "It's like a sandwich with a quarter pound of meat. It would be easier to show you than to explain."

She shrugs and faces forward again, using a fork to cut into her eggs. I take another bite of mine, and Juniper giggles.

"What are you laughing about?" I ask, smiling.

"Just...*you*."

"Me?"

"Yes." She sits up higher on her stool. "Caz fancies you. I've never seen anything like it from him."

I look her in the eyes briefly before lowering my gaze. My mind instantly goes back to that kiss, and my heart thumps in my chest.

"He wants me gone."

"Never in my life have I seen him carry a woman—let alone bring her into his house. *Never*. If there's one thing he hates more than someone touching him, it's touching someone else."

"That doesn't mean he likes me. I think he just feels obligated to take care of me because we're Tethered."

"Ah, yeah. That thing. Mum told me all about it. Still, it's true. He hates being touched." Juniper stretches her arms above her head, then winces and clutches her ribcage, a reminder of her pain. "That woman from the fight cracked my rib good. That bitch."

"I don't understand why they were making you and Killian fight."

"Because the Rippies are pieces of shit," she growls, and she cuts her eyes at me before sighing. "It's what they do when they catch people from Blackwater out of their territory. It's their way of degrading us before they...kill us."

"They were going to *kill* you and Killian?" I gasp.

"Of course they were. Right after they'd gotten what they wanted, which was rubies and gold from our fights. Rami figured with two people from Caz's clan gone, Caz would struggle to get us back and wouldn't enter Ripple Hills unless he had an army. This would've started a war, and Caz's goal is to *not* have them because he hates them. Rami would do that though. He'd push Caz to his limit, try to break him so that Caz will start one. And if Caz started it and killed a shit ton of

Rippies—which he's done in the past—Rami would run to The Council and cry over the damage, then Caz would pay for it with his rubies. It was all a numbers game to Rami. He was a terrible monarch who didn't care how many Rippies actually died as long as he got paid. He was a bloody idiot. Always underestimating Caz."

"Yeah. They asked Caz for rubies in exchange for you and Killian."

Juniper scoffs. "Sure, they wanted rubies, but that's not all they wanted. Their plan was to lure him there, in hopes that they could string him up and get him in the cage to fight too. I heard them talking about it. They were going to make him fight, make as much profit as possible, then set us free, just so Caz could come back with an army and start a war. But that's the last thing Caz will ever do again—*fight*." She shudders as if remembering something. "I'm surprised he even went to the ring to help us."

"What do you mean? He had to save you."

She pins her eyes on me, then shakes her head. "Never mind." I want her to elaborate, but someone clears their throat.

"Are we ready?" Caz's voice floats through the kitchen. When I look back, he's standing by the window, his leather-clad fingers crossed in front of him, as if he's been there for quite some time now. He's put on a black trench coat and the same black cap from the first day I met him is pulled over his brows, creating a shadow over his eyes.

"Sure." I climb off the stool, carrying my plate to the sink.

"So, you're leaving Vakeeli for good?" Juniper questions.

"I hope so." I feel a thump in my chest, and Caz shifts on his feet.

"Well, it was nice getting to know you for the short time I did." She smiles and climbs off her stool to hug me.

I hug her back, then turn to Caz who has cleared his throat

again, clearly wanting us to end the farewells. I'm not family or a friend to him. I'm just a woman in his way.

"I have the chant here," he says, holding a sheet of paper in the air. "Seeing as I can't take you there, to the portal where you'll return, Killian will guide you to the forest and send you off. I made sure this was a one-way chant. One that will send you home so that you can't return to Blackwater, or any of the Vakeeli territories, for that matter."

I walk to him, taking the paper and clutching it in my hand. My eyes don't leave his. *A one-way chant? Why?*

"This way," he says, leaving the kitchen and ignoring the telepathic question.

I follow him out, waving once more at Juniper who blows a kiss at me before I step around the corner. Caz pulls the front door open and leads the way out. The air is salty and cool, and the wind nips at my cheeks. The leaves of the trees sway with the breeze, and as I take a few more steps out, Silvera runs across the field to me.

I smile as I drop to one knee and rub her head. "You'll look after her?" I ask, pointing my gaze to Caz.

"Yes."

I look back down at her and sigh. "I wish I could get to know you more."

She pants, sitting on her hind. I don't expect her to understand, so I give her one more rub on her head, a scratch behind the ears, and then follow Caz down the rocky path leading to the forest.

Once he passes the gates, he stops and says, "This is as far as I go."

Killian is ahead, leaning against the trunk of a tree, using a knife to slice into a piece of bumpy-looking fruit. He pushes off the tree and walks off, and I assume I'm meant to follow him, so I turn to Caz and say, "Thank you for...getting me a way back home."

Caz steps back and nods, his hands clasping behind him. "Take care of yourself, Willow Woman." He looks me over twice, gaze lingering, before his throat bobs and he turns away, focusing on his house instead.

It's all I'll get, and I won't ever see him again. It's like our kiss didn't even happen. None of the time we spent together ever happened. It's all a wrap, and I get to go home.

I don't know why that thought pains me, but I accept his cold farewell and follow Killian into the forest. I fight every urge to look back, but something deep inside me begs me to turn back and go to him. I won't go running, but I do look.

Before a line of trees can cut off my view of him, I peer over my shoulder, and Caz is standing in the same spot, only he's not looking at the mansion anymore; he's looking at me.

Before the trees officially cut us off, he drops his head and clenches his jaw, and the sharpness in my chest intensifies.

FIFTY-TWO

CAZ

When I can no longer see her, I make the trek back to my house. The door is already open, and Juniper stands there with a bloom in her hand, pulling from it.

"Don't start," I grumble, walking past her.

"Why'd you let her go?" she demands, following me. Not that I didn't expect her to. She can be relentless.

"She *had* to go." I march to my office, picking up my transmitter.

"Did she?" Her question is laced with sarcasm.

"Yes. The longer she stays, the worse it becomes for me."

"Is that so? Because it seems the more she's around you, the *better* it is for you. She humanizes you."

I glance up, and she pulls from her bloom, a smug smile on her lips.

"Just leave me alone please, Juniper. I have work to do." I don't look at her, and I expect to hear her footsteps drifting away, but she doesn't go. She's still here, and I sit in my chair, pinching the bridge of my nose.

"I see the way you look at her, Caz." She steps deeper into the room. "The way you are when she's around, I've never seen you like this with anyone. You're so fiercely protective of her."

"She was my responsibility until I sent her back home. I couldn't just let her die."

"Oh, don't feed me that bullshit! I know you, Caz. And I know how you are with women. You don't treat her like the others."

"Look, Juniper, you're filling your mind with these romantic ideas to please yourself. None of what you're imagining is true."

"You know, the Caz I know would've found a way for her to stay, or at least found a way for her to pay us visits. Why? Because the Caz I know is selfish, and what he wants, he takes."

"Not the case here," I sigh, picking up a bloom of my own and sparking it. "She's not meant for repeated visits to our world. You saw her last night. She almost died from a fucking suppressant."

"Sure, but you saved her. Who hasn't almost died here?" She takes a step closer. "Yes, it's dangerous in Vakeeli, and sure there will be people here who will try to hunt her down, but she's *yours*, Caz, and we all see it. She was made for you." She scoffs, shaking her head. "I mean, seriously, I wish the universe would toss me a man who is my soulmate. If only it were that easy!"

"She *couldn't* stay." The words fall from my lips, but even I don't believe them. Surely there could've been a way, but what would be the point? I saw how fragile she was in the bathroom, how broken and alone she felt, and I feel that every day. Here, it would drive her mad. At least in her world, there are established relationships and people she can rely on who aren't so…*violent*, as she puts it.

Juniper sighs, as if annoyed, then turns away to leave the office. Before she's gone, she stops and says, "She may not be fit for our world, but she's fit for you, and that should be all that matters."

She's gone, and I finally hear those footsteps drifting away. I lean back in my chair, pulling from my bloom, hoping it'll ease the ache inside me, but it doesn't. Willow is leaving. She'll be a world apart, and I'll be...here. That's how it's supposed to be.

Juniper is a hopeless romantic. She wears her heart on her sleeve, hoping someone will see her for who she really is. She's the soft one, and I suppose that's why she fits here. She keeps us men practical when all we want is to be impractical...unless she's triggered. Then she becomes *worse* than us. But I don't have time for love. Love is a disadvantage I can't afford, and Willow is...different. She deserves far better than this world will give her. She deserves better than me.

FIFTY-THREE

WILLOW

"Did he give you the chant?" Killian asks, stopping in the middle of forest. It's the same place I'd fallen when I came to Vakeeli. The path looks different this time of day. Light filters through the leaves, not as yellow as the sunlight, but more like a brighter moonlight.

"Yes." I pull it out of my bra and unfold the paper.

"Right. Go on then." Killian takes a few steps back, folding his arms.

I look Killian up and down, and ask, "Is there a reason you don't like me?"

He frowns then blows a breath, clearly annoyed. "It's not that I don't like you. You're just a distraction we can't have."

"Excuse me?"

"To Caz, having you here is a distraction."

"How?"

"Because all he sees is you. He's blind to everything else."

"That's not true."

Killian raises a brow, pressing his lips.

"He's sending me away. That's not true," I tell him.

He sighs. "Just read your chant and go."

"Do you know that we're Tethered?" I ask.

"I'm aware," he replies dully.

"So, then you know that when I leave, he'll probably be in pain."

"He'll get through it, just like he does everything else." Killian shifts on his feet. "Pain is what keeps Caz going. Without it, he wouldn't be *Caz*."

"That's an awful way to live."

"It's the life he was destined." Killian's eyes flicker to the paper in my hand. "Read the chant."

I drop my eyes to the paper. Wow. Just four little lines and I'll be home, back to reality. It's what I wanted all this time, so why am I struggling to leave right now?

"If you stay, you'll become his weakness, Willow, and not having any is what keeps him in control here. Do you really want to become his burden? Because that's what you'll be. His burden. Think about that." Killian has dropped his arms and is rubbing a hand over his head. "I love Caz like he's my own brother and I always want what's best for him, but for the sake of his sanity and his life, you can't be here any longer. He knows this. *I* know this. It's what's best, and if you also want the best for him, then go. He'll be all right."

His words bring tears to my eyes, hot and thick. He's right, I guess. And it seems he and Caz already have it rough. I don't want to make things worse.

I draw in a breath, exhale, and read the chant.

. . .

The time has come.
   Be removed as one.
   Tether and pain.
   Break away again.

There's a crackle in the air as purple light surrounds me. I notice Killian backing away as I'm lifted off the ground, and beside him, Silvera appears, barking as I'm taken higher into the air.

It's just like the first time it happened. Purple everywhere and then complete darkness. Quiet. I close my eyes. Breathe in deep. Exhale. And when I open them, I'm staring up at the ceiling fan in my bedroom.

I sit up slowly, in the quiet of my apartment. The sun sits on the horizon, rays sweeping across the room. It's so quiet.

The purple light above me fades, and I glance at my nightstand, at my phone perched on a stack of books where I last left it.

I pick it up, but the battery is dead, so I plug it into the charger, then I look back up, and the purple light is completely gone. An ache clings to my chest, and the urge to cry is strong, but I keep the tears at bay because this is it.

I'm home, and I won't ever see Caspian Harlow again.

FIFTY-FOUR

CAZ

After Willow's departure, I didn't have much time to waste. I'd spent five days away from Blackwater trying to find a way for her to get home. I wasn't supposed to be away for so long, but because I was, a lot of things have fallen behind.

Fortunately, Della handled everything around my home, as she always does, but the tavern is another story. Shipments have fallen behind because I wasn't able to sign off on them, a group of people tried robbing one of the ruby warehouses, and Simpson has made the urgency about both very clear with all the contact he's made to my transmitter. He expected me back days ago, but I didn't foresee all the bumps in the road with the Rippies and Rami.

"It's about damn time you showed up!" he shouts when I enter the tavern. It's daylight, so not many people are in right now. Just the usual drunks slumped in the corners, sleeping in their own vomit. Paulina is taking down chairs and wiping down the tables.

"Get those people out of here, will you?" I demand.

"On it, but I need you to sign these first." Simpson places a clean glass down and walks around the counter with a stack of papers. "It's for the next shipment of gold and blue tonic, and essence elixir from Vanora. You know their queen won't ship until it's signed by you."

I take the papers from him. "How is the warehouse holding up?"

"Remaining steady. A couple of fuckers tried stealing some of the rubies when they found out you'd left Blackwater, but we handled most of them."

"Who were they?"

"Not sure. We didn't ask for names, just beat the asses of the fuckers we caught and took the rubies back. One of them got away, but we're finding out who he is."

"Well, when you do, give me his name. I'll deal with him myself. Paulina, send some tea to my office, please."

"Yes, sir," she calls.

I turn away, marching down the hallway that leads to my office. I unlock the door and step in, making my way to the desk. I sign the papers for Vanora first. The essence elixir is priority here. Without it, many people wouldn't be alive. They don't like waiting to purchase their jugs either. If they do, they go mad and start fights, commit arson, and other ridiculous crimes.

My office door creaks open, and Paulina trots in with a silver tray. She places it on my desk, then pours tea for me into a black teacup. With a smile, she goes, closing the door behind her.

I sip my tea, light a bloom, and begin signing the rest of the papers.

I spent as much effort as I possibly could blocking out

Willow's thoughts. It was hard, especially when I heard her talking to Killian. I couldn't bear hearing her thoughts when she finally left. I forced myself to stop tuning in, but I could feel her pain, her worry...her *heartache*. Even now, it continues to gnaw at me. I can't understand why she cares so much about me. I've given her nothing to care for. I jeopardized her safety more than once in less than a week. She should be glad I'm not a permanence in her life.

A knock raps on the door. "What?" I call.

Maeve opens the door and trots inside, dressed head to toe in a red suit. Her hair is in pin curls, and a black hat is on her head, crammed with red feathers.

"She's gone?" my aunt asks, walking deeper into the office.

"Yes."

"Hmm." She moves closer, sitting in the chair opposite of the desk. "Everything okay?"

"Everything's fine." I avoid her eyes, reading over another sheet of paper.

"You've never been a man of many words. Yet you wear your emotions all over your face."

I finally lower my pen, giving her my attention, and she looks me in the eyes while crossing her legs.

"Are you here to annoy me about this like Juniper has?"

"As much as I'd love to do that, no, I'm not." She pauses, concern on her face. "I heard about Rami."

I lean back in my chair. "What of it?"

"There will be consequences, Caspian. People are already talking."

"I'm well aware."

"You knew not to kill Rami. You agreed with The Council that to keep as much peace as possible in Vakeeli, the monarchs are to be untouched."

I pick the pen back up and hold it tight, going back to signing. "He drugged her."

"I understand, but—"

I slam the pen down. "He was going to *rape* her, Maeve. If I hadn't shot him, he'd have done it, or something much worse. And even if I did stop him by beating his fucking face in, he'd have found a way to get back at me for stopping him, probably through someone from my clan. He wanted a war but he took it too far this time."

Maeve stares at me a moment, then turns her head, looking away. She digs into the leather handbag on her lap and pulls out a bloom. After she finds her lighter and sparks the tip, she pulls from it, then releases a chain of smoke.

"Did you tell The Council these details?"

"I did. And that his people kidnapped Juniper and Killian. They know I had motive—that I reacted out of defense."

"And what did they say?"

"That I still have to pay a price for it."

Her eyes widen, worried. "Did they say how?"

"Not yet."

"For the love of Vakeeli, Caz." She pulls from her bloom again, shaking her head. "You know what they do. They either kill you or they use your fears against—the thing that makes you feel weakest."

"I have no fears."

Maeve eyes me. "We all have fears." Another pull from the bloom. "Well," she sighs, uncrossing her legs and standing. "Despite the barbarity of it, I'm glad you did it. You saved her life, plus I've always hated Rami." Maeve trots to the door but stops to look back at me. "Do you love her?"

I frown, my heart catching speed from her words. *"What?"*

"You heard me."

"She was just a woman who needed to be returned home. She was my responsibility, and I handled it."

"Yes, but you knew going into it that killing Rami could tarnish you, end your life even. I'm assuming she was worth that risk." When I don't say anything, Maeve smirks and leaves the office, and I shake my head, popping open the gray canister on my desktop and plucking out another bloom. I light the end and lean back in my chair, taking a long, hard pull.

"This family will be the death of me."

FIFTY-FIVE

WILLOW

"How the hell...?" I stare at the calendar on my phone screen. Only two days have passed since I dropped into Vakeeli. How is that even possible when I spent nearly five days there?

I expected to come back to missing posters with my face on it and cops swarming my apartment, but instead, all is normal. The bed is unmade, clothes still strewn all over the place. Even my takeout containers are still on the dining table.

The only difference is the note on the fridge from Garrett, who is concerned about my whereabouts. I'm not surprised by that, considering he visits me daily when he thinks I'm not working.

Call me when you see this. I've stopped by twice and you weren't here.

. . .

I pluck the sticky note off the fridge and place it on the counter, then grip the edge of it. The last thing I want is talk to Garrett, but I'm sure he's going to stop by again sometime, so I send him a quick text to let him know I'm fine.

He responds almost immediately, but not with a text. A call. I groan and reluctantly answer.

"Willow?" he hisses into the phone. "Where the hell have you been?"

"Why are you whispering?"

"I just walked out of the middle of a meeting," he says hurriedly. "That's not the point. I've been worried! You left your phone at home. What's going on with you?"

"Everything's fine."

"Where'd you go?" he demands.

I try to think of a lie, but I'm stumped. Surely there's no way I can tell him I was sucked into a vortex and dropped into another universe. He'd never believe me.

"I just needed some time away from everything, so I went to a hotel."

"And you couldn't tell me that?"

"I just needed time, Garrett. I didn't think I had to tell you or anyone."

"Well, that's seriously fucked up. I thought something happened to you!" He breathes hard into the phone, clearly agitated. "Anyway, I was worried about you, so I called Faye to see what was up."

Shit. I avoid groaning.

"You should check in with her if you haven't already, let her know you needed some *precious* time away."

I roll my eyes. "I will."

"Sure. Look, I have to get back, but I'll call you on my break."

"Kay."

Garrett hangs up, and I walk back to my bed, sitting on the edge. I send Faye a heart emoji, and she replies **BITCH!** and I laugh. I reply, **I'm okay. I promise.**

She replies, **You better be but don't think I'm letting it go that easily. After my shift you're telling me what the hell is going on with you.**

I debate whether I should tell Faye the truth or not. Surely, she would understand—or at least try to. Then again, trying to explain that I was in another world full of guns and violence, with a sexy, broody man I didn't know but made out with, sounds delusional. It sounds like something straight out of a book or movie, and don't get me wrong, Faye is all for swooning over a fictional hero, but she knows the difference between *reality* and *fiction*. For all I know, she'll be telling me to go to a psychiatric clinic to seek help, not a small practice therapist.

Regardless, it's nice to be back to normality, but as I look around my apartment, being back doesn't feel the same. It's all so *simple*, compared to Vakeeli. Cars drive by outside my window, people going about their lives, not even realizing mine has been altered.

I lock my phone for a moment and close my eyes, hoping I'll still hear Caz's voice, but I don't. I don't hear anything but silence and the footfalls of the neighbors in the apartment above me.

Will I ever hear him again, or did that chant end everything? Maybe by returning to my world, we're no longer Tethered. It's a thought...but I have a feeling it doesn't work that way.

Regardless, I can't sit here thinking about it. Or *him*. I have to get back to my life and forget all I went through. I check my phone again and have three missed calls from Lou Ann. Work will be a good distraction. It's better than lying around here.

I give Lou Ann a call back, and she asks to see me. It's a Sunday, but it must be important if she's wanting to meet on a weekend, so I agree to meet her for lunch.

I shower, get dressed, collect my satchel, and then check the mirror. There is nothing left of Vakeeli on me. I cleaned up, refreshed my hair, and the bruises and scars have somehow disappeared. They were already fading after the kiss from Caz but...

The thought fails me.

That kiss. That damn man. I need to forget him.

I tip my chin—reclaiming confidence—and leave the apartment, locking up and heading to my car.

FIFTY-SIX

WILLOW

I MEET Lou Ann for lunch at a sandwich shop uptown. She's already placed her order when I arrive (which doesn't surprise me as she waits for no one), and she's biting into her sandwich when I walk inside. A bit of avocado is on the corner of her lip as I approach, and she wipes it with a napkin, her eyes expanding when she sees me.

"Mmm, sorry!" she says, mouth full. "I didn't eat this morning, too busy with emails and calls, so I'm *starving*! And speaking of, why haven't you been picking up your phone, missy?"

"Oh, yeah, it broke and I had to wait for a replacement." The lie slips out without so much as a thought. I'm not usually one to flat out lie, so this lie takes me a little by surprise. Maybe some of Vakeeli has rubbed off on me. "But it was nice not having my phone for a few days."

"I'm sure it was, yes, but you know I always need you on call, Willow. Do you know Townsend reached out to us again?

"Did they?"

"Yes!" Her green eyes light up. "They want us to host another event for them next fall! It's also for charity, and they want it to be some kind of costume party, so we can have a lot of fun with this. Did you bring a notepad?"

"I did, yes," I tell her, pulling one out of my bag, along with a pen.

"Good. Of course, we can always work on this at the office, but I figured why not eat and chat, make it fun?" She beams, flashing her perfect white teeth, and I smile back. She bites into her sandwich again, and this time some avocado drips onto the collar of her black suit. I start to tell her, but she talks again, cutting me off. "We received a lot of praise for the cruise," she says. "That really was a wonderful idea. I'd love to hear what you have in mind for a costume event. Did you get the email I forwarded?"

"I did, yes." I open my phone and go to my inbox.

"Great. So, as you can see, they're asking for a..." Lou Ann continues talking, but her words become a buzz when I feel a cool draft float past me. A chill rides down my spine as the sandwich shop slowly disappears. Dark shelves replace the industrial ones of the shop, filled to the brim with books. The floors turn black. A spiky fan spins above me, and a fire is going in an oversized, familiar fireplace. I gasp as a man walks past me, muttering under his breath. It's Caz. I'm in his home office.

I watch him from an odd angle, one close to the ground as he paces back and forth. He's talking to himself, but I'm not sure what about, and I try and shake myself out of whatever trance I'm in, but it doesn't work.

I feel myself moving closer to him, and then I stop next to him, facing his legs. Caz sighs and bends down, and I'm staring deeply into his blue eyes. My heart beats harder, faster.

"What is it, eh, girl?" he asks, stroking the top of my head. "You miss your bonded mum? Is that it?"

What?

Caz blows a breath, still stroking the top of my head, and then I realize he's not talking to me. He's talking to someone else, or *something*, rather. Judging by the panting and whining, and the white fur on the paw, I'm assuming it's Silvera.

"I'm going to tell you something." He scratches behind one of her ears. "I think she was meant to stay. It hurts more without her, and none of the elixirs are working." He pauses, rubbing the center of his chest, as if it'll wipe some of the pain away. "Too bad I can't get her back. Suppose I'll have to live the rest of my life like this."

He drops his head, staring at the floor, and I have the urge to reach out to him, but when he pulls away and leaves the room, I'm sucked back to reality.

"Willow?" Pale fingers snap in my face. "Willow, are you okay?"

I blink rapidly, putting my focus on Lou Ann.

She smiles, sipping her drink. "Where'd you go?" she teases.

"Oh—I, um..." I look around the sandwich shop. All is the same, but I still feel cold. I try not to shiver as I focus on Lou Ann. "Sorry. Let's, um...let's do a masquerade. It's classy and never goes out of style." I push out of my chair. "Would you excuse me for a second? Need to run to the ladies' room."

I leave the table before Lou Ann can get another word in and race around the corner to the bathrooms. I burst into one of the stalls and slam it closed behind me, then take a moment to catch my breath.

I can see what he's doing through Silvera? That changes *everything*. Sure, I can't hear him, and maybe he's purposely blocking me out so that I can't hear a thing, and so that he can't hear me either, but Silvera is still there, and we're still connected. I close my eyes, trying to find my way back to her. I think of her—her soft fur, her silver eyes, and then I *feel* her.

She sits up in Caz's office.

Silvera. Can you hear me?

She whimpers, looking around the office. I can't control her, but I'm seeing everything from her viewpoint.

"Holy shit, this is incredible."

Hey, girl. It's me. I try to calm her—I feel her heart racing; she's startled.

I need you to do me a favor. Keep an eye on Caz. Make sure he doesn't hurt himself.

As if she understands, she walks out of the office and into the kitchen where Caz is standing, gripping the edge of the counter. His knuckles are white from holding it so tightly. She walks around him and jumps on the countertop, and Caz lets go of the counter with a deep frown.

"Oi! Get your ass off my counters!" he shouts.

Silvera defies him, sitting instead and staring at him. From her eyes, I see red pills on the counter, and there are black pills next to them. I've never seen the black ones before. What are they for? Silvera makes a noise of disapproval, and I feel a tightness in my gut, like something isn't right. Silvera moves a paw, swiping the black pills onto the floor.

"What the hell are you doing?" he snaps, watching the pills clatter. "Get the hell off my counter, Silvera," Caz warns, pointing a stern finger at the floor.

She can't keep an eye on him for me if she gets kicked out. And I have a feeling he'll send her off in a heartbeat if she doesn't listen, so I say, "*Down, Silvera.*"

Silvera listens to me, jumping off the counter and sitting on the black pills. They're clearly no good for him, and she knows this.

"Silvera, move," he commands, but she doesn't listen.

"For the love of Vakeeli," he gripes. "You're just like your owner! I tell you one little thing about me, and you make yourself too fucking comfortable." Caz collects what's left of the red pills and shoves them into a container. He then leaves the kitchen, and I smile when Silvera follows him, but she doesn't get the chance to follow him for long. Cerberus pops up as Caz storms up the stairs, growling at her. Silvera growls back, but Cerberus stands his ground, raising his large, bushy head. He won't let her pass. He knows Caz wants to be alone.

"Damn it," I whisper. *Leave him for now, girl.*

Silvera retreats, but not without purposely whacking her tail in Cerberus' face as she goes.

I open my eyes, bringing myself back to the present. Something is eating at Caz, and it's not just my leaving. No one is around to watch him, to help him, and I have a feeling he wants it to be that way.

I saw him with that gun the day I left, the way he pointed it at himself, the way his face melted, as if he could absolve himself of all weakness and sin if he pulled that trigger. He wanted that gun to take away whatever he was feeling, but why?

Why is he so broken?

What is he running away from?

Fifty-Seven

CAZ

It's been four days since Willow left, and I haven't slept. Not that I sleep much as it is, but without her here, I don't care to sleep at all.

I've kept myself occupied with work, or I've lain in my chambers, staring at the ocean, wishing a large wave would sweep through my house and take me.

Anything would be better than dealing with this pain. Nothing's working. The black tablets from Luxor have prevented sleep, as they should, but none of Della's elixirs are easing the ache in my chest.

She's tried everything, and it hardly takes the edge off. At this rate, I'll have to go back to Whisper Grove and request something stronger from Manx. But he'll read me, and he'll know what I'm truly feeling, and he'll say the only cure to it is *her*. I don't want anyone inside my head again, but I don't understand how someone who is so wrong for me can be the only thing to ease this pain.

Perhaps it's all wrong. Perhaps there is a way she *can* be here, and the Tether will strengthen us instead of break us. This Mournwrath feeds when we're together. If can find a way to get rid of Mournwrath, we'll be safe. There must be an anecdote, or a way to find Selah and rectify this whole thing.

The only downfall is that Willow would be back in this world—a world she doesn't deserve, and by the sounds of it, I don't think I'd fit in hers. So even if there is a way, where do we go from there?

There's a knock at my door, and I sigh, sitting up in the bed.

"What?"

"It's me." Juniper's voice is on the other side of the door. I walk to my closet, grabbing a shirt and tugging it over my head, then make my way to the door.

"Can we talk?" she asks when I've cracked the door open.

"What about?"

She sighs and steps back. "I think this conversation would be best over tea."

I MEET Juniper in the kitchen after putting on my coat and jeans. She's already sitting at the table, and from where I'm standing, I can see her leg bouncing beneath it. She's chewing on her thumbnail, something she only does when she's anxious. There's a brown folder on the table in front of her.

I sit at the opposite end of the table, and Della pops up with tea on a tray, pouring two cups for us.

"Thank you, Della." I grab my cup and take a sip, and she gives a slight bow of the head before leaving the kitchen. "What's this about, Juniper?"

"So, I've noticed your moping," she starts, sitting up taller.

"I haven't been moping."

"You have, but let's not get into that."

I sip my tea again, raising my chin. She's wasting my time.

"I spoke to Alora."

"About what?"

"Well, I went to her, and she took me to Beatrix again."

I frown. "Why?"

"Listen, before you get upset, I just want to tell you, there *is* a way for you and Willow."

I resist the urge to snap at her by sipping my tea and waiting for her to continue. She presses a hand on the folder before her and slides it across the oak table toward me. I glance down at it before lifting my gaze to hers again.

"Read it," she insists.

I don't read it right away because I have no clue what the hell I'm getting myself into. She's noticed my supposed moping and she's been speaking to Alora behind my back? What the hell else has she been doing?

"Did Maeve send you to Alora?"

Juniper blinks before dropping her eyes to her teacup. She cradles it in her hands, avoiding my eyes. "She wants what's best for you, Caz."

"I don't need anyone telling me what's best for me."

"Can you just read what's on the papers?"

I draw in a deep breath, snatching my eyes away from hers and focusing on the folder. I flip it open, and there's a white sheet inside, yellowing at the edges. The words are handwritten in black ink.

. . .

They will tell you there's no way to be with your mate due to the Cold Tether. They're lying. A simple Tether means you're soulmates, but a <u>Cold</u> Tether is much deeper than that. You're still soulmates, bound to one another lifetime after lifetime, but there is a beginning to your bond.

When you find out where your Cold Tether starts, it all makes sense. It's not a curse. It's a gift. And once that gift has been discovered, there will be others seeking to tear it apart for their own power. Together is the only way to keep your strength, even when they tell you not to be. Apart, and your soul suffers until you're left to be nothing but dust.

I LIFT my gaze to Juniper's, who is anxiously waiting for me to respond.

"What am I supposed to be gathering here?" I ask.

"Turn it over," she says.

I flip the page, and there's an address listed. "An address in The Trench." I raise a brow. She can't be serious.

"Yes. And from what Beatrix told me, she knows one couple who beat the Cold Tether who may still live there, but she also believes it's unlikely."

"Then why didn't she tell me this herself?"

"Because she didn't want to give false hope. I had to beg her for something—*anything* that could help you and Willow. This couple is from different worlds, just like you two, and it's believed that they're still together."

"How would they still be alive?"

Juniper stands. "I suppose we should go find out. If we can get to them, ask them how they did it, maybe this will help you get Willow back. She could stay here and—"

I shove back in my chair. "Juniper, do you hear yourself?

Willow doesn't *want* to be here! She can't be here! I don't give a fuck how this Cold Tether works, but she and I aren't meant to be, and the sooner you, Maeve, and anyone else who is plotting behind my back can get that through your thick fucking skulls, the better off you'll be."

"You don't have to be miserable, Caz! We've talked to Della! She's worried about you and so are we! You're in pain and you can't stop it."

"My pain has nothing to do with anyone," I grumble, turning away. "Now stop digging behind my back and leave it be."

"Willow wouldn't want this, and you know it. What happens when she starts to feel the pain too? Will you just let her suffer?" Juniper's voice echoes after me, but I've already left the kitchen. I march out the back door and cross the field to get to the stables. The door creaks on the hinges, and my stable boy, Pash, sees me and waves.

"Good morning, Mr. Harlow," the boy greets me, standing next to a bale of hay.

"Morning, Pash. Onyx behaving himself?"

"He is, sir. He loves his morning walks." Pash grins, standing closer.

I stand in front of Onyx, stroking his black mane. "How about a morning ride then, eh?" I murmur to the stallion.

Onyx huffs and stomps his front hooves, and I step away, opening his gate and mounting his back. As I settle on top of him, Cerberus comes rushing into the stables. Pash pets him when he approaches, scratching under his chin and causing one of Cerberus' back legs to thump.

I dig into my pocket, pulling out a satchel. I pluck out ten rubies and offer them to Pash. "Here."

Pash opens his palm, and I dump them in his hand. "Oh—sir, this is too much for today. It's enough to last us a month."

"You can take a month off, Pash."

His eyes well with tears. "Did I do something wrong, sir?"

"No, Pash. You did nothing wrong. Go enjoy your family. I'll contact you when I need a hand again." I replace the satchel, gripping Onyx's reins. "Feel free to clean the stables one last time. If any of the women come looking for me, tell them I don't want to be found."

I leave the stables with Onyx, and he dashes away as soon as we're outside, catching speed. The wind whips at my face, and the mist is stronger today, but the droplets feel good. It reminds me that I'm alive, if only for now. Moments like these can't be replaced.

My wolf catches up, chasing after us, enjoying the run.

"Yah!" Onyx gallops faster, and I peer over my shoulder at my home. It fades into the distance, and I hope the conversation I just had with Juniper does the same.

I can't even stay in my own bloody house without being bothered about Willow.

Where is the peace?

When does it end?

FIFTY-EIGHT

WILLOW

I COULDN'T SLEEP last night. I was and still am worried about Caz.

I searched the internet all night, trying to find information about the Cold Tether, but there's nothing. In my world, it doesn't exist...or maybe I'm just looking in all the wrong places.

Regardless, this Tether doesn't make any sense to me. How can two people who are supposed to be soulmates, not be able to be together? Something about it feels wrong. It's almost a form of torture—wanting something you know is yours, that you can't live without, yet being forced away from it.

Every hour, a deeper sensation builds in my chest. It grows stronger the more I think about Caz, and there's a sliver of pain when I try to get him out of my mind. A bond like this doesn't just go away, no matter what world we're in.

Something doesn't add up, and now that I'm back home, I feel there's only one person I can talk to openly about it. After my third cup of coffee, I collect my bag and phone and leave my apartment, but when I reach the parking lot, I spot Garrett closing his car door with his foot. A pink box is in one hand, probably full of pastries from one of his favorite bakeries, and in the other is a drink tray with two iced coffees. At the sight of him, my mouth becomes dry. What the hell is he doing here?

"Garrett, hi." I purposely give my keys a jingle, a clear indication that I'm about to leave. "I didn't know you were stopping by."

"Wanted to surprise you," he says, meeting up to me, his face solemn. For a surprise, he doesn't look very happy.

"Well, look at that. I'm surprised." I force a laugh. I really wish he would've called before popping up. I should start instilling boundaries.

"I know I should've called," he says, as if reading my mind. "I just stopped by to make sure you're okay."

"I'm fine. But yeah, you should've called first because I have a few things to do."

"Where are you headed? I can go with you."

"I'm going to see Faye and then grab a few groceries." The last part is a lie, though I do need groceries.

"Oh. Girl time?" He smirks, and I force another laugh. He then shifts on his feet. He's being weird, and it's making me uncomfortable. "Look, is there anything you need? Anything you want to talk about?"

"No, not really. I just need to see Faye first. I told her I'd swing by." That much is true. I just didn't say when, and since it's fall, she's busy at the bookstore, but I can help her there. There are always books needing to be shelved or tables to clean off in the café area. Plus, people love being there when the weather cools off and they're seeking a cozy place to hang out.

Garrett places the box of baked goodies on the trunk of my car as well as the drinks. Stuffing his hands into his front pockets, he says, "She told me about Warren."

I try not to flinch at the name. "What about him?"

"I know his birthday is tomorrow. Just like yours."

I look away, at anything but Garrett. "Okay?"

"I think you may have disappeared because you were thinking about him."

"I told you I just needed some time away, Garrett. Let's not make it a big deal."

"From your own home?" he asks, confused. There's urgency in his eyes as he silently demands answers and, truthfully, I don't feel like answering them right now. It's not the time to talk about Warren or our birthday. Not that it would even matter because he's not here to celebrate it anymore, and I'm not in the mood to celebrate my own.

"Look, Garrett, no offense, but you and I don't talk about things this personal, so forgive me if I don't want to talk about my brother right now."

His eyes grow bigger, as if shocked by my statement. Something about his eyes alarms me. They darken in a way I've never seen before. Taking his hands out of his pockets, he steps closer to me. "I get that, but I'm your *boyfriend*, Willow. And I'm trying to be here for you."

"You're not my boyfriend! When did we ever say we're a couple?"

"Are you fucking kidding? I bring you shit every day. I spend time with you, spend the night with you, check in on you!"

"Yeah, you do most of that *without* running it by me! You think you own me, but you don't!"

"What did you just say?" His eyes flare, his nostrils too. I was right. Something about his eyes has changed, and I can't put my finger on it. He takes another step closer, and I draw in a calming breath.

"Look, I really have to go."

"Why the hell are you trying to avoid me?" He's right in front of me now, and he grips my upper arm with both hands. It startles me to the point that tears creep to my eyes, and I'm reminded of Rami. The hopelessness. The fear.

"Garrett, let go of me," I say through clenched teeth.

"You're so fucking ungrateful," he growls in my face. "It's no wonder you're so alone and miserable."

His words are like a slap to the face. I stare at him, stunned, then shove him hard against the chest, forcing him off me. His back hits the side of a car, and his eyes widen.

"Fucking leave!"

"*What?*"

"You heard me! Leave!" I shout. "Or I'm calling the cops!"

He glares at me while shaking his head. "Fine. You know what?" He turns around, snatching up the iced coffees and box of pastries and chucking them on the ground. Cream and coffee spill on the blacktop, running toward the pile of muffins.

"You're a fucking bitch, Willow! You've wasted so much of my time and you're gonna regret that shit!" With those words in the air, he storms away. My heart pounds in my chest as I watch him return to his car, start the engine, and peel off, his tires screeching.

When he's gone, I close my eyes, draw in a deep breath, and then open them to climb into my car.

It won't be the last time I see him, I'm sure of it, but for now, he's not the priority. Getting back to Caz is.

FIFTY-NINE

WILLOW

THE SCENT of ground coffee beans envelopes me as I step into Lit and Latte's. The bell above the door chimes, and the warmth of the shop wraps around me, combining with the moisture that has accumulated on the back of my neck and upper lip. Nervous sweat.

Two employees stand behind the checkout counter, one working the café, chomping on a piece of gum as she shoves a pastry into the toaster oven. People are seated at tables by the window with books or laptops, peacefully sipping their drinks. It's all so simple, and I wonder if any of them realize there's a bigger world out there. There's so much more than we know. Hell, I bet Vakeeli isn't the only other universe that exists. There are probably thousands more waiting to be discovered.

I shake the thought away and make my way to the book checkout counter, where a girl with green hair and a septum piercing smiles as I approach. Her name badge is covered in *Harry Potter* and *Twilight* pins, and her name is Valeria.

"Hi. Is Faye in?" I ask.

"She is. I believe she's in the office. Do you want me to get her for you?"

"No, that's okay. I told her I was swinging by, so I'll just go meet her." I wander down the hallway and give the closed office door a quick knock.

"Come in!" Faye's voice is clear and distinct, and I feel such relief at the sound of it. I grip the doorknob and twist it open, stepping into the tight office. It's a box-sized room, one wall full of shelves, and no windows. A desk facing the door is in the center, atop with a Mac desktop, keyboard, and printer, and behind it is a cushioned rolling chair. Occupying the chair is Faye, who glances up from the book she's reading and does a double take when she realizes it's me.

"Willow!" she screeches, tucking a bookmark into the spine and then slapping it closed.

"Are you seriously hiding in your office to read?" I ask, laughing as she hops up and rushes to me.

"Yes! It's slow out there right now. A few chapters won't hurt." She squeezes me tight, and I smile over her shoulder. I've missed her hugs. "Are you okay?" She pulls away, her hands on top of my shoulders as she assesses me.

"I'm okay. But I really need to talk to you."

"Okay." She releases me and steps back. "Do you want to close the door?"

I look back at the empty hallway before nodding and closing the door again. She makes her way back to her chair and sits, crossing one leg over the other and placing her elbows on the desk, waiting with anticipation.

I drag one of the folded chairs from the corner toward the desk and sit, then release a slow exhale as I close my eyes.

"Willow?"

I open my eyes to meet hers again. Her anticipation has faded. There's nothing but concern filling her eyes now.

"So, this is going to sound crazy," I start.

"Nothing ever really sounds crazy to me," she says, shrugging. And it's true. Faye hasn't had the most decent upbringing. Her father tragically died when she was two and her mother had to raise her alone. One day, when she was seven, she came home after school and her mother wasn't there. Then, two days passed, and she still hadn't shown up. Fortunately, Faye was a very self-sufficient seven-year-old, so she fed, clothed, and bathed herself. But then her grandmother visited, and when she found out her mother had been missing, they put out a missing person's report. Long story short, Faye's mother was found in a motel, her face buried in a pile of coke. The only thing that stopped Faye from crying about the news was books. She still remembers the series she was reading—The Baby-Sitters Club. Her grandmother took her to the library every week, and there she'd stack up on books and stay in her room reading between school hours.

I don't think much can shock Faye, but I'm worried that if I tell her about Caz and all of Vakeeli, this'll tip her mind over the edge. There's only so much a person's mind can accept before they completely lose it.

"Okay, so let me start by telling the truth," I say. "I didn't go to a hotel to get away."

Faye shifts in her seat, her eyes rounding out, waiting for me to continue.

"The truth is that..." I stop, shuddering a breath. My heart is beating so fast—my pulse is in my ears. "I...was in another *world*, Faye."

Silence wraps around us, and we both stare at each other. The only thing we hear is the indie pop music playing from the bookstore, and the murmuring from those in the shop, clueless of our conversation.

"Another world? What do you mean by that?" she asks, blinking slowly.

"I mean literally in *another* world. I was...transported there. There was this purple light that took me there, to this other universe, and there was this guy who I'm apparently Tethered to, which means we're basically soulmates. And his world he's in is *way* more violent and darker than ours, and it's not like Earth, you know? The food and technology are different, and they have guns—*so many guns*. And there are wolves who are connected to us, and I can actually still see him through *my* wolf. My wolf protects me, and his protects him. And time is different there—it moves faster there than here, apparently because I spent nearly a week there, but only two days passed here, and they have this water that keeps them young, and some guy—he tried to take advantage of me, but Caz stopped him and now I'm back."

I suck in a breath, release it, then clamp my mouth shut as I lift my gaze to Faye's. Her eyes are still wide, and she doesn't blink. She just stares at me, not as if I've lost my mind, but as if she's trying to digest everything I've just told her.

"Faye?" I whisper. She probably thinks I'm insane. It does sound insane hearing it out loud. I'm not sure I'd believe anyone if they told me this. Not without proof.

She lifts a hand in the air, then slumps back in her seat, finally blinking. Her gaze drops to the desk; she's still processing.

"I know it sounds crazy," I continue. "But it really happened. I wouldn't make something like this up."

"I believe you."

"You do?" I look into her eyes.

"Yeah." She nods. "I—I mean, sure it sounds outrageous, but... surprisingly, I believe you." She smiles and shakes her head. "Wow, I always knew there was more to the world than this."

I let out a sigh of relief.

"So...how did you get back?"

I explain everything to Faye about Beatrix and the chant, and about how our Tether works.

"A *Cold* Tether?" she repeats after I say it.

"Yes."

"I've never heard of anything like that."

"Me neither. But it's real, and apparently when we're together for too long, it can kill one of us."

That causes her to frown. "That doesn't sound right."

"What do you mean?"

"I mean if you're meant to be someone's soulmate, it shouldn't *kill* you to be together. This can't be a Will Smith and Charlize Theron in *Hancock* situation. Clearly the universe created this Tether for a reason. Why would it create such a bond just for it to result in death?"

"That's what I've been asking myself." I scratch the crown of my head. "Something just seems off about it, but I don't know how to do research on something that doesn't exist here."

"Then that means you need to go back and find out more about it, right?"

I flinch as I look at her.

"What?" she asks. "What's wrong?"

"I—I don't know if I can go back there, Faye. That place is dangerous. Plus, the guy, Caz? He can be a real asshole." But man, do I want that asshole. I want him so bad it hurts. *Literally.*

"Well, how else are you supposed to find answers?"

"I don't know." I chew on my bottom lip. "What if I'm wrong, and I go back and it ends up killing him this time?"

"Well, you have to find out how this Tether thing works. Maybe there's a way you can go there and *not* be around him. Then you can figure it out." She taps her chin. "Wait...if it's as dangerous as you say, and he's such an asshole, why do you want to figure it out so badly? Wouldn't that make you want to forget about it?"

Her question punches me right in the stomach. I draw in a breath, ignoring the thoughts swimming through me. Sure, Caz is an asshole, but I care about that asshole. I care about him more than I want to admit, and it's strange because I hardly know him. I know some things, but not enough that I should care for his well-being, yet if something happens to him, I feel like it'll break me. If he's unhappy, I'm unhappy, and I can't shake that feeling, no matter how hard I try. I may not be able to hear him right now, but I *feel* him. I feel his pain, like a dull ache in my chest that won't go away, no matter how much I stretch and no matter how many ibuprofens I take. It's still there, and it lingers, proving that we *are* one. We're connected and we need each other, no matter how we feel about it.

I lock eyes on Faye again. "I have to get back to him before he does something to hurt himself." Then a reality hits me. "But he was so ready to send me back home."

Faye pushes out of her chair as I look up at her. "Well, we aren't going to find answers by sitting in here, sis."

"What are we supposed to do?"

"You say that Beatrix woman gave you a chant. Do you think if you say it again, that it'll take you back?"

"No. Caz made it clear it was a one-way chant. He doesn't want me coming back."

"And you don't know how you got there in the first place?"

"I was really, *really* high," I admit, huffing a laugh. "And I was in my bed, and I saw that light." I pause. "Oh—and that time in the basement when I was supposed to bring the wine to you. I was suddenly in a forest, and I could hear his voice. He was calling out to me, but it all went away when you came to find me."

"That's what that freakout was about?" she exclaims.

"Yes... that."

"I knew I wasn't overreacting! Why didn't you just say?"

"Because I would've sounded crazy! Hell, I feel like I sound crazy now!"

"I mean, you do, but also...I believe you. So I'm not sure what that says about us." She makes a warped face, then she's at the door as she says, "I guess we should go to the basement again. Maybe there's a connection there we can find."

SIXTY

CAZ

Killian and Rowan stand behind me, and I pluck the bloom from my lips, tossing it on the ground in front of the tattered house, then focusing on the front door. Smoke drifts from my lips, and I do wish the bloom would calm me down, but it won't at the moment. Right now, I'm annoyed and in pain, and this is just the distraction I need. Besides, I've warned this Moren fucker *twice* to stop stealing from my warehouse. Twice is too many. I don't allow third chances.

I pull out the steel wire from my pocket, raising it in the air to get a good look at it. I haven't used it in weeks. The thread is still strong.

"Right. Let's move in," I tell the boys. I march up what's left of the wooden stoop and kick the front door in.

The place reeks of gold dust and black opium. Rubies are scattered across the table, some of them tipped out of a familiar black satchel. They're the rubies from the safe in my warehouse. That's not what catches my attention most, though. It's the fucker lying on the sofa, a hand pressed to his bloated belly, his balding head tipped back. He's in his underpants, which are stained brown and yellow from shit and piss, his knobby knees chalky. He's so fucked up that he doesn't even wake when we burst in. However, a naked woman in the corner screams at the top of her lungs, grabbing a dirty throw pillow to cover herself.

"Leave," I grumble, and she whimpers as she collects her clothes and rushes past me, Killian, and Rowan. Rowan stands on one side of the room behind me, Killian on the other, and they glance at me before marching ahead to run a perimeter check.

"Clear," Killian calls when they return.

I walk deeper into the house, kicking the slanted table in the middle of the room and causing Moren's foot to fall. He jerks awake, gasping, a ring of black powder on one of his nostrils.

"Oi. Sit up," I snap at him, and his eyes fill with panic when he realizes it's me. Yes, me. Not a friend. Not a neighbor. *Me*.

"Mr. Harlow—sir, to what do I owe the pleasure?"

Rowan moves past me, reeling his arm back and punching Moren in the face with a solid fist. I tip my chin as Moren yowls and clutches his face, trying to stop the blood now gushing from his nose.

"Spare me the manners, Moren. If you had even an ounce of respect for me, I wouldn't be here. Now, I know what you've done, and I'm here to make sure you never do it again."

"Sir..." he blubbers.

"On your knees. "I step around the table where my rubies are.

Moren looks from me, to Rowan, then to Killian, who I'm sure he doesn't want trouble with either but will have it if he doesn't do what I say. With slight hesitation, Moren drops to his knees in front of the table, and I walk around, clutching the steel rope in my hand.

I glare down at the top of his bald head. "Place one of your hands on the table."

"Please, Mr. Harlow. Just kill me. Kill me, please," he moans.

My eye twitches and I give the man a fuller look before pulling out my gun and tipping his chin with it, forcing him to look at me. Blood has spread over his upper lip, his eyes filled to the brim with tears.

"Kill me," he begs. "*Please.*"

"Now, Moren," I sigh. "Would killing you teach you a lesson?" I bring the barrel of my gun to his forehead. "Killing you is much too beneficial for the mistake you've made. There is no suffering in death. It all just *ends* for you, and you'll live your life in the afterworld, gleeful and robbing souls, and what comes of it, eh, Moren?" I look him hard in the eyes. "*Nothing,* that's what. Hand on the table."

Moren's right hand trembles as he places it flat on the tabletop, and I put my gun back in place, pulling out my steel rope and wrapping it around his forefinger and middle finger. He's crying, praying, but what's the point of prayers? They'll get him nowhere.

Without another moment of mercy, I slice two of his fingers off with the rope and he screams, throwing his head back and hitting the edge of the filthy couch. He cradles his bleeding hand to his chest, sobbing, and I'm not sure what it is about the act, but it causes a wrenching in the center of my chest, like something is grabbing my heart and twisting it. The pain angers me. It defies everything I've built, everything I stand for, and I'm normally not one to let anger control me, but this time I do.

I stand there staring at Moren, realizing how easy he has it, despite how fucking poor he is. He has this life with no burdens, no lies, no torment, no pain, and no Tether hanging above his head, and he goes and fucks it up by stealing from me. *Me?* The fucking Monarch of Blackwater! He's a fucking idiot who has it so easy—it's all so simple for him! Why does he abuse it?

I don't think as I bring a foot up and kick him in his face. I kick and stomp until my vision turns red, and it isn't until a pair of hands grip my shoulders to yank me back that I stop the angry assault. The hands burn through my coat, increasing my anger.

"Get your fucking hands off me!" I snatch myself away from the hands and turn to face Killian, pointing my gun at him. Killian doesn't flinch, but he frowns, glaring at me.

"This is not you, brother," he rasps, and I lower my gun, breathing raggedly. I look back at Moren, whose face is bloody and swelling, but he groans. Still alive.

I switch my gaze to Killian again, then Rowan, who wears every emotion on his face—concern, confusion, a little bit of fear. He's not afraid *of* me. He's afraid *for* me.

"All right, Caz?" Rowan asks.

I stare at them, men who are basically my brothers. Both of them stare at me with pity in their eyes, and why shouldn't they? I'm not like them. We're all monsters, yes, but I'm head of this beast and I'm nosediving, dragging them down with me.

Another wave of pain hits me, and I clutch my chest. I nearly buckle to my knees, but I catch myself. *You're weak. Pathetic. You're a worthless bloody bastard.* As I draw in a sharp breath, Rowan reaches for me, but I step away before he can and leave the house. Once I'm outside, I mount Onyx and ride away, refusing to look back.

SIXTY-ONE

WILLOW

"Maybe if you think about something from the Vakeeli place?" Faye is standing near the end of a shelf in the basement, staring at me. I'm in front of it, like I was last time, staring at empty black crates, mimicking my actions when I found myself in the forest. I even picked up one of the leftover bottles of wine, but that didn't help.

I've been thinking about Caz. What more can I possibly do to get there?

"I don't think it works that way," I tell her. "Every time it happened, it was random, but it seemed the more I heard him in my head and interacted with him mentally, the closer I was getting to his world. Now that he's blocking me out, I don't know if it'll work the same."

"Well, surely, there's a way you can get back. Maybe certain events lead you there." Faye taps her chin, looking around—her signature moves when she's hatching a plan. "Can you try talking to him right now?"

"Not really. My words come back to me, like they're bouncing off a wall."

"How can he do that?"

"I have no idea."

We both sigh. "Well, one thing *mi abuelita* Mariana always did when she wanted to escape reality was meditating," Faye offers. "For that, you need to be somewhere comfortable. Not in the basement of an old bookstore."

"Right." And I did consider that. I've tried closing my eyes and picturing myself in Vakeeli again. I've only been able to get through Silvera, and she's hunting again. She hasn't been around Caz. Maybe she will be soon, but until then I need to find a way there that isn't through a hungry wolf.

Faye pulls her phone out of her back pocket, checking the screen. "I'm off in an hour. How about I meet you at your place? I'll use the bookstore's data base to try to find books or guides that may be able to help us."

"You don't have to do that, Faye. I can imagine how silly all of this sounds to you."

"Are you kidding me? All of this shit is fascinating! I *want* to help." She smiles, stepping closer to me. "Someone has to look out for you, Willow."

I smile back, then a thought occurs. "Speaking of looking out, I wish you hadn't told Garrett about Warren."

Faye gives me a puzzled look, her head going into a slight tilt. "What are you talking about? I've never told Garrett anything about him."

That takes me by surprise. I've never told Garrett much about Warren either, and I *definitely* didn't tell him he was my twin—just that I had a brother. How would he have known it was his birthday too? And why did he lie about it? Has he read up on me?

Found something in my apartment he shouldn't have been reading? See—this is confirmation that he needs to get the hell out of my life. Something isn't right about him. All these thoughts ping pong in my brain until someone shouts Faye's name.

"Down here!" Faye shouts back.

A door creaks open and Valeria appears, popping her head in. "The UPS guy is here and needs you to sign off on a shipment."

"Right." Faye huffs, then turns to me. "I guess I'll see you in a bit."

AN HOUR AND A HALF LATER, Faye is walking through my apartment door with a stack of books in her arms. I'm so glad it's her and not Garrett. Knowing him, he would show up to apologize, but there's no forgiving what he's done. It's a toxic cycle, and I have to end it.

Faye dumps the books on my bed, then she's rushing out of the apartment again, returning with an oversized cupcake in a plastic container and a Happy Birthday balloon.

"Aw, Faye!" I smile as she places the cupcake on the kitchen counter and releases the string of the balloon, letting it bump the ceiling.

"I didn't forget." I can't help my smile as she shuffles around in a drawer for a lighter. When she finds one, she digs into the grocery bag she brought with her and pulls out a pack of birthday candles. She sticks one into the center of the cupcake, lights it, and tilts her gaze to me as she starts singing the Happy Birthday song.

I can't fight the stupid smile on my face as she does, and when it's time for me to blow out my candle, she says, "For Warren too."

I lock on her eyes a split second before lowering my gaze to the single pink candle and studying it. I close my eyes and think of my brother. I think of the birthday party we had when we were eight. Our father couldn't afford much, but he'd tried. He'd made pigs in a blanket, decorated the house with items and balloons from the dollar store, and baked us a boxed cake. We were able to bring one friend over—I invited Faye, and Warren invited his friend Terry. We played with our friends, played with balloons, ran around our apartment complex playing tag, and then came back for cake. It was one of the best birthdays we'd ever had, and I remember telling Warren that. That was the last year our father put any effort into our birthdays. After that, it was almost like he forgot the day we were born.

"Willow?" Faye's voice is soft, and when I open my eyes, my vision of her is blurry. There's only flickering gold light from the candle flame and my tears.

"Sorry," I whisper.

She walks around the counter, rubbing my back. "Stop apologizing," she reprimands. "I'd rather you get it out than bottle it in."

"I know, I just..." I wipe one of the tears away. "I really miss Warren, Faye. I miss him every day, and it hurts not having him here. He was my brother, yes, but he was also my best friend, and now he's gone. I have no idea where he is or if I'll ever see him again."

"I know." She wraps her arms around me, pulling my head to her shoulder. "I know, Willow. I'm sorry. But I'm here. You can talk about him to me whenever. I know days like this hurt."

They do hurt. More than she realizes. She holds me a few seconds longer, and I try not to let every tear shed. When I feel strong enough, I pull away, and she smiles at me, tilting her head. "Okay?"

"Yeah. I'm okay."

"Good. Now blow out your candle. The wax is dripping all over the cupcake!"

I laugh and bend down, making an internal wish before blowing it out. My wish is stupid, and highly unlikely, but I think it anyway. I wish to see Caz again.

SIXTY-TWO

WILLOW

"So, I used our database to find what I could about Tethers, whether fictional or non-fictional, and these are the only books that popped up," Faye says. We shared the cupcake, popped open a bottle of champagne she'd brought along, and now it's time to focus.

"Four books?"

"Yes, and only one is nonfiction, so the fictional ones may not even help, ya know, since they're made up and all." She sits on the edge of the bed, picking one of them up. "So, I guess let's start with the nonfiction."

Two hours later, and nothing. I don't want to give up hope, but we're down to the last book and haven't come across anything that can help us. The final book is thin, which doesn't give me much to look forward to, and Faye exhales, handing it to me.

"I would read it, but I promised to spend time with abuela tonight. She knows I'm off early today so she's expecting dinner with me. You can join us if you want. You know she always makes plenty."

"No, that's okay. I don't want to interrupt your bonding time, plus I should probably keep reading. Tell her I said hello though." I take the book from her and smile, though it's the last thing I want to do right now. If I can't find a way back to Caz, will I ever be able to return? Why could I hear him so clearly before, even when I ended up in a frozen state in the forest, yet I can't hear him now?

"Okay. Well, let me know if you find out anything." Faye collects her purse and keys. "I'm sorry I couldn't help more."

"Don't worry. It obviously just means I should put it all behind me."

Faye presses her lips a moment, gripping the knob of the door. "I don't believe that for a second." Then she twists the knob, walks out, and closes the door behind her. As she leaves, I hear thunder in the sky. Rain is on the way.

I stare at the front of the book. The author's name is Leah Bianchi, and the cover isn't very enthusiastic. It's solid blue, with the title *The Cold Hearted* in white font.

Sighing, I walk with the book to my bed and flop backwards, staring at the ceiling. I've resisted the urge to get high, to cling to some feeling of escape, worried it would prevent me from hearing Caz. Now, I'm thinking that's not the case. Being sober seems to make me feel further away from him.

I open my nightstand and pluck out a joint and a lighter, spark the end of it, and lie back, taking a long pull. After two more long pulls, I feel relaxation come over me, and my racing thoughts slow down. I close my eyes, hoping to hear Caz. If I think about him, maybe I'll see his face.

But I don't. I take another pull before putting out the joint and then picking up the book, flipping it open to the first page. At first, nothing about the book stands out. A woman meets a man in another universe, which I find intriguing and can surprisingly say I relate to. The first few chapters explain their love, their connection, her dire need to have kids. But when I reach the tenth chapter, the dialogue changes. No longer is the author speaking about her great love with her wonderful man in another realm in first person. She's switched to second person, and when I see the words *Freezing Cold Tether* as the title of the next chapter, goosebumps crawl up my arms.

I spring up in the bed, reading the title of the new page again. The next sentence asks, **Is this you?**

You traveled to another universe, one unlike your own. You landed in a place unknown and were approached by someone who instantly connected with you. This person took you in, made you feel at home, and you fell in love. Everything in this world felt wrong but being with that significant other felt right. You only wanted to be with them.

And then something sent you away. Like the snap of fingers, you're gone, back to your world, yet all you can think about is your other half. Your soulmate. Your *Tether*.

You think for a while you don't belong together. The truth is, you do. And there is something in this world trying to stop your bond. I've concluded that a bond such as this one is too powerful for a single world, so it has split itself into different worlds. And due to some greater power—greater than anything I've ever imagined—we travel to this other world to

merge and form a bond. And this bond possesses good energy. It's pure, and wholesome, and it thrives and breathes…

But, of course, with anything that is good, along comes the bad.

The bad will rip you apart. The bad *will* lie. The bad will tell you that you don't belong, and you will believe it. Then the bad will attempt to kill you while you're apart because it is when you are most vulnerable. Apart, is when it truly feeds.

How do I know this? Because I've witnessed it. My love, my Tethered, was taken from me. I traveled back to his land, to his home, and there he lay on the floor; however, he was not himself. He was a hollow, sunken version of himself. His eyes were gone and had turned into black holes, as black and deep as a literal blackhole, and his mouth was ajar, as if he'd been screaming as whatever this evil being was sucked the life from him.

And then I heard it return. As if it'd sensed my presence, I felt the cold wrap around me, sinking into my bones, and I fled. I ran with tears in my eyes, begging for my world to swallow me back up, and it did.

Wrapped in a blue light, I returned home, but not without seeing that evil being. The red eyes, black body, black claws. It looked right at me, as if proving it would come for me next.

It'd taken my love. It'd taken half of me. And what they don't tell you is that when your Tether dies, so do you, just not right away. You weaken first, and you don't eat. You don't sleep. Your organs begin to freeze, and then they fail you. You always feel cold, even during summer. It lasts for months, a slow torture constantly reminding you of what you've lost.

As I write this, I'm on my deathbed, hoping what I have to say will help someone else out there with an unpredictable life such as mine.

Whatever you do, don't walk away from your Tether. Don't resist or fight it. Let it be. Don't give in to the lies that what you have is unnatural. It is as natural and wondrous as nature. Stay with your other, give in to it, or the coldness will follow suit. Together, you can defeat this evil. There is always an answer, and you must find it.

I EXHALE, staring at the passage, reading it repeatedly. This woman...she was just like me.

I scramble for my phone and do a quick Google search of the author. She's a beautiful Indian woman, born in New Jersey. She can't be any older than thirty, but her eyes look wise beyond their years. A link of her obituary appears, and in one of the images, she's holding up her book and smiling weakly. She's in a hospital bed wearing a chunky sweater, with dark circles around her eyes. She looks beaten and worn down, not like the other images of her on the internet. She died seventeen years ago—long before I'd even heard Caz's voice.

"So, I was right," I whisper to myself. The Tether doesn't make us weaker; it makes us stronger. But this completely contradicts everything Beatrix told us, which leads me to wonder who is telling the truth? And if Beatrix isn't, why the hell would she lie to us?

Lightning strikes the sky, and the lights in my apartment flicker. The rain falls harder, pitter-pattering on the windows.

How can I tell Caz what I read? If he's blocking me, how can I fill him in? There must be a way I can get back. How did Leah get the chance to go back?

Silvera. She's my only hope.

I clear my throat and sit on the middle of my bed, crossing my legs and closing my eyes. I think of my wolf, and at first nothing comes to mind. There's just darkness behind my eyelids—no images, no noise. Silence.

Then, gradually, I see something. Trees. Lots of them, towering above.

I hear breathing. She's panting. Paws beating into the land as she dashes through the forest, her heart pounding wildly.

"Hi, girl," I whisper, and I feel her heartbeat quicken. She feels me. "Still hunting?"

Silvera runs until she's made it to a river. She laps up some water then sits on her hind.

"Can you go back to Caz?"

She looks all around. The water trickles quietly, the tall blades of black grass swaying. The sun is nowhere in sight. It's gray, yet the boldness of the green leaves on the trees brings a soothing beauty. I think of what Alora said, about finding the beauty in Blackwater. She's right. I see it now in the dips and curves of the land, the dark sparkling waters, and swaying green leaves.

Silvera rises and leaves the river, dashing through the forest, and I squeeze my eyes tighter, not wanting to lose her. Within the span of ten minutes, she's running through a field that leads to Caz's castle. She curves around a corner, where a small door leads inside.

Huffing, she enters the house, and as she crosses a mud room full of black boots caked in mud, coats, and sweaters, we hear voices, loud and boisterous. Panic is in the air, and I feel Silvera's ears perk up as she slowly walks around a corner and into the large living area.

Four people stand in the room. Two are next to each other, Maeve and Rowan, and two of them are face to face, shouting. Killian and Juniper.

"I don't know where the fuck he ran off to, now lay off!" Killian barks in Juniper's face.

"Why would you let him out of your sight?" Juniper demands, shoving his chest. Anger seizes Killian and he stands taller, trying to intimidate Juniper, but he fails. "We told you not to let Caz out of your sight, and you let him go anyway! He isn't in the right state of mind right now! You never should've let him go to Moren!"

"I can't control Caz, and I'm not his keeper! We told him it wasn't a good idea, but he wanted to deal with Moren right away, so we went with him."

"You *are* his keeper! We all are!" she shouts back.

Maeve steps up to them, pressing a hand to both their chests. "You two shut up and sit down," she orders, but Juniper and Killian don't back away from each other. They're stubborn, refusing to be the first to move.

"Mum, if we don't find Caz, he'll hurt himself. I know it," Juniper pleads.

"Okay, but what comes of barking in each other's faces?" Maeve demands.

"She started with me," Killian growls.

"Oh, grow up, you big baby," Juniper shoots back.

"*Sit. Down.*" Maeve says the words through clenched teeth, and Killian shakes his head, turning away and sitting in one of the steel chairs, while Juniper folds her arms and sits on the leather sofa. "Now, which direction did he go?"

"West, from Moren's home," Rowan answers. He's standing in a corner, arms folded across his chest. I'd think he doesn't care about Caz's whereabouts if it weren't for the look in his eyes. It's not fear, more so worry. Just like Juniper.

"Have we tried his transmitter?" Maeve demands.

"Yes. He left it here," Killian responds.

"Damn it," she hisses. She turns and notices Silvera standing near the entrance of the room, and her brows pull together. "Is that Willow's wolf?"

"Yes. She comes and goes," Juniper murmurs.

"Do you think she's still connected?" asks Maeve.

"I'm not sure," replies Juniper. "It doesn't seem like it."

"So why is she still here? She's a wild wolf. They don't stay around humans for long...not unless they need to." Maeve walks toward Silvera in her long black gown, dropping to one knee and stroking the top of her head. "Once a wolf is connected to its owner, it stays with the owner. Which must mean Willow is still here somehow." Maeve looks deeply into Silvera's eyes—*my* eyes—and cocks her head ever so slightly.

"Are you here, Willow?"

"Mum, you're wasting your time," Rowan mutters.

"Silvera, give her your paw," I order.

Silvera does as told, lifting a paw and placing it on Maeve's arm. Maeve blinks down at the paw, stunned. "You're still here," she breathes. "You didn't give up." She says the last part to me. "You're still here."

My heart beats faster, and as badly as I want to cry, I bite my bottom lip and hold it in. "We need you back, Willow. We need you to find Caz."

Silvera barks, pulling away from Maeve, and Maeve stands up straight.

"Wait—Silvera, stay! Stay, girl!" The urgency drips from my voice, but she leaves the room anyway. I'm losing control of her now. Where is she going?

Silvera runs back out the door she came through. It's misting outside, and the micro droplets cling to her fur. I feel it on my skin, as if I'm there, but she's leading me, and though I've lost control, I sense she knows what she's doing. I trust her, so I stay quiet and let her go.

She dashes toward the forest where I dropped, paws pounding into the soil, until she stops in the same spot I was taken to before—where my portal is. Then she looks up and howls, and her howl echoes through me. It's loud and deafening, and when she stops, footsteps sound behind her.

Maeve, Rowan, Juniper, and Killian stop abruptly, about a foot away, staring at Silvera, and a sharp gasp falls from Juniper's lips before she cups her mouth.

"Willow?" she whispers. It sounds like she's in my room. I hear her voice, so close to me. I slowly open my eyes. I'm still seated on my bed, legs crossed, but my bed is now in the middle of the forest, and there is Caz's family, staring at me.

I look down at the purple haze radiating off my body and my bed.

"She's not physically here," Maeve says, taking a step closer. "But she is mentally. And she can go with her wolf."

I climb off the bed, but I feel weightless, like I'm floating. However, I feel the wet soil too, on my bare feet.

"Can you all hear me?" I ask, and Maeve nods.

Juniper's chin is practically on the ground, as well as Rowan's, and Killian holds steady, but I can tell he wants to react too.

"How do I find him?" I step closer to Maeve. She tries touching me, but her hand goes right through me. As if I'm a ghost—a passenger in this world.

"Your time is running out. Caspian must already be pulling away, and if he does that..." Maeve works hard to swallow, fighting tears. "Have Silvera find Cerberus. If you're Tethered to Caspian, then she shares a link with Cerberus." I drop my eyes to Silvera, who waits eagerly at my side.

"I'll find him," I tell Maeve, then I look at the rest of them, pressing a hand to the center of my chest. "I can feel him. He's in pain."

"Please hurry," Juniper pleads.

I nod, then turn to Silvera. She licks my hand as I try to pet her, and when I mentally give her the command to find Cerberus, she whips her head to the right, sniffs the air, then dashes away.

I follow her, looking back once at Caz's family before pointing my gaze ahead. I may not be here physically, but if they can see me, he can see me, and that should be enough. At least for now.

SIXTY-THREE

CAZ

THE WEIGHT of the gun feels too heavy in my hand. I can hardly lift it. Ever since leaving Moren's, a weakness has plagued me that's unlike anything I've ever felt before.

When I try bringing the gun to my head, it rolls out of my hand, clattering to the ground. I breathe in, exhale, and Cerberus whines at my feet.

My eyes move around the cabin, focused on the bare wooden walls, the green vines threading across them. The vines have taken over the place, and I swore to myself I'd take care of it, but it won't be long before the vines consume it entirely.

My eyes shift to the kitchen, where my mother used to cook. She'd hum her songs and knead the dough to bake fresh bread. Then she'd pull it out of the oven, slice several pieces for me, and bring it out to the garden, where I studied.

Her bread was good—sweet, but not too sweet. She'd sit with me, eat bread smothered with blackberry jam, then when I was done with my studies, she'd take me through the garden to pick out vegetables for dinner.

The memory slashes through me, and I close my eyes as the throbbing in my chest worsens. This pain isn't dull anymore. It's as sharp as the point of a knife, digging deeper and deeper into my flesh, ready to cut me in half. And the cold—the cold is like nothing I've ever felt before. It's in my bones, slithering through my bloodstream like ice. No matter how many coats or quilts I wear, I can't get warm.

I lift an arm, focusing on the black veins running down them. They slither to my hands now, dark and bold.

I lean forward, reaching for the gold tonic. My fingers tremble as I bring the cup to my lips and sip. It eases the pain, only temporarily.

Drunk and weak. That's what I am. Weak and pathetic, just like my father told me I'd be—just like *all of them* said I would be. It's impossible to deny fate, isn't it? Such simple words can haunt you until the day you die, and there's nothing you can do about it. Even in death, I'll be remembered as such.

I lie on my side, reaching for a black tablet on the table and bringing it to my mouth, gulping it down. If I die, I'd rather be alert. Dying in my sleep is too easy. I'd prefer to feel the pain. The black tablet keeps me awake, aware.

I close my eyes, hoping this is it. I plead to no one in particular, begging to be taken out of this world...out of this land.

Don't let the people I love find me. Don't let them see me like this.

Another chill shoots through me and I shiver. Cerberus growls and barks at the door as it swings open and slams into the wall. Through my periphery, I notice something black standing between the frames. A gust of wind swirls through the cabin, charging the atmosphere, and I turn my head just enough to see it. Its eyes are crimson red, its hands at its sides. The talons of it are revealed, sharp and twitching, as if aching for a touch.

Mournwrath.

The cabin becomes colder, and I shiver more. It's come for me. It's come to rob me of this torturous Tether. I close my eyes, listening as it approaches. Closer. *Closer.*

But then I hear a voice.

Caz, I'm here.

My eyes pop open, and the black figure stands only a few steps away, it's dark cape billowing in the cold wind. The inside of the cabin is now cloaked in ice that splinters across the walls and floors.

I sit up and look out the open door.

Show me where you are. Willow. Her voice rings through me, and that weakness I'd once claimed disappears. I stare at the dark figure as it stretches one of its taloned hands toward me.

"What are you waiting for?" I demand.

It doesn't move, and I realize this is clearly my choice. This is not an attack. It's a request of submission. If he touches me, I go. I'll leave this world, and all will fade.

But if I stay...

I use as much strength as my body will allow and climb off the couch, walking through the cabin and past the dark figure. When I reach the door, I look back at it, curious why I've been given the choice. I assumed there was none—that it'd come for me and be done with it.

"Go to her, and you'll die." Its voice is hollow. It crackles, echoes. It's a threat that feels anything but.

"I don't believe you."

It remains floating, reaching.

"Come with me. Make this simple...unless you wish to suffer."

"Caz!" Willow's voice is growing louder. She's close. I can feel her. Wherever she is, my body senses it. She beckons to me, and I have the sweet, sweet yearning to be with her.

"Well, if I must suffer," I murmur, dropping my gaze. "I'd rather it happen while I'm in her arms."

The cold wraps me up further as Mournwrath raises its hand higher. I feel the weight of its pull like a magnet, reeling me backward, but with one loud yell—one that slaps the air like a clap of thunder—I break the pull and stumble out of the cabin, hurrying to find my mate.

SIXTY-FOUR

WILLOW

SILVERA'S PACE picks up from a trot to a run.

"Wait!" I scream. If she goes any faster, I won't be able to keep up. She doesn't wait—she keeps running, maneuvering between the trees, jumping over dense, mossy logs.

"Willow!"

I gasp and stop running when I hear the voice. *His* voice.

"Willow, do ya hear me?"

"Caz," I whisper. It's just like the dream. I look all around me, his voice filling the void, then I look down at my arm, at the purple haze that's beginning to fade. My brown skin is breaking through. I'm returning to his world—to him. It's not too late.

I'm close.

I run in the direction Silvera went, as hard and as fast as I can. Darkness descends, swallowing the trees behind me, chasing me, but I keep running, refusing to let it catch me. The wind whips at my face, my locs, and a chill strikes me in my stomach. It takes everything in me not to double over in pain. I glance back as the darkness climbs behind me, moving faster. I clutch my belly with one hand and don't stop. My lungs work harder. They feel like they're freezing inside me.

Shit. Perhaps I was wrong. Maybe Leah Bianchi was wrong too. It could be possible that this Tether doesn't make you stronger at all, and what Beatrix said wasn't a lie.

"Willow!" Caz's voice is louder. Closer.

"I'm here!" I scream. The darkness is blinding now. My purple light is fading. The cold begins to paralyze me, my toes becoming numb, the soles of my bare feet pounding into the ground.

I'm here. I'm here. The thought is fleeting. I hope he can hear it.

And just when I feel I'll be engulfed in darkness and cold, swallowed whole by this evil that doesn't want us together, I spot Silvera, and her body clashes with a blur of black fur. Cerberus. And not too far behind Cerberus is Caz.

He's wearing his trench coat, no shirt beneath. His chest—the black veins that have taken over his pale body are prominent, but that's not what catches me off guard. It's the way he looks right now—his face sunken in and hollow, the dark bruises around his eyes, most likely from lack of sleep.

He's dying and Mournwrath is lingering, trying to take him before I can get to him.

When he sees me, my heart slows in rhythm, but I don't stop running, and neither does he. Every second counts. No breath can be wasted.

We run, racing against darkness, racing against the cold. The mist in the air clings to my skin, ice shooting through my limbs, but I don't care because he's here. I'm here.

And when we meet, we clash. We clash hard, my arms locking around his neck, his going around my middle. He holds me close, and I squeeze my eyes closed, waiting for the pain to sweep through me, waiting for the dark cold to steal us away and suck us dry.

"I'm here," I whisper. His body is chilly against mine, like a slab of ice. And then I hear voices above me—so many voices.

I open my eyes, and a cloud of purple swirls us. Caz grunts, as if he's been struck by something, but I hold on to him. Like we're in the eye of a hurricane, the thick cloud spins faster, faster, and three-dimensional figures pop out of the clouds.

A boy, holding the hand of a woman.

A boy, a little bit older, yanked away from her by a large man. The boy cries and reaches for his mother. She fights to get him back, screams, but someone covers her mouth and she faints.

The boy being tossed into the back of a wagon.

The boy alone in a dark cell, crying, whimpering.

Then, people are hollering, waving their fists in the air, and in the middle of the mad crowd are two boys fighting each other. Bones crunch and blood spills, as if they're fighting to the death.

With one punch from the opponent, the boy falls backward. He's taken back to a dark cell, holding his knees to his chest, trembling with fear.

The boy stands, a gunshot goes off, and he cries out, "Mama!" as he holds his chest. I wince. He bleeds as he crumbles to the floor, then another man enters the cell, giving the boy a tiny bottle, demanding him to drink it.

The boy drinks, and when he sits up, the bullet wound heals quickly. *Bang.* Another gunshot. The boy cries. Forced to drink another tiny bottle.

Another fight.

Another loss.

Back in the cell. A man enters, using a sharp razor to slice the boy's abdomen. The boy cries, another tiny bottle is handed to him, he heals instantly. Another slice of the razor.

It's a repetitive cycle, and with each gunshot, each slice of the razor on his skin, he's getting older, becoming a man.

People are around him again, shouting, waving fists, and the boy, I realize, is Caz. He can't be any older than fifteen or sixteen. He's in the middle of the ring, fighting a guy much larger than he is.

Blood gushing, bone crunching. He wins this time, and his arm is thrown in the air by the referee, despite the blood dripping out of his mouth.

Another vision appears, the boy sitting in a pristine room, a man standing by the door. "Where is my mother?" the boy demands.

The man leaves the room, slamming the door behind him.

Another vision, Caz standing on a dark shore in front of an ocean, dressed head to toe in black. A flat black cap is on his head, and beside him is an older woman. Maeve. Behind him, Juniper, Killian, and Rowan. Ahead of him, a body wrapped in black cloth, lying on top of a wooden board. Someone lights the body on fire and Caz watches the body float aimlessly across the ocean until he can no longer see it.

"You're safe now," Maeve tells him, her hand on his shoulder.

He pulls away from her, leaving the grave.

More gunshots.

More screaming.

More crying.

But none of it is happening *to* him. It's happening *because of* him.

I suck in a breath, and Caz groans again and buckles, but I catch him as the purple hurricane roars harder. It's all his inner turmoil being unleashed. All his rage, his bitterness, his pain...it's all here, laid out in front of me.

I clasp his face in my hands, giving him my attention again. "I see now. I understand."

"You shouldn't have come back," he says, looking away.

"Yes, I should have."

He finds my eyes, stares into them, then clutches my face in his hands too, his nostrils flaring.

"I'm no good for you, Willow," he rasps. "You can't be with me."

"I can," I counter.

He shakes his head, denying it, trying to pull his face out of my hands, but I hold steady.

"I *can*," I repeat, and he stops fighting me. Our gazes hold, and instead of cold this time, a blazing heat courses through me. Every chain wrapped around my heart breaks, and it comes alive.

This vulnerable act, us as one...I understand it now. Something this powerful is impossible to withstand. It's this moment that I understand what Leah was talking about in her book.

This Tether, it literally will make or break us, and if that's the case, we should choose for it to mend us. Every fragile, broken piece of us can be solidified with this bond. These vicious bonds that I never knew existed, they're here, dwelling in two sad, lonely people, combining into one cosmic union.

We're right where we need to be—at the right place, at the right time. Hardly knowing each other yet trusting that being together is the solution to our broken souls.

"You're right," Caz murmurs, his mouth moving closer to mine. He bows his head, and the hollowness in his face has filled again. He's being restored, back to the way he was. The man he was when I first met him. The bruises around his eyes fade, and color rises to his cheeks.

Let me in, I beg, holding his gaze.

I can't lose you too.

You won't.

He sighs, pursing his lips. **You don't need my permission to be let in.** His eyes fall to my mouth. **You're already here, within me. You've been here, long before we ever even met.** His voice swims through my mind, and I cave to them.

Our lips collide, and the hurricane of turmoil loses speed. The darkness that was chasing us fades away, and the longer I hold on to him, the more I feel myself opening—blossoming like a flower breaking through concrete.

A pressure builds at the center of my chest, but it's not one of pain. It's one filled to the brim with passion—a passion so profound I can feel it in the depths of my soul.

This connection is hard to explain. It can only be experienced. Never in my life have I felt so sure about something—or *someone*, rather. Yet this man in my arms, this man kissing me, holding me, filling my mind with his sweet, aching words—**You're in. We're one. I'm yours. You're mine.**—well, I'm sure about this.

Apart and in denial, the Tether will kill us. But together, in truth and harmony, we can thrive if we fight for it. And here we are, choosing the latter.

SIXTY-FIVE

WILLOW

THE WORLD IS JUST as it was. Well, *this* world anyway. The trees hover just as high as they did before, only the air is much clearer. There's a peace surrounding us that wasn't here prior. The darkness that loomed is completely gone.

Daylight remains, and the frogs croak, birds tweeting carefree songs while the leaves rustle in the wind, like nothing ever happened—as if we weren't almost swallowed whole by a hurricane of darkness.

Caz stands next to me, his head back and his face pointed up at the sky. His eyes are closed, and I watch as the youth slowly comes back to him. He inhales, and after exhaling, he drops his head and takes my hand.

"Come with me." He leads the way through the trees, stepping over wet leaves and grass, until he pushes a bush out of the way, revealing a small cabin.

The cabin is one story and can't be any bigger than an apartment. And that's me being generous. It's roped in green vines that wrap around every corner and even touch the roof. The front door is wide open; however, it's dark inside and I can't see much. Not too far from the cabin, tied to a tree, is a black stallion with a sleek black mane. It's just like the horse in that portrait from his mansion. A beauty. It stomps its thick hooves, huffs, then bows its head.

"Wait here." Caz leaves my side, walking ahead cautiously. I believe this is the first time I've seen him not carrying a gun. He approaches the door, takes a look inside, then turns to me and says, "Mournwrath was here."

"What?" My heart beats a little faster.

"I think it left. But I saw it. That darkness that was chasing you...I think that was it." Caz gestures for me to come. Sensing my hesitation, he says, "It's not here. And even if it were, I wouldn't let anything happen to you."

His words are enough for now. I walk ahead, taking his hand and walking up the stoop. He doesn't have gloves on, which I find all too surprising, and I look at him to see if he'll realize it. I think for a moment he'll read my mind, notice our hands touching and take his away, but his eyes avert to the open door of the cabin again. I let the thought pass me, fighting a satisfied smile.

The inside of the cabin can't be any bigger than my studio. A worn two-seater sofa is against the east wall, and on the west wall, a bed pressed against viny wood. A kitchen is straight ahead, equipped with a stove and sink, but I don't see a fridge. A two-top table with black tiles for the surface is wedged between the kitchen space and living area. There's bedding on the bed, a black sheet with a thick brown quilt folded at the bottom, and another quilt on the sofa, white with green threading.

I step deeper into the tiny cabin, and I'm not sure what it is about it, but it feels like *home*. Like I belong here...or like I've been here before.

"Watch your step there," he says, pointing at the floor. The floor is made of wood and one of the planks is splintered, as if someone stepped there before, creating the fracture.

"What is this place?" I ask.

Caz turns, then sighs. "It was me mum's place."

"Your mom?"

He nods, then walks across the cabin to the kitchen. "It's wedged between Blackwater and Whisper Grove. Not very easy to find." He swings open a cabinet above the stove and collects a silver flask, offering it to me.

"Water," he says.

I take it, unscrewing the cap and chugging some down. The water has a minty aftertaste, like the youth water. It's nice and cool, and I take a few more sips before giving the flask back to him. He drains it, then places it on the tile table.

"Why did you come here?" I ask as he stands by the table, his back to me.

"To get away."

"From what?"

He side-eyes me. "Everything."

"Your family is looking for you."

"I don't need them looking for me."

"They care about you, Caz."

He says nothing to that. Instead, he strips out of his coat and places it over the back of one of the steel chairs. He stands there, shirtless, his skin creamy between the black veins.

"Will those go away?"

"Not sure." He moves to a small door, swings it open, and takes out a long-sleeved shirt that looks to be made of black silk. When he slides his arms into it, he leaves the front of it unbuttoned, then digs into his back pocket, pulling out a platinum case. He takes a bloom out of it.

"How did you get back?" He sits at the table and lights the end of the bloom. He offers one to me from the case, but I shake my head.

"I thought of Silvera."

"You did, eh?" He takes another pull, then releases a cloud of smoke. "Didn't know it worked that way." He pauses, looking me all over. "And how'd you find me?"

"I followed her. Maeve told me Silvera might be linked to Cerberus, and I assume she found you through him."

"Hmm." He takes a few more pulls, releases the smoke, then grabs the ashtray on the table, stabbing the lit end out and killing the flame. "You weren't supposed to come back, Willow."

"I know, but I've been worried."

"About me?" He scoffs, a humorless smile riding his lips.

"Is it so hard to believe people actually care about you?"

His eyes flicker from the ashtray to mine, and he raises his chin. I realize that's a statement of bad timing. After seeing how he was treated in those hurricane visions, I get why he's afraid to trust.

"It was foolish of you to return. The Tether. It could kill us."

"I don't believe that anymore."

"And what makes you say that?"

"Because I found a book from my world. A woman talked about the same Tether we have—the Cold Tether. She believes those who are Tethered are *supposed* to be together. She says when she left the other world and went back to see her lover, he was dead."

He narrows his eyes briefly before dropping his hands. "Juniper thinks the same." He taps a finger on the tabletop. "Maeve sent her to speak to Alora and Beatrix behind my back."

"Why would Beatrix tell us to stay away from each other if we're actually supposed to be around each other?"

"I'm not sure, but either she's a liar or she had reason to warn us."

I sit against the back of the chair and take another look around the cabin. It's quiet here. Cozy. I can see why he came to this place.

"Does anyone else know about this place?"

"No one but you."

I don't know how that makes me feel, but it's not bad. I'm quiet another moment before asking, "Where is your mom now?"

He doesn't react on the outside, but I feel the heavy clench in his chest and the nerves shooting into his stomach. "No longer here." He pushes out of his chair, walking across the cabin, his boots thumping on the wood. He tosses logs into the fireplace and then lights a match, starting a fire.

"I saw you with the gun in your office." I stand but keep a distance between us. Sort of hard to do when we're in a house the size of a bedroom.

"I own lots of guns."

"You know what I mean."

He drops his head, agitated. "Just let it be."

"No, I won't just *let it be*." I walk closer, minimizing the gap between us. "Why do you want to die so badly?"

He turns to me. "What is there to live for? You've seen my world. It's cruel, and I didn't sign up for any of this shit."

"Sure, it's cruel, but you clearly bring order to it. If you go, who else will do it?

"There are plenty of people out there who can do a much better job than I can."

"There may be, but right now it's *you*. You're the one in charge. You're the one who can make the differences."

"I'm not in charge by choice. This role isn't something I went after. It was shoved into my hands."

I let his words marinate before walking around him. I stand in front of him and start to reach for his hands, but he stops me, clasping my wrists and holding them in the air.

"There's only so much I can take," he rasps.

"Do you mean of my touch?"

His eyes roam my face. "It doesn't feel like the others."

My head tilts. "How do you mean?"

"I mean...it doesn't...*burn* like the others. Doesn't hurt."

"No? So what does it feel like?"

His mouth twitches, and he strokes the flesh inside my wrists with the pads of his thumbs. I don't even think he realizes he's doing it as he looks into my eyes, trying to find the answer. Or maybe he won't answer me at all. Either way, I wait.

I don't understand...

"Understand what?"

He frowns and releases my wrists. "Get out of my head."

"I can't help what I hear. Tell me what you don't understand."

He sighs, a pained expression taking over his face. "I don't understand how it's all so different with you. It's as if my whole life has been a lie after meeting you."

"The Tether, apparently," I say, laughing a little. "That's what makes it different."

He looks like he wants to laugh, but he doesn't. Still, his eyes are lighter, his features not so heavy and somber.

"It's far too easy." He grabs my hands again, this time entwining our fingers. As he does, he brings me in closer until our bodies collide.

"What's wrong with it being easy?" I raise my chin, angling my lips. I want his lips again.

"Nothing in my life is ever this easy. What if I *do* die because you were too stubborn to listen?"

"Then we find a way to prevent that before it happens."

"And if there's no way?"

"Then...if you die, I die, and we go together."

My words seem like a slap to his face because he winces, but our eyes hold.

"You don't need your red pills," I whisper.

"Not with you, apparently. But I will need constraint."

"From what?"

His eyes spark. "*Ravishing* you."

"When's the last time you..." I swallow the rest of the words, but of course he hears them, and for the first time since meeting him, he cracks a smile, revealing a beautiful set of white teeth. He's so gorgeous when he smiles. "You find that funny, huh?" I laugh.

"Why does asking about my last time embarrass you?" His knees gently bump into my thighs, forcing me back. The backs of my legs hit the edge of the bed, and I gasp as I fall on it. When I'm seated, he's on top of me in an instant, cradling one side of my face in his hands.

"I don't know," I breathe as his mouth moves closer to mine.

"It was ages ago," he says on the hollow of my neck. "Fuck, why do I want to be *inside* you so badly right now? The way I'm feeling isn't normal. Is this what happens when you cave to your Tether?"

I'm not sure how to answer that, but that feeling he has, I feel it too. Every sense of mine is heightened now, all my desires bared. I want to blame it on the Tether, but it wouldn't be completely that, would it?

"You're changing the subject."

"Fine. Six months ago."

"That's not ages," I argue.

"It is to me."

I roll my eyes, and he dips his head back, looking at me. "You're angering yourself thinking about it."

"I'm not." Still, I'm annoyed.

"There's nothing to worry yourself about. For the last person, I needed *many* red pills to even take the edge off."

I want that answer to satisfy me, but it doesn't. What the hell? Since when have I become so jealous over what a man does? Never in my life have I cared what a man has done with his body, but Caz is different. His body, somehow, feels like it should only belong to me. He shouldn't share it, but knowing that he has…

"Who the fuck is Garrett?" he demands, frowning now.

"What?"

"You're thinking about your last time with a fucker named Garrett," he snaps, tipping his head back to get a fuller look at me.

"No, I'm not."

"You are. I hear you."

"Hmm. I guess that makes it fair then."

Caz's frown grows deeper, and I hear a growl building in the base of his throat. ***I'll rip his fucking heart out. She's mine. Fuck him.***

"We didn't know each other before you came here," he says, as if trying to justify it. "So long as it doesn't happen anymore."

"You're jealous."

He grunts, then plants an elbow outside my head. As he does, he scans my body with his eyes. "Do you wear these clothes around him?"

"Sometimes," I murmur. A tank top and pink shorts. No bra. I'd changed into the outfit when Faye and I started reading.

"Don't ever wear them around him again."

"Or what?" I challenge. Not that I'll wear this around him anymore. I never want to see Garrett again.

"Or I'll find a way to your world and fill his head with my bullets."

"You won't have to worry about that, trust me. But you should really get that temper of yours under control."

Caz looks down as I draw in a breath. His hand skims down my waist and I watch as he traces his fingers across the pink band, then drops his head, planting his lips on the hollow of my neck.

"I can't do this," he finally whispers.

"Why not?"

"I just...*can't*. It won't do either of us any good." A pause. "You should go back home."

Ugh. Why must he still put up a fight? I mean, I get that he's wary about the Tether, but come on. "What if I don't want to go back home? What if I want to be here? With you?"

He picks up his head, eyeing me. "Then I'd tell you what you want is unjust."

"For myself?"

"No," he says, and a breath falls through his parted lips. "For me. Staying here is suicide for you. If anyone outside of the people in my circle find out about you and me, that's not only a threat for myself, but you as well. I'm used to it, but I can't have that with you."

"Then we keep it here...right?"

"Not sure. Rami came close to knowing. Who's to say no one else noticed?" My breath hitches as he drags his hand down, farther, farther, until it's between my thighs. "I've never touched another person as much as this without..." He wrenches my thighs apart, gliding his fingers along the flesh inside of one of them. "No burning. No pain. Just...*pleasure*. I never thought it'd be possible."

I sit up as he does, and I sense that he wants to pull away. I hear him battling himself, wanting to retract, but finding it hard to. I don't want him to.

"Can I try something with you?" I ask.

He cuts his eyes to me. "Try what?"

I bite into my bottom lip, too nervous to say it out loud. My face becomes hot when the thought hits him, and when he gets a whisper of the idea, it registers all over his face. His eyes are rounder, brighter, and he blinks several times as he digests it.

He sits up straighter on the edge of the bed, drawing in a breath. "All right then."

I climb off the bed, moving in front of him. One of my knees presses outside his thigh, and I cradle one side of his face in my hands.

Trust me?

His eyes soften. ***I do.***

I hold his blue eyes a moment, and he stares back into mine, then I drop my leg and climb on the bed to get behind him. While he faces forward, I spread my legs outside of his, so my feet are dangling off the bed, then I guide my arms beneath his, wrapping them around his waist. From behind, I spread his shirt open a bit, splaying my fingers on his bare chest.

His breaths become ragged as my palms rest on his body, but I don't stop. I inch them farther down, spreading them over his abs and resting my cheek on his shoulder blade. He shudders as I reach for his belt buckle, then he rapidly grips my hand. I freeze, breathing evenly, and he slowly releases my hand, putting his back at his side.

I continue unbuckling his belt and listening to his heartbeat through his back. When the buckle is undone and the pants unbuttoned and unzipped, I lower them just enough to reach his briefs. He lifts his hips a bit, helping me get them down. When they are, I pull out his dick, freeing it, and he expels a trapped breath, dropping his head to watch what I'm doing.

"Is this too much?" I whisper, lifting my head.

"No." His voice is thick with arousal. "Keep going."

I wrap my hand around his hardening dick, sliding my thumb over the tip. It's wet with pre-cum, and I use it to dampen the head. I lower my hand and, slowly, I stroke him, working from the base to the top. As I swivel my wrist, his dick grows twice as hard in my palm.

"Has this been done to you before?"

"No. I don't let anyone touch me like this."

"And this doesn't hurt?" I ask, still going.

"Not at all." He places the back of his head on my shoulder, exposing his neck. He smells like sweet tobacco and ocean air. I place my lips on the crook of his neck, and he groans, body tensing.

"You'll make me come."

"That's the goal."

"I don't want to come in your hand." He reaches down, grabbing my hand and hissing as one of my fingers slips over the tip. Then he turns to face me again, laying me back and spreading my legs apart. He lowers himself, dragging his lips from my chest to my navel until I feel the heat of his mouth above my pussy.

"What are you doing?"

"Do you think it'll feel like a normal orgasm when I make you come?" Not if, *when*. "Or do you think, since we're Tethered and all, that the sensation will be heightened?"

"I—I don't know," I breathe.

"Shall we find out?"

Caz's mouth lowers and he kisses the lips of my pussy outside my shorts. He does this repeatedly until I find it hard to distinguish which is wetter—me, or my panties.

Finally, he uses a finger to move my shorts aside, and all that's left is the damp barrier of my panties. A guttural sound rips through him, and it travels through my body as he kisses the cotton fabric. The heat of his mouth is unbearable, and I twist below him. He presses a hand to my belly, silently demanding me to be still, to let him do this, and I gasp as he uses the other hand to shift my panties aside too.

"You're already wet," he rasps.

"Am I?"

A deep chuckle fills the cabin, and before I know it, his mouth is coming down and he's devouring me. Shit. He just goes straight for it and I knew it was coming, but I'm still not prepared.

His lips are hot, his tongue hotter as it wrestles with my clit. I clutch the bedsheets and a shrill gasp breaks out of me as I buck my hips, and as if he's taming a wild horse, he grips me and doesn't relent. His tongue feels incredibly delicious running over my clit, then sliding downward to enter my pussy. He guides a finger up and begins to fuck me with it while lapping his tongue around my swelling clit.

Pulling his mouth away, he says, "Fuck, you taste *incredible*," before diving back in. His tongue swirls, rolls, and dips. He even slows the licks down, teasing me, taunting himself, and I moan, pushing my hips upward, wanting his face buried deeper.

You're being greedy.

I want to slap him, but I also want to fuck his face at this point because the feeling building up inside me is excruciating. I need to come, but I'm also afraid to. I don't know what kind of sounds will escape me. Will they embarrass me? Will they embarrass *him*? Fuck, it's too much to think about. Regardless, I don't have much time to consider it because he takes his mouth away, flips me onto my stomach, and I hear the rustling of fabric.

You don't realize how much you're turning me on. Never felt like this before. Fuck, I need to come.

His voice is loud in my head, and it doesn't take a genius to know what comes next.

"I'll need your permission..." His voice is thick, raspy. The turmoil inside him is loud. He's torn.

I shouldn't. I'll lose control if I...

"You have my permission," I tell him. "Don't stop."

He pauses, as if contemplating it, then before I know it, he's hoisting my hips upward so that I'm on my knees, and he slowly enters me from behind. His dick is hard, swollen as he fills me, and I clutch the quilt on the bed, breathing deeply. I was *not* prepared for the size of him.

"Love of Vakeeli, your pussy is so wet," he groans. "And so tight. *Fuck.*" He leans forward, his mouth dropping to my shoulder blade to give it a small nip. It's enough to sting, for me to *feel* it, but not too much to take me away from the pleasure of this moment.

"I need a minute," he murmurs, voice thick.

"For what?"

"I just...I need to feel you right now, with all of me inside you. I need to remember this feeling." He clutches my hips, remaining perfectly still. Despite his body being motionless, though, I feel his cock pulsing, like it's taken on a life of its own. "Fuck, your pussy is too much to bear. What I imagined it would be like doesn't even come close." Again, he curses beneath his breath, then pulls his hips backwards before thrusting. He makes a noise of strained pleasure.

"Look back at me," he commands as I moan, and I turn my head, looking at him, moaning as he thrusts into me again. The eye contact only enhances the feeling. "Fucking hell, Willow. You've got me so hard."

Yeah, I can tell. He feels so big inside me, like he's swelling by the second. He works his hips faster, like an insatiable need has taken over him. Leaning forward, he brings a hand around to wrap around my throat, applying light pressure. He guides my body backwards, burying his dick deeper inside me. He does this repeatedly, his breath hot on my ear, his body hard like marble as it presses to me.

"Oh, fuck," I moan.

"Do you like how I feel inside you?"

"Yes," I breathe as his hand wraps tighter around my throat. He doesn't stop stroking, filling me to the brim, making sure I feel every inch of him.

I sink my teeth into my bottom lip as he pulls his hand away from my throat to grip a handful of my hair. He's definitely fucking me now—a primal being dominating what's his, and, my word, it's the best dick I've ever had.

He doesn't slow down until I hear him growl the words, "Oh, Willow. *Fuck*, I'm coming, baby."

Just when I think he won't have the restraint to pull out, he does, and his hot cum spills onto my lower back. I sigh, collapsing onto my belly as he groans and shudders with his release. I glance over my shoulder and he has his dick clutched in hand, pearly streaks dripping from the tip.

I have to brace myself at the sight of it because even after his release, his semi-hardness is massive. Sure, he felt big in my hand, and yes, he filled me up like never before, but *seeing* it brings forth a unique awareness. For a moment I can't believe something so big was inside of me. Is that how all the men in Vakeeli are? Violent, darker, broodier, and...*bigger*?

"Turn over," he commands after wiping his cum off my back with a towel.

"What?"

"Turn onto your back."

"I thought we were finished."

He cocks a brow. "Did *you* finish?"

I start to tell him no, but he grabs my hips and drags me toward the edge of the bed. To his knees he drops, and he glides his tongue through the lips of my pussy before sealing his mouth to my clit.

"Oh, my—"

I can't even finish my sentence. This man is just...*oh my goodness*. What kind of man is he, and how did I get so lucky?

He licks my clit, sucking away at it with dire need like his only priority is pleasing me. His eyes flicker up to mine, and they glaze over as he groans and buries his face deeper, like I'm the best thing he's ever tasted. And I watch him do this to me, a rush of coolness sweeping through me, fusing with a pleasurable heat—an icy-hot combination that's indescribable but *oh-so-good*.

"Oh, Caz!" I cry. *Oh, I'm gonna come.*

Come.

His voice makes me detonate. I rock my hips against his mouth, clutch a handful of his hair, arch my back, and come.

A loud cry breaks out of me, my body shattering into a million shards as he groans between my legs, drinking me all in.

When I look down, his cool gaze is on mine, and he's clearly pleased with what he's accomplished. His eyes are filled with pride, confidence, and a smidge of arrogance. "There," he says. "*Now* you're finished."

When he lets me go, my legs drop, and my feet hit the wooden floorboards. He steps away, using his thumb to wipe the edge of his bottom lip.

We stare at each other, breathing raggedly, the energy between us charged and palpable. It fills the room, striking every nerve in my body.

I don't know what comes over me—whether it's my insane attraction to him, our Tether, or a combination of both—but when I stand, I throw my arms around his neck, drag him back to bed, and one word runs through my brain as I kiss him.

Again.

SIXTY-SIX

CAZ

WE'VE FUCKED three more times, and I'm still insatiable. I don't know what it is about her that has me craving more, but when I had that first taste, I knew it wouldn't come close to being enough. She's so tight and wet, and the sounds that dispense from her body when I'm inside her...*fuck*. They're everything.

I've had to put up my mind's wall so she can't hear any more of what I'm thinking about her. I'm afraid if she hears too much, she'll assume I'm some sex-crazed lunatic. But that's not true. I've never craved sex like this before. Hell, I've hardly ever really enjoyed it. With the others, I'd have to get myself drunk enough to stand it, and I'd double up on red pills, just so their touch wouldn't bother me. Fortunately, my dick doesn't mind the pleasure or touch it receives. It's just the rest of me that doesn't like being touched, which makes enjoying sex virtually impossible for me unless I'm intoxicated.

But it's not like that with Willow. There's something about

her hands, her touch, her body. The voluptuous curve of her hips, the dimples in her thighs. Her full breasts and the way they bounce, her dark-brown nipples that peak to perfection when she's close. It awakes everything inside me—every atom, every blood cell, every single strand of my DNA. It's all connected to hers, and I have her. Fuck, do I have her.

We're lying in the bed, and she's in my arms. Her head is on my chest, a foreign affection to me, but it feels nice. She tried getting up once, thinking she was overwhelming me with her touch, but I held on to her. I don't want her going anywhere. Hell, I don't ever want to leave this cabin again, but I'm aware it's an unrealistic thought.

There's one small window next to the bed, no curtain. It's dark outside, the moon beaming into the cabin between thick branches of the forest. Moonlight bathes her skin and mine. We're a beautiful mixture, light and dark. Crème and cocoa.

Willow draws in a deep breath and exhales, and I glance down. I try listening to her thoughts, but I can't hear them. My brows dip. I *can't* hear her. That's a first.

"I think you're doing it," I say after trying to hear her again.

She lifts her head to eye me. "Doing what?"

"You're blocking me out. You've built a wall around your mind."

"Really? How can you tell?"

"I just tried to read you. Nothing came. It was like knocking on a door and not getting an answer."

She grins. "Really? That's how it feels when I try to hear you."

"How'd you do it?"

"I don't know." She pauses, rubbing the tip of her nose. "I just kept thinking to myself, 'I don't want him to hear that.'"

"You don't want me to hear *what*, exactly?"

She sighs and sits up, bringing the quilt with her to cover her bare chest. It takes some willpower to not move the blanket so I can see her naked, but I know that'll lead to another round and right now isn't the time. "I can't stop thinking about that book I read. And then you saying Juniper went to Beatrix again. Do you think we should go and see Beatrix ourselves? Find out what's really going on?"

"I'm not sure I'd trust her after going through all of this."

"Are there any other Mythics who'd be able to help?"

"There's Manx, but I don't think he knows much about Cold Tethers—not as much as Beatrix. Doesn't hurt to ask and see if he can dig deeper, but with him caring for those in Whisper Grove, I'm afraid he wouldn't have the time."

She twists her lips. "I think there's more that Beatrix isn't telling us."

"Like what?"

"I don't know, but..." She lowers her head and grabs my hand. "I *like* this, Caz. I like how I feel when I'm with you. And when I went back, I couldn't get you off my mind. Sure, it's terrifying being here again. I don't know what to ever expect, but when I'm around you I feel safe. Protected. To think that one day this could all end because of this Mournwrath thing..." She sucks in a sharp breath. "I don't want that for us. There has to be a way we can beat this."

"I like this too."

She looks me all over. "I'm sensing a *but*..."

I work hard to swallow and pull my eyes away from hers. There has been a tidbit I've left out, but only because I wasn't sure about this. *Us.* Is there even an us? We've kissed, yes, and we've had sex. I killed someone I was never supposed to kill (and trust me, Rami's demented ass deserved it) and it will result in some sort of punishment from The Council. She's been inside me mum's cabin, a place that's sacred to me, for the love of Vakeeli.

"Fuck," I groan, rubbing the wrinkles from my forehead. "There is an us."

"What?" She tilts a brow.

"Nothing. Listen, there is one thing Juniper told me." I sit up with her, pressing my back to the wall, and she locks on me, waiting with anticipation for me to continue. "She says there's a couple who were in a Cold Tether before. Apparently, they survived it and are still together."

"Really? Well, that proves it then! Why didn't you tell me this before?"

"Because there's a downfall to it."

"Well, what is it?"

My eyes flicker up to hers. "They live in a place called *The Trench*."

Her face turns a bit ashen. "I remember Juniper telling me about it."

"Yeah. It's a terrible place. People who are there don't choose to live there. They're banished there. It's one of the darkest, lowliest places, Willow. And most times, when you go there, you may not come out. I'd have to bring an army and all my guns with me if we went there."

"Is there a way this couple can come out of The Trench to meet us?"

"No. Once you're banished there, you're bound there. There's no escaping it, and it's assumed the Regals made it that way as a punishment for the worst people. That place is practically hell on Vakeeli. There's hardly any food, water, and there are no youth elixirs. You go there, work in dirty fields that provide corn and wheat once or twice a year, and eventually die. There are no authorities, no good people. There's no one to save you. That's why, if anyone like us entered without an army, they'd rob us on site. Wouldn't even hesitate. It's a terrible place."

"Yeah. It sounds like it." She bites on her bottom lip, and a hopelessness fills her eyes that tugs at my heart. I can't let this be it. She's right...there is something here. Something worth fighting for, at least. Even if we don't last, at least I won't regret the fact that I tried.

"We can return to Blackwater," I tell her. "Get to my place and get a word out to Alora to arrange a visit again. She can set us up with Beatrix, and then we can go from there. But I want you to promise me something, Willow." I lean forward, clasping her chin in my fingers.

"Sure. Anything."

"I want you to promise that you won't put all your faith into this tiny possibility. This couple who made it out of the Cold Tether? I'm sure they didn't do it without consequence. For them to wind up in The Trench means something terrible must've happened. You don't just get banished to The Trench for no reason. Sure, they may be without the Tether now and they're together, but we don't know what kind of hell that cost them. Whatever it is, I don't want that for you." I swallow. "For *us*."

She grabs my hand, tilting her head to cradle her cheek in my palm.

"I promise, but only if you promise that you'll try everything you can to find a way. I don't want this to kill us." Her warm brown eyes glisten.

"It won't kill you. I won't let it." I grab her hand, running my lips over her knuckles. Not a kiss, but an action that electrifies the both of us. A coolness ripples down the middle of my chest. "But if it comes down to it and you must return to your world, so be it. Even if there's a threat to me, you must go back. Do you promise?"

She hesitates a moment, then sighs, parts her lips, and says, "I promise."

SIXTY-SEVEN

WILLOW

"Can I show you something before we go?" Caz takes my hand before I can give him an answer.

He opens the front door of the cabin, and it creaks on its hinges. Walking out, he rounds shrubs and bushes that need trimming, and an unattended flower bed, until he reaches a dirt path. We take the path, my hand still clasped in his, until we're behind the cabin.

We stop in a fenced-in backyard that can't be any bigger than 100 square feet. And though it's dark out, the moonlight bathes all the outdoors, revealing a plush green garden. In the middle of the garden is a lopsided brown table and two chairs wrapped in vines, the nails rusting. Caz steps closer to the chairs.

Being out here was my favorite thing about this place when I was a kid.

I glance up at him as his voice whispers through my mind, and he tips his chin. The moonlight cloaks him, making his creamy skin more prominent. In the night, he reminds me of a beautiful ghost, standing tall in the darkness.

"It's beautiful," I tell him.

He's quiet a moment. "My mother would make me breakfast every morning, then she'd give me a book to read while she tended the garden. Then we'd have tea." A faint smile spreads across his lips. "It was always black or apple. I hated apple tea."

I smile. "What happened to her?"

He drops his chin, and a tightness buds in my chest, like someone has wrapped their hands around my heart and is squeezing tightly. The feeling is fleeting.

"Tell me who Warren is." I meet his eyes, and he's already staring down at me. I blink quickly, turning my gaze toward the forest.

"That's not fair."

"Why isn't it?"

"Because I asked you first."

"I'll tell you more about my mother eventually."

"Swear." I meet his eyes again.

"Swear on all of Vakeeli."

I narrow my eyes. "That's easy for you to say. You hate Vakeeli."

He smirks. "Not all of it."

I laugh, then sigh. No point in hiding my past anymore. In this world, it feels like all of it can be unleashed. I can be set free from the agony of my memories and never have to take any of it back with me. That's what this world does. It takes all the suffering, wraps it up in the wind, drags it to the sea, and washes it away, never to be felt again...or it just replaces it with a new form of torture.

"Warren is my brother," I finally say.

I feel Caz looking at me, but I don't want to face him right now.

"When you think about him, your heart aches."

"It's the same when you think about your mom."

He tilts his head slightly and shifts on his feet.

"Look at us," he sighs. "Two damaged people from two different worlds, with one major thing in common."

"What's that?"

"We're lonely in heart."

I reach for his hand again, wrapping mine around it. "Why are we this way?"

"I don't know." He shrugs. "Perhaps that's how this Tether works. Without you around, things were different." He pauses. "I can't explain it, but life felt emptier before. But now that you're here, I feel like I have purpose. I've been given a reason to keep fighting." His eyes find mine. "I'm certain that reason is so that I can protect you."

I squeeze his hand, and he lifts it in the air, spreading his fingers apart with mine. The pads of our fingers press together, a delicate touch, as he moves in closer, his mouth coming to my forehead.

"I feel safe here," he murmurs.

"Me too."

"I don't think we should ever leave."

I huff a laugh. "I don't think that's possible. Your family is looking for you."

"Eh. Let them keep looking. They'll be all right."

I tip my chin, smiling up at him.

"Your brother," he starts, dropping our hands again. "What happened to him?"

I start to look away, but he clasps my chin, keeping my head up. "Why can't you look at me when you talk about him?"

My emotions swirl into a hurricane. I want to cry at the thought, but I also want to be angry. Why *can't* I talk about Warren? Why does it hurt so badly? There are many factors, truly, but I suppose I've never cared to address them. Instead, I choose to ignore it and act like nothing ever happened. Hell, I don't even have pictures of him in my apartment because seeing him hurts, and I don't want anyone asking me who he is. It's been easier to pretend he didn't exist, but deep inside, it's impossible to pretend when that person was your twin. Someone you shared a womb and every birthday with.

As if Caz can feel the cocktail of emotion brewing inside me, he strokes my chin with his fingers. I release a breath and pull away from him, focusing on a thick log not too far away, by the fence. I walk over to sit on it, and Caz watches me a moment before joining me. Crickets chirp, and a cool breeze floats by that smells of salt, a reminder that an ocean is nearby.

"The truth is that I don't talk about him much, with anyone."

"Your memories of him bring you pain?" he asks.

"Yes...and no." I twist my lips. "The memories from when we were kids, those bring me joy, of course. It's just...there are so many questions and things left unanswered about his death. I try to block it all out and distract myself with working, or men who think they can control me, because it's better than being alone and constantly thinking about it. I'd drive myself crazy with all the what ifs and wondering."

Caz nods, then frowns. "Who's trying to control you? That Garrett fucker you're always thinking about?"

I nod reluctantly.

"Has he hurt you?"

I press my lips, nodding again, and Caz clenches the fist on his lap. "I'll kill him."

"How?" I laugh. "He's in a whole other world."

"I'm sure there's a way to get there. I'll find a way, believe me." I huff a laugh. "Garrett is a conversation for another time."

"Fine." Caz sits taller, but it doesn't stop his jaw from ticking. "You were going to tell me about Warren."

I clear my throat. "Yeah. So, um...he used to travel a lot, my brother. He visited so many countries. All he ever talked about was marking countries off his bucket list, and he used to have this stupid scratch off map that he'd use whenever he came back home." I laugh at the reminder. I still have that map, folded up and buried deep in a shoe box in my closet. "We shared an apartment when we turned twenty-five, right after we graduated college. We felt it would be better to split the bills, plus our dad was a piece of shit who didn't want us living with him anymore when we turned eighteen, so we had each other. But that was the year my brother didn't come back." I glance at Caz. His eyes are still on me, clearly invested and waiting to hear what comes next.

"At first, I figured his phone was dead, or that he lost it or something. He called me every single day to update me, or just to bother me about something—you know, the annoying sibling thing. But after a week passed and I still hadn't heard from him, I got worried. The last place he visited was a small country called New Zealand, so I got ahold of authorities there, and they looked into him, went to the Airbnb he was staying in, and all of his stuff was there...but *he* wasn't." I squeeze my eyes shut and bring my hands up, pressing my fingers into my face and dragging them downward. I can't believe I'm talking about this.

Caz rubs my upper thigh, bringing me back to the present, and I drop my hands to look at him.

"This clearly pains you to talk about. You don't have to go on."

I shake my head. "No. It's fine. Surprisingly, I...want to." I draw in a deep breath, then exhale. "Anyway, the police told me they'd look into it. Long story short, they never found him, and his disappearance never made sense to me. I know my brother and he'd *never* just disappear on me unless something terrible happened to him, and if he was in some kind of trouble, he would have told me first before going off the grid. He knew what it was like to be abandoned and we promised each other we'd always keep in touch. *Always*. No matter what." My voice cracks with the last sentence and I clear my throat again. "He's been gone for almost two years now, and if I haven't heard from him yet, I'm assuming he's dead. Probably got kidnapped and killed or something."

Silence swims around us. Fortunately, the crickets are louder, and all the sounds of the night, so it's not so awkward.

"Wow." Caz's voice is full of sorrow. "I'm sorry, Willow. I didn't realize..."

"Yeah. Now you can see why it's something I don't like talking about much."

"I do see." He pauses and the silence lingers between us a bit. When I look at him, he appears to be thinking. His eyes have narrowed, his lips twisting a bit. "You know, when we were in Whisper Grove, I went to the library while you were sleeping to find out more about how the Tether originated. Apparently, the original Tethered people had babies, and Selah created a spell for them to be constantly recreated if they die." Another pause. "If Warren is your twin...it is possible that he's not dead—that he may be in Vakeeli somewhere."

I swing my eyes to his. "Are you serious? And you're just now telling me?"

"I didn't know your brother had gone missing. I mean, I heard you thinking about him, but I figured maybe he'd just left you alone or walked out of your life. And it's just a possibility that he's in Vakeeli. I'm not sure. But if you have a mate, I'm certain he does too."

I don't even know how to take this news, and for a moment I have to sit there, absorbing the possibilities. If Warren is still alive—if he's here, in Vakeeli like I am...

"If I had a portal come here, that means he did too! Maybe he went through one in New Zealand just like I did but never came back." I jump to a stand. "Caz, do you realize what this means? We have to find him! He could be here somewhere!"

"I'll put my best people on it when we get to Blackwater."

"That would explain so much," I murmur. "Why a body was never found, how he randomly disappeared. Oh my God, it all makes sense now!"

I look up at him, and he's watching me, clearly delighted with my reaction, but also apprehensive.

"Sorry—I'm jumping the gun. I just... it's been so long. He could still be alive and if he is..." I swallow down my emotions before they get the best of me.

"Look, I don't want you getting your hopes up, Willow," he says when I sit again. "It's a possibility that he's here, yes, but he could be anywhere. And there were only four babies. You and I make two of them. If another Tethered couple is out there, he could be with his mate in The Trench. And if so, he may as well be dead. Or, for all we know, he found his mate, fell in love with her, and Mournwrath got to them. I'm not sure what to make of it, or why they could possibly be there."

"I know, I know. You're right." Silence descends, and as badly as I want to take my mind off warren being alive, I can't. "I'd give anything to see his face again—to hug him, laugh with him, crack a joke on him. Please, for all the love in Vakeeli, or however you guys say it, let my brother be alive."

Caz laughs at that, a deep, warming timbre that makes me warm inside.

To take my mind off Warren, I say, "How about you tell me about your mother."

He lowers his gaze a bit, his smile slipping away. "I will...but not tonight. It's heavy enough hearing you talk about your brother's disappearance. Telling you about my mother will tip us over the edge."

I press my lips and nod as he places a kiss on my forehead. It must be bad, plus I don't want to force him to talk about her. On another note, Faye would be proud to know I finally talked to *someone* else about Warren. I've only ever told her, and even with her I was vague with the details because I wanted to spare myself the pity, and she's my best friend. What I've just told Caz, I've never told anyone before.

"I'll be right back." Caz's words snap me out of my thoughts, and I watch him jog toward a line of trees, to return moments later with something shining in his hand. When he's closer, I see it's a flower he's holding—and not just any flower, a *gold* one. It's shaped similar to a rose, with thorns and all, and I gasp when I spot blood on his fingers.

"You grabbed it by the thorns?" I ask.

He shrugs. "I'll be fine." He digs into his pocket, pulling out a pocketknife. When he flings it open, the silver blade catching the moonlight, he sits next to me again and starts slicing off the thorns. "It's a Vanorian Blossom. I used to steal them from Vanora when me and my mum would visit the markets, and I'd come back and plant them around the cabin. It wasn't legal then to take plants from other lands. Each territory had a rule about their flowers and herbs being sacred, for trading purposes, but that's all changed since my generation of monarchs. Anyway, my mum would find the flowers around this cabin when we returned and she'd scold me about taking them, always telling me I could get in trouble. She loved them, though. Always admired them. She used to tell me often how she wanted a bouquet of them just to place on the table and look at, but they were quite expensive." He takes a long pause, focused on removing the thorns. "All I ever wanted was for her to be happy, so I'd steal them. And sure, she'd scold me, but she'd never deny them. She'd water them and keep them alive, let them flourish. She loved them. They grow on their own now, which is nice." He cuts off the final thorn, chops half of the stem, and then turns to me with it, tucking it behind my left ear. Dropping his hand, his eyes light up as he smiles at what he's done, then says, "It looks nice with your hair. What do you call this style by the way?"

I can't help the smile that takes over my whole face, or the bombardment of heat swimming through me. "Thank you," I say, voice soft. "For the flower...and the story. As for my hair, they're called locs. Lots of Black women have them."

"They look great on you." He lowers his gaze, a small smile on his lips. "You're right about my family, though." His head lifts back up. "We should get going before they get concerned for both of us."

"Yeah."

"Cerberus!" he shouts, and in only a matter of minutes, I hear his paws pounding into the ground. Cerberus appears, panting, his black fur shimmering in the moonlight. Caz drops to one knee and rubs the top of his large head.

"A good boy, eh?" He strokes him under the chin, and Cerberus leans into Caz's touch.

"Do you think Silvera will come?" I ask.

"I'm sure she will if you call for her."

I look ahead, in the direction Cerberus came from. "Silvera?" I don't call her as loudly as Caz called Cerberus, but she appears just as quickly as he did, her tail wagging, silver eyes glowing in the dark.

"There you are!" She stands beside me, and I smile as I scratch behind her ears. "Thank you for leading me here, homegirl."

She rubs her muzzle on my leg.

"*Homegirl?*" Caz asks. "What the hell does that mean?"

"Oh—it's a saying." I crack a smile. "It's like calling someone your bestie."

"*Bestie?*" He raises a confused brow.

"Wow. I have so much to teach you about my world," I laugh.

He chuckles. "Right. Well, fill me in on the way back," he says, fixing his collar. He walks toward the cabin, Cerberus at his side, and I follow his lead. As he goes up the single step in front of the door, I watch him fish around in his coat pocket for his gloves and slip them on, and I'm reminded that the Caz I'm with tonight won't be the same man once we walk into his real home. He'll have to return to his violent acts, his nonchalance, and his take-no-shit mentality because he *has* to. It's how he protects himself, and how he maintains order of Blackwater.

I see why he wants to stay here at the cabin. Here, he can be himself. There's no point in hiding what he wants or how he wants things. But to everyone else, he has to put up a shield because any sign of weakness can lead to his demise.

Caz has me put on a shirt to conceal my upper half. He's still not satisfied with my legs being out, but in his words, "It'll do for now." Afterward, he collects his guns and a few other items from the cabin, then walks outside again to untie his horse.

"What's his name?" I ask.

"Onyx," Caz says, then wraps his hands around my waist. "Up you go." He helps me onto the horse, and I gasp as I sit on his back.

"I've never ridden a horse before, Caz."

"Do you not have horses where you're from?"

"Yes, we have horses, but people aren't really getting by on them in the city. Everyone drives cars."

"Well, this isn't the city," he says, climbing on behind me. He slides in close, his breath trickling past my ear. Goosebumps sweep across my skin, and I feel a clench between my legs as he drops his hands to clutch the reigns. "And he's a wild horse at heart, so you better hang on." When he says that, he loosens the reins and Onyx takes off, jerking us backward. Our wolves run on either side of him, and at first, it's terrifying riding on the back of a horse—especially at night. It's dark and I'm not sure how he can see anything, but he gallops flawlessly between the gaps of the trees, leaping over fallen trunks and ducking under low-hanging branches like he's done this many times before.

My heart beats a mile a minute, but as I look ahead and we reach a clearing, I realize how freeing this is. The air is cool and comforting, running through my hair. Caz steers his stallion, tugging on the reins to control Onyx's speed, and never in my life have I felt so liberated.

As we ride through the clearing, mist sprinkles from the sky, droplets clinging to my skin.

"You're radiating joy," Caz says on shell of my ear.

"You can feel that too?"

"I can."

"Well, I can't help it! This is a first for me!" I laugh.

"Yeah." He chuckles, a comforting sound from him. "It's a first for me too."

SIXTY-EIGHT

WILLOW

AT THE SIGHT of Caz's mansion standing like a gothic tower in the night, I'm filled with relief. There are lights on inside, casting a gold glow, and smoke billows out of one of the chimneys.

After Caz takes Onyx to the stables, we journey across the field to get to the door. Caz opens it and walks inside, and I follow after him while our wolves decide to stay outdoors. When the door creaks and slams shut, he walks down the foyer, checks the den, and then his office, until finally stopping at the kitchen entrance.

"Caz!" Juniper's voice echoes through the house. I meet up to him just as Juniper comes rushing his way, throwing her arms around his neck. "If you *ever* disappear like that again, I'll feed you to the sharks!"

Caz grunts, but pats Juniper on the back anyway as a form of his affection.

She pulls away from him, looking him all over, then swings her eyes to me. "You found him."

"Sort of," I say, smiling.

Juniper steps back, and I look around her, spotting Maeve sitting at the head of the table with a lit bloom between her fingers. She pulls from it, then exhales, blowing out a cloud of smoke.

"I knew he wasn't far," Maeve proclaims.

"And yet you didn't come looking for me," Caz mumbles, walking toward the table. There's a teapot on the center of the table, as well as a few empty teacups. He grabs the pot, pours some into two cups, and sits. He slides the other cup toward the chair next to him and eyes me.

I walk over, taking the chair beside him and cupping the tea in my hand. On the other side of the table is Killian, who's frowning of course, and beside Killian is Rowan, cleaning one of his guns. Juniper sits opposite Caz, close to Maeve. She picks up a glass cup, but it's not tea in there. It's blue tonic most likely.

"I'm glad you're back, brother," Killian says. "I hate to be the bearer of bad news, but The Council sent someone to come for you at the tavern."

Caz presses his lips before asking, "What did they want?"

"They asked for you. They said they need you in Luxor immediately."

Caz sips his tea carefully, letting Killian's words marinate. "I'll deal with them later. For now, there's something more important I feel should be addressed. Something I must tell you all."

"Well spit it out then," Rowan says, sitting up in his chair.

"As you're all aware, Willow and I are Tethered. And we are not a simple Tether, we are a Cold Tether, which apparently makes us rare and endangered. We were told that by being together, it would make us weaker. However, Willow and I sense that by being together, it makes us stronger." Caz clears his throat, and I shift in my seat. "When she left Vakeeli, I could feel myself becoming weaker. There came a point where I could hardly even lift my gun." He looks at everyone around the table. "Which leads me to believe that someone has lied to us, and I need to know why. I'm sure Juniper has told you all about what Beatrix said—that there is a couple who has survived this Cold Tether. What she hasn't told you, and what you're unaware of, is that there is something out there called Mournwrath who feeds on Cold Tethers like the one Willow and I share. He almost did it tonight, but I believe that my acceptance of the bond with Willow sent him away, if only for now." He folds his fingers on the table. "I would like to get to Beatrix again, which means paying yet another visit to Alora. I'm sure she won't like it, but I need answers, and I need them immediately, before Mournwrath makes a return."

"So, what do you need us to do?" Maeve asks, putting out her bloom.

"I need you all to keep the talk about the Tether quiet. As I told Willow, if anyone outside this circle finds out, they'll know I have a weakness and they'll use it against me." He glances at me, a pained expression gripping him, before dropping his blue eyes to the table. "And while she's in my world, she's my responsibility. I can't let anything happen to her."

"So, is she going back to her world anytime soon?" Killian asks, and I cut my eyes at him, frowning.

"Killian," Maeve interjects.

"I'm just saying, if the Beatrix woman says she's not meant to be here, she shouldn't be here," Killian goes on. "She poses a threat for all of us, Caz, not just you."

"As long as everyone in this room agrees to keep their mouths shut about the Cold Tether, she brings no threat." Caz's jaw ticks as he glares into Killian's eyes. "Beatrix lied—that, or someone lied to her. We need to get to Vanora right away to figure out what's really going on. The sooner we do, the less of a threat there'll be."

"I don't like this," Killian grumbles, slouching back in his chair. "All our heads on a guillotine for a bloody woman who isn't even *family*. It's fucking stupid."

Caz shoves back in his chair, standing tall. "Killian, meet me out back. *Now*." He storms out of the kitchen, and Killian's nostrils flare as he looks at me before gripping the table with his big hands and lumbering out of the kitchen himself.

"Ah, he'll get over it," Rowan says, crossing his arms and leaning against the back of his chair. "Killian's always so paranoid."

"Yeah," Juniper agrees, after sipping her drink. "Killian's always been a bit afraid of everything."

"It's not that he's afraid," Maeve says, pouring herself some tea. "It's that he feels he must protect everyone at all times. Now that Willow has been tossed into the mix and he has no idea what it's doing to Caz, he feels like he's losing control."

"But you heard him, Mum. Caz almost died because Willow wasn't here," Juniper says.

A nod from Maeve. "I know."

"And with her around, he could very well die because she's attached to him, or whatever," Rowan adds.

"Possibly."

Silence fills the air, deafening.

"But she saved him," Maeve adds, smiling with her teacup in hand. She gives me a wink. "And he knows that. So right now, we have to trust whatever comes next. If Caz believes he's better with her here, so be it. She stays."

Just as the words of Maeve are expressed, we hear a loud thump, deep grunting, and the breaking of glass.

SIXTY-NINE

WILLOW

"Oh, no." Juniper presses a hand to her forehead when I gasp from the noise. Maeve rolls her eyes, remaining seated, while Rowan groans, pushing out of his chair.

"Why do I always have to split these two up?" he shouts, charging out of the kitchen. Juniper follows him but Maeve remains seated, sitting farther back in her chair, and sipping her tea.

I follow Juniper and Rowan out the kitchen and down the hallway that leads to a back door. They step outside, onto a tall black deck that overlooks a black sea. Glass from a window is on the ground, and standing not too far away from that glass is Caz and Killian. Caz has Killian in a chokehold, and Killian is clawing at Caz's arm, his face turning purple as he struggles to breathe.

"Fucking stop it, Caz! He can't breathe!" Juniper yells.

"He shouldn't have shoved me into the window then," Caz growls.

"Knock it off!" Rowan snaps, stepping forward, but he doesn't touch Caz. I get the sense that if anyone tried touching him right now, they'd be a fool. Caz looks from Rowan, to Juniper, and then at me. It's when his eyes lock with mine that he releases Killian, who tumbles onto his knees on the deck. The ocean roars as Killian works hard to catch his breath, and Caz steps back, breathing raggedly.

"Why are you two always fighting?" Juniper demands, bending down to try to help Killian off the ground.

"Get off me." Killian swats Juniper's hand away, slumping onto his bottom, his back hitting the guardrails.

"He started it," Caz pants.

"Vakeeli's sake, Caz! What are you, twelve?"

"He's the one who has a problem with Willow! I was setting him straight!"

Killian frowns and immediately stands, getting in Caz's face again. "I never said I have a problem with her!"

"You don't have to say it for me to know it," Caz snaps back.

"You keep going at me at this rate and I'll rip your fucking head from your shoulders, Caz. Don't fuck with me."

"Go on, then," Caz says, spreading his arms out wide. "Try it."

Killian, being an inch or so taller than Caz, glowers down at him, but Caz doesn't back away. However, Killian does reel his arm back and punches him in the face.

I gasp as Caz stumbles backward, his lower back hitting the railing. He doesn't allow himself much time to settle into the blow because he's rushing Killian again, tackling him to the ground.

"Caz! Stop it!" Juniper screams.

Rowan grips Caz by the shoulders, ripping Caz away from his brother and pushing him into the farthest corner. "Stay there!" Rowan barks, pointing a finger at Caz as he swipes the back of his hand over his bloody nose.

Killian lies flat on his back on the deck, panting, and Juniper sighs, planting her hands at her waist.

"Are you two done acting like hooligans?" Maeve's voice is near, and she's walking toward the door, another bloom between her fingers. When she steps out, she looks down at Killian, then at Caz, who's jaw is ticking furiously.

"He takes cheap shots," Caz grumbles. "Doesn't fight fair."

I roll my eyes at the same time Juniper does. "Is this a common occurrence?" I ask, not to anyone in particular.

"Oh yes, it is, and it's *maddening*!" Juniper groans.

"Killian, whether you like it or not, Willow *is* family now. She's a part of Caz, which makes her a part of us, so suck it up." Maeve walks to the center of the deck, offering a hand to Killian. He mutters something beneath his breath but takes his mother's hand and allows her to help him up.

"Is the air clear?" Maeve demands, looking from him to Caz.

Caz doesn't answer, just turns his back to face the black waters.

"Killian." She glares at him.

"Fine. Whatever," her son grumbles.

"Good. Now while you two were having your fight over who's balls are bigger, I contacted Alora. Willow can ride to Vanora; however, Caz, I'm afraid you can't go with her."

"What?" he snaps. "Why the hell not?"

"The Council has been in touch with Alora. She apologizes, but she can't let you into Vanora until you've gone to Luxor to speak to them."

"There's no way I'm sending Willow to Beatrix's place without me. Not after what happened with the Rippies."

"Yes, well it is *because* of what happened with the Rippies and Rami that The Council needs to see you. Look, the sooner you get to them and deal with this and the Rami mess, the better. I'm assuming they don't want you dead, otherwise they'd have come to do it already. Juniper, Rowan, and I will take Willow to Vanora to get to Beatrix. And we will go prepared this time."

"And what about me?" Killian asks, frowning.

"You'll be going to Luxor with Caz and making amends with him." Maeve pulls from her bloom with a satisfied smirk as both men glare at each other.

"Why should I stay here watching after his ass when all he cares about is himself?" Killian counters.

"Oh, just shut the hell up already, Killian!" Rowan snaps. "You're not making any of our lives easier by complaining about everything, so for once in your life, just *shut up*, brother."

Killian squares his shoulders and points a stern finger at Rowan. "*Fuck you.*" He storms back into the house, but not without purposely bumping into Rowan's shoulder along the way.

"Great. Now he's off to throw a tantrum. I need a bloody bloom." Rowan leaves the deck as well, and Juniper follows, shaking her head. Maeve walks toward Caz and says something I can't make out, then she's in the house too.

Only Caz and I are left on the deck, the roaring of the ocean filling the void. His nose is still bloody, and his bottom lip now has a cut on it and is starting to swell. Walking up to him, I wipe some of the blood from his lip and then sigh.

"You know violence doesn't settle violence," I tell him.

"No, it doesn't, but I lost my temper."

"What did he say to you?"

Caz's nostrils flare at the edges. "He doesn't want any part of the Tether. He thinks it's going to get us all killed."

"So you were about to choke him to death because of that?"

"No. I was about to choke him to death because he referred to you as a *bitch*. I had to let him know you're not just some random Vakeeli whore he can talk shit about."

I blink, stunned to hear that. "Oh. I see."

"He won't call you that ever again. I'm sure of it."

"I guess I should say thanks?"

He side-eyes me before facing the water again, and I step next to him. "I don't want you going to Vanora without me," he mutters. "But if they're telling Alora to keep me away from Vanora, it means they're close to putting a bounty on my head. If I don't go willingly, they'll make a scene. I'm surprised they haven't already."

"All of this—a bounty on your head—just for killing that piece of shit, Rami?" I ask incredulously. Because seriously, fuck Rami.

He says nothing to that. Instead, he wipes his nose again, then steps back. "We can't let too much time pass us by. We don't know when Mournwrath will return and we need answers, so... though I don't want you going without me, you'll have to." He takes my hand, wrapping his gloved fingers around it. "I can meet you there, after seeing The Council. I'll take the quickest train back."

"What if The Council doesn't let you go so quickly?"

"I'm the Blackwater Monarch. They can't keep me long without chaos erupting here." He clasps my hand in his. "You'll be fine going to Vanora with Maeve, Rowan, and Juniper, but you'll need weapons once you get to Beatrix—lots of them—so come with me."

SEVENTY

CAZ

I SEND Juniper and Maeve to dress Willow in clothing more appropriate for Vakeeli. Walking around in what she's wearing —shorts, a tank top, and no bra—won't do. I'd given her one of my silk shirts to cover her upper half when we left the cabin, but her legs are still revealed. Not to mention she's been barefoot this entire time. I can't have anyone else looking at what's mine.

Juniper helps Willow to the shower, finds clothes for her from her wardrobe, and once Willow is done and has eaten something, she meets me on the third floor, in the armory.

The armory is a sacred place for us. It's where we store our weapons, rubies, good steel, records, and everything else of value. I keep the armory in my house because no one will dare break into it. Doing so would be like committing suicide. In Blackwater, my home is to remain untouched by anyone other than my respective team, and as Monarch, not only do I have the people's highest respects, but I also have their *fear*. No one fucks with the Blackwater Clan and gets away with it.

"A whole room dedicated to guns." Willow's voice comes out of nowhere, and I glance over my shoulder as she steps into the armory. "Why am I not surprised?"

"You're getting good at keeping your thoughts quiet."

"Thanks. I've been practicing." She smiles at me, and I can't help smirking. My eyes fall to her clothes, and a wave of satisfaction rides over me. Juniper did well picking the outfit. All black, with a black cloak that'll hide her weapons. Thick boots with silver chains are on her feet, spiked platinum bangles on her wrists. The bangles, I know, are a touch from Juniper. They're unnecessary, but it wouldn't be Juniper without some sort of fashion tossed in. Still, it works. She blends right in, and no one will suspect that she isn't a member of Blackwater.

"Do people not own guns in your world?" I ask.

"Some people do," she says, running her fingers over the handle of a silver handgun. "But I don't."

"Why not?" I pick up the gun she just touched, weighing it in my hand.

"I don't know. I guess I just felt like I never really needed one."

"That's a backwards way of thinking."

"Not everyone's lives revolve around violence and guns where I'm from," she says, smirking.

"That may be so," I murmur, turning toward her with the gun. "But in *my* world, it does." I place the gun in her palm, and she looks down at it. She bounces it in her hand, and I turn for a belt clip. It'll work best strapped around her waist, beneath the cloak. Easy to access in case anyone tries to make any sudden moves.

"I'll be safe with your family, I'm sure," she says when I turn to face her with the clip. My eyes swivel up to hers briefly before dropping and focusing on the clip. I attach it to the leather belt around her waist, then grab a sheath for a knife that's large enough to strap around her upper thigh.

"It's not that I don't think they'll protect you. Leg up."

She lifts her boot-clad foot, placing it on one of the shelves. "So, what is it then?"

I wrap the sheath around her thigh, then turn for the wall of knives and daggers. "I just don't want you getting the answers without me. Beatrix lied once. What if she lies again? What if this is all a bloody trap?"

She thinks on that a moment, and while she does, I select a few of the sharpest knives that are also lightweight and take down a jagged dagger for good measure. The dagger has a ruby on the center of the black handle, the blade a sharp, sparkling platinum. Perfect for slicing someone's throat.

"We'll try to be careful. You deal with whatever The Council wants, and I'll try to tap in with you mentally to fill you in."

"Right. Fine." I carry the knives to the nearest counter and set them down one by one. She approaches the counter too, gawking at each one.

"Do I *really* need all of that?" she asks.

"Yes, you do. As a matter of fact, you should be taking more than this, but I don't want to overwhelm you."

She moves closer to me, brushing against my side. I don't know how she does it, but that simple touch is enough to send a current through me. It charges me, making me hyperaware of everything about her. Her soft breaths, the sweet scent of her skin. The heat of her body.

"I know it's hard, but I really think you should stop worrying," she says near my ear.

"I wish I could. In truth, I'm trying not to care, but everything in my mind and body goes against the effort."

She steps closer, and I turn toward her, cupping one side of her face, my fingers tangling in the hairs at the nape of her neck. "I just have a bad feeling about this. I don't think we should be separated right now. If Mournwrath comes to you when I'm not there..."

"I'll beg Beatrix for a protection morsel or something—whatever—that can help."

"And if she doesn't give it to you?"

"Then I'll take one of those knives and point it at her throat."

That makes me laugh, much harder than I anticipate. I haven't laughed in ages, so it feels weird coming out, all raspy and dry.

"Wait a minute. Was that a laugh?" she teases.

"No, it wasn't," I counter.

"Yes, it was! I got a laugh out of Serious Caspy! Aww, do it again, please! You have a beautiful laugh."

I chuckle. "Blackwater is clearly starting to rub off on you. And what the hell is a *Caspy*?"

"It's you." She pats my chest. "I've decided that's what I'll call you from now on. My own little thing. It's got a ring to it, don't you think?"

"Why not just Caz, like everyone else?"

"Meh. That name gets boring to say after a while. You could let me call you Caspian."

"Have our relationship gotten to that level yet?"

"I think it has."

I reel her in by the waist, my lips a breath away from hers. At this point, it's getting harder to control my urges and the way I touch her. All I want to do is hold her, keep her close. Kiss her. *Fuck* her. It's an odd feeling. Makes me feel weak and thoughtless. But, at the same time, I'm okay feeling weak in her presence.

"We should finish gearing you up," I murmur on her lips.

She leans into my mouth, her plump lips brushing mine. "Yeah. We probably should."

"So why aren't we?"

She shudders a breath as I plant a kiss on her lips, so soft I feel the ripple effects travel through both of us. "Not sure," she breathes.

A groan fills my throat as she drops her head an inch to kiss my neck. Fuck, she's too good at that. My dick instantly hardens, and I press it into her.

"If you don't stop, I'll fuck you around my weapons."

"Sounds dangerous."

"It is, but that won't stop me." I grab her by the waist and pick her up, placing her bottom on the counter.

"Maeve and Juniper are waiting for me to come back down."

"I suppose they'll come looking for you soon then, eh?" I kiss her on the throat this time, my lips dragging from the crook to the soft skin above her collarbone.

"Probably."

"Then we better make this quick."

She attempts a weak argue with, "I'll have to take all of these clothes off."

"I'll help you put them back on."

A giggle bubbles out of her, and she drops her head to meet my eyes. "These clothes took me thirty minutes to put on. Explain to me why the bras here are so complicated."

"I wouldn't be able to tell you. I don't have breasts."

She laughs again. "Funny." Then her mouth is on mine, and she tastes like Blackfruit and mint. Her fingers comb through my hair, and I reel her in by the hips, my tongue colliding with hers. She reaches down, groping my dick through my pants, and I groan into her mouth.

"Your touch," I groan. "Fuck, Willow. How am I so weak for it?" I unzip my jeans and lower them, then work to unbutton hers. She lifts her hips, allowing me to ease them down. Her panties are white lace and fresh, and I so badly want to rip them off.

"You do that, and we're fighting," she says, narrowing her eyes at me.

I smirk. "What? Your panties can always be replaced."

"Then what will I tell Juniper when she sees them ripped?"

"I don't know. "I reach down, pushing her panties aside. My finger grazes the lips of her pussy, and she sucks in a breath. "But you'll have to forgive me if I do."

"Caz," she breathes as I thrust a finger inside her, and then another. Her lips part, and she looks so damn sexy as I play with her. Her pussy tightens around my fingers, and she moans, looking into my eyes. There's so much desire swirling in her eyes. I feel the aching, her hips rolling with my fingers, begging for more.

I can't hold off any longer. I pull my fingers away, and she nearly whines.

Why'd you stop?

I fight a smile, lowering my pants just enough to free my dick. I lick my palm, wrapping it around my shaft and stroking it, making it wet.

Sliding her hips to the edge of the counter, I angle the head of my dick at her entrance, slowly pushing my way inside her. With each deliberate inch, she moans louder, and when I'm all in, I say, "That's why I stopped. To *feel* you, like this."

She wraps her arms around the back of my neck, and I pick her up off the counter, bouncing her up and down the length of my dick. I clutch her ass in my hands, groaning because she feels so good.

"You're so wet for me. *Fuck*, Willow. The things we do to each other." She moans again, dropping her head and kissing me, and I guide her body up and down, fast then slow, and it's damn near impossible not to come right away. Her pussy is dripping down the length of my dick, making wet, sticky noises in the quiet of the armory.

I place her on the counter again, and she lies flat on her back. I wrap a hand around her throat and thrust harder into her.

"Oh, Caz!" she cries, her back arching. I watch her like this, my hand around her throat, my dick buried deep inside her, to the hilt, and that's all it takes for her to cry out again.

"You take me so well," I breathe.

She moans.

"Do you like feeling me inside you?"

"Yes," she breathes.

"I can tell. You're gripping the hell out of my dick, baby."

She clutches my wrist. "Oh, I'm gonna come. Don't pull away," she breathes again. It takes everything in me to jerk my hips back, taking away what she so desperately needs.

"What are you doing?" she asks raggedly. She starts to sit up, but I hold her by the throat, keeping her pinned down. "Why'd you stop?"

"You want to come around my dick, you'll have to beg."

"*Beg*?" she huffs a laugh, rolling her eyes. "You're so full of yourself, my goodness."

"Do it."

"I'm not begging for anything," she counters.

"No?" I push the head of my dick inside her, just enough for her to feel me there, and she sighs.

"You're such an asshole," she moans.

"Beg for me to make you come, and I'll do it."

"Deeper, Caz," she breathes.

"This isn't a negotiation."

"Please," she pleads.

I thrust deeper, halfway in.

"You want it all, don't you?"

"Yes." She wriggles beneath me. There's desperation in her voice.

Driving me crazy. Please, Caz!

"Out loud," I murmur, sliding my thumb over her jaw and chin.

Her eyes shoot up to mine, her legs wrapping around my waist. She uses her legs to guide me deeper, and I let her because I can't resist either. I'm as hard as a rock, swollen and throbbing, wanting so badly to fill her with my come.

"Please make me come," she finally says, and I loosen my grip around her throat, burying myself deeper. When I jerk back and stroke deep again, her body bucks, and a sharp gasp bursts out of her. Her fingernails drag down my arms as her back arches again, and then she crumbles beneath me, crying my name. The sticky noises are louder and her grip around me is insane. When I look down, my dick is wetter, milky at the base.

"Shit, Willow. Look what you've done. Look how wet you are for me." I wrap my hand around the back of her neck and bring her upward just enough to look at me again. Her warm brown eyes latch with mine, and that look, as well as her pussy gripping my dick, is enough to make me detonate. "You're so beautiful when you come." She clasps my face in her hands, kissing me again.

Oh, fuck. Now I'm about to come.

Come for me, baby.

Love of Vakeeli, her voice. A groan bursts out of me, and I pull out just before I cum, gripping my pulsing dick, jacking it, and letting the semen spill on her pelvis. Some of it drips through the lips of her pussy and witnessing it makes me groan. I lower the tip of my dick, running it through the slickness. She twitches and moans as the tip of my dick meets her clit, then cups the back of my neck, bringing me down low enough to kiss me. Her lips are soft and warm. Sweet. Fuck, she's *everything*.

"You're bad." She shudders again when I skim the head of my softening dick over her clit. If I wasn't going soft, I'd put it in again. "Now find me a new pair of panties because these are most definitely ruined."

SEVENTY-ONE

WILLOW

Caz saves me a ton of embarrassment by asking Della to find panties for me. She goes into the village for some and returns within twenty minutes with several pair in a paper bag.

Afterward, Caz leads me to his bedroom, and it's nothing like the other rooms. For starters, his room is enormous. The walls are painted black, including the ceiling. Two sharp-bladed fans hang from the ceiling on opposite sides of the rooms, and a large bed is positioned against the north wall. To my right is a tall black curtain. Caz walks over to separate the velvet curtains and reveals floor to ceiling windows, and just outside the windows is a balcony made of wood with steel railings. I take a look out at the black sea, the water rippling. There's nothing but water for miles and miles, dark waves that are alluring yet terrifying beneath the gray sky.

"So...this is your room," I say, looking around. A gray recliner is in one of the corners, next to a nightstand stacked haphazardly with books. Just around the corner is a bathroom, the walls gray, with a large silver tub—large enough to fit at least four people. His shower is built into the corner—no curtain, just a glass wall and a large silver showerhead.

"This is my room," he confirms, looking around with me.

"It's nice."

"Yes. It's unfortunate that I don't get to spend much time in it."

"Why not?"

"Work. Running an entire territory. Blackwater Tavern. I always have my hands full."

I press my lips. Makes sense. Still, I'd never leave a bedroom like this. I run a hand over his bedding. It's fluffy and soft, his pillows cool to the touch. My eyes travel up the wall the bed is against, at the portraits hung there. This wall is made of gray wood paneling, the portraits hanging in sections. There are five portraits total, all of them sharp, dark, abstract designs of horses and guns, except the one in the middle, which stands out most.

I focus on the picture in the middle, of a woman and a boy. The woman has dark skin like mine, her hair as dark as the wings of a raven, wild and curly around the edges, the rest collected into one single braid that rests on her shoulder. A smile graces her lips, similar to the Mona Lisa smile—there, but just a whisper of it.

She's in an emerald dress and she's holding the hand of a boy. The boy doesn't look any older than six or seven. He's smiling hard and missing a tooth. His hair is just as dark as hers, and he has the woman's eyes—icy blue and bold. He's barefoot in black trousers and an ivory shirt. He looks happy...and I know exactly who he is.

"Is that your mother?" I ask, turning to look back at Caz.

"It is."

"Wow." I face the portrait again. "She's gorgeous."

"She was quite beautiful."

The question from earlier hits me again. *What happened to her? Where is she now?*

Caz walks up to me. "After we find out what's going on with the Tether, I'll tell you about my mother. Deal?"

"Okay." I look into his eyes. "Deal."

"Now take this." He raises the bag of panties Della gave him. "Go and change, then meet me downstairs."

I take the bag from him, and he leaves the room, closing the door behind him.

When he's gone, I look around once more, but I can't help going back to the picture of him and his mom. He looked so happy then, so carefree and full of life. Who ruined that little boy and turned him into the hardened man he is now? There is hardly any softness left in him. Who robbed him of that?

The question lingers as I go to the bathroom to wash up, slide into a new set of panties, and then leave the bathroom. I start to leave the bedroom, but something outside the balcony catches my eye.

Outside the window is a floating black figure. It hovers above the water, red eyes pointed in my direction, its black talons revealed. It's cape billows in the wind, and my heart beats hard in my chest as I stare at it, waiting to see what it will do, but it does nothing. Just floats there, looking at me.

"Did I not tell you that if you go to him, he'll die?"

The voice rings in my head, coming out like a painful croak. I try to move, but I'm frozen solid.

"The closer you are to the answers, the quicker your death. Accept your fate."

"You're full of shit. Tell me, if you're so powerful, why haven't you already killed us?"

"It was never that simple," it says.

"Yeah, because it's all a lie."

"*There are no lies.*" It moves closer to the balcony. I'm still paralyzed, nothing moving but my eyes and my mouth. "*I will keep coming for you. If you do not accept your fate right now, both of you will die a painful death once I obtain your Tether.*"

"We'll never accept it. Not when there's a choice."

"*What a stupid, stupid girl.*"

"Fuck you," I seethe.

Mournwrath makes a throaty, croaking noise, like nails on a chalkboard, and I wince. Finally able to move, I cover my ears and crouch to the ground. The walls begin to shake, and the balcony doors rattle relentlessly.

In a matter of seconds, the glass shatters and shards fly across the room. A gust of wind sweeps in, so powerful it knocks me backward against the edge of the bed. I grunt, tumbling onto the floor, and when the wind stops, I look toward the balcony again.

Mournwrath is gone. Nothing is left but a broken window, open air, and sea.

Breathing raggedly, I push to a stand, and glass scatters off my clothes. The bedroom door swings open, and Caz comes charging in with Juniper and Rowan behind him.

"What the hell happened?" he asks, rushing toward me.

"Mournwrath was here," I tell him.

"Shit. Did it hurt you? Let me see." He reaches for my face and rubs my jawbone. I wince from the sting. The glass must've cut me there.

"I'm fine," I tell him.

Maeve, Killian, and Della barge into the room next, and when they see the shattered glass and one side of the room now destroyed as if hit by a hurricane, their jaws go slack.

"What happened here?" Maeve asks.

"Mournwrath," Caz grumbles, finally pulling away from me.

He then hisses through his teeth and tugs the sleeve of his shirt up, revealing his forearm. The black veins are spreading there, and I feel my heart drop as I watch them slither up his arm.

"We need to move out. *Now*. There isn't much more time. Maeve, Juniper, Rowan, get Willow out of here and head to Vanora. The sooner you can get there, the better. Killian," he sighs, looking into his eyes. "I need you, brother. Stick with me." Killian tips his chin, looks Caz over, then nods. The disagreement from earlier is no longer an issue. He's dropping it, if only for now.

It's all a frenzy after we leave Caz's bedroom. Everyone hustles down the spiral staircase, and from there, Juniper, Maeve, and Rowan strap up to the teeth with weapons. Caz helps me put on the weapons he selected for me, then makes sure to cover them with my cloak.

Right after, we're being shuttled into an SUV with Rowan climbing behind the wheel. Silvera hops in and sits in the middle, Juniper on the other side.

"Always be aware of your surroundings," Caz says before I get into the car.

I nod. "I will.

"And if Mournwrath comes again, don't let it touch you."

"I'll try not to."

"Good." He guides me into the car, and I sit on the seat, looking back at him. He looks me over, and I don't know what it is about the way he looks at me, but it *terrifies* me. It's like he's looking at me for the last time.

"Hey," I call, grabbing his hand and squeezing it. "Everything will be okay."

He nods. Lifting my hand, he turns it over and runs his lips over my knuckles like he's done before—not kissing them, just feeling my flesh on his lips—then he releases me and steps back to close the door.

He gives the passenger window a knock, Rowan bobs his head, and the SUV takes off. I look back as we go, and Caz and Killian stand in front of the house, watching us drive away.

I sink my teeth into my bottom lip, fighting the wave of emotion running over me, but it's hard, because with each mile away, I feel that ache building in my chest again. The one that longs for him, desires his touch, and wants to be near him, and I know he feels it too.

As badly as I'd love to stay in his house, lying in his big bed, staring at the ocean, we can't. If we don't figure this Tether out and find a way to get rid of Mournwrath, we'll never be able to do any of that—so for the greater good, we'll take this time apart.

Silvera rests her head on my lap, and I sigh, stroking the top of it while Juniper rubs her back. My eyes meet Juniper's, and the words are spoken between us silently.

We'll figure this out. We'll be okay.

That's what I hope, anyway.

SEVENTY-TWO

CAZ

THE BLACKWATER TRAIN STATION consists of numerous gray booths and grumpy Blackwater citizens behind thick glass, swapping tickets for rubies. Lots of robberies happen here, hence the thickness of the glass, but they won't today. Not while I'm here.

It's not surprising having everyone stare at me. Their monarch is amongst them, going about his business, to a place unbeknownst to them. I don't often take the train to reach other destinations, I drive. But today calls for it. It's much faster taking the flash train, going an average of 180 miles per hour.

After ordering two tickets to Luxor from a booth, I walk to Killian who is standing near the tracks. A train speeds by, powerful enough to knock a bypasser down if they stand too closely. There've been many deaths because of the flash train—some accidental, others committed out of suicidal desires.

I offer Killian a ticket and he glances down at it, his arms folded across his chest. He faces ahead again, not taking it.

"Are you going to be this way the whole time?"

"What way?" he grumbles.

"Pouting."

"I'm not pouting," he counters.

"Yes, you are. Your arms are folded, and you won't look me in the eye. You're pouting because I whipped your ass earlier."

He finds that funny because he smirks, then puts his focus on me. "You didn't whip my ass. I *let* you win."

I smile, offering him the ticket again. He takes it, then sighs, stuffing it into the pocket of his dark pants. I take out my case of blooms, offer one to him, and after grabbing it, he pulls out a lighter and sparks the end of mine first before lighting his.

"Sometimes I wonder what the hell I've gotten myself into by working for ya," Killian murmurs, taking a pull.

"Ah, Kill. If only I knew."

"This Tether of yours. It doesn't frighten you?"

I look ahead at a mother with four children. She's shuttling them forward like sheep, trying not to miss the train stationed on the other side.

"A little," I admit.

"Do you think it's wise to keep her here?"

"I don't know."

"Well, I won't lie to you. I don't think it's wise." He exhales, a cloud of smoke surrounding him. "I think once someone finds out her attachment to you, you're dead, brother. Or she is."

"So, what do you expect me to do, eh? Send her back again? Forget all about her? I tried that and it damn near killed me, remember?"

"There has to be a way to break this Cold Tether—something that will set you apart from her."

I don't say anything to that. What is there to say? A part of me hates that Willow is Tethered to me, only because of the peril it places her in, but the other half enjoys it because for once, someone understands my angles. For once, there is someone who vouches for me, and probably always will, no matter what I do. She feels me and understands everything I do without me having to say a word, whether she agrees with it or not.

"The Council will have your head for killing Rami," he goes on.

"Nah." I take one last pull, exhale, and then drop the bloom, stepping on the lit end. "They've been wanting to get rid of Rami for a long time. They're probably glad he's gone. Besides, if they wanted me head, they'd have gotten it already. There's a reason they want me coming to Luxor. I'm not sure what that reason is yet, but I get the sense that I have nothing to worry about as far as what was done to Rami."

"With Rami gone, do you think…" Killian drops his head, working his jaw.

"His son," I mumble.

"He's only twenty-seven," Killian says. "Still a boy. Knowing his father is dead and that you killed him, he'll likely seek his own revenge. If not him, someone else in Rami's clan will."

"We'll make sure that doesn't happen. As you said, he's just a boy, and from what I've heard, Rami was never really a present father. We get to the boy, get him on our side, squash this brewing war with the Rippies, and finally clear the air."

A train zips by, the wind causing my jacket to flap. When it stops, the brakes squealing, I say, "This is us."

We board the train, people moving out of our way as we maneuver to VIP. It's vacant, so I take a seat by the window. Killian takes the seat across from me, and a trainwoman approaches, asking if we'd like anything to drink. I request a whiskey. Killian goes for blue tonic, most likely to keep him calm. He hates the train.

"I'm surprised you're willing to come," I say when the train lurches and departs.

Killian inhales, then exhales slowly. "I've said this once, and I'll say it again. When we had that feud—the one against the Rippies near Shadow's Peak—and that one fucker gassed me and dragged me to that Rippie pit to torture me, you found me, and you saved my life." Killian eyes me, a serious stare mixed with sincerity. "You didn't ask questions, and you didn't hesitate. You killed every bloody Rippie in there and got me out when I thought I was as good as dead, and for that, I'll owe you forever." He leans forward, capping my shoulder with his large hand. I feel his touch searing through my clothes, and as badly as it hurts, I don't move. "Wherever you go, I go, brother. And no matter how much your decisions piss me off, you'll never face your threats alone. Not while I'm still breathing."

I nod, clapping his shoulder too, smiling. "I appreciate you, brother. I really do."

THREE HOURS IS ALL it takes to get to Luxor on the flash train.

As soon as we step off, I draw in a breath. The air is much different in Luxor than it is in other territories. It's clearer, with a sweet scent that reminds me of honey. But it's also cold, so it's like frosted honey, if it were a thing.

The train moves away, and Killian and I leave the station. Mountains farther than the eye can see are ahead, capped with snow. A chill rides through me, and I turn my head left as a silver X-Stinger approaches. It stops in front of us, and a man climbs out from behind the driver's side.

"Monarch Harlow?" he asks, eyeing me.

"That's me."

"I'm Garan of Luxor, and I will be taking you to Council Castle." He pulls the back door of the car open, and I glance at Killian, who throws me a cautious look, before I walk ahead, climbing inside. Killian marches to the other side to get in, and Garan is behind the wheel again, driving away from the station.

"It's a cold one out there, innit?" Garan smiles as he looks through the rearview mirror.

I'm not in the mood for small talk. Their drivers always do this—try to ask questions to pose distractions. I know how The Council works. They want me to lower my guard, butter me up.

Killian and I already agreed that we won't be having drinks or any food while in Council Castle. I've heard the stories, how they slip poison in drinks and give it to those who've done wrong. They'll offer food that looks delectable but is actually rotten. Only they can see that it's rotten, due to some sort of spell they put on the food.

Garan takes a sharp right off the main road and drives up a winding mountain. Snow falls, trickling onto the windshield, pattering on the windows. I look at the village below. The lights gleam and cars whizz by, like tiny bugs.

Up Garan goes until the dark tips of Council Castle appears, surrounded in a thick blanket of fog. The roof is black, the building made of gray concrete. Several stories high and so big, I'm sure the entire population of Luxor could live there.

Garan drives across the bridge that leads to the front of the castle, a three-hundred-foot drop. Fall off it, and you're landing on jagged rocks and icicles shaped like daggers. When Garan finally parks, he hops out of the car and pulls my door open for me.

I step out, fixing my jacket, my cap, and when I look up the steps, three people are already standing there. They're in pure white suits and silver cloaks, their skin a rich dark brown, and their hair as white as the snow on the mountaintops.

Two men and a woman. The woman stands in the middle, Calista, her hair braided on the sides and pulled back into a neat ponytail. The two men are her brothers, Vassilis and Arie. Vassilis is much larger than Arie, twice Killian's size. He has coily, spring-like hair, while Arie's is wavy. I can't stand Vassilis; however, with Arie, it's easy to make peace with him.

"Welcome, Monarch Harlow." Calista calls her greeting.

"Go on up then," Garan insists. I cut my eyes at him before looking at Killian.

"Right, Killian," I sigh, digging into my pocket to retrieve a bloom. "We know how The Council are. Heads are always up their asses, and they'll do their best to get under our skin, but we won't let them." I light the end of it, inhale, then exhale as I stare at the trio atop the stairs. "They know how hard Blackwater Territory is to handle, so at the end of the day, they need us. We don't need them."

Killian grunts, squaring his shoulders.

"Right. Let's go on up and deal with whatever the fuck their problem is so we can be on our way."

"Easier said than done," Killian grumbles.

"I know, brother." I cap his shoulder. "But today, we do our best to behave."

I march up the stairs first, and when I'm at the top, The Council takes a step back. Calista smiles, revealing stark white teeth behind blood-red lips. Arie, as always, wears a proud smirk, and Vassilis frowns. Nothing new there.

"I trust your trip to Luxor went smoothly?" Arie asks.

"It was fine." I fold my fingers in front of me. "Now tell me why I'm here."

"Are you in a hurry?" Vassilis asks, a hint of agitation in his voice.

I switch my gaze to his. "I am, actually. I have pressing matters to tend to."

"Matters more important than facing your Council?"

"Yes, believe it or not."

A growl forms in the pit of Vassilis' throat, and his eyes flash silver. Those are his *angry* eyes. I fight a smile, putting my focus on Calista.

"Listen, I know that I'm not here for you to have my head. If that were the case, you'd have done it yourselves in Blackwater, or at least hired someone to do the job for you. Since that hasn't happened, I believe it's safe for me to assume Rami's death has become a *convenience* for you. So, what is it that I'm here for?"

Calista laughs, a soft noise that is hardly audible in the cold wind. "You have always been a smart man, Monarch Harlow. And you're right, we don't need your head. At least, *not yet*." She raises her chin, then turns away, moving past two guards near the colossal double doors that lead into the castle. "Let us continue this conversation inside, next to food and a fire. There, we will discuss why we've really asked you here."

SEVENTY-THREE

CAZ

Council Castle isn't a place welcoming to visitors. Their dark walls, thin windows, and sharp corners create an atmosphere that screams, *"We're better and stronger than you, now bow to us or get the fuck out."*

I'll be damned if I bow to these people–silver little terrors who hide behind their powers and their walls. Calista leads the way through the castle, Arie and Vassilis walking at mine and Killian's side.

"You think we're gonna run?" Killian eyes Vassilis.

"You'd be wise not to, lest you want your brains splattered all over our walls."

"Ha. Good luck with that, you Mythic bitch."

Vassilis' jaw ticks. He hates Blackwater people, I'd say with a very strong passion. He hates that we don't fear The Council the way other territories do. In his mind, because they're in charge, everyone should cater to them, run at their beck and call, and fear them.

They have a constant need for respect, yet they hardly do shit for anyone but themselves. That's why there's so much chaos in Vakeeli. They let us all run rampant while they pick and choose which crimes matter most, and which will be least problematic.

I suppose I shouldn't take away all their credit. They *are* the most powerful beings of Vakeeli right now, but with powers like theirs comes massive responsibility. Their actions can't stem from cruel or unjust intentions, courtesy of the Regals. My mother informed me of this when I was a child, back when she had me studying Vakeeli hierarchy. Which is probably why Vassilis hasn't blasted us to smithereens quite yet, but I'm sure he's looking for a solid enough reason to.

Due to his honor of protecting those in Vakeeli, he can't be as ruthless as he desires or he'll be stripped of his powers, and the thought of it makes me want to laugh in his face.

Calista rounds a corner, entering a large room with an intricately designed ceiling. Sharp icicles run up the black columns, threaded with twinkling lights and silver flowers. A table that can seat at least twenty people is in the middle, an iron chandelier with dagger-like jewels glinting above. A decanter of wine, a tray of fruit, and a roasted lump of meat (boar, most likely) is on the table. Calista points a hand in the direction of the fireplace and a large flame appears, instantly warming the room.

"Please, sit," she insists, already taking the throne-like chair at one end of the table. Her brothers sit on either side of her, and Killian and I take several seats down.

With a snap of her fingers, three servants dressed in silver with scarves covering their hair appear.

"Wine," Calista commands, and they hurry to the table, pouring wine into each crystal. One of them, a girl who can't be any older than fifteen, sets a glass in front of me then bows. She takes off, rounding a corner with the others.

"We have an idea of what caused your attack on Rami," Calista starts, diving right into it.

"*My* attack?" I shake my head. She's fucking with me, I know it. "He started it. I just finished it."

"You defied the rules," Vassilis snarls. Love of Vakeeli, I would really love to punch him in the fucking face, just once to make him stop all that unnecessary snarling and growling.

"As I'm sure you're aware, Rami attacked me while I was seeing a Mythic, took two people from my clan, made them fight in his bloody caves, and then assaulted someone I was meant to protect."

"You mean your mate," Calista says, smiling and I expected one of them to bring Willow up, but hearing her say it with that vicious smirk doesn't calm my nerves. I clench a fist on the table, and Killian adjusts in his chair. I eye him, and there's a warning in his eyes—one we pass to each other often when dealing with others. *Remain calm. Don't let them get a reaction out of you.*

"I've just discovered she's my mate, yes," I state.

"And you killed another Monarch because he was about to assault her?" Arie asks.

"He would have raped her."

Arie looks at Calista, and then Vassilis. "Can't say I wouldn't have done the same—not that I know what it's like having a mate. But if I did, I'd do what I have to do to honor and protect her. I personally think Rami crossed the line there."

This is why I like Arie most. Though naive at times, he thinks sensibly and with understanding.

"Despite what Rami has done, he was still Ripple Hills' appointed Monarch," Calista goes on. "And now that territory is up in metaphorical flames because he is dead."

"You knew the law of killing a Monarch. It's a cause for *death*," Vassilis adds with snark. "You've been trouble since becoming a monarch yourself. Tell us why we shouldn't kill you right here, right now."

"Because you need me."

Vassilis scoffs, glancing at Calista, who watches me carefully, eyes narrowed, her head in a slight tilt.

"You are very wise, Monarch Harlow. I can appreciate that. As you stated before, Rami was becoming a nuisance. You are not the first territory he's tried inciting wars with." She sighs, then sips her wine, as if bored. "But we cannot let what happened go unpunished. Many of the Rippies saw you and your clan in his club, and they're angry. They're ready to start their own war—create an act of vengeance for their fallen monarch."

"I understand." I sit forward, pushing my wine glass away from me and folding my hands on the table. Calista's eyes flicker to my glass before lifting back up again to mine. "So, what will the punishment be?"

She leans back in her chair, bringing her glass to her crimson lips again. "There is a boy of Rami's. He's next in line to become Monarch there and now that Rami is dead, he'll be sworn in within a year." She swirls her wine. "We don't want another Rami taking over Ripple Hills. We'd prefer to keep the peace, and though you can be a pain in the ass yourself, well...you're a better alternative than Rami or any Rippie and the boy will need proper guidance."

I frown. "You want me to guide Rami's son?"

"We want you to train him, look after him, show him the ropes of being a monarch. Someone will have to be in charge there. He'll need to plant his roots, get things in order. Consider this an opportunity for you to create a treaty with them."

Killian shifts in his chair, grunting. I know what he's thinking. A treaty with the Rippies is impossible. It's never been done.

"And as we all know," Arie chips in, "Rippies love rubies. They'll do *anything* for them. To ease their concerns and kill those metaphorical fires my sister speaks of, you will give reparations to their guards. We're thinking about five million rubies. That should be enough to pay them all off and shut them up. And if it isn't, we will see to it ourselves that they have more reason to hate Rami than to grieve for him."

"Five million rubies?" Killian blurts. "Are you out of your fucking minds? Our men will have to mine for those rubies day and night. Some of them may even die in the ruby caves."

Calista shrugs as her wine magically refills. "A small price to pay for the murder of a king."

"Rami was far from a king," I grumble.

"You're right. He was a piece of shit, scum on our shoe. Listen, this will be done. There is no negotiating it. You'll look after the boy, take him under your broken wings, and you'll pay the Rippies, so everyone forgets Rami and all of the mess it's created."

"Fine," I mutter, but it doesn't sit well with me. I care for my people, unlike Rami, and having them dig in the caves for rubies, it'll be endless. They'll grow to hate me, and the men's families will wish me dead. It's no better than sending them off to war. I'll have to come up with a solution that doesn't put my people in danger but still gets those bloody Rippies paid.

"Very good," says Calista, and Vassilis puts on a shit-eating grin. My fingers ache for my gun.

"Anything else?" I ask.

"Yes, actually, there is one more thing." Calista plucks an iceberry from the tray, a gray fruit I'm not fond of. "We know you've been trying to shield your thoughts about your Tether. You want to keep that part of your life sacred, but you forget we know everything that goes on in Vakeeli, whether we interfere or not."

"What does my Tether have to do with this?"

"Your Tether, believe it or not, is our link to setting Selah free."

"Elaborate."

"Your kind–the ones who carry the Cold Tether–are constantly recreated. Every couple of years, there is a new version of you that is born, most times through different parents, and there has not been a version quite like you. You have the combination of a Monarch, a hybrid Mythic, and the Cold Tether from the Regals, and what a rare mixture that is."

I sit back in my seat, waiting for her to elaborate further.

"With your gifts–your *blood*–it can help us find Selah. However, there's something out there trying to stop that from happening."

A chill runs down my spine. "You're talking about Mournwrath."

"Decius, yes."

"Why can't you defeat him yourselves?"

"Unfortunately, we were created only to defend the commoners and the gilded. Decius is a being created before our time. He can't harm us, and we can't harm him. In fact, it's impossible for us to even be in the same room as him."

"Why?"

"It weakens our energy," Vassilis states. "And his, so he purposely avoids us. We can thank Selah for that."

"Some Council you are," Killian huffs.

"Anyway, we've had the location of Selah for a very long time, and she can only be awakened with your blood. You, I'm afraid, are the cure to her awakening. Right now, she rests in the tombs of an island, far off the Vanorian coast, Inferno Isle. We believe Decius has put a spell on her that weakened her, caused her to fall into a sleep that lasts forever, and took her there to hide the body. We've tried everything in our power to wake her from where we are, nothing has worked, and after doing our studies, we realized it was never *us* who could do it. She can only be awakened with the blood of the three most powerful individuals of Vakeeli. And that's where you come in."

"Every man knows if you even make it through the treacherous waters, it's impossible to survive Inferno Isle. You can forget it," I tell her. "It'll kill me."

"Death is a possibility." Calista examines her silver nails. "But we are willing to do everything we can to protect you. We'll give you fireproof armor and other things to withstand the heat and flames. And to get there, we'll have a boat built, made with the finest Vakeeli iron and Vanorian gold."

"And if it still sinks?"

Calista smirks. "Then we hope another version like you is born with the blood you have now in the near future."

"Highly unlikely," Arie mutters.

"'Tis true," Calista sighs. "We've waited centuries for you."

"And why come to me now? Mournwrath has attacked us more than once. Who's to say he won't kill us the next time?"

"Well, you had to mate first. The Tether had to be in full effect, which is why we opened the portal for your tether and brought her here."

"*You* did that?" I grimace. "You put her whole life in jeopardy, and for what? To get me to bond with her so you can awake Selah?"

"Exactly. It took a while, actually. We couldn't get it right the first time—Arie was too drunk and stupid to stay awake." Calista side eyes her brother just as he takes a sip of wine. "We managed, though. And don't be so glum about it. You can't deny that she's the best thing that's ever happened to you. You should be thanking us."

Fucking bitch.

"We knew you'd look after her," Calista goes on. "It's what you do. You protect the ones you love and eliminate anyone who comes after them, and that's why we're glad *you* are the chosen one. You should be elated! This is an honor. Not even we can awake a Regal. Now that you've mated, it's all come full circle. Your blood is charged."

"You must be forgetting about Decius," I counter. "If he kills me before your boat is built, I can't help you with Selah."

"That's why you must go immediately–before he can capture you," Vassilis says. "We'll find the strongest men in Vakeeli and have them build the boat within three days. That's more than enough time for you to prepare for the trip. And while you go, your mate can come here, where she'll be better protected from Decius."

"Like I'd let you get anywhere near her." I glare him down a moment before clasping my fingers in my lap. "What if I don't want to do this? What if I fail?"

"Wouldn't be wise to reject," Arie says, twirling the stem of his wine glass between his fingers. "As for failing, just stop it, alright? You've survived some crazy shit. If anyone in Vakeeli can do it, it's you." He sets the glass down a little too roughly and leans forward. "Now can we be done with this? I need to drain my fucking balls and this meeting is *incredibly* boring."

"*Disgustingly* vulgar," Vassilis hisses, side-eying his brother, who grins and waves a middle finger at him.

"You *will* do this, Caspian," Calista says, voice firm. "You have no choice. Remember, we saved you from Magnus. And if you awake Selah, this favors all of Vakeeli, not just us. There will be restoration, retribution. She will kill Decius like she's always had planned and you and your mate will be freed from his shackles of the Cold Tether. You can live your life as normal people, doing normal things without worrying about a billion-year-old monster sucking the life out of you."

"Enticing, but I can't help feeling like there's a catch with this whole Selah thing—other than me boarding a boat and navigating waters that are likely to kill me." As I survey each of them, I know they aren't telling me the whole truth. There's something being left off the table, I can sense it.

"No catch," Calista says, her voice light. "You're the only one who can complete this mission right now. You, the tormented, damaged, cold, but *brilliant* Monarch Harlow. You've been through and have done so much. You'll be able to get to her. We need our Regal back for a more fruitful life. For more gifts from the Regals, and to truly limit the violence of Vakeeli. With Selah thriving and awake, the world will be as it was. It will be a place where we all can live without threats, or wars, or hostility. We'll be able to mind our own and sing our praises to her for creating us, and in return she'll bestow her gifts and blessings upon us. Tell me that doesn't sound promising?"

"Not really, but if that's what you want..."

Her eyes flash, clearly agitated by my response. "It is. And in three days, you will board the boat and go to her. Now do we have your word?"

"Fine. You have my word, but if Decius gets to me before that boat is built, you're out of luck."

"We'll do what we can to hold him off," Vassilis declares.

"Sure," I mutter.

"I will see to it that you and your mate are covered by our eyes, just as we've been doing since your mate returned," Calista says. "That means Decius will not attack while we need you."

"How so?"

"Consider it a bubble of sorts, an invisible one that surrounds you and keeps you safe. Nothing can breakthrough this bubble of our energy unless you allow it."

"This covers Willow as well?"

"Yes." Calista rises, her cloak swimming down to her ankles. "Please enjoy your stay at the Luxor Inn," she says as Arie hops out of his chair and scatters out of the room. "Our driver will take you back down to the town. We have rooms ready for you and your guest and any food or drink you want is on the house. And no, Caz, the food and drinks are *not* poisoned. The last thing we want is a roll of bread ending a chosen man's life. We've waited far too long to let that ruin it."

"I feel I should be honored." I stand, fixing my coat. "We'll be going now."

A smile from Calista. "Of course."

Killian is already across the room, making his way to the closed doors.

As I walk his way, Vassilis says, "There's one thing you should consider, Harlow." I turn to look at him. "If you don't keep your promise, or you pull back on your word, there will be consequences. And I'm certain one of them will involve that pretty little mate of yours."

I look him in the eye and my jaw ticks as he sits there, reveling in his threat. The urge to pull my gun out is intense and as badly as I'd love to pop a bullet in his skull and be done with him, I keep my hands at my side and draw in a breath, exhaling.

"I am a man of my word," I inform him. "But let me be clear about something. If you *ever* use my mate as a threat again, I'll rip those shiny eyes out of your fucking head and shove them down your throat."

Vassilis smirks, his eyes glowing, a stark silver in the dimly lit room.

"Caz. Let's go." Killian grips my shoulder, urging me to move. I stare Vassilis in the eyes a moment longer, envisioning what it would be like to wrap my hands around his throat to strangle him. It would satisfy the hell out of me, but now isn't the time, so I turn away, leaving.

SEVENTY-FOUR

WILLOW

I step out of the car in front of Alora's palace and raise my hands above my head to stretch, glad we've finally made it. Night has fallen, the sun nowhere in sight. The stars twinkle in the indigo sky, the moon a sweet crescent.

We're taken up to the palace by one of Alora's guards, and when she sees us, seated on her throne in a red dress, she smiles.

"Welcome back, my Blackwater friends."

"Thank you for having us again, your majesty," Maeve says, giving a slight bow. "Will we be seeing Beatrix tonight?"

"Ah, if only. I was unaware that tonight is the night Beatrix hunts for food and berries. She does it once a week—it's a Mythic thing, so she won't be home until tomorrow night, I'm afraid."

"Oi, I'm not sure if we have that much time," Maeve sighs. "Is there any way you can request for her to come back sooner?"

"I try not to disrupt Beatrix during her hunting." Alora walks down the golden steps from her throne. "As a Mythic, hunting is how she restores her energy. You know how it is for them—they stick to their old ways. If she does her hunting unbothered, she'll be more inclined to see us tomorrow."

"Are we to stay here again, then?" Juniper asks, looking around.

"I would prefer it. I apologize, but after what happened in Iron Class last time, I'll need everyone from Blackwater to remain in the palace."

"Understandable." Maeve eyes Juniper. "Is that understood, Juniper?"

"Fine," Juniper mutters.

"Shall we break open some wine, then?" Alora's eyes light up.

She leads us to one of the balconies on the second floor. Tables that face the ocean are set up, fairy lights draped from column to column, and a bar is already set up with drinks. A man in a gold suit stands behind it, prepping glasses, and ready to serve. Juniper and Maeve go straight for the bar, and Rowan slumps down in a chair, sighing as he rests the back of his head on it.

I take a seat at the table closest to the edge of the balcony, with the best view of the water. I attempt to tap in with Caz, but all my words bounce back. He's blocking me out right now, which means he's probably with The Council. He did say he'd have to block me once he was in Luxor. He doesn't trust them with his thoughts and doesn't want them knowing about our Tether. The people of Luxor are different, so I've been told. They're much more calculating.

Alora has a small band come to the balcony to play music. The band's instruments consist of a harp, a violin, and something that looks like a guitar, but is much wider and has way more strings. It's nice outside, a warm, gentle breeze going, and a part of me wishes Caz were here too. I hope he's okay.

"Let me guess," Juniper says, turning a chair backwards and

sitting on it. There's a drink in her hand and goofy smile on her face, like she's already tipsy. "You're thinking about Caz."

I fight a smile. "Is it that obvious?"

"I assure you, he's fine. If anyone can handle The Council, it's him."

"They sound like scary people."

"Hmm...they can be. But only when you cross them. They normally like keeping the peace, but of course there are the few who don't care about that, so The Council handles them."

"Handles them how?"

"Depends. Sometimes a person is sent to The Trench, which is basically a wasteland. Other times, The Council will just end you themselves, if it's a crime punishable enough. One of the main rules of Vakeeli from The Council revolves around children. If someone hurts a child, they kill them, plain and simple. There is no trial or anything—they just end you."

"Oh." I press my lips, and my eyes travel to Alora, who is dancing between the tables with Proll. Proll has his hand on her waist in a protective way. I tilt my head. That is *not* the touch of two people dancing for fun. I study them as they waltz, how their eyes link, the way Proll keeps her close and buries his large fingers into her slim waist. She's completely relaxed in his arms.

"Wait a minute. Is the queen sleeping with her guard?" I ask softly, and Juniper looks over her shoulder.

"Oh, yeah. She's been sleeping with him for ages."

"Wow." I continue watching them. Proll tips Alora backwards, and she releases a harmonious laugh before being reeled back up like she's the weight of a feather.

"Alora's had her fair share of men," Juniper proclaims.

"Really? It seems she wouldn't bother with any since she's so powerful."

"Well, she's very picky about who she sleeps with. The men

normally work for her in the palace, or they're monarchs themselves. I've heard she's even slept with Mythics."

"Monarchs?" I ask. That catches me off guard, and Juniper locks eyes with me briefly before gulping the rest of her drink.

"Shit. I've said too much, haven't I?"

"No, tell me what you mean. Which monarch has she slept with?"

"Willow, it's nothing. Forget I even said it." Juniper starts to stand, but I catch her hand.

"Are Caz and Alora sleeping together?" I ask, softening my voice.

"Love of Vakeeli, no!" Juniper exclaims, but her answer doesn't satisfy me. My heart is pumping faster, and there's a burning in my chest that's bubbling up to my head.

As if she notices my irritation, Juniper sighs and sits back down. "Okay, look, it was many years ago. Literally when they first met. And I only know because I saw him coming out of her chambers that night. I don't think it was serious. They never did anything like it again. They've only remained allies. Trust me, you have nothing to worry about."

I look from Juniper to Rowan and Maeve who are standing near the balcony, chatting. I'm not sure why it bothers me so much, knowing this. I mean, I didn't know Caz before a few weeks ago, and yet this reality stings.

I realize *why* it stings as I look at Alora. She's graceful, patient, kind, and beautiful. Any man would want her. Even mine...

Then again, is Caz really *my* man? Or are we just bound to this Tether, sinking into the satisfaction it provides?

I stand and walk around the table. "I'm gonna get some sleep."

"Oh, come on, Willow!" Juniper groans. "Don't leave!"

"I'm fine," I tell her, forcing a smile. "I'm just really tired after that ride here." It's a boldface lie, but she takes it, so I leave the balcony, and as I go, I feel eyes on me. I glance over my shoulder to find Alora watching me leave.

I wander through the palace until I find the chambers I was in last time and close the large door behind me, lock it, and then take off my boots. After removing my cloak, blouse, and pants, I pull down the thick quilt and climb into the bed, pulling it over me. Lying down doesn't calm my racing heart, though. And my mind races even faster.

I thought he didn't like to be touched. Did he enjoy whatever he did with Alora? God, why do I even care? It was a long time ago, and we've only just met.

I flop onto my back, staring up at the ceiling. Gold stars are painted up there, glowing in the night. It's like staring up at the night sky.

Willow.

I gasp when I hear his voice, and damn it, even when I'm upset with him, I get butterflies from it.

I hear you.

Good. I've just left The Council. Apologies for blocking you out for so long.

How did it go?

It was...a lot. I'll fill you in when I see you.

Fine.

There's silence for a moment. Then: **Everything all right?**

Yep. Everything's fine.

Doesn't sound like it. Have you gone to see Beatrix yet?

No. We're staying until tomorrow. Beatrix is hunting or something.

Quiet again. **I sense some anger. Why are you upset?**

I'm not upset.

You can't lie when I can feel it, Willow. What's going on? Has someone hurt you?

"No!" I say out loud, then I sigh, sitting up against the upholstered headboard.

Well, if no one's hurt you, what's the matter? You're stewing about something.

I close my eyes a moment, then sigh.

I found out...about you and Alora.

Silence again, only this time it's deafening.

That was a long time ago, Willow.

I know.

So why be angry about it?

I'm not angry.

Jealous, then.

I'm not jealous, I counter, rolling my eyes, and I can't believe it, but he chuckles.

You are.

You know what? Just leave me alone please. I'm not jealous. It just caught me off guard, that's all.

Another laugh. ***Sure, okay.***

I sink lower in the plush bed, pulling the quilt over my face.

You have nothing to worry about. It was just a stupid, drunk night for both of us. Nothing even happened.

I don't respond. I don't want to, and I'm not quite sure I believe him.

What can I do to prove it to you? he asks.

"There's nothing you can do. Whatever you had with her happened, and it is what it is," I say out loud, as if that will solidify it. "I'm over it."

Are you? Because it sure doesn't sound or feel like it.

"Well, I am." I fold my arms. Goodness, what the hell is wrong with me? Acting like a spoiled brat. What is this man doing to me?

I'm at an inn, in Luxor. Killian and I will be leaving in the morning on a fast train to Vanora.

Great.

He lets out a loud sigh that washes through me.

What are you wearing?

"What?"

I didn't stutter.

I frown, lowering my eyes to my tank top. Beneath the quilt, I'm only in my panties.

Ah. So, you're half naked then? I hope you're alone.

Shut up. I fight a smile.

I plan on taking a shower.

Good for you, I think sarcastically. He gives pause.

I can't stop thinking about you, Willow.

His words make my heart hammer in my chest. I feel myself lowering my guard, anticipating his next words.

Will you do me a favor?

What? I wonder, as if bored.

Slide your fingers into your panties and play with yourself.

Are you serious right now?

I'm dead serious.

I fidget in the bed, then shake my head. *No. Why should I?*

I want to try something.

Well, whatever it is, I'm not doing it.

Caz is quiet again, and I think he's not going to say much else. But then I feel a sensation down below, and I squeeze my thighs together, gasping.

"What the hell are you doing?" I whisper.

You felt that, eh? Didn't think it would work.

"Caz, what was that? What are you doing?"

I'm in the shower.

Okay...

And my dick is in my hand.

I squeeze my thighs together again, trying to fight the throb that rocks through me.

"How are you doing that?" I breathe.

He ignores me. **Put your fingers in your panties**. It's a demand. No longer an option.

I sink my teeth into my bottom lip when I feel the throbbing again. I can't help following his lead, slipping my fingers beneath the waistband of my panties, sighing as I graze the tips over my pelvis. When my middle finger presses down on my clit, I gasp and throw my head back.

Oh yeah. I feel you now. Play with your pussy for me. I want to hear you come around your fingers.

"This is crazy," I breathe.

Do you feel me? he rasps and, insanely enough, I do. **I'm stroking my dick in the shower while I think about you, Willow.** He releases a gruff groan that sets me ablaze. **You're all I can ever think about these days.**

It feels like you're inside me.

I'm wishing that I were, he rasps. **And imagining that I am.**

How is this happening?

I don't know, but don't you stop.

I don't. I continue circling my clit with my finger, and as I do, I swear I feel Caz pushing his way inside me. The girth of his dick filling me up inch by savory inch, just like the real thing. A guttural groan echoes in my head, and I hiss through my teeth as I feel him going faster.

Is this my pussy?

"Yes," I breathe.

Are you my mate?

"Yes," I breathe again.

You're the only woman I'll ever enjoy feeling. The only one who can make me weak like this. There is no comparison.

I don't need to use my fingers anymore. I feel him, as if he's right here in the bedroom with me, thrusting inside me, groaning in my ear. My back curves, my breathing becomes wilder, and before I know it, I'm coming. I'm coming so hard the stars on the ceiling blur.

Ah, shit, Willow, he groans. ***I'm going to cum. Fuck, I wish I were coming in your pussy instead of my hand right now.***

His words tip me over the edge. They're so primal, so guttural, that I come again, crying out his name and clutching the bedding. Never in my life have I felt something so intense.

Look at that. My naughty mate. Coming for me again, are you? I suppose you aren't that angry with me after all.

Caz's groans are louder. He growls the words, **oh fuck**, and then there's silence. As if he's pulled his way out, I don't feel him buried within me anymore. The imaginary weight of him is gone, and I feel open, raw.

Silence washes over the room, and it takes me a moment to realize what just happened. He just fucked me telepathically and made me orgasm. *Twice.* Holy shit.

"Caspy?" I call when the silence has gone on for too long.

Get some rest, Willow. It's the last thing he says to me before blocking me out again.

SEVENTY-FIVE

WILLOW

A whole day passes because Beatrix still isn't home. Alora allows us to stay in the palace (really, we have no choice. She refuses to let anyone go into the city), and while we do, we eat, wander the grounds, and collect berries from one of the gardens, and by the time the sun sets, she sends three girls to paint my, Juniper's, and Maeve's nails.

Our nails aren't painted using the same method my world does. In Vanora, they use paint brushes and a thick liquid that hardens on the nail. One coat is all they need. I go with gold—it seems fitting for us being in Vanora—while Juniper goes for black, and Maeve chooses a blood red.

Alora doesn't get her nails painted. Instead, she sits in a chaise in a corner, chatting away with Maeve and Juniper. I find it hard to have a conversation with her right now. In fact, I've been mostly avoiding Alora after finding out about her and Caz.

I'm not sure where this jealous, territorial side of me has come from, but it bothers me that he was ever with her. It's possible he may have been on those red pills, and yeah, maybe he was drunk, but it's the fact that it happened. I never would've guessed they'd done something together.

Luzian and Clara enter the room with food and drinks on gold trays, setting them on a table nearby. They offer a glass of something bubbly to me, but I pass on it. Juniper takes her glass and walks to the balcony, standing next to Maeve who is smoking a bloom.

"Something's troubling you." Alora's voice is close. I swing my eyes to hers, and she has her head in a slight tilt.

"Why do you say that?" I ask.

"I can see it all over you."

She narrows her eyes, studying my face. I look toward the balcony where Juniper and Maeve are.

"Ah." I turn my head again as Alora snaps her fingers.

"What?"

"It's about Caz and me."

I avoid a frown. "What do you mean?"

"Let's not play ignorant, Willow. I know that you know. It's why you can no longer look me in the eye."

I'm not sure what to say to that, so I don't say anything at all. Alora stands and walks across the room, sitting on the edge of my ivory chaise. She's so close I can smell her floral perfume. It's a delightful scent.

"Do you want to know the truth?"

I sigh. "I think I already know the truth."

"No, you don't."

I meet her eyes.

"The truth is, I'm a woman who loves a challenge. And here was this man, coming into my palace, acting as if he were untouchable. I mean, he literally did *not* want to be touched.

Wouldn't even shake my hand!" Her head moves side to side in disbelief. "So, sure, I flirted with him, and I invited him to my room. And he stopped by...but do you want to know what happened?"

"I don't need the details," I mutter. The nerve of her.

"When he came to my room, he told me he wasn't going to sleep with me. In fact, he specifically came to my room to *reject* me."

My eyes stretch and my jaw drops a bit. "Wait...so, nothing happened?"

"Other than a long, long chat about the things he was going to change about Blackwater, nothing happened. But I can tell you what happened for me?"

"What?"

"I developed a deep respect for Caz that night. Never had a man been so certain about what he *didn't* want. I always come across these arrogant men boasting about the things they have, or the things they want or can steal, but never a man who is so passionate about what doesn't interest him." She huffs a laugh, as if tickled by the thought. "It's how I knew Caz was different. He's not like other Vakeeli men. He's more, and my dear, he's *yours*. He is literally bonded to you. No one can take that. Not even the queen herself." She places a hand on my shoulder, smiling. "Now please quit your moping, my love. This side of you is *extremely* boring."

I laugh as she stands and strolls across the room toward the balcony with the others.

SEVENTY-SIX

CAZ

After I've packed what little I brought with me, I leave my room at Luxor Inn, giving Killian's door a knock as I pass it.

He opens it, eyeing me through a crack, before pulling the door a bit wider.

"Heading down for a bite. Coming?"

"I'll meet you downstairs," he says, standing taller.

I cock a brow and try to look over his shoulder, but he blocks my view. My eyes move to his again. "A Luxorian? That's a new low for you, Kill."

"She's only visiting Luxor. She's from Kessel."

"Where'd you meet her?"

"At the bar, now fuck off. I'll be down in a minute." He shuts the door in my face as the woman giggles, and I huff a laugh, pulling out a bloom from my pocket and sparking it.

I enter the pub after marching down the stairs, grateful it's mostly vacant. Most people are shuttling into this place at nightfall, filling up on tonics and stuffing their faces with greasy Luxorian food. This morning, there's a maximum of four people, all drinking tea or eating at tables, and the barman.

I bob my head at the barman, who nods back with hesitancy, before sitting at a table in the corner. A waitress approaches, her hair silver, dressed head to toe in black.

"What can I get you?" she inquires.

"A whiskey and toast will do, thank you."

She nods and takes off, walking behind the bar to a door leading to the kitchen.

The barman cleans out a glass, eyeing me again. I pull from my bloom, eyeing him back. Then he sets his glass down and walks around the counter, and I slide my hand to the gun at my waist.

"Don't worry. I'm not coming over to cause you trouble," the barman announces, then he extends an arm, offering me a hand. "Name's Harold."

"Nice to meet you, Harold." His extended hand lingers, and I inhale again before stabbing out my bloom. "Might as well put that hand down. I don't shake with strangers."

"Oh." Harold drops his hand and stands up straight, dusting himself off.

"Why are you staring at me, Harold?"

"Was I staring?" He looks around, his face turning as red as his hair. "I apologize, it's just that...well, you don't remember me, do you?"

I tip my chin, assessing him—his green eyes, freckles splattered across his nose and upper cheeks—but nothing about him rings a bell.

"Can't say that I do."

Harold pulls the chair on the opposite side of the table back, and I draw my gun out. He pauses halfway. "Mind if I sit?"

I press my lips but keep the gun on top of the table. I don't know who he is. For all I know, he's a distraction, and the woman in the room with Killian is too.

"Buckley's Fight Club," Harold says, and my eyes widen as I glare at him.

"What?"

"We met at Buckley's Fight Club—well, it's not called that anymore. Do you remember? I was the water boy. I fetched the pails, brought water back from the Ripple Hill Riverbank for the fighters. Oh, man, I used to love watching those fights! Especially when *you* were in the ring! You'd really rein it in for those wins! Beating those bastards to mush!"

I stare at Harold a moment. Probably a moment too long because he begins to look uneasy, fidgeting in his chair. A disgusting feeling slithers down to my stomach, causing it to churn, and my jaw ticks.

"Look, I—I'm sorry to bother you. I—I'll go now."

I grip my gun, sliding it closer to me, ready to pick it up and point it at him. "Yes. You'd better."

Harold skitters off, rushing behind the bar and into the kitchen. When he's gone, I close my eyes briefly and draw in a breath.

"Guns on the table. Don't you have any manners?"

My eyes pop open, and Manx stands in the center of the pub. His white hair gleams, and if I'm not mistaken, he looks younger. The wrinkles around his eyes seem to have faded—then again, he's a jolly man. He never lets stress settle in his body.

"Manx. What the hell are you doing here?" I ask as he pulls the chair out at my table to sit.

"Oh, don't you mind me. I'm here to see The Council. Apparently, someone ran off and eradicated Rami, and now I must testify since that *someone* made a stop in Whisper Grove beforehand." He leans in, smirking. "They believe I told you to do it."

"That's ridiculous. It had nothing to do with you. Besides, they saw me last night about it and we settled things. Why bother you?"

"I don't know." Manx sits back in his chair with a sigh. "Perhaps they're just checking off a list of people to interrogate about it to make themselves feel accomplished."

The waitress approaches my table, setting down my whiskey and toast. She asks if there will be anything else, I tell her no, and she walks off again.

"I know you killed Rami for her," Manx goes on as I pick up my whiskey. I try swallowing the bile that built up in my throat from Harold's conversation. It doesn't go away.

"And how would you know that?" I ask.

"Well, why else would you have broken the Law of Monarchs, if not for her? Let me guess, she was your bait and it backfired?"

"She wasn't bait," I counter, despite the guilt gnawing at me. "She wanted to help."

Manx chuckles. "You've never been one to accept blame."

I bite into my toast, mulling that over. "You're right, Manx. As I told The Council, I did kill Rami, but only to save her. He was forcing himself on her, and he had two members of my clan in his fight club. He was breaking two laws. I only broke one."

"That isn't the first time Rami has forced himself on a woman, and you know it."

"It wasn't just about that," I mutter.

"No. Then what was it about?"

I look around before leaning in a bit and murmuring, "As you're aware, she's my Tether."

"That she is," he murmurs back. "And have you decided to accept it?"

"What do you mean *accept it*?"

"You know what I mean."

I lean back again, eyeing him. His eyes drop to the half of toast left on my plate and when I don't say anything, he asks, "Do you remember when the Whisper Grove army saved you from Buckley?"

"What the hell is going on here? You're the second person to bring up Buckley today." I take another gulp of whiskey.

"But do you remember?"

"Of course, I do."

"You were so angry. You trusted no one," Manx says.

I don't say anything, but I do watch his face, the way it crumples with concern. "I remember thinking there was no saving you. Getting into fights with everyone. Running away from Maeve's. But I promised your mother I would look out for you...and I did. I still do, right?"

"At times." I smirk.

He cracks a smile, folding his hands on his lap. "I remember the boy who lived on the border of Whisper Grove and Blackwater—the free spirit who was full of life. With eyes as blue as his mother's, and a heart of gold. I suppose your heart would be more of steel now," he chuckles.

I lean forward, resting my elbows on the table. "What are you getting on about, Manx?"

"I'm just glad you didn't turn out to be like your father," he murmurs, and hearing that causes me to sit back again, slowly, as I watch his eyes. Where is this coming from? "I know Blackwater is tough terrain, but I see a much bigger difference now that you're in charge compared to when he was in charge. And your mother, she would be proud of where you are now and all you've overcome. Just remember to keep that promise you gave me."

"To never be like Magnus."

"You've kept your promise thus far. Keep being the change Blackwater needs. With Willow at your side, perhaps it'll become easier to attract peace in your territory."

"Perhaps," I mumble.

Manx smiles, then he looks toward the bar, at Harold who is looking between us. "Right. Well, The Council is waiting for me," Manx says, standing. "And don't you worry. I'll be vouching for you. I've always hated Rami."

I huff a laugh as he turns away. "Oh, before I go." He faces me again, digging into the pocket of his jacket and taking out a brown pouch. "I was hoping to run into you sometime. I've tried your transmitter but hadn't gotten contact. You probably won't need these, but it's more protection morsels for you and Willow. I wish I had other ways to help you than these gross things."

I take the brown pouch from him. "Thank you, Manx."

"Always." He leaves the pub, and when he's gone, I turn my head to look at Harold again, who is avoiding looking at me now.

Putting my gun away, I turn in my chair to face the bar and ask, "Harold, do you remember my fight against Dimitri?" and Harold lights up, rushing back around the counter to my table again.

"Do I? You practically murdered him!" As he gushes about the fight—one of the worst ones of my life that I almost didn't survive—I remember one thing Manx always told me. He said to never let my pain fester. If it does, it'll stink up the whole place and drag around me like I'm carrying a dead body, and who wants that weight?

I've done it for years—allowed the pain to swallow me up, weigh me down—and it has only caused me trouble. Perhaps he's right about Willow. With her in Vakeeli with me, things can change. Peace can come, and the solution to our problem isn't far away. My visit with The Council has declared it, no matter how unsettling. I do this for them, and awakening Selah can remove Decius. Willow and I can be ourselves, no one hunting us, tormenting us. We'll be free of the burdens of this Tether. We'll be able to be together, prospering as one. For the first time in my life, there's hope.

My traumas are mine to deal with, and I won't be someone who passes those traumas on to someone else, like my father did to me. I suppose to be a great monarch, you must be willing to sacrifice, and if my pain is what has this Harold stranger smiling and reliving what were probably wonderful days of *his* life, so be it. The change starts now.

SEVENTY-SEVEN

WILLOW

By nightfall, we're moving out. Juniper helps me with my weapons at the car before we leave, and instead of having Veno tag along, Rowan drives through Vanora to get to Beatrix's.

"Ugh," Rowan groans. "I have a bloody headache."

"How much tonic did you drink?" Maeve asks from the passenger seat.

"Too much." Rowan cracks a smile at his mother. "Got to dance with those Vanorian girls, though, so it was worth it."

"Oh, keep driving," Maeve hisses, swatting at him.

I laugh at their interaction before peering out the window. The farther we get from Vanora, the more my smile disappears. I'm not sure what it is, but going out of the city to get to Beatrix's doesn't feel right. Maybe it's because of what happened with Ripple Hills last time—the attack and all. Or maybe it's because the farther we get, the less light there is. We're swarmed in darkness, the headlights the only thing giving way.

A car follows us—Alora and three of her best guards. Even she's prepared for the worst. I reach into my cloak, feeling for the gun at my waist. My fingertips find the cool metal and I sigh.

Caz?

I'm here.

How far out are you?

Not far. Fifteen minutes or so from Beatrix's.

Okay. Relief washes over me.

Don't worry. I'll be there soon. Nothing will happen to you.

That's easy for him to say. He's used to this. I'm not.

Rowan drives over the long bridge that leads to Beatrix's, and when he's off it, I spot her little cottage at the top of the hill. It's been repaired since the attack, but the color of the door is different. It's gold, which I assume is a courtesy of Alora. Rowan drives closer, and I spot smoke puffing out the chimney. Her lights are on inside, glowing in the night, and that swirl of dread washes away when I realize how cozy the place looks.

When Rowan parks, he shuts the car off and climbs out first. I step out, and Silvera jumps out behind me, Juniper getting out on the other side.

I face Beatrix's house while Rowan says, "Gonna have a look around." He pulls out a gun and walks the perimeter of the house, disappearing around a corner.

"You have nothing to worry about," Juniper says, approaching me.

"Sheesh. Is my worry that obvious?" I ask, smiling.

"Oh, yes. But it's okay. You're still getting used to all this. I can't imagine how daunting it is."

"Yeah. This is a chaotic lifestyle. I'm not sure how you all just embrace it."

"With these," she says, whipping out her gun and holding it in the air. It's a thick silver handgun with a wide barrel and a black handle. "A gun is a man's best friend. Well, that's what we say in Blackwater." She grins.

"Let me go up first, see if Beatrix is ready for us," Alora says as she passes us.

She moves along in a copper two-piece outfit and sandals, taking the stairs up and giving the door a knock.

"Beatrix?" she calls. "We're here! I trust your hunt went well!"

Alora takes a step back, waiting. We all watch her and the door, waiting for it to open, but after a minute passes and not a peep is heard, Alora glances at Proll. Proll nods and walks around the back of the house, but before he can make it, we hear a bang, one loud enough to be a gunshot.

SEVENTY-EIGHT

WILLOW

"Stay here!" Juniper yells at me before dashing toward the back of the house. Maeve rushes to me, pulling me aside and crouching next to the car. A growl is coming from Silvera as she glares at the house, her back hunched and her teeth bared. Proll, who was just at the side of the house, is now running to Alora and whisking her away.

"What's happening?" I breathe.

"I'm not sure, dear," Maeve answers.

"Is it another attack?"

Maeve looks at me a moment before focusing on the house. "I believe so."

Another gunshot goes off, then some clattering and glass breaking. Maeve places her purse down and digs into it, pulling out her own gun.

"Caz will be here any moment. You stay here."

"But I—" I'm unable to ask her a thing because she's gone, rushing around Beatrix's house in her heels.

I glance back, and Proll is tucking Alora into their car. He runs to the trunk and pops it open, and when he emerges, he has a large axe-like weapon in his hand. The blade is gold, shimmering from the light of Beatrix's house. The two other guards grab theirs and follow Proll behind the house. Silvera chases after them.

"No, Silvera! Come back!" But she's gone. "Shit."

I can't sit here. Everyone is back there. And I have guns. I can probably help. I pull out the handgun at my waist and rush to the side of the house. I don't run to the back, despite hearing the metal of swords clashing, men grunting, and more gunshots. My heart beats wildly in my chest as I pass a window. I look inside, and gasp when I spot Beatrix lying on the ground, a pool of blood beneath her.

"Oh my God!" I run to the porch and grip the doorknob, but it's locked, so I kick the door in. It takes me two attempts before it swings open, dangling by the hinges. I rush to Beatrix, dropping to my knees. Her eyes are open, but she's staring blankly at the ceiling.

"What happened?" I ask, panicked.

"I've been stabbed," she croaks.

"Where? Let me take a look."

Beatrix winces as she lifts a hand and points to her rib.

"Who did this?"

She uses that same bloody hand to point toward her back door. The back door is wide open, and I see Rowan fighting someone in all black with a hood. Two other people in all black are out there, fighting Proll and the other guards with long, silver bladed swords.

"The blue vial," Beatrix says. "On the shelf."

"What?"

"The shelf," she says again, pointing. I look where her hand is pointed, and on the shelf is a collection of vials, all in various colors.

"The blue?" I ask.

She nods, and I rush across the room to grab it. When I bring it back, I pop it open and she takes it from me, chugging the liquid down rapidly. Some of the blue liquid dribbles out the side of her mouth. Her hand falls with the vial as she sucks in a breath, then she exhales, looking at me. Reaching for my cloak, she clutches a handful of it, reeling me closer.

"You must forgive me," she wheezes. "I...I lied to you before. I felt I had no choice."

"What do you mean?"

"Your Tether...it's not meant to be carried alone."

"Elaborate," I demand.

"It's...a gift, passed down from Regals."

"Aren't they the creators of Vakeeli?"

"Yes," a voice says behind me. I glance over my shoulder, and Alora is walking into the house, a bow and arrow in her hand.

"There's only one Regal left," Beatrix goes on. "She can help you, but you'll have to find her." She winces. "No one has seen her for centuries."

"Which Regal is she?"

"Selah," Alora murmurs, crouching next to Beatrix. "Oh, Beatrix. Who did this to you?"

"He threatened to kill me. He knew I was meeting with you all today, and he's trying to stop it before they find a way to reach Selah."

"Stop what?"

Someone roars loudly, barging into the house from the back door. He's in all black—a hood over his head, so I can't see his face

—and he comes charging toward us, a sword in hand. I realize he's not coming for us—he's going for Beatrix.

Fortunately, he doesn't make it far. A gunshot goes off, the man in black freezes, and then he collapses on the floor, his sword clattering on the old wood.

I look back to see where the gunshot came from, and Caz stands in the front door, his gun pointed forward, where the man once stood.

"Caz! Back here!" Rowan yells. "One of them is getting away!"

Caz rushes around us, barreling out of the house. I look ahead, and Rowan, Juniper, and Killian are running toward the trees, chasing a figure in black. Proll and the other guards are standing above two bodies in black on the ground. With a grunt, Proll lifts his gold axe in the air and brings it down, chopping one of their heads off.

I snatch my eyes away, focusing on Beatrix.

"Help me get her to her room," Alora insists.

"Will she be okay?"

"She'll be fine. She took a healing elixir, so it'll stabilize her." Alora grunts as she grabs Beatrix's feet. I grab Beatrix's upper body, and we carry her through the tiny house, rounding a corner and entering an even smaller bedroom. "It should help her heal within a few hours. If we had gotten here later, there may not have been enough time for healing."

I focus on Beatrix, who winces as we lay her down. "Who would do this?"

"I don't know." Alora shakes her head, sighing. "But it's clearly someone she's afraid of."

"Your majesty!" someone shouts, and Alora glances at me before leaving the bedroom to find the voice. She weaves her way through the tiny house to get out the back door, and I follow her, stepping onto plush green grass.

Rowan and Killian are dragging a limp body down the hill while Caz and Juniper march ahead. When they're in Beatrix's backyard, Killian and Rowan drop the body on the ground.

Killian kicks the person onto their back and bends down to snatch the hood off. The entire right side of their head is gone, like it was blasted the right half of the face so mutilated I can hardly make it out. Despite it, Caz takes a step forward, studying the body, his eyes narrowed.

Why does he seem familiar?

Caz's voice rings in my head and I switch my gaze to his, just as he locks his eyes on me. I look at the man again, but his face is so destroyed, I'm afraid if I look any longer, I'll throw up.

"I'll have my guards get an ID on these people," Alora declares, sighing. "In the meantime, perhaps it'll be best for you all stay at the palace."

SEVENTY-NINE

WILLOW

I'M NOT sure what to make of what just happened. Even now, as I drink tea while sitting on the balcony that faces the waterfalls with the others, none of what happened makes sense. Who were those people, and why did they attack Beatrix? The questions sink deep as I chew on a chunk of the protection morsel Caz gave me moments ago.

Luzian and Clara bring out more tea for us to settle in. We'll be staying another night in the palace, in hopes that Beatrix will feel better enough to fill us in by morning.

Music plays, the sound of harps and violins, and everyone chats amongst themselves as if nothing happened, and I don't understand it. How can they just move on after all that? Drink their tea and laugh and continue life, like they weren't just facing death? It's a good thing Alora sent two of her guards to look over Beatrix while she's healing. At least she isn't dead.

My eyes swing to Caz, who is standing near the balcony. He's been quiet since we've gotten here. Something is clearly on his mind that he doesn't want me to hear because he's blocking me out.

Luzian and Clara bring out a tray of fruits and crackers, offering some to me, but I pass. Instead, I walk over to Caz and stand next to him, absorbing the sounds of the trickling water.

"You okay?"

He glances at me. "Define okay."

I rest my elbows on the marble guardrail. "I didn't expect that at Beatrix's."

"Yeah. Me neither. But I suppose it comes with the territory. There are ears everywhere and whoever they were, they were probably looking for me. Not even Mythics are safe." He pauses. "It's just...I keep thinking they were Rippies, but they didn't look like Rippies. Their body types weren't the same...and that one who almost got away..." His head shakes. I can't help feeling like I knew him or saw him before, I just don't remember where."

"How could you tell with his face so butchered?" I ask, shuddering at the reminder.

"It was the angle of his chin that I could see, the hair..." Caz sighs, digging into his pocket and pulling out a bloom. "Or maybe I'm just being paranoid and it's all in my head." He lights the bloom, takes a pull from it, then offers it to me. I take it, pull, and exhale. "I'll be glad when that boat is built and I get this shit over with for The Council. Perhaps they're right and waking Selah will take away some of our burdens."

Right. He filled me in about that—his mission to ride a boat through a dangerous sea to an island practically made of *fire*. He claims the island isn't fully made of fire, and that there are paths to take that are safe, but either way it, sounds like a death trip. I can't believe he agreed to that. But at least the Council has agreed to protect us from Mournwrath aka Decius so Caz can fulfill his end of the bargain. So much can happen in three days, though.

"I've been thinking," I start. "It might be best if I go back home until you complete your mission."

His eyes find mine—sharp, serious. "Why do you say that?"

"It just seems like me being here is bringing you more trouble, and you and I both know so much can happen between now and when that boat is built."

"There's always trouble for me, Willow Woman. That'll never change."

I laugh at the nickname, and he moves in closer. "Tell me what's on your mind."

"I just don't think I should stay, Caz. I don't know why, but it feels like those people were trying to kill Beatrix because of *us*. And there's no telling how many people know about our Tether by now. I hate saying it, but Killian was right. They can use me as leverage against you and that can prevent what you need to do."

"I won't let them get to you."

"You can't promise that."

He takes another pull before putting out his bloom. Then he wraps his arms around me, bringing my cheek to his chest and holding me close.

"I've missed this," he sighs, and I smile, taking a deep breath and then burying my face deeper into his chest. "You must understand. I don't think I can let this go again. *Us*."

I'm not sure what to say to that, so I remain quiet.

"But if you want to go back—if you don't feel safe here—I understand, and I won't make you stay."

I lean back, tipping my chin to look up at him. "You think I *want* to go back?"

"Don't you?"

"I'm not in a hurry to go, Caz. I *want* to be here, with you. I want more moments like this, on a balcony that faces a waterfall. Beneath starry night skies, with your family laughing around us." I pause. "I don't have this at home. Family. But if there's danger everywhere...we have to be careful. We have to play our cards right."

He looks from me to everyone else. He studies them a moment, then takes my hand and leads me away from them. We venture along the rest of the wraparound balcony until we're alone, still facing the moon. When we are, he brings me to him and cups my face in his hands, pressing his lips to mine. I expect his lips to be warm, but they're not. They're cold. But I take it because I've been dying for another kiss since he left for Luxor.

I lace my arms around the back of his neck, press my chest to his, but his body feels cold too. I break the kiss. "Are you okay? You feel cold."

"I'm fine. Just a bit nippy out here." He smiles, bringing his mouth down to mine again, then he picks me up, pressing my back against a marble column.

"Maybe there are ways I can come and go?" I offer.

"There may be. But we won't know until tomorrow when we see Beatrix." He drags his lips over the crook of my neck, and I shudder.

"Caz, you're really cold."

He frowns then, studying my face before placing me back on my feet. I grab his hands, and even through the gloves, they feel like blocks of ice.

"Let's go to your room and light a fire," I insist. Worry tugs at my gut, but I keep it at bay as I grab his hand and lead the way to his chambers. I enter the room swathed in gold and ivory and hurry to the fireplace, tossing logs into it and then asking for his lighter. He hands it to me, and I get the fire going, and suddenly I'm shivering so hard my teeth are chattering.

"You all right?" he asks.

"I'm f-fine."

"Willow." He steps closer. "Your lips are turning blue."

I try to speak again, but I can't. Though the fire is going now, I can't feel the heat of it. And then I hear a chuckle, deep and sinister. When I look at Caz, his eyes are as black as coals.

I gasp, stumbling away, but he walks closer to me, smirking.

"Did you think it would be that easy?" he asks, but his voice is different. Darker. The air around me freezes, ice splintering up the walls. The fire is no longer burning hot. The flames are frozen solid. He steps closer.

"Caz," I whisper.

"You didn't listen to me, now I'm taking him. But don't worry. It won't be long before I take you too."

"W-who are you?"

He puts on a wicked smile. And right before my very eyes, he vanishes.

"Willow!" someone shouts, and I gasp when Juniper's face comes into view. "Love of Vakeeli, what's happened to you?" I look around. I'm back on the balcony, seated. But Caz isn't where he was last standing. In fact, he's not on the balcony at all.

"Where's Caz?" I ask, shooting out of my chair.

"He's in his chambers. He said he wasn't feeling well after you guys were all lip-locked and goo-goo-eyed around the corner."

Wait...what? "When was this?"

"About five minutes ago."

"Is everything all right?" Rowan asks, concern etching his face. I shake my head. "No. It's not."

Then I run down the corridor and into the palace. "Caz!" I scream, storming up the stairs. I scream his name repeatedly, my heart beating harder. As I run, I feel the cold still in my lungs, as if I've inhaled that nightmare. I don't stop, even when the cold seems it will paralyze me.

I run to his room and shove the door open. And when I see him, my heart drops to my stomach.

EIGHTY

WILLOW

He's lying on the floor, shirtless, his body paler than I've ever seen it before. "Caz!" I yell. I run to him, lifting his head up. His body has black veins all over it, and he's as cold as ice.

Footsteps approach, and Juniper and Maeve rush into the room.

"What's happened?" Maeve shouts.

"I—I don't know!" I wail.

Maeve drops to her knees, pressing two fingers to the pulse on Caz's neck. "He still has a pulse, but it's faint." I'm glad to hear that, but he doesn't look well. His lips are dark blue, and black veins slither along his eyelids.

"He's freezing cold, Maeve."

"Juniper, go for your brothers," Maeve commands, and Juniper doesn't hesitate to flee the room.

"What do we do?" I'm panicking now.

"Did you see anything when you spaced out on the balcony?" she asks.

"I—I saw Caz. I was in this room, but...it wasn't Caz. It was like something darker had taken over him."

Maeve's eyes widen with shock. "What could that possibly mean?"

"I don't know."

Alora rushes into the room in a flurry, her gold gown catching the light. "I just got IDs on the men who attacked Beatrix." She hands a small stack of cards to Maeve, who takes them and rapidly flips through them with a frown.

"I don't know any of these men," Maeve mutters.

"What happened to Caz?" Alora asks, walking deeper into the room.

I let go of Caz to look over Maeve's shoulder as she shuffles through the cards, and at first none of them are familiar. But then...

"Wait!" I step around her, taking one of the cards out of her hands. On the card is a man, handsome, with a strong jawline, a wide smile, and shoulder-length brown hair.

I *know* this man. He carried me, gave me verdeberries. And right beside his photo is a name that confirms it.

"This is Alexi," I say, pointing at his picture. "H—he lives in Whisper Grove." But why would he attack Beatrix? He had to have been the one Caz said was familiar, despite how mutilated his face was.

As the questions haunt me, Caz lets out a pained groan that catches all of our attention, and when I look back, his body is upright and floating in the air.

EIGHTY-ONE

CAZ

When I stir awake, there's a chill in the air. I open my eyes, realizing there are two major things wrong.

One: I was in one of Alora's chambers, and I had a fire going. Now, whether it's still going or not, there should be heat in my room, but there isn't.

Two: I don't remember falling asleep. In fact, I hardly ever sleep, which tells me something is seriously wrong.

I snatch my gun from beneath the pillow and turn over in the bed, but when I look up, there are trees above me, tall, with branches that seem to stretch for miles. Their ends are spiky, snow capping the thicker branches.

When I breathe, tufts of my breath linger, and I sit up on the bed, looking around me. I'm in a forest—a cold, dark, empty forest. Nothing is here but me and the bed from Alora's. I'm shirtless, and when I look down, black veins are spread over my body, long and unorderly.

Then there's a deep, wicked laugh that I hear in the hollows of my mind. I climb off the bed, my gun already aimed, but at what, I'm not sure.

"Who's there?" I call. I spin around when I hear leaves rustle behind me, a twig snapping.

"Show yourself," I demand.

"The Council has told you the truth. They're leading you to Selah. This is *not* a good thing for me."

"I don't know what you're talking about."

"You awake Selah, and you slip out of my grasp. I've worked much too hard to let that happen."

I clench my jaw, trying to find the voice. I can't find it. It seems to be everywhere, echoing all around me. Then I feel something hit me from behind. A blur of black swoops past as I land on the ground, and then it's gone.

"You're a coward," I grumble.

"Am I the coward, or are you? Hiding behind your guns. Pleading with a hunk of metal to take your life. Let me guess, you've had a taste of your mate and don't feel that way anymore. Now you feel like you must live for her, forever and ever. How romantic."

I push to a stand again, dirt wedging between my fingers and toes. "Stop hiding and show yourself!"

"If I do that, there will be no turning back."

A branch snaps. The wings of a bird flap. I spin around when I hear another snap, pointing my gun ahead. A dark figure walks through a line of trees. At first, I can't see it well. It's too dark, too far, but the closer it gets, the temperature drops around me, and the colder I become.

When it steps into the light, my eyes widen because I can't believe it. I lower my gun, staring at the figure that smiles back at me, speechless. It wears a sly smile, it's eyes dark like coals. It's shirtless, just like me. In fact, it *is* me...

Only its skin is gray. And when it smiles, it's teeth are sharp, like daggers. Black veins canvas his body, just like mine, and when he cocks his head, my heart drops.

"You want to kill yourself so badly, well go ahead then," the other me says.

It steps closer, and I lift my gun in the air again. "One more step and I'll blow your fucking head off."

It steps forward anyway. I pull the trigger. The bullet pierces it in the chest. It doesn't flinch, nor does it bleed.

"Another step, and it's your head."

It steps.

I shoot a bullet through its forehead.

It collapses on its back, and I draw in a breath, staring at the body as it lies on the ground. But it doesn't lie there for long. It begins to shake, as if having a seizure, and then the body shoots from the ground to the sky. It floats there, eyes red like hot coals, teeth bared, talons out, staring down at me.

"Did that satisfy you?" it screeches.

I raise my gun, shoot at it, but the bullet passes right through it, like it's a ghost.

"This," it moans, sneering. "Will satisfy me."

It flies toward me, knocking me into the nearest tree. All the wind leaves my body as the bark scratches my back before I crumple to the ground. When I look up, the figure is floating above me.

Caz! Wake up, please! Willow's voice rings in my head.

"Willow!" I shout, my voice cracking. "Willow, can you hear me?"

"She can't hear you." The figure drops to the ground. "She'll never hear you again, I'm afraid."

I expect to see that wicked version of myself staring back.

Instead, I see the face of someone I know. Someone I trust...or so I thought.

"Oh, Caspian," Manx sighs, and my heart drops to my stomach. "You were so close."

"Why?" I croak. "Manx, how could you?"

"You shouldn't trust everything a Mythic gives you."

What? I stare at him until a realization dawns on me. Something Calista said rings loudly in my head: *Nothing can breakthrough this bubble of our energy unless you allow it.*

Unless you allow it. I allowed this. The protection morsels he gave me in Luxor...I ate one at Alora's palace and even gave one to Willow. What he gave us, it wasn't to protect us. It was to break through The Council's protection. *Fuck.* I let him right in to sabotage us.

"I tried to resist, I really did," Manx goes on. "But you must understand, Caspian. This hunger has become *unbearable* for me, and the moment you fell for her, the scent of your Tether grew even sweeter. I could only resist for so long. Now that I know you were going to wake Selah, well, it's best I get this over with now. No use in prolonging the inevitable."

"You fucking backstabber," I growl through clenched teeth.

"Don't worry," he murmurs, stepping closer and clasping my head in his hands. "I like you, so I'll make this quick."

Those are the last words I hear before my body is chained in ice and my vision turns black.

If you've made it to this part of the book, I want to personally thank you for reading Vicious Bonds! I know that wasn't the ending you were expecting, but listen...book 2 , Wicked Ties, will be released in November 2023!

Expect more violence, more answers about the Cold Tether and Regal Selah, and most of all MORE ROMANCE between Caz + Willow.

Sign Up For My Newsletter on my website to stay updated and to receive exclusive information, teasers, graphics, and much more! www.shanorawilliams.com

For updates, teasers, and more fun exclusives:

Follow Me on Instagram @reallyshanora
Follow Me on TikTok: @theshanorawilliams
Twitter: @shanorawilliams

Visit www.shanorawilliams.com for more info and details.
psssttt... by the way, I'm most active on Instagram and TikTok

ACKNOWLEDGMENTS

Well, dang! We're here, at the part of the book where I get to praise my loving readers!

This is the first full romance novel I've published in two years. I have over thirty-five books written and all of them are special to me but writing THIS one in particular was...*different*.

I rarely get the chance to sit with my novels for longer than a year, to analyze them, dream about them, wake up at 2 A.M. to write notes like mad about them, but I did with this one. This was a book that had no pressure applied because no one knew about it until I was ready, and I enjoyed that so much.

Caz and Willow are two characters I truly wanted to get to know. I wanted to start from scratch, figure them out from the inside out, and I was able to do that with them in more ways than I thought possible. I wanted a diverse world, something unexpected and fresh and exciting. I wanted to challenge myself, and damn was this book a challenge. This book is a work of fiction I couldn't really put into words, only something I could experience as I wrote it, and I did that. I experienced each and every moment, chapter by chapter, and it turned out ten times better than I ever imagine.

There are moments when it didn't feel worth continuing, I won't lie, but I wouldn't have been able to keep going without my best friend Hannah. I thank you so much for sharing your passion with these characters, for our chats in Kentucky and tossing ideas with me out loud. That was the best, and truly so inspiring. Thank you for making this feel real to me.

To Traci Finlay – thank you for always making my stories top tier! Your advice, critique, and ideas really made the final result AMAZING! You're a queen, girl! Absolute royalty! Thank you, thank you!

To my husband Juan, who is forever supporting me, pushing me to "get some work done" even when you know I don't feel like it, or when I want to lounge on the sofa like a lazy cat. You encourage me every single day and I love that I get to spend life with an incredible man like you.

And to my readers. I honestly am not sure what to say to y'all other than THANK YOU. As I type this, I'm tearing up because I never thought I'd have people in my corner, rooting for me and sticking with me when I hadn't published a single morsel of romance. Like...I'm not even kidding when I say your endless support keeps me going. And I know I say this every book, but I would *not* be doing this without y'all. I wouldn't have the career I have without you, wouldn't be able to support my boys without you, and I wouldn't be **Shanora Williams** without you. Thank you for loving my characters, for loving *me*, and for all the support you give. It means so much to me. So, so much.

More Books by Shanora

WARD DUET
THE MAN I CAN'T HAVE
THE MAN I NEED

CANE SERIES
WANTING MR. CANE (#1)
BREAKING MR. CANE (#2)
LOVING MR. CANE (#3)
BEING MRS. CANE (#4)

NORA HEAT COLLECTION
CARESS
CRAVE
DIRTY LITTLE SECRET
MY PROFESSOR

STANDALONES
BAD FOR ME

COACH ME
TEMPORARY BOYFRIEND
MY FIANCE'S BROTHER
DOOMSDAY LOVE
DEAR MR BLACK
FOREVER MR. BLACK
UNTIL THE LAST BREATH

SERIES
FIRENINE SERIES
THE ACE CROW DUET
VENOM TRILOGY

THRILLERS:
The Perfect Ruin
The Wife Before
The Other Mistress

Most of these titles are available in Kindle Unlimited. Visit www.shanorawilliams.com for more information.

Printed in Great Britain
by Amazon